W9-DAY-047

THE CAMBRIDGE EDITION OF THE WORKS OF
F. SCOTT FITZGERALD

First page of the holograph, "The Guest in Room Nineteen," here entitled "Room Nineteen." Marie Shank Additions, Fitzgerald Papers, Princeton University Libraries.

THE LOST DECADE

Short Stories from *Esquire*, 1936–1941

* * *

F. SCOTT FITZGERALD

Edited by
JAMES L. W. WEST III

CAMBRIDGE UNIVERSITY PRESS
Cambridge, New York, Melbourne, Madrid, Cape Town, Singapore, São Paulo, Delhi

Cambridge University Press
The Edinburgh Building, Cambridge CB2 8RU, UK

Published in the United States of America by Cambridge University Press, New York

www.cambridge.org
Information on this title: www.cambridge.org/9780521885300

First published 2008

Printed in the United Kingdom at the University Press, Cambridge

A catalogue record for this publication is available from the British Library

Library of Congress Cataloguing in Publication data

Fitzgerald, F. Scott (Francis Scott), 1896–1940.
The lost decade : short stories from Esquire, 1936–1941 / F. Scott Fitzgerald; edited by James L.W. West, III.
p. cm. – (The Cambridge edition of the works of F. Scott Fitzgerald)
Includes bibliographical references.
ISBN 978-0-521-88530-0
I. West, James L. W. II. Title. III. Series.
PS3511.I9L67 2008
813′.52 – dc22 2007053045

ISBN 978-0-521-88530-0 hardback

CONTENTS

ACKNOWLEDGMENTS

I am grateful to Eleanor Lanahan, Thomas P. Roche, Jr., and Chris Byrne, the Trustees of the F. Scott Fitzgerald Estate, for their interest, advice, and support. I thank Phyllis Westberg of Harold Ober Associates, Inc., for assistance and counsel.

The illustrations in this volume taken from originals in the F. Scott Fitzgerald Papers and the F. Scott Fitzgerald Additional Papers are reproduced with permission from the Manuscript Division, Department of Rare Books and Special Collections, Princeton University Libraries. My thanks to Don Skemer, Meg Rich, and AnnaLee Pauls at Princeton for their continuing help and good humor during my visits. Christine A. Lutz, an archivist at the Mudd Manuscript Library, Princeton, was most helpful with the annotations for "The Ants at Princeton."

Sarah Hartwell of the Rauner Special Collections Library, Dartmouth University, assisted with the annotations. The photograph of Arnold Gingrich is reproduced with permission from the Arnold Gingrich Papers, Box 25, Bentley Historical Library, University of Michigan. The *Esquire* cover for May 1936 is reproduced from the copy in the Bruccoli Collection, Thomas Cooper Library, University of South Carolina.

Support for the Cambridge Fitzgerald Edition is provided by Susan Welch and Ray Lombra of the College of the Liberal Arts, Pennsylvania State University, and by Robert L. Caserio and Robin Schulze, both of whom served as head of the Penn State English Department during the preparation of this volume. Transcription, collation, annotation, and proofing chores were ably performed by Gregg Baptista, Audrey Barner, and Jeanne Alexander.

J.L.W.W. III

ILLUSTRATIONS

(*Beginning on page 249*)

INTRODUCTION

During the last six years of his life F. Scott Fitzgerald was an *Esquire* author. For most of his career he had been identified with the *Saturday Evening Post*: between 1920 and 1934 he had appeared there some sixty-five times and in 1932 had even attempted, for tax purposes, to have himself declared "virtually an employee" of the magazine.[1] Around 1934, however, Fitzgerald's relationship with the *Post* began to lose momentum. He managed to sell a few more manuscripts to the magazine over the next three years, but he was no longer able to manufacture the kinds of short fiction that the *Post* editors wanted, and they were not interested in the autobiographical and confessional writing he was producing.

Enter *Esquire*. Between 1934 and 1940 (the year of his death) Fitzgerald sold some forty-five manuscripts to *Esquire*—three essays in the "Crack-Up" series, seventeen stories in the Pat Hobby series, and twenty-five other pieces of writing. Fitzgerald came to rely on the magazine as a source of income and an outlet for his work. *Esquire* helped to support him during his difficult final years and played an important role in establishing and maintaining his posthumous reputation.

I. HISTORY

Esquire grew out of *Apparel Arts*, a large-format magazine created by the merchandiser David A. Smart for the men's fashion industry.[2]

[1] *As Ever, Scott Fitz—Letters between F. Scott Fitzgerald and His Literary Agent Harold Ober, 1919–1940*, ed. Matthew J. Bruccoli and Jennifer McCabe Atkinson (Philadelphia and New York: J. B. Lippincott Co., 1972): 193. Ober gave a sworn deposition to the effect that Fitzgerald was employed by the *Post*—this so Fitzgerald would not be taxed as a self-employed freelance author. The deposition is reproduced in *As Ever*, pp. 192–93.

[2] The account that follows is taken from James L. W. West III, "Fitzgerald and *Esquire*," in *The Short Stories of F. Scott Fitzgerald: New Approaches in*

Originally planned as a quarterly, *Esquire* was to have been sold or given away at men's clothing stores, with a few sales by subscription and a few more at tobacco shops and newsstands. The initial issue in autumn 1933, however, was an instant hit with readers, and Smart decided to turn the magazine into a monthly. Editorial offices were established at 919 North Michigan Avenue in Chicago, and the magazine went into operation.

Arnold Gingrich, the founding editor, quickly built an impressive stable of writers. His most prominent contributor, Ernest Hemingway, wrote a monthly letter to the magazine; Hemingway's agreement with Gingrich was that he would receive twice the fee paid to the other authors.[3] Those other writers during the 1930s included Dashiell Hammett, John Dos Passos, Theodore Dreiser, Conrad Aiken, Erskine Caldwell, Ezra Pound, Morley Callaghan, Stephen Vincent Benét, Thomas Wolfe, H. L. Mencken, George Jean Nathan, Ford Madox Ford, André Maurois, Aldous Huxley, William Saroyan, Bertrand Russell, Thomas Mann, Sinclair Lewis, Frank O'Connor, Langston Hughes, D. H. Lawrence, John Steinbeck, Waldo Frank, John Gould Fletcher, and E. E. Cummings—as impressive a line-up as any American magazine of the time could boast.

Esquire was a leisure magazine for men, printed in color on glossy stock and in an oversized format. A special feature of *Esquire* was its full-page cartoons and illustrations; the magazine also printed photographs and drawings of beautiful, scantily clad women. Each copy sold for 50 cents, a high price in the 1930s when a copy of

Criticism, ed. Jackson R. Bryer (Madison: University of Wisconsin Press, 1982): 149–66. Also useful is chapter 5, "The *Esquire* Period," in Bryant Mangum, *A Fortune Yet: Money in the Art of F. Scott Fitzgerald's Short Stories* (New York and London: Garland, 1991): 129–76. For information about the founding of *Esquire*, see Arnold Gingrich's memoir *Nothing but People* (New York: Crown, 1971). An account of the history of the magazine is included in Theodore Peterson, *Magazines in the Twentieth Century* (Urbana: University of Illinois Press, 1964): 273–81.

3 Initially the standard payment for an article or story was $200, with Hemingway receiving $400. The base fee was later raised to $250. The buying power of $250 in 1935 was equivalent to approximately $3,200 in 2005 dollars. A current website for making such conversions is www.measuringworth.com/calculators/compare.

a comparable magazine cost a nickel or a dime. Advertisements in *Esquire* were for the better brands of men's clothing, automobiles, liquor, and accessories. The magazine was launched at an inauspicious time, during one of the worst years of the Great Depression, but it flourished. When Fitzgerald began publishing in *Esquire* in 1934 its readership was approximately 130,000; by his death in 1940 the circulation had grown to almost 470,000.[4]

2. FITZGERALD AND GINGRICH

Fitzgerald was guided to *Esquire* in the spring of 1934 by his friend and supporter, the Baltimore journalist H. L. Mencken. Fitzgerald was living in Baltimore near Johns Hopkins University where his wife, Zelda, was receiving psychiatric treatment. Mencken, who was friendly with Gingrich, suggested to Fitzgerald that he might find a market for his writing at *Esquire*. Years later Gingrich recalled receiving Fitzgerald's first manuscript:

> He wrote me enclosing a script entitled "'Show Mr. and Mrs. F. to Number—'" by Zelda and F. Scott Fitzgerald. And, since I was a great Fitzgerald fan from 1920 on (had read *This Side of Paradise* in high school) I moved right in on him with long fan letters, and began an intensive correspondence and frequent exchange of phone calls, from February '34 onward.[5]

"'Show Mr. and Mrs. F.'" was a long free-association piece, composed by Zelda and revised by Fitzgerald, in which they recalled details about the many hotels in which they had stayed during their marriage.[6] Gingrich purchased the manuscript and published it in two parts in May and June 1934. Gingrich's letters and telephone

[4] *N. W. Ayer and Son's Directory of Newspapers and Periodicals* (Philadelphia: N. W. Ayer, 1935, 1941).

[5] Gingrich to James L. W. West III, 18 December 1969, quoted in "Fitzgerald and *Esquire*," 152.

[6] A corrected and annotated text of "'Show Mr. and Mrs. F.'" is included in *My Lost City: Personal Essays, 1920–1940*, ed. James L. W. West III, Cambridge Edition of the Works of F. Scott Fitzgerald (Cambridge and New York: Cambridge University Press, 2005): 116–29. For an account of the collaboration, see pp. xxiii–xxiv of that volume's introduction and Appendix 1, pp. 301–38.

calls brought in another effort, a similar collaboration entitled "Auction—Model 1934" in which the Fitzgeralds imagined what a sale of their miscellaneous possessions might be like. Gingrich accepted that manuscript and published it in July 1934.

Fitzgerald did not make a submission under his name alone until several months later. He was heavily in debt to his publisher, Charles Scribner's Sons, and to his literary agent, Harold Ober. He continued his attempts to market short stories to the *Post* during this period, but with little success. In the late fall of 1934 he sent Gingrich a short essay on insomnia called "Sleeping and Waking"; two stories followed—"The Fiend" and "The Night before Chancellorsville." Gingrich took all three manuscripts and published them in December 1934, January 1935, and February 1935.

Fitzgerald's relationship with Gingrich now fell into a pattern. He would borrow ahead at the magazine, then send in manuscripts to reduce the debt. Gingrich remembered the procedure many years later:

> The $250 we charged off against every accepted manuscript simply reduced by that amount his outstanding account with us which, while seldom much over a thousand dollars, never stayed much below that amount for very long either. The advances were made in dribs and drabs, as he would wire for them, sometimes at night and sometimes on holidays, and the money was usually wired to him, most often for fifty or a hundred dollars at a time.[7]

This arrangement was similar to the one Fitzgerald had maintained for years with Harold Ober, borrowing from his literary agent as he needed money and reducing the debt whenever Ober sold a manuscript. Fitzgerald seems to have considered this a comfortable way to do business; his correspondence with Ober, in fact, suggests that he needed the guilt produced by debt to bring him to the work table.[8] The money from *Esquire* covered his living expenses and some of the costs for Zelda's treatments. He dealt directly with

[7] Gingrich to West, 13 April 1970, quoted in "Fitzgerald and *Esquire*," 153.

[8] See James L. W. West III, "F. Scott Fitzgerald, Professional Author," in *A Historical Guide to F. Scott Fitzgerald*, ed. Kirk Curnutt (New York: Oxford University Press, 2004): 49–68.

Gingrich and did not channel his work through Ober, thus avoiding the agent's 10-percent fee. The amounts that Fitzgerald earned from *Esquire* did not approach those he had received from the *Post*, but *Esquire* helped to keep him afloat and kept his name visible in the literary marketplace.[9]

3. STORIES

Fitzgerald's best-known publications in *Esquire*, the three "Crack-Up" essays, brought him much notice, not all of it favorable, when they appeared in February, March, and April 1936. But Fitzgerald also published some important short fiction in the magazine, especially during his first period as a contributor—a stint that ended in the summer of 1937 when he left Asheville, North Carolina (to which he had moved from Baltimore), and went to Hollywood to work as a screenwriter for Metro-Goldwyn-Mayer. During this first period, *Esquire* published two of his best late stories, "Three Acts of Music" (May 1936) and "The Long Way Out" (September 1937). Three other worthy efforts also appeared in the magazine: "An Alcoholic Case" (February 1937), "The Guest in Room Nineteen" (October 1937), and "Financing Finnegan" (January 1938).

Fitzgerald trained himself to write to the requirements of *Esquire*. During his years as a *Post* author he had mastered the kind of story published by that magazine—a discursive, loosely organized narrative of from 6,000 to 8,000 words, plotted chronologically, featuring passages of lyrical description, and with a love story at its center. For *Esquire*, Fitzgerald learned to write a very different kind of narrative—the brief, unplotted, elliptical tale typical of Chekhov, Turgenev, and De Maupassant. Fitzgerald's reasons for writing in this form were probably more professional than artistic; *Esquire* did not want long stories, and Gingrich had made it clear that he would pay only $250 for a manuscript, no matter what the length. But the discipline imposed by these new requirements was probably good for

[9] Gingrich was indulgent with Fitzgerald, upon occasion enduring bad behavior. For an account of one incident, see Sheilah Graham and Gerold Frank, *Beloved Infidel* (New York: Holt, 1958): 206–10.

Fitzgerald: he learned to write in his "late style"—the stripped, compressed prose that one finds in *The Last Tycoon*, the novel on which he was working when he died. He was also able to deal frankly with subjects that had been off-limits at the *Post*: alcoholism, depression, suicide, adultery, and violence.

Fitzgerald's contract with Metro-Goldwyn-Mayer (MGM) was not renewed at the end of 1938. He had not been able to adapt to the demands of screenwriting and now found himself dependent again on writing for the magazines. In mid-July 1939 he asked Gingrich for an advance of $100 and, within a short time, sent in two excellent stories—"Design in Plaster" (November 1939) and "The Lost Decade" (December 1939). Early in September 1939, Fitzgerald decided to attempt a series of stories for *Esquire* about an aging Hollywood hack writer named Pat Hobby. This was the fifth story-series that Fitzgerald had undertaken in his career. During the late 1920s and early 1930s he had written nine stories about an adolescent boy named Basil Duke Lee and five more about a teenaged girl named Josephine Perry. These two series had appeared in the *Post* and are today considered to be among Fitzgerald's best writings from that period. The next series, centering on a medieval count named Philippe, was an attempt at historical fiction; the next after that had as its central character a young girl named Gwen Bowers who was patterned after Fitzgerald's daughter, Scottie. Neither of these series (published during the 1930s in *Redbook* and the *Post*, respectively) was a success, and neither was completed. Still, the advantages of writing stories in a series were obvious to Fitzgerald. One did not have to invent fresh characters and settings each time out, and ideally one built a following for the series in the magazine.

The Pat Hobby stories came easily to Fitzgerald. Between 16 September and 13 November 1939, he sent seven of them to Gingrich; by the end of the following March he had produced nine more. A final story, making seventeen in all, was sold to Gingrich in June 1940. A few of these stories are fully developed narratives, but most are sketches based on bits of Hollywood lore, fragments of movie history, and items of studio gossip. Pat, a "script-stooge" from the silent-movie era, scrambles through the narratives in search of a temporary writing assignment, a screen credit, a drink, or a loan. Though sometimes labored, these stories have their moments; many of them are funny in an offbeat way. Fitzgerald considered the best four to be "A Man in the Way" (February 1940), "'Boil Some Water—Lots of It'" (March 1940), "Pat Hobby's Christmas Wish" (January 1940), and "No Harm Trying" (November 1940).[10]

The Pat Hobby stories saturated Fitzgerald's market with *Esquire*. He therefore hit upon a plan for Gingrich to publish two of his stories in each issue—a Pat Hobby story under his own name and another story under a pseudonym. Fitzgerald floated this idea to Gingrich in February 1940, claiming that his ultimate motive was to receive "a fan letter from my own daughter."[11] In reality his intention was probably to dispose of the backlog of his manuscripts at *Esquire*. Gingrich agreed to the scheme and scheduled a story called "On an Ocean Wave" (a satire of the tough-guy narratives of the *Black Mask* writers) for publication in the February 1941 issue. But by the time this story appeared, under the *nom de plume* "Paul Elgin," Fitzgerald was dead. No other pseudonymous fiction by him was published in *Esquire*.[12]

4. POSTHUMOUS REPUTATION

When he died in December 1940, Fitzgerald was eight stories ahead with *Esquire*. Five were Pat Hobby efforts; the other three were "On an Ocean Wave," "The Woman from '21'" (June 1941), and "Three Hours between Planes" (July 1941)—this last story a well-wrought narrative based on Fitzgerald's reunion in October 1937

10 Fitzgerald left among his papers a "Rating of Stories" for the Pat Hobby series; the document is reproduced in the illustrations section of this volume.

11 Fitzgerald to Gingrich, 7 February 1940, quoted in F. Scott Fitzgerald, *The Pat Hobby Stories*, ed. Arnold Gingrich (New York: Scribners, 1962): xvii.

12 Initially Fitzgerald wanted to use the pseudonym "John Darcy"—a nod to Monsignor Thayer Darcy, a character in *This Side of Paradise*. Later he proposed "John Blue" to Gingrich, but the editor thought the name too obvious an invention. Fitzgerald eventually settled on "Paul Elgin." Other than some apprentice work in Princeton student publications, "On an Ocean Wave" was Fitzgerald's only piece of writing published under a pseudonym.

with Ginevra King, his first serious love.[13] The eight stories were published in 1941. Gingrich wrote a tribute to Fitzgerald for the March 1941 issue, and letters from readers praising Fitzgerald's work appeared in the correspondence section as late as September of that year. Stories by Fitzgerald were reprinted in the popular *Esquire* anthologies of the 1940s and 1950s, and the magazine published several substantial articles about him during the 1950s and 1960s. Gingrich collected and edited the Pat Hobby stories for Scribners in 1962; unpublished letters and stories by Fitzgerald appeared at various times in the 1950s, 1960s, and 1970s.[14] The *Esquire* connection, helpful to Fitzgerald during his life, was even more important to his reputation after his death.

5. INCLUSIONS AND EXCLUSIONS

This volume of the Cambridge Fitzgerald Edition brings together all seventeen of the Pat Hobby stories and thirteen of the eighteen other Fitzgerald stories published in *Esquire*.[15] Five *Esquire* stories are omitted. "The Fiend" (January 1935) and "The Night before Chancellorsville" (February 1935) were both reprinted by Fitzgerald in *Taps at Reveille* (New York: Scribners, 1935), the last of the four short-story collections that he assembled and published during his lifetime. These two will be included in the Cambridge edition of *Taps*, in preparation. Three other *Esquire* stories—"Shaggy's Morning" (May 1935), "'Send Me In, Coach'" (November 1936), and "The Honor of the Goon" (June 1937)—are excluded in accordance with the wishes of Scottie Fitzgerald Smith, the author's daughter, who judged them to be unworthy of reprinting.[16] The remaining thirteen *Esquire* stories are published in Section I of this volume, arranged chronologically by date of appearance in the magazine.

[13] James L. W. West III, *The Perfect Hour: The Romance of F. Scott Fitzgerald and Ginevra King* (New York: Random House, 2005): 87–88.

[14] West, "Fitzgerald and *Esquire*," notes 26–31.

[15] All of Fitzgerald's nonfiction writings for *Esquire* are included in the Cambridge edition of *My Lost City*, cited earlier.

[16] Texts of the three stories can be acquired through the interlibrary loan services available at most academic and public libraries.

The seventeen Pat Hobby stories appear in Section II, likewise in chronological order of publication.

6. EDITORIAL PRINCIPLES

The procedures used to establish the texts for this volume are derived from G. Thomas Tanselle's "Editing without a Copy-Text," *Studies in Bibliography*, 47 (1994): 1–22. No copy-texts are declared; equal authority is vested in holograph, typescript, proof, and serial texts. This is an intentionalist approach, derived from the principles of Greg-Bowers editing, but without reliance on a copy-text. Emendation decisions are recorded in the apparatus.[17]

Pre-publication evidence for establishing the texts of these *Esquire* stories survives in profusion at Princeton University Library, both in the Fitzgerald Papers (the original archive, donated to the library in 1951 by his daughter) and in the Fitzgerald Additional Papers (materials given to the library or purchased for the collection after 1951). The *Esquire* Additions include typescripts (most of them reproduced from microfilm) and correspondence between Fitzgerald and Gingrich. The Marie Shank Additions and the Bertie Barr Additions contain pre-publication material for nearly all of the *Esquire* stories.[18] A holograph draft of "The Guest in Room Nineteen" is among the Marie Shank Additions, and at least one typescript is extant in the archive for every story in this volume, with the exception of "In the Holidays" and "Financing Finnegan." Frequently the *Esquire* setting copy survives; often one or more of the extant typescripts has been revised by Fitzgerald.[19] This abundance

[17] See "Editorial Principles" in *This Side of Paradise*, ed. James L. W. West III, Cambridge Edition of the Works of F. Scott Fitzgerald (Cambridge: Cambridge University Press, 1995): xl–xlii.

[18] Marie Shank was the proprietor of a secretarial service in Asheville, North Carolina, where Fitzgerald lived off and on during the mid-1930s before going to Hollywood in 1937. He used her typing services, and she preserved some of his manuscripts and early drafts. Bertie Barr was a friend from the 1930s with whom Fitzgerald left a great many typescripts of his *Esquire* writings. Both women donated their materials to Princeton during the 1960s.

[19] An early typescript of "The Woman from '21'" has been facsimiled in *F. Scott Fitzgerald Manuscripts*, vol. 6, part 3, ed. Matthew J. Bruccoli (New York:

of evidence has made it possible to establish the texts of these stories with considerable confidence. The materials extant for each story are described in the apparatus. Each story represents a separate editorial problem.[20]

Fitzgerald's habit with *Esquire* was to sell an early typescript to the magazine, then to send in revisions in the months that followed. Sometimes he sent a fully re-typed draft; more often he sent a full or partial carbon of the typescript already at *Esquire*, with his handwritten revisions added; at still other times he mailed in a typed list of changes. Some of these typescripts and lists survive, but other materials were apparently discarded. The *Esquire* copy-editors, however, appear to have transcribed Fitzgerald's revisions onto the setting copies in these cases. Using these various forms of evidence it has been possible to ensure that Fitzgerald's late revisions are present in the texts published here.

One revised version—a fresh typescript for the Pat Hobby story "A Patriotic Short"—arrived at *Esquire* too late. The earlier version had already been set up in type and appeared in the December 1940 issue of the magazine. In 1962, Gingrich edited *The Pat Hobby Stories* for Scribners (with an informative introduction) and included, as an appendix, the revised version of "A Patriotic Short." That text is published in this volume; it has been established from the revised typescript mailed in by Fitzgerald on 14 October 1940.

No proofs bearing corrections by Fitzgerald are known to survive for the *Esquire* stories. The extant correspondence does not mention proofs; in fact, it is not certain that proofs were ever sent to him. But collation of setting-copy typescripts with the published texts has revealed, for some of the stories, minor revisions and tight-

Garland, 1991): 429–35. This volume also includes, on pp. 437–59, reproductions of working materials for an unfinished Pat Hobby story entitled "Reunion at the Fair" or "Pat at the Fair," together with some of Fitzgerald's memoranda on the Pat Hobby series and a plan by him for a play featuring Pat as a character.

20 Microfilm printouts of some of Fitzgerald's *Esquire* letters and typescripts are present among Arnold Gingrich's papers at the Bentley Historical Library, University of Michigan. Everything at Michigan is also at Princeton. The locations of the original letters from Fitzgerald to Gingrich are unknown; carbons and photocopies survive at Princeton and Michigan.

enings of language that look, on first inspection, to be authorial. Most of these changes, however, occur toward the ends of the stories, in paragraphs that were published in the back pages of the *Esquire* issues. From examination of those back pages it appears that some of the revisions might have been executed by copy-editors who were trimming the texts in proofs to make them fit into limited space surrounded by blocks of advertising. Often the revisions remove an adverb or a prepositional phrase; sometimes they do away with expendable bits of action. Usually the goal seems to be to save a line in the narrow-width columns at the back of the issue so as to compress the story, one slug of type at a time. In these cases, the Cambridge texts follow the wording of the typescript. The passages there were surely written by Fitzgerald, while the trimming in proofs might not have been his work. The tendency in scholarly editing to follow the version that is unquestionably authorial, in cases of doubt, has proved useful here.

Fitzgerald collected only two of these *Esquire* stories during his lifetime—"The Fiend" and "The Night before Chancellorsville," both mentioned earlier and both to be included in the Cambridge edition of *Taps at Reveille*. He revised these two stories for *Taps*, as was his habit, but since he did not live to collect any of the other *Esquire* short fiction, there are no collected texts against which to collate the serial versions in search of authorial variants. With one exception, every story in this volume was published only once during Fitzgerald's life: he left no marked-up tearsheets with late revisions, and none of the stories was published in England before his death. The exception is "Design in Plaster," included in *The Best Short Stories 1940*, edited by Edward J. O'Brien and published by Houghton Mifflin in Cambridge. Collation of this text with the *Esquire* version has revealed minor copy-editing of punctuation and word-division but no substantive revisions.

Two stories rejected by *Esquire* survive. The first, "Dearly Beloved," was sent to Gingrich by Fitzgerald on 23 February 1940.[21]

[21] For the text of Fitzgerald's cover letter, see James L. W. West III, "F. Scott Fitzgerald to Arnold Gingrich: A Composition Date for 'Dearly Beloved,'" *Papers of the Bibliographical Society of America*, 67 (Fourth Quarter, 1973):

No rejection letter from Gingrich is extant, but the story was never published in the magazine, and there is no record of its being submitted elsewhere. Four typescripts of "Dearly Beloved" are preserved in Fitzgerald's papers at Princeton; the story appeared first in the *Fitzgerald/Hemingway Annual* 1969, pp. 1–3, and has been reprinted in *The Short Stories of F. Scott Fitzgerald: A New Collection* (New York: Scribners, 1989): 773–75. "Dearly Beloved" is published in Appendix 1 of this volume; its text has been established from the last in the sequence of typescripts. A second story, this one entitled "Salute to Lucy and Elsie," was rejected by Gingrich in September 1939. The story suffers from confused plotting; Alfred Smart, one of the editors at *Esquire*, also noted in a memo to Gingrich that the story would need to be "washed and laundered" of anti-Catholic elements before it could be published. Fitzgerald attempted to revise the story but abandoned it. Though a typescript survives at Princeton, "Salute to Lucy and Elsie" is not included in this volume of the Cambridge edition. It might be published with other unfinished work in a later volume pending a decision by the Fitzgerald Trust, which administers the author's literary estate.

Three titles are at issue for these stories. "The Long Way Out" bears the title "Oubliette" on the surviving typescript and on a set of proofs in the Bertie Barr Additions. The change in title must have been executed between proofs and published text (September 1937). No correspondence or other evidence survives to indicate who made the alteration. It seems unlikely that such a change would have been made without Fitzgerald's approval—but perhaps it was. The title "The Long Way Out" is accepted for the text published in this volume; "Oubliette" is printed also at the head of the story, within brackets. Fitzgerald did object to a change in title for one of the Pat Hobby stories. "Pat Hobby, Putative Father" was a title

452–54. In this letter Fitzgerald mentions to Gingrich that the actor Edward Everett Horton, from whom Fitzgerald was renting a house in Encino, was interested in using the Pat Hobby stories as a "theatrical vehicle." Horton never followed up on the idea. Fitzgerald also submitted a poem to Gingrich with this same letter, but Gingrich did not accept it for *Esquire*. The poem was "Beloved Infidel," which Fitzgerald had written for Sheilah Graham in 1937. The poem was first published in chapter 17 of *Beloved Infidel*.

substituted at *Esquire* for "Pat Hobby's Young Visitor." Fitzgerald complained about the alteration in a 25 June 1940 letter to Gingrich; the new title "anticipated the first climax," he said. The story is known to Fitzgerald's readers as "Pat Hobby, Putative Father." That title is retained, but "Pat Hobby's Young Visitor" is also printed within brackets at the head of the story. The same policy is followed for "Three Hours between Planes," which Fitzgerald sold to *Esquire* under the title "Between Planes." The title change was made for the July 1941 issue, seven months after his death. No letter or document survives to indicate that Fitzgerald ordered the change before he died. Both titles appear at the head of the text, the second within brackets.

7. CRUXES

The texts of two stories require special attention. The first is "An Alcoholic Case," published in *Esquire* in February 1937 and reprinted by the critic Malcolm Cowley in *The Stories of F. Scott Fitzgerald* (New York: Scribners, 1951)—the first major collection of Fitzgerald's short fiction to be issued after his death. Cowley made three changes in the story in an attempt to clarify its action and to alter its chronology. These changes will be disallowed in the Cambridge text.[22]

"An Alcoholic Case" is a study by Fitzgerald of the psychology of alcoholics and of those who care for them. In the story a cartoonist who lives in a resort hotel is being looked after by a young nurse. He is a charming man but a difficult patient: he begs her for alcohol and, when she refuses, attempts to wrest a bottle of gin from her grasp. She becomes angry and threatens to break the bottle. "Once more you try to get it I'll throw it down," she tells him, and adds:

[22] Cowley made textual changes in at least one other story that he chose for this collection. See Barbara Sylvester, "Whose 'Babylon Revisited' Are We Teaching? Cowley's Fortunate Corruption—and Others Not So Fortunate," in *F. Scott Fitzgerald: New Perspectives*, ed. Jackson R. Bryer, Alan Margolies, and Ruth Prigozy (Athens: University of Georgia Press, 2000): 180–91. See also Christa E. Daugherty and James L. W. West III, "Josephine Baker, Petronius, and the Text of 'Babylon Revisited,'" *F. Scott Fitzgerald Review*, 1 (2002): 3–15.

"I will—on the tiles in the bathroom." The cartoonist again attempts to seize the bottle. In the setting-copy typescript of the story and in the published *Esquire* text, the nurse makes good on her threat, deliberately dropping the bottle on the bathroom floor. "She dropped it like a torpedo," reads the text, "sliding underneath her hand and slithering with a flash of red and black and the words: SIR GALAHAD, DISTILLED LOUISVILLE GIN." The bottle shatters, and the cartoonist calms down. The nurse reads to him from *Gone with the Wind*, and he falls asleep. She puts a robe over his shoulders and, when her shift ends, leaves him alone in his room. She then rides a bus across town to the nursing agency for which she works.

During her struggles with the cartoonist, the nurse has vowed never to take on another "alcoholic case." After she leaves him, however, her resolve softens. She likes the cartoonist and sympathizes with him, though she knows that she will not change him or even help him very much. At the nursing agency she decides to go back and continue caring for him that evening and night. Her supervisor can find no one else to take this second shift. The nurse returns to the hotel room, finds the cartoonist awake, and helps him dress for dinner. In the midst of his preparations, the cartoonist allows his mind to drift. He pauses and fixes his eye "on some place just ahead." In the typescript and the *Esquire* text, the nurse notices that the cartoonist is "looking at the corner where he had thrown the bottle this afternoon." But it was the nurse, earlier in the story, who had dropped the gin bottle on the bathroom floor. The cartoonist had not thrown it.

While revising an earlier version of "An Alcoholic Case," Fitzgerald must have changed the text in such a way as to have the nurse, instead of the cartoonist, break the bottle. But Fitzgerald seems not to have followed through by changing the sentence, later in the story, in which the cartoonist is given responsibility for having thrown the bottle. There is no way to test this reconstruction since only one pre-publication document survives—the setting-copy typescript, which contains the confusion, as does the published *Esquire* text. No early typescripts are extant to make clear the sequence of revision.

Cowley attempted to fix "An Alcoholic Case" in his edition by inventing a sentence and adding it to the end of the twelfth paragraph. Cowley's sentence follows the words "DISTILLED LOUISVILLE GIN" in the passage quoted above. The sentence reads: "He took it by the neck and tossed it through the open door to the bathroom." Now it is the cartoonist, not the nurse, who is responsible for shattering the gin bottle—though she still drops it in the Cowley version. (We are apparently to assume that it does not break.) Cowley's added sentence changes the psychology of the story. The cartoonist now breaks the bottle in a fit of pique; the nurse does not make good on her promise to "throw it down." Certainly Cowley's revision was well-meaning—he must only have wanted the story to make sense—but the alteration changes something about the nurse's character. One of the points that Fitzgerald makes about her is that she is a woman of strength and principle, willing to follow through on what she says she will do.

The editor has three possible courses of action here: to leave the text as it appeared in the typescript and in *Esquire*; to incorporate Cowley's invented sentence; or to make a different emendation. The third option has been chosen for the Cambridge text. A change of two words will clear up the confusion and allow the nurse to break the bottle. By emending "he had thrown" to "she had dropped" in the third paragraph from the end, responsibility for breaking the bottle is given to the nurse, and the contradiction is erased from the text. This emendation has been made and is recorded in the apparatus.

Cowley also changed the chronology of "An Alcoholic Case." Fitzgerald had written the story to cover an afternoon and evening of the same day—about four or five hours of time. The nurse and the cartoonist struggle over the bottle during the afternoon; she breaks it, he goes to sleep, and she leaves to ride to the nursing agency. There she talks with the supervisor and decides to work another shift. She takes the bus back to the cartoonist's hotel. They have their final exchange, and the story ends. Cowley seems to have thought that the narrative should occupy an extra day. He invented this sentence—"It was early the next evening."—and added it at the very beginning of section II of the story. Now the nurse is given a full day, instead of an hour or so, to think about her decision not to care for the alcoholic. This added sentence necessitated a further change, later in the story, to the same sentence discussed above—the sentence that reads (in typescript and in the *Esquire* text): "He was looking at the corner where he had thrown the bottle this afternoon." Cowley changed "this afternoon" to "the night before." Why Cowley should have made these two alterations is unclear. Perhaps he felt that the nurse needed more time to think about her vow. Fitzgerald, however, had wanted the action of the story to cover only four or five hours. The nurse, in his version of the narrative, made her decision quickly and emotionally. Cowley's two alterations in the chronology of "An Alcoholic Case" are not accepted for the Cambridge text.

A second textual problem involves the ending of "On the Trail of Pat Hobby," the thirteenth of the Pat Hobby stories, published in the January 1941 *Esquire*. The editorial decision here is complicated by missing documents.

"On the Trail of Pat Hobby" is typical of many of the stories in the Pat Hobby Series. Pat, who is trying to get onto the payroll at the movie studio, is loitering around the Writers' Building, hoping for a break. He is also trying to dodge the Los Angeles police. He has been making ends meet by working under an assumed name ("Don Smith") as the night clerk at the Selecto Tourist Cabins, a seedy motel at which immoral goings-on take place. The police raid the motel, arrest some of the guests, and tell Pat that he will be wanted later as a witness. He gives them his false name, ducks out of a side door, sneaks off the property, buys a half-pint of gin at a nearby drugstore, and hitchhikes across the city to the studio lot. In his hasty flight from the motel he has left his hat behind, so he goes to the studio commissary and steals one from the hat-check room. He chooses a "sturdy grey Homburg which looked as if it would give him good service." Now he feels relatively safe—and he has a presentable hat to wear.

Pat's sometime friend, the producer Jack Berners, is offering a fifty-dollar prize to any writer who can come up with a good title for a B-movie (just going into production) about a motel clerk. Pat hears about the prize and wanders into Berners' office. Finding it empty, he helps himself to the producer's brandy—having already consumed his own half-pint of gin. He falls asleep on Berners' couch. The producer returns, wakes Pat, and reports that all filming on the lot has been stopped until a missing hat belonging to Harold Marcus, the most important movie mogul at the studio, has been located. The hat, a grey Homburg, is said to be Mr. Marcus' favorite. Of course it is the grey Homburg that Pat has just pinched.

A few paragraphs later Pat and a female writer friend, Bee McIlvaine, begin tossing title suggestions at Berners. Pat is exhausted from his flight across Los Angeles and queasy from the ill-advised mixture of gin and brandy in his stomach, but he wants the fifty dollars and summons his best effort. To warm up he recites the titles of several famous movies: *Test Pilot*, *The Birth of a Nation*, *It Happened One Night*, and *Grand Hotel*—this last a classic film from 1932 starring Greta Garbo, John Barrymore, Joan Crawford, and Lionel Barrymore. Pat is not entirely serious: one of the oddities of his character is that he is proud of the best efforts of the film industry, despite the fact that he has never worked on anything other than trashy B-movies. He would never affix the title of a masterpiece to anything that Jack Berners would produce. Berners, however, has no such qualms. Throughout the Pat Hobby stories, he plays the role of the philistine with his eye only on the box-office. He hears Pat incorrectly and selects "*Grand Motel*" as the winning title. Pat will receive the fifty-dollar prize, but the entire experience has made him ill. As he leaves Berners' office, Bee McIlvaine hands him the grey Homburg. In the original typescript, the story ends this way:

> "Good work, old timer," she said.
>
> Pat seized the hat, retched suddenly into it with a roar and stood holding it there like a bowl of soup.
>
> "Feel—better—now," he mumbled after a moment, "Be right back."
>
> And carrying his dripping burden he shambled toward the lavatory like a hunted man.

This ending is appropriate for the story; probably it represents what Fitzgerald thought of the commercial side of the movie industry. The ending, however, did not appear in the published text of "On the

-6-

"No, you didn't. You said Grand Motel--and for my money it wins the fifty."

"I've got to go lie down," announced Pat, "I feel sick."

"There's an empty office across the way. That's a funny idea Pat, Grand Motel--or else Motel Clerk. How do you like that?"

As the fugitive quickened his step out the door Bee pressed ~~his~~ the hat into his hands.

"Good work, old timer," she said.

Pat seized ~~the~~ Mr. Marcus' hat, ~~retched suddenly into it with a roar~~ and stood holding it there like a bowl of soup.

"Feel--better--now," he mumbled after a moment, "Be ~~right~~ back for the money."

And carrying his ~~dripping~~ burden he shambled toward the lavatory, ~~like a hunted man.~~

Trail of Pat Hobby." Instead, the text in the January 1941 *Esquire* ends as follows:

"Good work, old timer," she said.

Pat seized Mr. Marcus' hat, and stood holding it there like a bowl of soup.

"Feel—better—now," he mumbled after a moment. "Be back for the money."

And carrying his burden he shambled toward the lavatory.

This passage was "created" by the *Esquire* copy-editor on the final leaf of the setting copy. (This setting copy survives in the Bertie Barr Additions at Princeton; the final leaf is reproduced on the facing page.) Using a red pencil, this copy-editor revised the last three paragraphs to remove all mention of Pat's nausea. Everything offensive is gone from the ending; what remains is thoroughly bland.

Under whose orders was the copy-editor working? It's possible that Gingrich, or one of the other editors at the magazine, was put off by the vomiting and ordered the revisions. *Esquire* was a publication for men; it allowed much more in the way of crudity, profanity, and sexual innuendo than, for instance, the *Saturday Evening Post* did, but Pat's retching into Mr. Marcus' hat and holding it "like a bowl of soup" might have been too much even for *Esquire*. Perhaps the ending of the story was rewritten without Fitzgerald's permission.

It's also possible, of course, that Fitzgerald himself rewrote the ending. Perhaps he was afraid that someone in Hollywood—a producer who might be thinking of hiring him—would read the story. Fitzgerald mailed revisions for many of the Pat Hobby stories to Gingrich: sometimes he sent a fresh typescript, sometimes a revised carbon, sometimes a typed list of changes. Several of the carbons and lists survive in the *Esquire* Additions at Princeton, and in each case the copy-editor has faithfully transferred Fitzgerald's changes to the setting copy. Not all of the carbons and lists survive, however: other setting copies show similar revisions in the copy-editor's hand, with no carbon or list to certify the revisions as Fitzgerald's. This is the case for "On the Trail of Pat Hobby." The copy-editor has changed the ending; there is no document that identifies the new conclusion as Fitzgerald's work—but it might have been. Perhaps the carbon or list sent in by Fitzgerald was discarded after the copy-editor had transferred the revisions to the setting copy.

Did Fitzgerald see the story in proofs? If so, and if the ending had been changed on the setting copy without his permission, then he might have protested to Gingrich in a letter. But no set of proofs for any one of the *Esquire* stories survives with corrections in Fitzgerald's hand, and proofs are never mentioned in the letters between Fitzgerald and Gingrich. A set of proofs is extant at Princeton for "On the Trail of Pat Hobby," but the markings, in blue pencil, are by the *Esquire* copy-editor and are corrections of minor typographical errors.

Did Fitzgerald object to the new ending once it was published? This too is impossible to know: Fitzgerald died on 21 December 1940, just about the time that the January 1941 issue of *Esquire* would have been delivered from the printer. The last extant letter from Fitzgerald to Gingrich is dated 27 November 1940. If Fitzgerald was unhappy about the new ending, no letter survives to express his dissatisfaction. Indeed, it is possible that he never saw the published text.

Any attempt to reconstruct the sequence of revision for "On the Trail of Pat Hobby" or to assign responsibility for the changed ending is therefore highly speculative. Not enough evidence survives. Fitzgerald sent in revisions for many of the Pat Hobby stories, but nearly all of these changes were minor—small adjustments in style, corrections of misspelled words, substitutions of one word for another. None of the mailed-in revisions was nearly as significant as the altered ending of "On the Trail of Pat Hobby."

The editor has two choices here: to print the ending as it appeared in *Esquire* or to publish the original ending from the typescript. The decision for the Cambridge text is to publish the original ending, with Pat retching into the hat. The revised ending might have been affixed on Fitzgerald's orders, but there is no document or letter to prove it. The original ending, on the other hand, is undeniably Fitzgerald's work, embodied in the typed text that he submitted to *Esquire*—the same document that was altered by the copy-editor. The unrevised ending of this typescript is accepted for the Cambridge text.

8. REGULARIZED FEATURES

For most words Fitzgerald used standard American spellings, though he did favor some British forms—"spectre," "glamour," and "grey," for example. These British spellings have been preserved. Like most authors Fitzgerald was inconsistent about division of compound words; study of his holograph drafts has established his preferences for most words: "good-bye," for example, and "drug store" and "bookkeeper" and "tiptoe" and many others.

Fitzgerald preferred to use italics only for words in other languages and for emphasis in dialogue, often italicizing only one or two syllables of a word. These practices are followed here; names of books, newspapers, literary works, and movies appear within quotation marks. Question marks and exclamation points that follow italicized words are italicized. The paragraphing, italics, and section breaks of the surviving typescripts are followed unless otherwise indicated in the apparatus.

Seasons of the year are in lower-case, years in Arabic numerals. "Mother" and "Father," used as proper nouns, are capitalized. Numbered avenues in New York City are spelled out; cross-streets are in Arabic numerals. All dashes are one-em in length. Block quotations from movie scripts in the Pat Hobby stories employ underscoring rather than italics—the better to mimic the look of a typescript.

Lines of dialogue in Fitzgerald's manuscripts and typescripts are often punctuated as follows: "I wonder whether he remembers me," she said, "it's been so many years." The second comma in these readings has been altered to a full stop, and, when necessary, the first word of the second clause has been capitalized. Fitzgerald's usual practice was to omit the comma between two adjectives of equal weight, and he nearly always left out the comma between the last two elements in a series. These habits of punctuation are allowed to stand. Commas are often missing before the conjunctions in compound sentences; these commas are supplied only in sentences that might cause confusion for the reader if left unpunctuated.

The editor has not attempted to create a system of pointing typical of Fitzgerald's usages and to impose that system on his texts. This would only subject the texts to a new round of house-styling. The accidentals of the texts in this volume follow, as closely as possible, the pointing, word-division, and capitalization of the typescripts.

SECTION I

ESQUIRE STORIES, 1936–1941

THREE ACTS OF MUSIC

They could hardly hear it for awhile. It was a slow gleam of pale blue and creamy pink. Then there was a tall room where there were many young people and finally they began to feel it and hear it.

What were they—no. This is about music.

He went to the bandstand; the piano player let him lean over his shoulder to read:

"From 'No, No, Nanette' by Vincent Youmans."

"Thank you," he said. "I'd like to drop something in the horn but when an interne has a dollar bill and two coins in the world he might get married instead."

"Never mind, Doctor. That's about what I had when I got married last winter."

When he came back to the table she said:

"Did you find out who wrote that thing?"

"*No!* When do we go from here?"

"When they stop playing 'Tea for Two.'"

Later as she came out of the women's dressing room, she asked the man: "Who played it?"

"My God, how do I know. The band played it."

It dripped out the door now:

Tea . . .
. . . two
Two . . .
. . . tea

"We can never get married. I'm not even a nurse yet."

"Well, let's kill the idea—let's spend the rest of our lives going around and listening to tunes. What did you say that writer's name was?"

"What did *you* say? You went over and looked, dint you?"

"*Didn't* you," he corrected her.

"You're so swell all the time."

"Well, at least I found out who wrote it."

"Who?"

"Somebody named Vincent Youmans."

She hummed it over:

And you . . .
. . . for me
And me . . .
. . . for you
Al—
o-
o-
n-n . . .

Their arms went about each other for a moment in the corridor outside the red room.

"If you lost the dollar bill and the other nickel I'd still marry you," she said.

II

This is now years later but there was still music. There was "All Alone" and "Remember" and "Always" and "Blue Skies" and "How About Me." He was back from Vienna but it didn't seem to matter so much as it had before.

"Wait in here a moment," she said outside the operating room. "Turn on the radio if you want to."

"You've got mighty important, haven't you?"

He turned on:

Re-mem-ber
the night
the night
you said—

"Are you high-hatting me," she inquired, "or did medicine begin and end in Vienna?"

"No, it didn't," he said humbly. "I'm impressed—evidently you can supervise the resident or the surgeons—"

"I've got an operation of Dr. Menafee's coming in and there's a tonsillectomy that's got to be postponed. I'm a working girl. I'm supervising the operating room."

"But you'll go out with me tonight—won't you? We'll get them to play 'All Alone.'"

She paused, regarding him.

"Yes, I've been all alone for a lot of time now. I'm somebody—you don't seem to realize it. Say who is this Berlin anyhow? He was a singer in a dive, wasn't he? My brother ran a roadhouse and he gave me money to get started with. But I thought I was away from all that. Who is this Irving Berlin? I hear he's just married a society girl—"

"He's just married—"

She had to go: "Excuse me. I've got to fire an interne before this gets going."

"I was an interne once. I understand."

They were out at last. She was making three thousand a year now and he was still being of a conservative old Vermont family.

"This Irving Berlin now. Is he happy with this Mackay girl? Those songs don't sound—"

"I guess he is. The point is how happy are you?"

"Oh, we discussed that so long ago. What do I matter? I matter in a big way—but when I was a little country girl your fambly decided—

"Not *you*," she said at the alarm in his eyes. "I know *you* never did."

"I knew something else about you. I knew three things—that you were a Yonkers girl—and didn't pronounce the language like I did—"

"And that I wanted to marry you. Let's forget it. Your friend Mr. Berlin can talk better than we can. Listen to him."

"I'm listening."

"No. But *lis*den, I mean."

Not for just a year but—

"Why do you say my friend Mr. Berlin? I never saw the guy."

"I thought maybe you'd met him in Vienna in all these years."

"I never saw him."

"He married the girl—didn't he?"

"What are you crying about?"

"I'm not crying. I just said he married the girl—didn't he? Isn't that all right to say? When you've come so far—when—"

"You are crying," he said.

"No, I'm not. Honest. It's this work. It wears down your eyes. Let's dance."

–o
–ver
–head

They were playing.

Blue
skies
o
ver
head

She looked up out of his arms suddenly.

"Do you suppose they're happy?"

"Who?"

"Irving Berlin and the Mackay girl?"

"How should I know whether they're happy? I tell you I never knew them—never saw them."

A moment later she whispered:

"We all knew them."

III

This story is about tunes. Perhaps the tunes swing the people or the people the tunes. Anyhow:

"We'll never do it," he remarked with some finality.

Smoke gets in your eyes, said the music.

"Why?"

"Because we're too old. You wouldn't want to anyhow—you've got that job at Duke's hospital."

"I just got it."

"Well, you've just got it. And it's going to pay you four thousand."

"That's probably half what you make."

"You mean you want to try it anyhow?"

When your heart's on fire

"No. I guess you're right. It's too late."

"—Too late for what?"

"Just too late—like you told me."

"But I didn't mean it."

"You were right though. . . . Be quiet."

Lovely
to look at
Romantic
to know

"You're all those things in the song," he said passionately.

"What? Lovely to look at and all that? You should have told me that fifteen years ago. Now I'm superintendent of a women's hospital." She added: "And I'm still a woman." Then she added: "But I'm not the woman you knew anymore. I'm another woman."

—lovely to look at

the orchestra repeated.

"Yes, I was lovely to look at when I was nothing—when I couldn't even talk plain—"

"I never knew—"

"Oh let's not go over it. Listen to what they're playing."

"It's called 'Lovely to Look At.'"

"Who's it by?"

"A man named Jerome Kern."

"Did you meet *him* when you went back to Europe the second time? Is he a friend of yours?"

"I never saw him. What gives you the impression I met all these big shots? I'm a doctor. Not a musician."

She wondered about her own bitterness.

"I suppose because all those years I met nobody," she said finally. "Sure, I once saw Dr. Kelly at a distance. But here I am—because I got good at my job."

"And here I am, because—"

"You'll always be wonderful to me. What did you say this man's name was?"

"Kern. And I didn't say it *was*. I said it *is*."

"That's the way you used to talk to me. And now both of us are fat and—sort of middle-aged. We never had much. Did we?"

"It wasn't my fault."

"It wasn't anybody's fault. It was just meant to be like that. Let's dance. That's a good tune. What did you say was this man's name?"

"Kern."

They
asked me how I
knew-ew-ew—

"We've had all that anyhow, haven't we?" she asked him. "All those people—that Youmans, that Berlin, that Kern. They must have been through hell to be able to write like that. And we sort of listened to them, didn't we?"

"But my God, that's so little—" he began but her mood changed and she said:

"Let's not say anything about it. It was all we had—everything we'll ever know about life. What were their names—you knew their names."

"Their names were—"

"Didn't you ever know *any* of them in that fifteen years around Europe?"

"I never saw one of them."

"Well, I never will." She hesitated before the wide horizon of how she might have lived. How she might have married this man, borne him children, died for him—of how she had lived out of sordid poverty and education—into power—and spinsterhood. And she cared not a damn for her man anymore because he had never gone off with her. But she wondered how these composers had lived. Youmans and Irving Berlin and Jerome Kern and she thought that if any of their wives turned up in this hospital she would try to make them happy.

THE ANTS AT PRINCETON

Sufficient time having elapsed it is now possible to tell the facts about a case concerning which little is known, but about which the wildest speculations have been made. As a Princeton man and a friend of certain University officials the present author is in a position to know the true story, from its beginning at a faculty meeting to its nigh tragic ending at an intercollegiate football game.

One detail will forever elude me—which member of the faculty first conceived the idea of admitting *ants* as students to the University. The reasons given, I remember, were that the insects by their highly complicated organizing power, their discipline and above all their industry would set an example to the other students.

In any event the experiment was inaugurated one autumn under what seemed the best auspices. It was possible, through the efforts of Professor ______ of the bacteriological department, and through the generosity of Mr. ______ of the Board of Trustees, to find a number of ants suitable to the experiment. And so tactfully was it managed that many of the students were totally unaware of the presence of their new classmates, and, but for a certain incident which forms the basis of this story, might have remained so all through college.

Some of the ants, because of their diminutive stature, found difficulty in "keeping up" with their fellow students and these were reluctantly dropped at midyear examinations. The majority of them did well, however, and all progressed favorably through the year in spite of a growing inferiority complex among them. This complex was strongest in an especially large, well-developed ant, in whom the conviction gradually grew that it was his destiny to justify his people and their abilities before the rest of the student body.

As I say, his stature approached that of a man, and it was natural that his ambition should take the form of making for himself a berth on the varsity football team.

This was not so difficult, for during the previous year the team had been disorganized. It was between regimes, so to speak, and Fritz Crisler had been called East from the University of Minnesota to take the reins.

One of Mr. Crisler's first acts in assuming control was to ask for full independence in molding a newer and better team—and the first matter that came up in this connection naturally centered about the ant.

For the ant by this time was playing running guard on the second varsity and to older alumni it seemed almost a disgrace that a team which had in other days contained such legendary heroes as Hillebrand, Biffy Lea, Big Bill Edwards and the Poes should have an *ant* on it, no matter what his personal character or ability.

But Crisler was firm.

"At Minnesota," he would say, "we have no racial discriminations on our teams—except of course against Scandinavians."

So as spring practice turned to fall practice the older alumni became resigned to the situation. And meanwhile the ant was moved up to the first varsity, in which he became an important cog because of his versatility, playing secondary defense on the offense and secondary offense on the defense.

By the beginning of the season the coaches were beginning to think of him as a potential All-American. He was big and rugged and the dazzling way in which he twisted through the line on all fours, as well as his confusing ability to carry the ball under any of his eight arms, seemed to inaugurate a new era in American football. The whole offense was gradually built about him.

Every old Princetonian will remember that season—how in turn Cornell, Pennsylvania, Dartmouth, Columbia and Yale, and the two "breathers" (as the easy games were called), the Lawrenceville Seconds and the New Jersey School for Drug Addicts, fell before the onslaught of the Tiger—or rather of the ant, for it was to him that the sportswriters gave full credit. When his head was torn off in the Yale game there was dismay on the campus and a sigh of relief went over the undergraduate body when it was once more fixed in place.

Only one obstacle lay in the way of a victorious season and a sure trip to the Rose Bowl. The last game that year was with Harvard;

and the captain of the Crimson, Cabot Saltonville, who also played running guard, declared that he would rather cancel the game than play against an ant.

"I do not think it necessary to give any reasons," he declared to an eager press, "but I assure you on my word as an old Groton man it is not a question of fear."

The battle raged in the newspapers and on the two campuses. The Princetonians naturally saw in it a disingenuous desire to get rid of their star player. The claim was made that a Maeterlinck had written about ants while only an Adams had written about Bostonians. The Cambridgians stood almost unanimously behind their captain and broke up a radical meeting which considered the matter an aspect of the class war.

In the end Princeton yielded. The ant would sit on the sidelines. Saltonville had won.

As the game progressed the result was as prophesied. Without their quintuple threat the Princeton team was as paralyzed. Steadily the score mounted 7-0, 14-0, 50-0, 65-0—while the cheering from the Tiger stands gradually took on the semblance of a groan.

Finally someone—legend ascribes it to a freshman—started a sing-song slogan:

"We want 'Aunty'.
We want 'Aunty'."

Those nearby took it up and finally the whole orange-and-black section were chanting it.

"We want Aunty!"

It was here that Captain Saltonville of Harvard made his great mistake. There were only ten minutes to play and in the overweening confidence engendered by the score he was moved to one of those gestures of chivalry inherited from a long line of New England ancestors.

He called time out and shouted to the Princeton sidelines:

"Send in that insect."

They sent him in. He was in his civilian clothes for he had not expected to play, but before ten seconds had passed that seemed to make no difference, for once he was on the field a new spirit possessed the Princeton players. They swung into their old formations and with the ant leading the tandems rushed down the field. Crisler, as has been said, had built an offense around him that had carried them through an undefeated season. As "Aunty" bucked, tackled, spun, reversed, kicked and passed, hundreds of other smaller ants making their way cautiously through the grass swarmed over the Harvard players, and at each starting signal nipped them with such vehemence as to completely destroy their charge and spoil any vestige of an offense. (Some of them, by penetrating the players' nether garments, gave rise to a famous phrase which would be indelicate to set down here.)

Captain Saltonville, his face black with ants so that he could scarcely see, cursed his generosity. But still he saw the score roll up 6-65, 25-65, 55-65, 64-65—until Princeton was ahead at last. Then he decided on a desperate measure. He would "get" Aunty. He would violate all the traditions of his family and play dirty.

The signal was given and in he rushed.

"Bim!" went his fist, under the scrimmage. "Bim! Bam! Bim!"

Something warned him even at the moment that he was being rash.

And presently the huge throng was treated to a strange sight. Out of the pile burst Captain Saltonville, running at full speed, and after him, with a ferocious light in his beady eyes, came the ant. Past his own goal posts ran the Cambridgian, and then with a glance behind and a terrified cry, up he went over the barrier into the stands, up the aisle he climbed with the ant always behind him.

Terrified, the crowd watched knowing that eventually Captain Saltonville would reach the top of the stadium with no alternative to a fifty-foot leap to the ground.

The stricken Massachuten reached the press box and paused, white with anguish. Nearer and nearer came the ant, impeded only a little by the efforts of Harvard men to head him off.

And then another anonymous figure walks into this story. It was a young resourceful sportswriter.

"If you will give the proper statement to the press," he said, "I think I can calm him down."

"Anything!" cried Saltonville.

Carefully the reporter dictated and Saltonville repeated after him into the mike, his blood quivering with shame at the words.

"This anim— I mean my honorable opponent, is superior to me . . . in industry, character and courage. . . ." He hurried on for his adversary was within hearing: "He is a gentleman and sportsman and I am proud to have encountered him even in defeat."

The ant heard and stopped. Flattery is sweet and his fighting nature was mollified.

The pressman spoke for him.

"Do you mean that, Captain Saltonville?" he asked.

"Of course I do," faltered the son of John Harvard. "That's why I hurried up to the press box. I couldn't keep back the truth any longer."

And that is the true story of the ants at Princeton. That they became a nuisance and had to be exterminated the following spring does not detract from the credit of their achievement.

The extermination order did not of course apply to "Aunty." You can see him any day now, if you are curious, for he has specialized in the future of his own people and holds down with credit the Harkness Chair of Insectology at Yale and in his spare time coaches the team. And Captain Saltonville is still remembered as one of the fastest running guards the Crimson ever knew.

“I DIDN’T GET OVER”

I was ’sixteen in college and it was our twentieth reunion this year. We always called ourselves the “War Babies”—anyhow we were all in the damn thing and this time there was more talk about the war than at any previous reunion, perhaps because war’s in the air once more.

Three of us were being talkative on the subject in Pete’s back room the night after commencement, when a classmate came in and sat down with us. We knew he was a classmate because we remembered his face and name vaguely, and he marched with us in the alumni parade, but he’d left college as a junior and had not been back these twenty years.

“Hello there—ah—Hib,” I said after a moment’s hesitation. The others took the cue and we ordered a round of beer and went on with what we were talking about.

“I tell you it was kind of moving when we laid that wreath this afternoon.” He referred to a bronze plaque commemorating the ’sixteeners who died in the war. “To read the names of Abe Danzer and Pop McGowan and those fellows and to think they’ve been dead for twenty years and we’ve only been getting old.”

“To be that young again I’d take a chance on another war,” I said, and to the new arrival: “Did you get over, Hib?”

“I was in the army but I didn’t get over.”

The war and the beer and the hours flowed along. Each of us shot off our mouths about something amusing, or unique, or terrible—all except Hib. Only when a pause came he said almost apologetically:

“I would have gotten over except that I was supposed to have slapped a little boy.”

We looked at him inquiringly.

“Of course I didn’t,” he added. “But there was a row about it.” His voice died away but we encouraged him—we had talked a lot and he seemed to rate a hearing.

"Nothing much to tell. The little boy, downtown with his father, said some officer with a blue M. P. band slapped him in the crowd and he picked me! A month afterwards they found he was always accusing soldiers of slapping him, so they let me go. What made me think of it was Abe Danzer's name on that plaque this afternoon. They put me in Leavenworth for a couple of weeks while they investigated me, and he was in the next cell to mine."

"Abe *Danzer!*"

He had been sort of a class hero and we all exclaimed aloud in the same breath. "Why he was recommended for the D.S.C.!"

"I know it."

"What on earth was Abe Danzer doing in Leavenworth?"

Again Hibbing became apologetic.

"Oddly enough I was the man who arrested him. But he didn't blame me because it was all in line of duty, and when I turned up in the next cell a few months later he even laughed about it."

We were all interested now.

"What did you have to arrest him for?"

"Well, I'd been put on Military Police in Kansas City and almost the first call I got was to take a detail of men with fixed bayonets to the big hotel there—I forget the name—and go to a certain room. When I tapped on the door I never saw so many shoulder stars and shoulder leaves in my life; there were at least a brace apiece of generals and colonels. And in the center stood Abe Danzer and a girl—a tart—both of them drunk as monkeys. But it took me a minute's blinking before I realized what else was the matter: the girl had on Abe's uniform overcoat and cap, and Abe had on her dress and hat. They'd gone down in the lobby like that and run straight into the divisional commander."

We three looked at him, first incredulous, then shocked, finally believing. We started to laugh but couldn't quite laugh, only looked at Hibbing with silly half-smiles on our faces, imagining ourselves in Abe's position.

"Did he recognize you?" I asked finally.

"Vaguely."

"Then what happened?"

"It was short and sweet. We changed the clothes on them, put their heads in cold water, then I stood them between two files of bayonets and said, forward march."

"And marched old Abe off to prison!" we exclaimed. "It must have been a crazy feeling."

"It was. From the expression in that general's face I thought they'd probably shoot him. When they put me in Leavenworth a couple of months later I was relieved to find he was still alive."

"I can't understand it," Joe Boone said. "He never drank in college."

"That all goes back to his D.S.C.," said Hibbing.

"You know about that too?"

"Oh yes, we were in the same division—we were from the same state."

"I thought you didn't get overseas."

"I didn't. Neither did Abe. But things seemed to happen to him. Of course nothing like what you fellows must have seen—"

"How did he get recommended for the D.S.C.," I interrupted, "—and what did it have to do with his taking to drink?"

"Well, those drownings used to get on his nerves and he used to dream about it—"

"What drownings? For God's sake, man, you're driving us crazy. It's like that story about 'what killed the dog.'"

"A lot of people thought he had nothing to do with the drownings. They blamed the trench mortar."

We groaned—but there was nothing to do but let him tell it his own way.

"Just what trench mortar?" I asked patiently.

"Rather I mean a Stokes mortar. Remember those old stove-pipes, set at forty-five degrees? You dropped a shell down the mouth."

We remembered.

"Well, the day this happened Abe was in command of what they called the 'fourth battalion,' marching it out fifteen miles to the rifle range. It wasn't really a battalion—it was the machine-gun company, supply company, medical detachment and Headquarters Company. The H.Q. Company had the trench mortars and the one-pounder and the signal corps, band and mounted orderlies—a whole menagerie in itself. Abe commanded that company but on this day most of the medical and supply officers had to go ahead with the advance, so as ranking first lieutenant he commanded the other companies besides. I tell you he must have been proud that day—twenty-one and commanding a battalion; he rode a horse at the head of it and probably pretended to himself that he was Stonewall Jackson. Say, all this must bore you—it happened on the safe side of the ocean."

"Go on."

"Well, we were in Georgia then, and they have a lot of those little muddy rivers with big old rafts they pull across on a slow cable. You could carry about a hundred men if you packed them in. When Abe's 'battalion' got to this river about noon he saw that the third battalion just ahead wasn't even half over, and he figured it would be a full hour at the rate that boat was going to and fro. So he marched the men a little down the shore to get some shade and was just about to let them have chow when an officer came riding up all covered with dust and said he was Captain Brown and where was the officer commanding Headquarters Company."

"'That's me, sir,' said Abe.

"'Well, I just got in to camp and I'm taking command,' the officer said. And then, as if it was Abe's fault, 'I had to ride like hell to catch up with you. Where's the company?'

"'Right here, sir—and next is the supply, and next is the medical—I was just going to let them eat—'

"At the look in his eye Abe shut up. The captain wasn't going to let them eat yet and probably for no more reason than to show off his authority. He wasn't going to let them rest either—he wanted to see what his company looked like (he'd never seen a Headquarters Company except on paper). He thought for a long time and then he decided that he'd have the trench mortar platoon throw some shells across the river for practice. He gave Abe the evil eye again when Abe told him he only had live shells along; he accepted the suggestion of sending over a couple of signal men to wigwag if any farmers were being bumped off. The signal men crossed on the barge and, when they had wigwagged all clear, ran for cover themselves because a Stokes mortar wasn't the most accurate thing in the world. Then the fun began.

"The shells worked on a time fuse and the river was too wide so the first one only made a nice little geyser under water. But the second one just hit the shore with a crash and a couple of horses began to stampede on the ferry boat in midstream only fifty yards down. Abe thought this might hold his majesty the captain but he only said they'd have to get used to shell fire—and ordered another shot. He was like a spoiled kid with an annoying toy.

"Then it happened, as it did once in awhile with those mortars no matter what you did—the shell stuck in the gun. About a dozen people yelled, 'Scatter!' all at once and I scattered as far as anybody and lay down flat, and what did that damn fool Abe do but go up and tilt the barrel and spill out the shell. He'd saved the mortar but there were just five seconds between him and eternity and how he got away before the explosion is a mystery to me."

At this point I interrupted Hibbing.

"I thought you said there were some people killed."

"Oh yes—oh but that was later. The third battalion had crossed by now so Captain Brown formed the companies and we marched off to the ferry boat and began embarking. The second lieutenant in charge of the embarking spoke to the captain:

"'This old tub's kind of tired—been overworked all day. Don't try to pack them in too tight.'

"But the captain wouldn't listen. He sent them over like sardines and each time Abe stood on the rail and shouted:

"'Unbuckle your belts and sling your packs light on your shoulders—' (this without looking at the captain because he'd realized that the captain didn't like orders except his own). But the embarking officer spoke up once more:

"'That raft's low in the water,' he said. 'I don't like it. When you started shooting off that cannon the horses began jumping and the men ran around and unbalanced it.'

"'Tell the captain,' Abe said. 'He knows everything.'

"The captain overheard this. 'There's just one more load,' he said. 'And I don't want any more discussion about it.'

"It was a big load, even according to Captain Brown's ideas. Abe got up on the side to make his announcement.

"'They ought to know that by this time,' Captain Brown snapped. 'They've heard it often enough.'

"'Not this bunch.' Abe rattled it off anyhow and the men unloosened their belts, except a few at the far end who weren't paying attention. Or maybe it was so jammed they couldn't hear.

"We began to sink when we were halfway over, very slowly at first, just a little water around the shoes, but we officers didn't say anything for fear of a panic. It had looked like a small river from the bank but here in the middle and at the rate we were going, it began to look like the widest river in the world.

"In two minutes the water was a yard high in the old soup plate and there wasn't any use concealing things any longer. For once the captain was tongue-tied. Abe got up on the side again and said to stay calm and not rock the boat and we'd get there, and made his speech one last time about slipping off the packs, and told the ones that could swim to jump off when it got to their hips. The men took it well but you could almost tell from their faces which ones could swim and which couldn't.

"She went down with a big *whush!* just twenty yards from shore; her nose grounded in a mud bank five feet under water.

"I don't remember much about the next fifteen minutes. I dove and swam out into the river a few yards for a view, but it all looked like a mass of khaki and water with some sound over it that I remember as a sustained monotone but was composed, I suppose, of cussing, and a few yells of fright, and even a little kidding and laughter. I swam in and helped pull people to shore, but it was a slow business in our shoes. . . .

"When there was nothing more in sight in the river (except one corner of the barge which had perversely decided to bob up) Captain Brown and Abe met. The captain was weak and shaking and his arrogance was gone.

"'Oh God,' he said. 'What'll I do?'

"Abe took control of things—he fell the men in and got squad reports to see if anyone was missing.

"There were three missing in the first squad alone and we didn't wait for the rest—we called for twenty good swimmers to strip and start diving, and as fast as they pulled in a body we started a medico working on it. We pulled out twenty-eight bodies and revived seven. And one of the divers didn't come up—he was found floating down the river next day, and they gave a medal and a pension to his widow."

Hibbing paused and then added: "But I know that's small potatoes to you fellows in the big time."

"Sounds exciting enough to me," said Joe Boone. "I had a good time in France but I spent most of it guarding prisoners at Brest."

"But how about finishing this?" I demanded. "Why did this drive Abe hell-raising?"

"That was the captain," said Hibbing slowly. "A couple of officers tried to get Abe a citation or something for the trench mortar thing. The captain didn't like that, and he began going around saying that when Abe jumped up on the side of the barge to give the unsling order, he'd hung on to the ferry cable and pulled it out of whack. The captain found a couple of people who agreed with him but there were others who thought it was overloading and the commotion the horses made at the shell bursts. But Abe was never very happy in the army after that."

There was an emphatic interruption in the person of Pete himself who said in no uncertain words:

"Mr. Tomlinson and Mr. Boone. Your wives say they calling for the last time. They say this has been one night too often, and if you don't get back to the inn in ten minutes they driving to Philadelphia."

Tommy and Joe Boone arose reluctantly.

"I'm afraid I've monopolized the evening," said Hibbing. "And after what you fellows must have seen."

When they had gone I lingered.

"So, Abe wasn't killed in France."

"No—you'll notice all that tablet says is 'died in service.'"

"What did he die of?"

Hibbing hesitated.

"He was shot by a guard trying to escape from Leavenworth. They'd given him ten years."

"God! And what a great guy he was in college."

"I suppose he was to his friends. But he was a good deal of a snob wasn't he?"

"Maybe to some people."

"He didn't seem to even recognize a lot of his classmates when he met them in the army."

"What do you mean?"

"Just what I say. I told you something that wasn't true tonight. That captain's name wasn't Brown."

Again I asked him what he meant.

"The captain's name was Hibbing," he said. "I was that captain, and when I rode up to join my company he acted as if he'd never even seen me before. It kind of threw me off—because I used to love this place once. Well—good-night."

AN ALCOHOLIC CASE

"Let—go—that—oh-h-h! Please, now, will you? *Don't* start drinking again! Come on—give me the bottle. I told you I'd stay awake givin it to you. Come on. If you do like that a-way—then what are you goin to be like when you go home. Come on—leave it with me—I'll leave half in the bottle. Pul-lease. You know what Dr. Carter says—I'll stay awake and give it to you, or else fix some of it in the bottle—come on—like I told you, I'm too tired to be fightin you all night. . . . All right, drink your fool self to death."

"Would you like some beer?" he asked.

"No, I don't want any beer. Oh, to think that I have to look at you drunk again. My God!"

"Then I'll drink the Coca-Cola."

The girl sat down panting on the bed.

"Don't you believe in anything?" she demanded.

"Nothing you believe in—please—it'll spill."

She had no business there, she thought, no business trying to help him. Again they struggled, but after this time he sat with his head in his hands awhile before he turned around once more.

"Once more you try to get it I'll throw it down," she said quickly. "I will—on the tiles in the bathroom."

"Then I'll step on the broken glass—or you'll step on it."

"Then let go—oh you promised—"

Suddenly she dropped it like a torpedo, sliding underneath her hand and slithering with a flash of red and black and the words: SIR GALAHAD, DISTILLED LOUISVILLE GIN.

It was on the floor in pieces and everything was silent for awhile and she read "Gone with the Wind" about things so lovely that had happened long ago. She began to worry that he would have to go into the bathroom and might cut his feet, and looked up from time to time to see if he would go in. She was very sleepy—the last time she looked up he was crying and he looked like an old Jewish man she had nursed once in California; he had had to go to the bathroom many times. On this case she was unhappy all the time but she thought:

"I guess if I hadn't liked him I wouldn't have stayed on the case."

With a sudden resurgence of conscience she got up and put a chair in front of the bathroom door. She had wanted to sleep because he had got her up early that morning to get a paper with the Yale-Harvard game in it and she hadn't been home all day. That afternoon a relative of his had come in to see him and she had waited outside in the hall where there was a draft with no sweater to put over her uniform.

As well as she could she arranged him for sleeping, put a robe over his shoulders as he sat slumped over his chiffonier, and one on his knees. She sat down in the rocker but she was no longer sleepy; there was plenty to enter on the chart and treading lightly about she found a pencil and put it down:

Pulse 120
Respiration 25
Temp 98—98.4—98.2
Remarks—
—She could make so many:
Tried to get bottle of gin. Threw it away and broke it.
She corrected it to read:
In the struggle it dropped and was broken. Patient was generally difficult.

She started to add as part of her report: *I never want to go on an alcoholic case again*, but that wasn't in the picture. She knew she could wake herself at seven and clean up everything before his niece awakened. It was all part of the game. But when she sat down in the chair she looked at his face, white and exhausted, and counted his breathing again, wondering why it had all happened. He had been so nice today, drawn her a whole strip of his cartoon just for fun and given it to her. She was going to have it framed and hang it in her room. She felt again his thin wrists wrestling against her wrist and remembered the awful things he had said, and she thought too of what the doctor had said to him yesterday:

"You're too good a man to do this to yourself."

She was tired and didn't want to clean up the glass on the bathroom floor, because as soon as he breathed evenly she wanted to get him over to the bed. But she decided finally to clean up the glass first; on her knees, searching a last piece of it, she thought:

—This isn't what I ought to be doing. And this isn't what *he* ought to be doing.

Resentfully she stood up and regarded him. Through the thin delicate profile of his nose came a light snore, sighing, remote, inconsolable. The doctor had shaken his head in a certain way, and she knew that really it was a case that was beyond her. Besides, on her card at the agency was written, on the advice of her elders, "No Alcoholics."

She had done her whole duty, but all she could think of was that when she was struggling about the room with him with that gin bottle there had been a pause when he asked her if she had hurt her elbow against a door and that she had answered: "You don't know how people talk about you, no matter how you think of yourself—" when she knew he had a long time ceased to care about such things.

The glass was all collected—as she got out a broom to make sure, she realized that the glass, in its fragments, was less than a window through which they had seen each other for a moment. He did not know about her sisters, and Bill Markoe whom she had almost married, and she did not know what had brought him to this pitch, when there was a picture on his bureau of his young wife and his two sons and him, all trim and handsome as he must have been five years ago. It was so utterly senseless—as she put a bandage on her finger where she had cut it while picking up the glass she made up her mind she would never take an alcoholic case again.

II

Some Halloween jokester had split the side windows of the bus and she shifted back to the negro section in the rear for fear the glass might fall out. She had her patient's check but no way to cash it at this time of night; there was a quarter and a penny in her purse.

Two nurses she knew were waiting in the hall of Mrs. Hixson's agency.

"What kind of case have you been on?"

"Alcoholic," she said.

"Oh yes—Gretta Hawks told me about it—you were on with that cartoonist who lives at the Forest Park Inn."

"Yes, I was."

"I hear he's pretty fresh."

"He's never done anything to bother me," she lied. "You can't treat them as if they were committed—"

"Oh, don't get bothered—I just heard that around town—oh, you know—they want you to play around with them—"

"Oh, be quiet," she said, surprised at her own rising resentment.

In a moment Mrs. Hixson came out and, asking the other two to wait, signaled her into the office.

"I don't like to put young girls on such cases," she began. "I got your call from the hotel."

"Oh, it wasn't bad, Mrs. Hixson. He didn't know what he was doing and he didn't hurt me in any way. I was thinking much more of my reputation with you. He was really nice all day yesterday. He drew me—"

"I didn't want to send you on that case." Mrs. Hixson thumbed through the registration cards. "You take T. B. cases, don't you? Yes, I see you do. Now here's one—"

The phone rang in a continuous chime. The nurse listened as Mrs. Hixson's voice said precisely:

"I will do what I can—that is simply up to the doctor. . . . That is beyond my jurisdiction. . . . Oh, hello, Hattie, no, I can't now. Look, have you got any nurse that's good with alcoholics? There's somebody up at the Forest Park Inn who needs somebody. Call back will you?"

She put down the receiver. "Suppose you wait outside. What sort of man is this, anyhow? Did he act indecently?"

"He held my hand away," she said, "so I couldn't give him an injection."

"Oh, an invalid he-man," Mrs. Hixson grumbled. "They belong in sanitaria. I've got a case coming along in two minutes that you can get a little rest on. It's an old woman—"

The phone rang again. "Oh, hello, Hattie. . . . Well, how about that big Svensen girl? She ought to be able to take care of any alcoholic. . . . How about Josephine Markham? Doesn't she live in your apartment house? Get her to the phone." Then after a moment, "Joe, would you care to take the case of a well-known cartoonist, or artist, whatever they call themselves, at Forest Park Inn? No, I don't know, but Dr. Carter is in charge and will be around about ten o'clock."

There was a long pause; from time to time Mrs. Hixson spoke:

"I see. . . . Of course, I understand your point of view. . . . Yes, but this isn't supposed to be dangerous—just a little difficult. I never like to send girls to a hotel because I know what riff-raff you're liable to run into. . . . No, I'll find somebody. Even at this hour. Never mind and thanks. Tell Hattie I hope the hat matches the negligee. . . ."

Mrs. Hixson hung up the receiver and made notations on the pad before her. She was a very efficient woman. She had been a nurse and had gone through the worst of it, had been a proud, idealistic, overworked probationer, suffered the abuse of smart internes and the insolence of her first patients, who thought that she was something to be taken into camp immediately for premature commitment to the service of old age. She swung around suddenly from the desk.

"What kind of cases do you want? I told you I have a nice old woman—"

The nurse's brown eyes were alight with a mixture of thoughts—the movie she had just seen about Pasteur and the book they had all read about Florence Nightingale when they were student nurses. And their pride, swinging across the streets in the cold weather at Philadelphia General, as proud of their new capes as debutantes in their furs going in to balls at the hotels.

"I—I think I would like to try the case again," she said amid a cacophony of telephone bells. "I'd just as soon go back if you can't find anybody else."

"But one minute you say you'll never go on an alcoholic case again and the next minute you say you want to go back to one."

"I think I overestimated how difficult it was. Really, I think I could help him."

"That's up to you. But if he tried to grab your wrists."

"But he couldn't," the nurse said. "Look at my wrists: I played basket-ball at Waynesboro High for two years. I'm quite able to take care of him."

Mrs. Hixson looked at her for a long minute. "Well, all right," she said. "But just remember that nothing they say when they're drunk is what they mean when they're sober—I've been all through that; arrange with one of the servants that you can call on him, because you never can tell—some alcoholics are pleasant and some of them are not, but all of them can be rotten."

"I'll remember," the nurse said.

It was an oddly clear night when she went out, with slanting particles of thin sleet making white of a blue-black sky. The bus was the same that had taken her into town but there seemed to be more windows broken now and the bus driver was irritated and talked about what terrible things he would do if he caught any kids. She knew he was just talking about the annoyance in general, just as she had been thinking about the annoyance of an alcoholic. When she came up to the suite and found him all helpless and distraught she would despise him and be sorry for him.

Getting off the bus, she went down the long steps to the hotel, feeling a little exalted by the chill in the air. She was going to take care of him because nobody else would, and because the best people of her profession had been interested in taking care of the cases that nobody else wanted.

She knocked at his study door, knowing just what she was going to say.

He answered it himself. He was in dinner clothes even to a derby hat—but minus his studs and tie.

"Oh, hello," he said casually. "Glad you're back. I woke up a while ago and decided I'd go out. Did you get a night nurse?"

"I'm the night nurse too," she said. "I decided to stay on twenty-four-hour duty."

He broke into a genial, indifferent smile.

"I saw you were gone, but something told me you'd come back. Please find my studs. They ought to be either in a little tortoise-shell box or—"

He shook himself a little more into his clothes, and hoisted the cuffs up inside his coat sleeves.

"I thought you had quit me," he said casually.

"I thought I had, too."

"If you look on that table," he said, "you'll find a whole strip of cartoons that I drew you."

"Who are you going to see?" she asked.

"It's the President's secretary," he said. "I had an awful time trying to get ready. I was about to give up when you came in. Will you order me some sherry?"

"One glass," she agreed wearily.

From the bathroom he called presently:

"Oh, nurse, nurse, Light of my Life, where is another stud?"

"I'll put it in."

In the bathroom she saw the pallor and the fever on his face and smelled the mixed peppermint and gin on his breath.

"You'll come up soon?" she asked. "Dr. Carter's coming at ten."

"What nonsense! You're coming down with me."

"Me?" she exclaimed. "In a sweater and skirt? Imagine!"

"Then I won't go."

"All right then, go to bed. That's where you belong anyhow. Can't you see these people tomorrow?"

"No, of course not."

"Of course not!"

She went behind him and reaching over his shoulder tied his tie—his shirt was already thumbed out of press where he had put in the studs, and she suggested:

"Won't you put on another one, if you've got to meet some people you like?"

"All right, but I want to do it myself."

"Why can't you let me help you?" she demanded in exasperation. "Why can't you let me help you with your clothes? What's a nurse for—what good am I doing? Do you think I never took care of a man?"

He sat down suddenly on the toilet seat.

"All right—go on."

"Now don't grab my wrist," she said, and then: "Excuse me."

"Don't worry. It didn't hurt. You'll see in a minute."

She had the coat, vest and stiff shirt off him but before she could pull his undershirt over his head he dragged at his cigarette, delaying her.

"Now watch this," he said. "One—two—three."

She pulled up the undershirt; simultaneously he thrust the crimson-grey point of the cigarette like a dagger against his heart. It crushed out against a copper plate on his left rib about the size of a silver dollar, and he said "Ouch!" as a stray spark fluttered down against his stomach.

Now was the time to be hardboiled, she thought. She knew there were three medals from the war in his jewel box, but she had risked many things herself: tuberculosis among them and one time something worse, though she had not known it and had never quite forgiven the doctor for not telling her.

"You've had a hard time with that, I guess," she said lightly as she sponged him. "Won't it ever heal?"

"Never. That's a copper plate."

"Well, it's no excuse for what you're doing to yourself."

He bent his great brown eyes on her—shrewd, aloof, confused. He signaled to her, in one second, his Will to Die, and for all her training and experience she knew she could never do anything constructive with him. He stood up, steadying himself on the wash basin and fixing his eye on some place just ahead.

"Now, if I'm going to stay here you're not going to get at that liquor," she said.

Suddenly she knew he wasn't looking for that. He was looking at the corner where she had dropped the bottle this afternoon. She stared at his handsome face, weak and defiant—afraid to turn even halfway because she knew that death was in that corner where he was looking. She knew death—she had heard it, smelt its unmistakable odor, but she had never seen it before it entered into anyone, and she knew this man saw it in the corner of his bathroom; that it was standing there looking at him while he spit from a feeble cough and rubbed the result into the braid of his trousers. It shone there . . .

crackling for a moment as evidence of the last gesture he ever made.

She tried to express it next day to Mrs. Hixson:

"It's not like anything you can beat—no matter how hard you try. This one could have twisted my wrists until he sprained them and that wouldn't matter so much to me. It's just that you can't really help them and it's so discouraging—it's all for nothing."

THE LONG WAY OUT
[OUBLIETTE]

We were talking about some of the older castles in Touraine and we touched upon the iron cage in which Louis XI imprisoned Cardinal Balue for six years, then upon oubliettes and such horrors. I had seen several of the latter, simply dry wells thirty or forty feet deep wherein a man was thrown to wait for nothing; since I have such a tendency to claustrophobia that a Pullman berth is a certain nightmare, they had made a lasting impression. So it was rather a relief when a doctor told this story—that is, it was a relief when he began it for it seemed to have nothing to do with the tortures long ago.

There was a young woman named Mrs. King who was very happy with her husband. They were well-to-do and deeply in love but at the birth of her second child she went into a long coma and emerged with a clear case of schizophrenia or "split personality." Her delusion, which had to do with something about the Declaration of Independence, had little bearing on the case and as she regained her health it began to disappear. At the end of ten months she was a convalescent patient scarcely marked by what had happened to her and very eager to go back into the world.

She was only twenty-one, rather girlish in an appealing way and a favorite with the staff of the sanitarium. When she became well enough so that she could take an experimental trip with her husband there was a general interest in the venture. One nurse had gone into Philadelphia with her to get a dress, another knew the story of her rather romantic courtship in Mexico and everyone had seen her two babies on visits to the hospital. The trip was to Virginia Beach for five days.

It was a joy to watch her make ready, dressing and packing meticulously and living in the gay trivialities of hair waves and such things. She was ready half an hour before the time of departure and she paid some visits on the floor in her powder blue gown and her hat that looked like one minute after an April shower. Her frail lovely face, with just that touch of startled sadness that often lingers after an illness, was alight with anticipation.

"We'll just do nothing," she said. "That's my ambition. To get up when I want to for three straight mornings and stay up late for three straight nights. To buy a bathing suit by myself and order a meal."

When the time approached Mrs. King decided to wait downstairs instead of in her room and as she passed along the corridors with an orderly carrying her suitcase she waved to the other patients, sorry that they too were not going on a gorgeous holiday. The superintendent wished her well, two nurses found excuse to linger and share her infectious joy.

"What a beautiful tan you'll get, Mrs. King."

"Be sure and send a postcard."

About the time she left her room her husband's car was hit by a truck on his way from the city—he was hurt internally and not expected to live more than a few hours. The information was received at the hospital in a glassed-in office adjoining the hall where Mrs. King waited. The operator, seeing Mrs. King and knowing that the glass was not sound proof, asked the head nurse to come immediately. The head nurse hurried aghast to a doctor and he decided what to do. So long as the husband was still alive it was best to tell her nothing, but of course she must know that he was not coming today.

Mrs. King was greatly disappointed.

"I suppose it's silly to feel that way," she said. "After all these months what's one more day? He said he'd come tomorrow, didn't he?"

The nurse was having a difficult time but she managed to pass it off until the patient was back in her room. Then they assigned a very experienced and phlegmatic nurse to keep Mrs. King away from other patients and from newspapers. By the next day the matter would be decided one way or another.

But her husband lingered on and they continued to prevaricate. A little before noon next day one of the nurses was passing along the corridor when she met Mrs. King, dressed as she had been the day before but this time carrying her own suitcase.

"I'm going to meet my husband," she explained. "He couldn't come yesterday but he's coming today at the same time."

The nurse walked along with her. Mrs. King had the freedom of the building and it was difficult to simply steer her back to her room, and the nurse did not want to tell a story that would contradict what the authorities were telling her. When they reached the front hall she signaled to the operator, who fortunately understood. Mrs. King gave herself a last inspection in the mirror and said:

"I'd like to have a dozen hats just like this to remind me to be this happy always."

When the head nurse came in frowning a minute later she demanded:

"Don't tell me George is delayed?"

"I'm afraid he is. There's nothing much to do but be patient."

Mrs. King laughed ruefully. "I wanted him to see my costume when it was absolutely new."

"Why, there isn't a wrinkle in it."

"I guess it'll last till tomorrow. I oughtn't to be blue about waiting one more day when I'm so utterly happy."

"Certainly not."

That night her husband died and at a conference of doctors next morning there was some discussion about what to do—it was a risk to tell her and a risk to keep it from her. It was decided finally to say that Mr. King had been called away and thus destroy her hope of an immediate meeting; when she was reconciled to this they could tell her the truth.

As the doctors came out of the conference one of them stopped and pointed. Down the corridor toward the outer hall walked Mrs. King carrying her suitcase.

Dr. Pirie, who had been in special charge of Mrs. King, caught his breath.

"This is awful," he said. "I think perhaps I'd better tell her now. There's no use saying he's away when she usually hears from him twice a week, and if we say he's sick she'll want to go to him. Anybody else like the job?"

II

One of the doctors in the conference went on a fortnight's vacation that afternoon. On the day of his return in the same corridor at the same hour, he stopped at the sight of a little procession coming toward him—an orderly carrying a suitcase, a nurse and Mrs. King dressed in the powder blue colored suit and wearing the spring hat.

"Good morning, Doctor," she said. "I'm going to meet my husband and we're going to Virginia Beach. I'm going to the hall because I don't want to keep him waiting."

He looked into her face, clear and happy as a child's. The nurse signaled to him that it was as ordered so he merely bowed and spoke of the pleasant weather.

"It's a beautiful day," said Mrs. King, "but of course even if it was raining it would be a beautiful day for me."

The doctor looked after her, puzzled and annoyed—why are they letting this go on, he thought. What possible good can it do?

Meeting Dr. Pirie he put the question to him.

"We tried to tell her," Dr. Pirie said. "She laughed and said we were trying to see whether she's still sick. You could use the word unthinkable in an exact sense here—his death is unthinkable to her."

"But you can't just go on like this."

"Theoretically no," said Dr. Pirie. "A few days ago when she packed up as usual the nurse tried to keep her from going. From out in the hall I could see her face, see her begin to go to pieces—for the first time, mind you. Her muscles were tense and her eyes glazed and her voice was thick and shrill when she very politely called the nurse a liar. It was touch and go there for a minute whether we had a tractable patient or a restraint case—and I stepped in and told the nurse to take her down to the reception room—"

He broke off as the procession that had just passed appeared again, headed back to the ward. Mrs. King stopped and spoke to Dr. Pirie.

"My husband's been delayed," she said. "Of course I'm disappointed but they tell me he's coming tomorrow and after waiting so long one more day doesn't seem to matter. Don't you agree with me, Doctor?"

"I certainly do, Mrs. King."

She took off her hat.

"I've got to put aside these clothes—I want them to be as fresh tomorrow as they are today." She looked closely at the hat. "There's a speck of dust on it, but I think I can get it off. Perhaps he won't notice."

"I'm sure he won't."

"Really I don't mind waiting another day. It'll be this time tomorrow before I know it, won't it?"

When she had gone along the younger doctor said:

"There are still the two children."

"I don't think the children are going to matter. When she 'went under,' she tied up this trip with the idea of getting well. If we took it away she'd have to go to the bottom and start over."

"Could she?"

"There's no prognosis," said Dr. Pirie. "I was simply explaining why she was allowed to go to the hall this morning."

"But there's tomorrow morning and next morning."

"There's always the chance," said Dr. Pirie, "that some day he will be there."

The doctor ended his story here, rather abruptly. When we pressed him to tell what happened he protested that the rest was anticlimax—that all sympathy eventually wears out and that finally the staff at the sanitarium had simply accepted the fact.

"But does she still go to meet her husband?"

"Oh yes, it's always the same—but the other patients, except new ones, hardly look up when she passes along the hall. The nurses manage to substitute a new hat every year or so but she still wears the same suit. She's always a little disappointed but she makes the best of it, very sweetly too. It's not an unhappy life as far as we know, and in some funny way it seems to set an example of tranquility to the other patients. For God's sake let's talk about something else—let's go back to oubliettes."

THE GUEST IN ROOM NINETEEN

Mr. Cass knew he couldn't go to sleep so he put his tie on again and went back to the lobby. The guests were all gone to bed but a little aura of activity seemed to linger about a half-finished picture puzzle, and the night watchman was putting a big log on the fire.

Mr. Cass limped slowly across the soft carpet, stopped behind him and grunted, "Heavy?"

The watchman, a wiry old mountaineer, looked around sharply. "A hundred pound. It's wet—it'll be one o'clock before it's burning good."

Mr. Cass let himself into a chair. Last year he had been active, driving his own car—but he had suffered a stroke before coming south last month and now life was like waiting for an unwelcome train. He was very lonely.

The watchman built burning chunks about the wet log.

"Thought you was somebody else when you came in," he said.

"Who did you think I was?"

"I thought you was the fella who's always coming in late. First night I was on duty he came in at two without any noise and give me a start. Every night he comes in late."

After a pause Mr. Cass asked:

"What's his name?"

"I never did ask him his name."

Another pause. The fire leapt into a premature, short-lived glow.

"How do you know he's a guest here?"

"Oh, he's a guest here." But the watchman considered the matter for the first time. "I hear him go down the corridor and around the corner and then I hear his door shut."

"He may be a burglar," said Mr. Cass.

"Oh, he's no burglar. He said he'd been coming here a long time."

"Did he tell you he wasn't a burglar?"

The watchman laughed.

"I never asked him that."

The log slipped and the old man adjusted it; Mr. Cass envied his strength. It seemed to him that if he had strength he could run out of here, hurry along the roads of the world, the roads that led back, and not sit waiting.

Almost every evening he played bridge with the two clerks, and one night last week he simply passed away during a bridge hand, shrinking up through space, up through the ceilings like a wisp of smoke, looking back, looking down at his body hunched at the table, his white fist clutching the cards. He heard the bids and his own voice speaking—then the two clerks were helping him into his room and one of them sat with him till the doctor came. . . . After awhile Mr. Cass had to go to the bathroom and he decided to go to the public one. It took him some time. When he came back to the lobby the watchman said:

"That fella came in late again. I found out he's in number nineteen."

"What's his name?"

"I didn't like to ask him that—I knew I could find out from his number."

Mr. Cass sat down.

"I'm number eighteen," he said. "I thought there were just some women next to me."

The watchman went behind the desk to the mail rack. After a moment he reported.

"Funny thing—his box ain't here. There's number eighteen, that's Mr. Cass—"

"That's me."

"—and the next one is twenty, on the second floor. I must of understood him wrong."

"I told you he was a burglar. What did he look like?"

"Well, now he wasn't an old man and he wasn't a young man. He seemed like he'd been sick and he had little holes all over his face."

Despite its inadequacy the description somehow conjured up a picture for Mr. Cass. His partner, John Canisius, had never looked old or young and he had little holes in his face.

Suddenly Mr. Cass felt the same sensation stealing over him that he had felt the other night. Dimly he was aware that the watchman had gone to the door and dimly he heard his own voice saying: "Leave it open"; then the cold air swept in and his spirit left him and romped around the room with it. He saw John Canisius come in the open door and look at him and advance toward him, and then realized it was the watchman, pouring a paper cup of water into his mouth and spilling it on his collar.

"Thanks."

"Feel all right now?"

"Did I faint?" he muttered.

"You fell over kind of funny. Reckon I better help you get back into your room."

At the door of number eighteen Mr. Cass halted and pointed his cane at the room next door.

"What's that number?"

"Seventeen. And that one without a number is the manager's rooms. There ain't any nineteen."

"Do you think I'd better go in?"

"Sure thing." The watchman lowered his voice. "If you're thinking about that fella, I must of heard him wrong. I can't go looking for him tonight."

"He's in here," said Mr. Cass.

"No, he ain't."

"Yes, he is. He's waiting for me."

"Shucks, I'll go in with you."

He opened the door, turned on the light and took a quick look around.

"See—ain't nobody here."

Mr. Cass slept well and the next day was full spring, so he decided to go out. It took him a long time to walk down the hill from the hotel and his progress across the double tracks took a good three minutes and attracted solicitous attention, but it was practically a country stroll compared to his negotiation of the highway which was accompanied by a great caterwauling of horns and screech of brakes. A welcoming committee awaited him on the curb and helped him into the drug store where, exhausted by his adventure, he called a taxi to go home.

Because of this he fell asleep while undressing and waking at twelve felt dismal and oppressed. Finding it difficult to rise he rang, and the night watchman answered the bell.

"Glad to help you, Mr. Cass, if you'll wait five minutes. It's turned cold again and I want to get in a big log of wood."

"Oh," said Mr. Cass. And then: "Has the guest come in yet?"

"He just got in now."

"Did you ask him if he's a burglar?"

"He's no burglar, Mr. Cass. He's a nice fella. He's going to help me with this big log. I'll be right back."

"Did he say what room—" But the watchman was gone and Mr. Cass could only wait.

He waited five minutes, he waited ten. Then he gradually realized that the watchman was not coming back. It was plain that the watchman had been sent for.

Everyone tried to keep distressing things from Mr. Cass, and it was not until the following evening that he heard what had happened from some whispering at the desk. The watchman had collapsed trying to lift a log too heavy for him. Mr. Cass said nothing because he knew that old people have to be careful what they say. Only he knew the watchman had not been alone.

After Easter the hotel's short season faded out and it was not worth while to hire a new watchman, but Mr. Cass continued to have lonely nights and often he sat in the lobby after the other guests went to bed. One April night he dozed there for awhile, awakening to find that it was after two and he was not alone in the lobby.

The current of cooler air might have roused him, for a man he did not know had just come in the door.

The man was of no special age but even by the single light left burning Mr. Cass could see that he was a pale man, that there were little holes in his face like the ravages of some disease, and he did not look like John Canisius, his partner.

"Good evening," said the stranger.

"Hm," said Mr. Cass, and then as the man turned down the corridor he spoke up in a strong voice:

"You're out late."

"Yes, quite late."

"You a guest here?"

"Yes."

Mr. Cass dragged himself to his feet and stood leaning on his cane.

"I suppose you live in room nineteen," he said.

"As it happens, I do."

"You needn't lie to me," said Mr. Cass. "I'm not an ignorant mountaineer. Are you a burglar—or did you come for someone?"

The man's face seemed to grow even whiter.

"I don't understand you," he said.

"In any case I want you to get out of here," said Mr. Cass. He was growing angry and it gave him a certain strength. "Otherwise I'm going to arouse the hotel."

The stranger hesitated.

"There's no need of doing that," he said quietly. "That would be—"

Mr. Cass raised his cane menacingly, held it up a moment, then let it down slowly.

"Wait a minute," he said. "I may want you to do something for me."

"What is it?"

"It's getting cold in here. I want you to help me bring in a log to put on the fire."

The stranger was startled by the request.

"Are you strong enough?" he asked.

"Of course I'm strong enough." Mr. Cass stood very upright, throwing back his shoulders.

"I can get it alone."

"No, you can't. You help me or I'll arouse the house."

They went out and down the back steps, Mr. Cass refusing the stranger's arm. He found, in fact, that he could walk much better than he thought and he left his cane by the stoop so that both hands were free for the log.

It was dark in the woodshed and the stranger lit a match. There was only one log, but it was over a hundred pounds, quite big enough to amply fill the small fireplace.

"Hadn't I better do this?" said the stranger.

Mr. Cass did not answer, but bent and put his hands on the rough surface. The touch seemed to stimulate him, he felt no pain or strain in his back at all.

"Catch hold there," he ordered.

"Are you sure—"

"Catch hold!"

Mr. Cass took a long breath of cool air into his lungs and shifted his hands on the log. His arms tightened, then his shoulders and the muscles on his back.

"Lift," he grunted. And suddenly the log moved, came up with him as he straightened, and for a triumphant moment he stood there squarely, cradling it against him. Then out into space he went, very slowly, carrying the log which seemed lighter and lighter, seeming to melt away in his arms. He wanted to call back some word of mockery and derision to the stranger, but he was already too far away, out on the old roads that led back where he wished to be.

Everyone in the hotel was sorry to lose Mr. Cass, the manager especially, for he read the open letter on Mr. Cass's desk saying that no further money could be remitted that year.

"What a shame. He'd been here so many years that we'd have been glad to carry him awhile until he made arrangements."

Mr. Cass was the right sort of client—it was because of such guests that the manager had tried to keep his brother out of sight all winter.

The brother, a tough number, was considerably shaken by what had happened.

"That's what I get for trying to be a help," he said. "I should have known better. Both those old guys looked exactly like death itself to me."

IN THE HOLIDAYS

The hospital was thinly populated, for many convalescents had taken risks to get home for the holidays and prospective patients were gritting their teeth until vacation was over. In the private ward one interne took on the duties of three, and six nurses the duties of a dozen. After New Year's it would be different—just now the corridors were long and lonely.

Young Dr. Kamp came into the room of Mr. McKenna, who was not very ill, and snatched rest in the easy chair.

"How's back feel?" he asked.

"Better, Doc. I thought I'd get up and dress tomorrow."

"All right—if you haven't any fever. The X-ray plates didn't show a thing."

"I've got to be out of here day after tomorrow."

"When you get home you better see your own doctor, though I never have felt you were seriously ill—in spite of the pain. We've got a patient downstairs with a dizzy head that we can't find a thing the matter with—there's probably faulty elimination of some kind, but he came through every test sound as a dollar."

"What's his name?" McKenna asked.

"Griffin. So you see sometimes there just isn't any diagnosis to be made. Say, were you in the war?"

"Me? No, I was too young."

"Did you ever get shot?"

"No."

"That's funny—the X-ray showed a couple of things that looked like slugs in your buttocks."

"Oh, that was a hunting accident," said McKenna.

When the doctor left, the nurse came in—she was the wrong one, not the beautiful little student nurse, dark and rosy, with eyes as soft as blue oil. Miss Hunter was plain and talked about the man she was marrying next month.

"That's why I'm here on New Year's Eve. We need the money and a girl gave me five dollars to take her place over the holidays. I can't see him but I write him a whole book every night."

"It certainly is some life in here," said McKenna. "The food makes me sick."

"Aren't you ashamed—it's better than we get. You ought to see that little student nurse go for the dessert you left today."

He brightened momentarily.

"The pretty one?" Maybe this was an angle.

"Miss Collins." She proffered him a vile liquid. "You can drink her health with this cocktail."

"Oh, skip it. This doctor thinks I'm just bluffing—me and some other fellow that's dizzy in the head. Name's Griffin—do you take care of him?"

"He's down on the first floor."

"What does he look like?"

"Well, he wears glasses, about your age."

"Is he handsome like me?"

"He's very pale and he's got a big bald place in his mustache. What's the use of having a mustache if you have a bald place in it."

He shifted in bed restlessly.

"I think I'd sleep better if I got up for awhile—just around the corridors. I could get a paper in the office and all that."

"I'll ask the doctor."

Without waiting for permission McKenna got up and dressed. He was tying his tie when the nurse returned.

"All right," Miss Hunter said, "but come back soon and wear your overcoat. The corridors are cold. And would you please drop this letter in the box for me?"

McKenna went out and downstairs and through many halls to the main office. He stopped at the registry desk and asked a question, afterwards writing down something on the back of an envelope.

Out in the damp, snowless night he inquired the way to a drug store; he went directly to the phone booth and closeted himself for some minutes. Then he bought a movie magazine and a hip flask of port, and asked for a glass at the fountain.

All around the hospital the streets were quiet and the houses, largely occupied by medical people, were dark and deserted. Across the street the dark fortress of the hospital was blocked out against a pink blur in the downtown sky. There was a mailbox on the corner and after a moment he took out the nurse's letter, tore it slowly into four pieces, and dropped it in the slot. Then he began thinking of the little student nurse, Miss Collins. He had a vague idea about Miss Collins. She had told him yesterday that she was sure to be flunked from her class in February. Why? Because she had stayed out too late with boy friends. Now, if that wasn't a sort of come-on—especially when she added that she wasn't going back to the old homestead and had no plans at all. Tomorrow McKenna was leaving town but in a couple of weeks he could ride down again and keep her out late in a big way, and if he liked her get her some clothes and set her up in Jersey City where he owned an apartment house. She was the double for a girl he once went with at Ohio State.

He looked at his watch—an hour and a half till midnight. Save for several occasions when he had been deterred for reasons contingent on his profession, all his New Year's were opaque memories of whoopee. He never made resolves or thought of the past with nostalgia or regret—he was joyless and fearless, one of the still-born who manage to use death as a mainspring. When he caused suffering it made his neck swell and glow and yet he had a feeling for it that was akin to sympathy. "Does it hurt, fella?" he had asked once. "Where does it hurt most? Cheer up—you're almost out."

McKenna had intended to leave the hospital before the thing came off, but the interne and nurse had only just spilled what he wanted to know into his lap and it was too late at night to leave without attracting attention. He crossed the street in order to re-enter the hospital by the door of the dispensary.

On the sidewalk a man and a woman, young and poorly dressed, stood hesitating.

"Say, mister," the man said, "can you tell us something—if doctors look to see what's wrong with you is it free? Somebody told me they sting you."

McKenna paused in the doorway and regarded them—the woman watched him breathlessly.

"Sure they sting you," McKenna said. "They charge you twenty bucks or they take it out on your hide."

He went on in, past the screen door of the dispensary, past the entrance to the surgical unit where men made repairs that would not wait for the year to turn, past the children's clinic where a single sharp cry of distress came through an open door, past the psychiatric wards, exuding a haunted darkness. A group of probationers in street clothes chattered by him, an orderly with a wheel chair, an old negress leaning on a grizzled man, a young woman weeping between a doctor and a nurse. Through all that life, protesting but clinging, through all that hope of a better year, moved McKenna, the murderer, looking straight ahead lest they see death in his eyes.

II

In his room he rang for the nurse, had a quick drink and rang again. This time it was Miss Collins.

"It took you long enough," he said. "Say, I don't think I'll go to bed yet. It's so near twelve I think I'll stay up and see the New Year in and all that stuff; maybe go out on the porch and hear the noise."

"I suppose it's all right."

"You'll stick with me, won't you? Want a little port wine?"

Miss Collins wouldn't dare do that but she'd be back presently. She was the prettiest twitch he had seen in a year.

After another glass of port he felt a growing excitement. He pictured "Mr. Griffin" on the floor below, feeling so hidden and secure, possibly asleep. He pictured Oaky and Flute Cuneo and Vandervere strapping on the arsenal; he wished he could be in on the finish but that was no play for a front man.

At a quarter of twelve Miss Collins came back and they went down the corridor to a glassed-in porch overlooking the city.

"I'm afraid this is my last New Year's here," she said.

"What do you care—you've got too much on the ball to go around washing mummies."

At a minute before twelve a din started—first thin and far away, then rolling toward the hospital, a discord of whistles, bells, firecrackers and shots. Once, after a few minutes, McKenna thought he heard the pump sound of a silencer, once and again, but he could not be sure. From time to time Miss Collins darted in to the desk to see if there was a call for her, and each time he kept carefully in her sight.

After fifteen minutes the cacophony died away.

"My back hurts," McKenna said. "I wish you'd help me off with my clothes and then rub me."

"Certainly."

On the way to his room he listened carefully for the sounds of commotion but there was nothing. Therefore, barring the unforeseen, all had gone off as planned—the State of New York's intended witness was now with his fathers.

She bent over the bed, rubbing his back with alcohol.

"Sit down," he ordered. "Just sit on the bed."

He had almost finished the flask of port and he felt fine. There were worse ways to spend New Year's—a job all mopped up, the good warming wine and a swell girl to rub his back.

"You certainly are something to look at."

Two minutes later she tugged his hand from her rumpled belt.

"You're crazy," she exclaimed, panting.

"Oh, don't get sore. I thought you kind of liked me."

"Liked you! You! Why your room smells like a dog's room. I hate to touch you!"

There was a small knock and the night superintendent called Miss Collins, who went into the hall, hastily smoothing her apron. McKenna got out of bed, tiptoed to the door and listened—in a minute he heard Miss Collins' voice:

"But I don't know how to do it, Miss Gleason. . . . You say the patient was shot. . . ."

And then the other nurse:

". . . then you simply tie the hands and feet together and . . ."

McKenna got back into bed cautiously.

"Last rites for Mr. Griffin," he thought. "That's fine. It'll take her mind off being sore."

III

He had decided to leave next afternoon, when the winter dusk was closing down outside. The interne was uncertain and called the resident, just back from vacation. The latter came in after lunch when the orderly was helping McKenna pack.

"Don't you want to see your doctor tomorrow?" he asked.

He was big and informal, more competent-looking than the interne.

"He's just a doctor I got at the hotel. He doesn't know anything about it."

"Well, we've got one more test to hear from."

"I haven't got any fever," said McKenna. "It must have been just a false alarm."

The resident yawned.

"Excuse me," he said—"they called me at two o'clock last night."

"Somebody die?"

The resident nodded.

"Very suddenly. Somebody shot and killed a patient on the floor below."

"Go on! You're not safe anywhere now, are you?"

"Seems not."

McKenna rang the bell at the head of the bed.

"I can't find my hat, and none of those nurses have been in here all day—only the maid." He turned to the orderly. "Go find a nurse and see if they know where my hat is."

"And oh—" the resident added, "tell them if they have that test ready to send it in."

"What test?" McKenna asked.

"Just a routine business. Just a part of your body."

"What part?"

"It ought to be here now. It's hard to get these laboratory tests on a holiday."

Miss Hunter's face appeared in the doorway but she did not look toward McKenna.

"The message came," she said. "It was just to tell you that the test was positive. And to give you this paper."

The resident read it with interest.

"What is it?" demanded McKenna. "Say, I haven't got—"

"You haven't got anything," said the resident, "—not even a leg to stand on. In fact, I'd be sorry for you—if you hadn't torn up that nurse's letter."

"What nurse's letter?"

"The one the postman put together and brought in this morning."

"I don't know anything about it."

"We do. You left your finger prints on it—and they seem to belong to a man named Joe Kinney who got three slugs in his bottom in New York last June."

"You got nothing on me—what do you think you are, a tec?"

"That's just what I am. And I know now that you work out of Jersey City and so did Griffin."

"I was with Miss Collins when that happened."

"What time?"

Catching his mistake McKenna hesitated.

"I was with her all evening—till one o'clock."

"Miss Collins says she left you after five minutes because you got tough with her. Say, why did you have to pick a hospital? These girls have work to do—they can't play with animals."

"You got nothing at all on me—not even a gun."

"Maybe you'll wish you had one when I get done with you down at the station. Miss Hunter and I are engaged to be married and that letter was to me."

By nightfall the hospital showed signs of increasing life—the doctors and nurses back early to go to work in the morning, and casualties of riot and diet, victims of colds, aches and infections saved since Christmas. Even the recently vacated beds of Messrs. Griffin and McKenna would be occupied by tomorrow. Both of them had better have celebrated the holidays outside.

FINANCING FINNEGAN

Finnegan and I have the same literary agent to sell our writings for us, but though I'd often been in Mr. Cannon's office just before and just after Finnegan's visits, I had never met him. Likewise we had the same publisher, and often when I arrived there Finnegan had just departed. I gathered from a thoughtful sighing way in which they spoke of him—

"Ah—Finnegan—"

"Oh yes, Finnegan was here."

—that the distinguished author's visit had been not uneventful. Certain remarks implied that he had taken something with him when he went—manuscripts I supposed, one of those great successful novels of his. He had taken "it" off for a final revision, a last draft, of which he was rumored to make ten in order to achieve that facile flow, that ready wit, which distinguished his work. I discovered only gradually that most of Finnegan's visits had to do with money.

"I'm sorry you're leaving," Mr. Cannon would tell me. "Finnegan will be here tomorrow." Then after a thoughtful pause, "I'll probably have to spend some time with him."

I don't know what note in his voice reminded me of a talk with a nervous bank president when Dillinger was reported in the vicinity. His eyes looked out into the distance and he spoke as to himself:

"Of course he may be bringing a manuscript. He has a novel he's working on, you know. And a play too."

He spoke as though he were talking about some interesting but remote events of the cinquecento; but his eye became more hopeful as he added: "Or maybe a short story."

"He's very versatile, isn't he?" I said.

"Oh yes," Mr. Cannon perked up. "He can do anything—anything when he puts his mind to it. There's never been such a talent."

"I haven't seen much of his work lately."

"Oh, but he's working hard. Some of the magazines have stories of his that they're holding."

"Holding for what?"

"Oh for a more appropriate time—an upswing. They like to think they have something of Finnegan's."

His was indeed a name with ingots in it. His career had started brilliantly, and if it had not kept up to its first exalted level, at least it started brilliantly all over again every few years. He was the perennial man of promise in American letters—what he could actually do with words was astounding, they glowed and coruscated—he wrote sentences, paragraphs, chapters that were masterpieces of fine weaving and spinning. It was only when I met some poor devil of a screenwriter who had been trying to make a logical story out of one of his books that I realized he had his enemies.

"It's all beautiful when you read it," this man said disgustedly, "but when you write it down plain it's like a week in the nuthouse."

From Mr. Cannon's office I went over to my publishers on Fifth Avenue and there too I learned in no time that Finnegan was expected tomorrow.

Indeed he had thrown such a long shadow before him that the luncheon where I expected to discuss my own work was largely devoted to Finnegan. Again I had the feeling that my host, Mr. George Jaggers, was talking not to me but to himself.

"Finnegan's a great writer," he said.

"Undoubtedly."

"And he's really quite all right you know."

As I hadn't questioned the fact, I inquired whether there was any doubt about it.

"Oh no," he said hurriedly. "It's just that he's had such a run of hard luck lately—"

I shook my head sympathetically. "I know. That diving into a half-empty pool was a tough break."

"Oh, it wasn't half empty. It was full of water. Full to the brim. You ought to hear Finnegan on the subject—he makes a side-splitting story of it. It seems he was in a rundown condition and just diving from the side of the pool you know—" Mr. Jaggers pointed his knife and fork at the table, "and he saw some young girls diving from the fifteen-foot board. He says he thought of his lost youth and went up to do the same and made a beautiful swan dive—but his shoulder broke while he was still in the air." He looked at me rather anxiously. "Haven't you heard of cases like that—a ball player throwing his arm out of joint?"

I couldn't think of any orthopedic parallels at the moment.

"And then," he continued dreamily, "Finnegan had to write on the ceiling."

"On the ceiling?"

"Practically. He didn't give up writing—he has plenty of guts, that fellow, though you may not believe it. He had some sort of arrangement built that was suspended from the ceiling and he lay on his back and wrote in the air."

I had to grant that it was a courageous arrangement.

"Did it affect his work?" I inquired. "Did you have to read his stories backward—like Chinese?"

"They were rather confused for awhile," he admitted, "but he's all right now. I got several letters from him that sounded more like the old Finnegan—full of life and hope and plans for the future—" The faraway look came into his face and I turned the discussion to affairs closer to my heart. Only when we were back in his office did the subject recur—and I blush as I write this because it includes confessing something I seldom do—reading another man's telegram. It happened because Mr. Jaggers was intercepted in the hall and when I went into his office and sat down it was stretched out open before me.

WITH FIFTY I COULD AT LEAST PAY TYPIST AND GET HAIRCUT AND PENCILS LIFE HAS BECOME IMPOSSIBLE AND I EXIST ON DREAM OF GOOD NEWS DESPERATELY FINNEGAN.

I couldn't believe my eyes—fifty dollars, and I happened to know that Finnegan's price for short stories was somewhere around three thousand. George Jaggers found me still staring dazedly at the telegram. After he read it he stared at me with stricken eyes.

"I don't see how I can conscientiously do it," he said.

I started and glanced around just to make sure I was in the prosperous publishing office in New York. Then I understood—I had misread the telegram. Finnegan was asking for fifty thousand as an advance—a demand that would have staggered any publisher no matter who the writer was.

"Only last week," said Mr. Jaggers disconsolately, "I sent him a hundred dollars. It puts my department in the red every season so I don't dare tell my partners anymore. I take it out of my own pocket—give up a suit and a pair of shoes."

"You mean Finnegan's broke?"

"Broke!" He looked at me and laughed soundlessly—in fact I didn't exactly like the way that he laughed. My brother had a nervous—but that is afield from this story. After a minute he pulled himself together. "You won't say anything about this, will you? The truth is Finnegan's been in a slump, he's had blow after blow in the past few years, but now he's snapping out of it and I know we'll get back every cent we've—" He tried to think of a word but "given him" slipped out. This time it was he who was eager to change the subject.

Don't let me give the impression that Finnegan's affairs absorbed me during a whole week in New York—it was inevitable, though, that being much in the offices of my agent and my publisher, I happened in on a lot. For instance, two days later, using the telephone in Mr. Cannon's office, I was accidentally switched in on a conversation he was having with George Jaggers. It was only partly eavesdropping, you see, because I could hear only one end of the conversation and that isn't as bad as hearing it all.

"But I got the impression he was in good health . . . he did say something about his heart a few months ago but I understood it got well . . . yes, and he talked about some operation he wanted to have—I think he said it was cancer. . . . Well, I felt like telling him I had a little operation up my sleeve too, that I'd have had by now if I could afford it. . . . No, I didn't say it. He seemed in such good spirits that it would have been a shame to bring him down. He's starting a story today, he read me some of it on the phone. . . .

". . . I did give him twenty-five because he didn't have a cent in his pocket . . . oh, yes—I'm sure he'll be all right now. He sounds as if he means business."

I understood it all now. The two men had entered into a silent conspiracy to cheer each other up about Finnegan. Their investment in him, in his future, had reached a sum so considerable that Finnegan belonged to them. They could not bear to hear a word against him—even from themselves.

II

I spoke my mind to Mr. Cannon.

"If this Finnegan is a four-flusher you can't go on indefinitely giving him money. If he's through he's through and there's nothing to be done about it. It's absurd that you should put off an operation when Finnegan's out somewhere diving into half-empty swimming pools."

"It was full," said Mr. Cannon patiently—"full to the brim."

"Well, full or empty the man sounds like a nuisance to me."

"Look here," said Cannon, "I've got a talk to Hollywood due on the wire. Meanwhile you might glance over that." He threw a manuscript into my lap. "Maybe it'll help you understand. He brought it in yesterday."

It was a short story. I began it in a mood of disgust but before I'd read five minutes I was completely immersed in it, utterly charmed, utterly convinced and wishing to God I could write like that. When Cannon finished his phone call I kept him waiting while I finished it and when I did there were tears in these hard old professional eyes. Any magazine in the country would have run it first in any issue.

But then nobody had ever denied that Finnegan could write.

III

Months passed before I went again to New York, and then, so far as the offices of my agent and my publisher were concerned, I descended upon a quieter, more stable world. There was at last time to talk about my own conscientious if uninspired literary pursuits, to visit Mr. Cannon in the country and to kill summer evenings with George Jaggers where the vertical New York starlight falls like lingering lightning into restaurant gardens. Finnegan might have been at the North Pole—and as a matter of fact he was. He had quite a group with him, including three Bryn Mawr anthropologists, and it sounded as if he might collect a lot of material there. They were going to stay several months, and if the thing had somehow the ring of a promising little house party about it, that was probably due to my jealous, cynical disposition.

"We're all just delighted," said Cannon. "It's a godsend for him. He was fed up and he needed just this—this—"

"Ice and snow," I supplied.

"Yes, ice and snow. The last thing he said was characteristic of him. Whatever he writes is going to be pure white—it's going to have a blinding glare about it."

"I can imagine it will. But tell me—who's financing it? Last time I was here I gathered the man was insolvent."

"Oh, he was really very decent about that. He owed me some money and I believe he owed George Jaggers a little too—" He "believed," the old hypocrite. He knew damn well. "—so before he left he made most of his life insurance over to us. That's in case he doesn't come back—those trips are dangerous of course."

"I should think so," I said, "—especially with three anthropologists."

"So Jaggers and I are absolutely covered in case anything happens—it's as simple as that."

"Did the life-insurance company finance the trip?"

He fidgeted perceptibly.

"Oh, no. In fact when they learned the reason for the assignments they were a little upset. George Jaggers and I felt that when he had a specific plan like this with a specific book at the end of it, we were justified in backing him a little further."

"I don't see it," I said flatly.

"You don't?" The old harassed look came back into his eyes. "Well, I'll admit we hesitated. In principle I know it's wrong. I used to advance authors small sums from time to time, but lately I've made a rule against it—and kept it. It's only been waived once in the last two years and that was for a woman who was having a bad struggle—Margaret Trahill, do you know her? She was an old girl of Finnegan's, by the way."

"Remember I don't even know Finnegan."

"That's right. You must meet him when he comes back—if he does come back. You'd like him—he's utterly charming."

Again I departed from New York, to imaginative North Poles of my own, while the year rolled through summer and fall. When the first snap of November was in the air, I thought of the Finnegan expedition with a sort of shiver, and any envy of the man departed. He was probably earning any loot, literary or anthropological, he might bring back. Then, when I hadn't been back in New York three days, I read in the paper that he and some other members of his party had walked off into a snowstorm when the food supply gave out, and the Arctic had claimed another sacrifice.

I was sorry for him, but practical enough to be glad that Cannon and Jaggers were well protected. Of course, with Finnegan scarcely cold—if such a simile is not too harrowing—they did not talk about it, but I gathered that the insurance companies had waived *habeas corpus* or whatever it is in their lingo, and it seemed quite sure that they would collect.

His son, a fine-looking young fellow, came into George Jaggers' office while I was there and from him I could guess at Finnegan's charm—a shy frankness together with an impression of a very quiet brave battle going on inside of him that he couldn't quite bring himself to talk about—but that showed as heat lightning in his work.

"The boy writes well too," said George after he had gone. "He's brought in some remarkable poems. He's not ready to step into his father's shoes, but there's a definite promise."

"Can I see one of his things?"

"Certainly—here's one he left just as he went out."

George took a paper from his desk, opened it and cleared his throat. Then he squinted and bent over a little in his chair.

"*Dear Mr. Jaggers*," he began, "*I didn't like to ask you this in person—*" Jaggers stopped, his eyes reading ahead rapidly.

"How much does he want?" I inquired.

He sighed.

"He gave me the impression that this was some of his work," he said in a pained voice.

"But it is," I consoled him. "Of course he isn't quite ready to step into his father's shoes."

I was sorry afterwards to have said this, for after all Finnegan had paid his debts, and it was nice to be alive now that better times were back and books were no longer rated as unnecessary luxuries. Many authors I knew who had skimped along during the depression were now making long-deferred trips or paying off mortgages or turning out the more finished kind of work that can only be done with a certain leisure and security. I had just got a thousand dollars advance for a venture in Hollywood and was going to fly out with all the verve of the old days when there was chicken feed in every pot. Going in to say good-bye to Cannon and collect the money, it was nice to find he too was profiting—wanted me to go along and see a motorboat he was buying.

But some last-minute stuff came up to delay him and I grew impatient and decided to skip it. Getting no response to a knock on the door of his sanctum, I opened it anyhow.

The inner office seemed in some confusion. Mr. Cannon was on several telephones at once and dictating something about an insurance company to a stenographer. One secretary was getting hurriedly into her hat and coat as if upon an errand, and another was counting bills from her purse.

"It'll be only a minute," said Cannon. "It's just a little office riot—you never saw us like this."

"Is it Finnegan's insurance?" I couldn't help asking. "Isn't it any good?"

"His insurance—oh, perfectly all right, perfectly. This is just a matter of trying to raise a few hundred in a hurry. The banks are closed and we're all contributing."

"I've got that money you just gave me," I said. "I don't need all of it to get to the coast." I peeled off a couple of hundred. "Will this be enough?"

"That'll be fine—it just saves us. Never mind, Miss Carlsen. Mrs. Mapes, you needn't go now."

"I think I'll be running along," I said.

"Just wait two minutes," he urged. "I've only got to take care of this wire. It's really splendid news. Bucks you up."

It was a cablegram from Oslo, Norway—before I began to read I was full of a premonition.

AM MIRACULOUSLY SAFE HERE BUT DETAINED BY AUTHORITIES PLEASE WIRE PASSAGE MONEY FOR FOUR PEOPLE AND TWO HUNDRED EXTRA I AM BRINGING BACK PLENTY GREETINGS FROM THE DEAD

FINNEGAN.

"Yes, that's splendid," I agreed. "He'll have a story to tell now."

"Won't he though," said Cannon. "Miss Carlsen, will you wire the parents of those girls—and you'd better inform Mr. Jaggers."

As we walked along the street a few minutes later, I saw that Mr. Cannon, as if stunned by the wonder of this news, had fallen into a brown study, and I did not disturb him, for after all I did not know Finnegan and could not wholeheartedly share his joy. His mood of silence continued until we arrived at the door of the motorboat show—just under the sign he stopped and stared upward, as if aware for the first time where we were going.

"Oh, my," he said, stepping back. "There's no use going in here now. I thought we were going to get a drink."

We did. Mr. Cannon was still a little vague, a little under the spell of the vast surprise—he fumbled so long for the money to pay his round that I insisted it was on me.

I think he was in a daze during that whole time because, though he is a man of the most punctilious accuracy, the two hundred I handed him in his office has never shown to my credit in the statements he has sent me. I imagine, though, that someday I will surely get it because someday Finnegan will click again and I know that people will clamor to read what he writes. Recently I've taken it upon myself to investigate some of the stories about him and I've found that they're mostly as false as the half-empty pool. That pool was full to the brim.

So far there's only been a short story about the polar expedition, a love story. Perhaps it wasn't as big a subject as he expected. But the movies are interested in him—if they can get a good long look at him first—and I have every reason to think that he will come through. He'd better.

DESIGN IN PLASTER

"How long does the doctor think now?" Mary asked.

With his good arm Martin threw back the top of the sheet, disclosing that the plaster armor had been cut away in front in the form of a square, so that his abdomen and the lower part of his diaphragm bulged a little from the aperture. His dislocated arm was still high over his head in an involuntary salute.

"This was a great advance," he told her. "But it took the heat wave to make Ottinger put in this window. I can't say much for the view but—have you seen the wire collection?"

"Yes, I've seen it," his wife answered, trying to look amused.

It was laid out on the bureau like a set of surgeons' tools—wires bent to every length and shape so that the nurse could reach any point inside the plaster cast when perspiration made the itching unbearable.

Martin was ashamed at repeating himself.

"I apologize," he said. "After two months you get medical psychology. All this stuff is fascinating to me. In fact—" he added, and with only faint irony, "it is in a way of becoming my life."

Mary came over and sat beside the bed, raising him, cast and all, into her slender arms. He was chief electrical engineer at the studio and his thirty-foot fall wasn't costing a penny in doctor's bills. But that—and the fact that the catastrophe had swung them together after a four months' separation, was its only bright spot.

"I feel so close," she whispered. "Even through this plaster."

"Do you think that's a nice way to talk?"

"Yes."

"So do I."

Presently she stood up and rearranged her bright hair in the mirror. He had seen her do it half a thousand times but suddenly there was a quality of remoteness about it that made him sad.

"What are you doing tonight?" he asked.

Mary turned, almost with surprise.

"It seems strange to have you ask me."

"Why? You almost always tell me. You're my contact with the world of glamour."

"But you like to keep bargains. That was our arrangement when we began to live apart."

"You're being very technical."

"No—but that *was* the arrangement. As a matter of fact I'm not doing anything. Bieman asked me to go to a preview, but he bores me. And that French crowd called up."

"Which member of it?"

She came closer and looked at him.

"Why, I believe you're jealous," she said. "The wife of course. Or *he* did, to be exact, but he was calling for his wife—she'd be there. I've never seen you like this before."

Martin was wise enough to wink as if it meant nothing and let it die away, but Mary said an unfortunate last word.

"I thought you liked me to go with them."

"That's it," Martin tried to go slow, "—with 'them,' but now it's 'he.'"

"They're all leaving Monday," she said almost impatiently. "I'll probably never see him again."

Silence for a minute. Since his accident there were not an unlimited number of things to talk about, except when there was love between them. Or even pity—he was accepting even pity in the past fortnight. Especially their uncertain plans about the future were in need of being preceded by a mood of love.

"I'm going to get up for a minute," he said suddenly. "No, don't help me—don't call the nurse. I've got it figured out."

The cast extended half way to his knee on one side but with a snake-like motion he managed to get to the side of the bed—then rise with a gigantic heave. He tied on a dressing gown, still without assistance, and went to the window. Young people were splashing and calling in the outdoor pool of the hotel.

"I'll go along," said Mary. "Can I bring you anything tomorrow? Or tonight if you feel lonely?"

"Not tonight. You know I'm always cross at night—and I don't like you making that long drive twice a day. Go along—be happy."

"Shall I ring for the nurse?"

"I'll ring presently."

He didn't though—he just stood. He knew that Mary was wearing out, that this resurgence of her love was wearing out. His accident was a very temporary dam of a stream that had begun to overflow months before.

When the pains began at six with their customary regularity the nurse gave him something with codeine in it, shook him a cocktail and ordered dinner, one of those dinners it was a struggle to digest since he had been sealed up in his individual bomb-shelter. Then she was off duty four hours and he was alone. Alone with Mary and the Frenchman.

He didn't know the Frenchman except by name but Mary had said once:

"Joris is rather like you—only naturally not formed—rather immature."

Since she said that, the company of Mary and Joris had grown increasingly unattractive in the long hours between seven and eleven. He had talked with them, driven around with them, gone to pictures and parties with them—sometimes with the half comforting ghost of Joris' wife along. He had been near as they made love and even that was endurable as long as he could seem to hear and see them. It was when they became hushed and secret that his stomach winced inside the plaster cast. That was when he had pictures of the Frenchman going toward Mary and Mary waiting. Because he was not sure just how Joris felt about her or about the whole situation.

"I told him I loved you," Mary said—and he believed her. "I told him that I could never love anyone but you."

Still he could not be sure how Mary felt as she waited in her apartment for Joris. He could not tell if, when she said good-night at her door, she turned away relieved, or whether she walked around her living room a little and later, reading her book, dropped it in her lap and looked up at the ceiling. Or whether her phone rang once more for one more good-night.

Martin hadn't worried about any of these things in the first two months of their separation when he had been on his feet and well.

At half-past eight he took up the phone and called her; the line was busy and still busy at quarter of nine. At nine it was out of order; at nine-fifteen it didn't answer and at a little before nine-thirty it was busy again. Martin got up, slowly drew on his trousers and with the help of a bell-boy put on a shirt and coat.

"Don't you want me to come, Mr. Harris?" asked the bell-boy.

"No thanks. Tell the taxi I'll be right down."

When the boy had gone he tripped on the slightly raised floor of the bathroom, swung about on one arm and cut his head against the wash bowl. It was not so much, but he did a clumsy repair job with the adhesive and, feeling ridiculous at his image in the mirror, sat down and called Mary's number a last time—for no answer. Then he went out, not because he wanted to go to Mary's but because he had to go somewhere toward the flame, and he didn't know any other place to go.

At ten-thirty Mary, in her nightgown, was at the phone.

"Thanks for calling. But, Joris, if you want to know the truth, I have a splitting headache. I'm turning in."

"Mary, listen," Joris insisted. "It happens Marianne has a headache too and has turned in. This is the last night I'll have a chance to see you alone. Besides, you told me you'd *never* had a headache."

Mary laughed.

"That's true—but I *am* tired."

"I would promise to stay one half-hour—word of honor. I am only just around the corner."

"No," she said and a faint touch of annoyance gave firmness to the word. "Tomorrow I'll have either lunch or dinner if you like, but now I'm going to bed."

She stopped. She had heard a sound, a weight crunching against the outer door of her apartment. Then three odd, short bell rings.

"There's someone—call me in the morning," she said. Hurriedly hanging up the phone she got into a dressing gown.

By the door of her apartment she asked cautiously:

"Who's there?"

No answer—only a heavier sound—a human slipping to the floor.

"Who is it?"

She drew back and away from a frightening moan. There was a little shutter high in the door, like the peephole of a speakeasy, and feeling sure from the sound that whoever it was, wounded or drunk, was on the floor Mary reached up and peeped out. She could see only a hand covered with freshly ripening blood, and shut the trap hurriedly. After a shaken moment, she peered once more.

This time she recognized something—afterwards she could not have said what—a way the arm lay, a corner of the plaster cast—but it was enough to make her open the door quickly and duck down to Martin's side.

"Get doctor," he whispered. "Fell on the steps and broke."

His eyes closed as she ran for the phone.

Doctor and ambulance came at the same time. What Martin had done was simple enough, a little triumph of misfortune. On the first flight of stairs that he had gone up for eight weeks, he had stumbled, tried to save himself with the arm that was no good for anything, then spun down catching and ripping on the stair-rail. After that a five-minute drag up to her door.

Mary wanted to exclaim "Why? Why?" but there was no one to hear. He came awake as the stretcher was put under him to carry him to the hospital, repair the new breakage with a new cast, start it over again. Seeing Mary he called quickly, "Don't you come. I don't like anyone around when—when— Promise on your word of honor not to come!"

The orthopedist said he would phone her in an hour. And five minutes later it was with the confused thought that he was already calling that Mary answered the phone.

"I can't talk, Joris," she said. "There was an awful accident—"

"Can I help?"

"It's gone now. It was my husband—"

Suddenly Mary knew she wanted to do anything but wait alone for word from the hospital.

"Come over then," she said. "You can take me up there if I'm needed."

She sat in place by the phone until he came—jumped to her feet with an exclamation at his ring.

"Why? Why?" she sobbed at last. "I offered to go see him at his hotel."

"Not drunk?"

"No, no—he almost never takes a drink. Will you wait right outside my door while I dress and get ready?"

The news came half an hour later that Martin's shoulder was set again, that he was sleeping under the ethylene gas and would sleep till morning. Joris Deglen was very gentle, swinging her feet up on the sofa, putting a pillow at her back, and answering her incessant "Why?" with a different response every time—Martin had been delirious; he was lonely; then at a certain moment telling the truth he had long guessed at: Martin was jealous.

"That was it," Mary said bitterly. "We were to be free—only I wasn't free. Only free to sneak about behind his back."

She was free now though, free as air. And later, when he said he wouldn't go just yet, but would sit in the living room reading until she quieted down, Mary went into her room with her head clear as morning. After she undressed for the second time that night she stayed for a few minutes before the mirror arranging her hair and keeping her mind free of all thoughts about Martin except that he was sleeping and at the moment felt no pain.

Then she opened her bedroom door and called down the corridor into the living room:

"Do you want to come and tell me good-night?"

THE LOST DECADE

All sorts of people came into the offices of the news-weekly and Orrison Brown had all sorts of relations with them. Outside of office hours he was "one of the editors"—during work time he was simply a curly-haired man who a year before had edited the Dartmouth "Jack-o-Lantern" and was now only too glad to take the undesirable assignments around the office, from straightening out illegible copy to playing call-boy without the title.

He had seen this visitor go into the editor's office—a pale, tall man of forty with blond statuesque hair and a manner that was neither shy, nor timid, nor otherworldly like a monk, but something of all three. The name on his card, Louis Trimble, evoked some vague memory, but having nothing to start on Orrison did not puzzle over it—until a buzzer sounded on his desk, and previous experience warned him that Mr. Trimble was to be his first course at lunch.

"Mr. Trimble—Mr. Brown," said the Source of all luncheon money. "Orrison—Mr. Trimble's been away a long time. Or he *feels* it's a long time—almost twelve years. Some people would consider themselves lucky to've missed the last decade."

"That's so," said Orrison.

"I can't lunch today," continued his chief. "Take him to Voisins or '21' or anywhere he'd like. Mr. Trimble feels there're lots of things he hasn't seen."

Trimble demurred politely.

"Oh, I can get around."

"I know it, old boy. Nobody knew this place like you did once—and if Brown tries to explain the horseless carriage just send him back here to me. And you'll be back yourself by four, won't you?"

Orrison got his hat.

"You've been away ten years?" he asked while they went down in the elevator.

"They'd begun the Empire State Building," said Trimble. "What does that add up to?"

"About 1928. But as the chief said, you've been lucky to miss a lot." As a feeler he added, "Probably had more interesting things to look at."

"Can't say I have."

They reached the street, and the way Trimble's face tightened at the roar of traffic made Orrison take one more guess.

"You've been out of civilization?"

"In a sense." The words were spoken in such a measured way that Orrison concluded this man wouldn't talk unless he wanted to—and simultaneously wondered if he could have possibly spent the thirties in a prison or an insane asylum.

"This is the famous '21,'" he said. "Do you think you'd rather eat somewhere else?"

Trimble paused, looking carefully at the brownstone house.

"I can remember when the name '21' got to be famous," he said, "about the same year as Moriarty's." Then he continued almost apologetically, "I thought we might walk up Fifth Avenue about five minutes and eat wherever we happened to be. Some place with young people to look at."

Orrison gave him a quick glance and once again thought of bars and grey walls and bars; he wondered if his duties included introducing Mr. Trimble to complaisant girls. But Mr. Trimble didn't look as if that was in his mind—the dominant expression was of absolute and deepseated curiosity, and Orrison attempted to connect the name with Admiral Byrd's hideout at the South Pole or flyers lost in Brazilian jungles. He was, or he had been, quite a fellow—that was obvious. But the only definite clue to his environment—and to Orrison the clue that led nowhere—was his countryman's obedience to the traffic lights and his predilection for walking on the side next to the shops and not the street. Once he stopped and gazed into a haberdasher's window.

"Crêpe ties," he said. "I haven't seen one since I left college."

"Where'd you go?"

"Massachusetts Tech."

"Great place."

"I'm going to take a look at it next week. Let's eat somewhere along here—" They were in the upper Fifties. "—you choose."

There was a good restaurant with a little awning just around the corner.

"What do you want to see most?" Orrison asked, as they sat down.

Trimble considered.

"Well—the back of people's heads," he suggested. "Their necks—how their heads are joined to their bodies. I'd like to hear what those two little girls are saying to their father. Not exactly what they're saying but whether the words float or submerge, how their mouths shut when they've finished speaking. Just a matter of rhythm—Cole Porter came back to the States in 1928 because he felt that there were new rhythms around."

Orrison was sure he had his clue now, and with nice delicacy did not pursue it by a millimeter—even suppressing a sudden desire to say there was a fine concert in Carnegie Hall tonight.

"The weight of spoons," said Trimble, "so light. A little bowl with a stick attached. The cast in that waiter's eye. I knew him once but he wouldn't remember me."

But as they left the restaurant the same waiter looked at Trimble rather puzzled as if he almost knew him. When they were outside Orrison laughed:

"After ten years people will forget."

"Oh, I had dinner there last May—" He broke off in an abrupt manner.

It was all kind of nutsy, Orrison decided—and changed himself suddenly into a guide.

"From here you get a good candid focus on Rockefeller Center," he pointed out with spirit "—and the Chrysler Building and the Armistead Building, the daddy of all the new ones."

"The Armistead Building." Trimble rubber-necked obediently. "Yes—I designed it."

Orrison shook his head cheerfully—he was used to going out with all kinds of people. But that stuff about having been in the restaurant last May. . . .

He paused by the brass entablature in the cornerstone of the building. "Erected 1928," it said.

Trimble nodded.

"But I was taken drunk that year—every-which-way drunk. So I never saw it before now."

"Oh." Orrison hesitated. "Like to go in now?"

"I've been in it—lots of times. But I've never seen it. And now it isn't what I want to see. I wouldn't ever be able to see it now. I simply want to see how people walk and what their clothes and shoes and hats are made of. And their eyes and hands. Would you mind shaking hands with me?"

"Not at all, sir."

"Thanks. Thanks. That's very kind. I suppose it looks strange—but people will think we're saying good-bye. I'm going to walk up the avenue for awhile, so we *will* say good-bye. Tell your office I'll be in at four."

Orrison looked after him when he started out, half expecting him to turn into a bar. But there was nothing about him that suggested or ever had suggested drink.

"Jesus," he said to himself. "Drunk for ten years."

He felt suddenly of the texture of his own coat and then he reached out and pressed his thumb against the granite of the building by his side.

ON AN OCEAN WAVE

Gaston T. Scheer—the man, the company, the idea—five feet eight, carrying himself with dash and pride, walking the deck of the ocean liner like a conqueror. This was when it was something to be an American—spring of 1929.

O'Kane, his confidential secretary, met him in the morning on the open front of the promenade deck.

"See her?" Scheer asked.

"Yes—sure. She's all right."

"Why shouldn't she be all right?"

O'Kane hesitated.

"Some of her baggage is marked with her real initials—and the stewardess said—"

"Oh hell!" said Scheer. "She should have had that fixed up in New York. It's the same old story—girl's not your wife she's always sensitive, always complaining about slights and injuries. Oh, hell."

"She was all right."

"Women are small potatoes," said Scheer disgustedly. "Did you see that cable from Claud Hanson today that said he'd gladly die for me?"

"I saw it, Mr. Scheer."

"I liked it," Scheer said defiantly. "I think Claud meant it. I think he'd gladly die for me."

Claud Hanson was Mr. Scheer's other secretary. O'Kane let his natural cynicism run riot in silence.

"I think many people would, Mr. Scheer," he said without vomiting. Gosh, it was probably true. Mr. Scheer did a lot for a lot of people—kept them alive, gave them work.

"I liked the sentiment," said Scheer gazing gravely out to sea. "Anyhow Miss Denzer oughtn't to grouse—it's just four days and twelve hours. She doesn't have to stay in her cabin, just so she doesn't make herself conspicuous or talk to me—just in case."

Just in case anyone had seen them together in New York.

"Anyhow—" he concluded, "my wife's never seen her or heard of her."

Mr. O'Kane had concluded that he himself would possibly die for Mr. Scheer if Mr. Scheer kept on giving him market tips for ten years more. He would die at the end of the ten—you could cram a lot into ten years. By that time he himself might be able to bring two women abroad in the same load, in separate crates so to speak.

Alone, Gaston T. Scheer faced a strong west wind with a little spray in it. He was not afraid of the situation he had created—he had never been afraid since the day he had forced himself to lay out a foreman with a section of pitch chain. It just felt a little strange when he walked with Minna and the children to think that Catherine Denzer might be watching them. So when he was on deck with Minna he kept his face impassive and aloof, appearing not to have a good time. This was false. He liked Minna—she said nice things.

In Europe this summer it would be easier. Minna and the children would be parked here and there, in Paris and on the Riviera, and he would make business trips with Catherine. It was a willful, daring arrangement but he was twice a man in every way. Life certainly owed him two women.

The day passed—once he saw Catherine Denzer, passing her in an empty corridor. She kept her bargain, all except for her lovely pale head which yearned toward him momentarily as they passed and made his throat warm, made him want to turn and go after her. But he kept himself in control—they would be in Cherbourg in fifty hours.

Another day passed—there was a brokerage office on board and he spent the time there, putting in a few orders, using the ship-to-shore telephone once, sending a few code wires.

That evening he left Minna talking to the college professor in the adjoining deck chair and strolled restlessly around the ship, continually playing with the idea of going to Catherine Denzer, but only as a form of mental indulgence because it was twenty-four hours now to Paris and the situation was well in hand.

But he walked the halls of her deck, sometimes glancing casually down the little branch corridors to the staterooms. And so, entirely by accident, in one of these corridors he saw his wife Minna and the professor. They were in each other's arms embracing, with all abandon. No mistake.

II

Cautiously Scheer backed away from the corridor. His first thought was very simple: it jumped over several steps—over fury, hot jealousy and amazement—it was that his entire plan for the summer was ruined. His next thought was that Minna must sweat blood for this and then he jumped a few more steps. He was what is known medically as a "schizoid"—in his business dealings, too, he left out intermediate steps, surprising competitors by arriving quickly at an extreme position without any discoverable logic. He had arrived at one of these extreme positions now and was not even surprised to find himself there.

An hour later there was a knock on the door of Mr. O'Kane's cabin and Professor Dollard of the faculty of Weston Technical College came into the room. He was a thin quiet man of forty, wearing a loose tweed suit.

"Oh yes," said O'Kane. "Come in. Sit down."

"Thank you," said Dollard. "What do you want to see me about?"

"Have a cigarette."

"No thanks. I'm on my way to bed, but tell me, what's it about?"

O'Kane coughed pointedly—whereupon Cates, the swimming-pool steward, came out of the private bathroom behind Dollard and went to the corridor door, locking it and standing in front of it. At the same time Gaston T. Scheer came out of the bathroom and Dollard blushed suddenly dark as he recognized him.

"Oh, hello—" he said, "—Mr. Scheer. What's the idea of this?" He took off his glasses with the thought that Scheer was going to hit him.

"What are you a professor of, Professor?"

"Mathematics, Mr. Scheer—I told you that. What's the idea of asking me down here?"

"You ought to stick to your job," said Scheer. "You ought to stick there in the college and teach it and not mess around with decent people."

"I'm not messing around with anybody."

"You oughtn't to fool around with people that could buy you out ten thousand times—and not know they spent a nickel."

Dollard stood up.

"You're out of your class," said Scheer. "You're a school teacher that's promoted himself out of his class."

Cates, the steward, stirred impatiently. He had left the two hundred pounds in cash in his locker and he wanted to have this over with and get back and hide it better.

"I don't know yet what I've done," Dollard said. But he knew all right. It was too bad. A long time ago he had decided to avoid rich people and here he was tangled up with the very worst type.

"You stepped out of your class," said Scheer thickly, "but you're not going to do it anymore. You're going to feed the fishes out there, see?"

Mr. O'Kane, who had bucked himself with whiskey, kept imagining that it was Claud Hanson who was about to die for Mr. Scheer—instead of Professor Dollard, who had not offered himself for a sacrifice. There was still a moment when Dollard could have cried out for help but because he was guilty he could not bring himself to cry out. Then he was engrossed in a struggle to keep breathing, a struggle that he lost without a sigh.

Minna Scheer waited on the front of the promenade deck, walking in the chalked numbers of the shuffle-board game. She was excited and happy. Her feet as she placed them in the squares felt young and barefoot and desperate. She could play too—whatever it was they played. She had been a good girl so long, but now almost everybody she knew was raising the devil and it was a thrilling discovery to find that she could join in with such pleasure. The man was late but that made it all the more tense and unbearably lovely, and from time to time she raised her eyes in delight and looked off into the white hot wake of the steamer.

THE WOMAN FROM "21"

Ah, what a day for Raymond Torrence! Once you knew that your roots were safely planted outside megalopolitanism what fun it was to come back—every five years. He and Elizabeth woke up to the frozen music of Fifth Avenue and 59th Street and first thing went down to his publishers on Fifth Avenue. Elizabeth, who was half Javanese and had never been in America before, liked it best of all there because her husband's book was on multiple display in the window. She liked it in the store where she squeezed Ray's hand tensely when people asked for it, and again when they bought it.

They lunched at the Stork Club with Hat Milbank, a pal of Ray's at college and in the war. Of course no one there recognized Ray after these years but a man came in with the Book in his hands, crumpling up the jacket. Afterwards Hat asked them down to Old Westbury to see the polo in which he still performed, but they went to the hotel and rested as they did in Java. Otherwise it would all be a little too much. Elizabeth wrote a letter to the children in Suva and told them "everyone in New York" was reading Father's book and admired the photograph that Janice had taken of a girl sick with yaws.

They went alone to a play by William Saroyan. After the curtain had been up five minutes the woman from "21" came in.

She was in the mid-thirties, dark and pretty. As she took her seat beside Ray Torrence she continued her conversation in a voice that was for outside, and Elizabeth was a little sorry for her because obviously she did not know she was making herself a nuisance. They were a quartet—two in front. The girl's escort was a tall and good-looking man. The woman leaning forward in her seat and talking to her friend in front distracted Ray a little, but not overwhelmingly until she said in a conversational voice that must have reached the actors on the stage:

"Let's all go back to '21.'"

Her escort replied in a whisper and there was quiet for a moment. Then the woman drew a long, long sigh, culminating in an exhausted groan in which could be distinguished the words "Oh, my God."

Her friend in front turned around so sweetly that Ray thought the woman next to him must be someone very prominent and powerful—an Astor or a Vanderbilt or a Roosevelt.

"See a little bit of it," suggested her friend.

The woman from "21" flopped forward with a dynamic movement and began an audible but indecipherable conversation in which the number of the restaurant occurred again and again. When she shifted restlessly back into her chair with another groaning "My God!"—this time directed toward the play—Raymond turned his head sideways and uttered a prayer to her aloud:

"Please."

If Ray had muttered a four-letter word the effect could not have been more catalytic. The woman flashed about and regarded him—her eyes ablaze with the gastric hatred of many dying martinis and with something more. These were the unmistakable eyes of Mrs. Richbitch, that leftist creation as devoid of nuance as Mrs. Jiggs. As they burned with scalding arrogance—the very eyes of the Russian lady who let her coachman freeze outside while she wept at poverty in a play—at this moment Ray recognized a girl with whom he had played Run, Sheep, Run in Pittsburgh twenty years ago.

The woman did not after all excoriate him but this time her flop forward was so violent that it rocked the row ahead.

"Can you bel*ieve*—can you im*ag*ine—"

Her voice raced along in a hoarse whisper. Presently she lunged sideways toward her escort and told him of the outrage. His eye caught Ray's in a flickering embarrassed glance. On the other side of Ray, Elizabeth became disturbed and alarmed.

Ray did not remember the last five minutes of the act—beside him smoldered fury and he knew its name and the shape of its legs. Wanting nothing less than to kill, he hoped her man would speak to him or even look at him in a certain way during the entr'acte—but when it came the party stood up quickly, and the woman said: "We'll go to '21.'"

On the crowded sidewalk between the acts Elizabeth talked softly to Ray. She did not seem to think it was of any great importance except for the effect on him. He agreed in theory—but when they went inside again the woman from "21" was already in her place, smoking and waving a cigarette.

"I could speak to the usher," Ray muttered.

"Never mind," said Elizabeth quickly. "In France you smoke in the music halls."

"But you have some place to put the butt. She's going to crush it out in my lap!"

In the sequel she spread the butt on the carpet and kept rubbing it in. Since a lady lush moves in mutually exclusive preoccupations just as a gent does, and the woman had passed beyond her preoccupation with Ray, things were tensely quiet.

When the lights went on after the second act, a voice called to Ray from the aisle. It was Hat Milbank.

"Hello, hello there, Ray! Hello, Mrs. Torrence. Do you want to go to '21' after the theatre?"

His glance fell upon the people in between.

"Hello, Jidge," he said to the woman's escort; to the other three, who called him eagerly by name, he answered with an inclusive nod. Ray and Elizabeth crawled out over them. Ray told the story to Hat who seemed to ascribe as little importance to it as Elizabeth did, and wanted to know if he could come out to Fiji this spring.

But the effect upon Ray had been profound. It made him remember why he had left New York in the first place. This woman was what everything was for. She should have been humble, not awful, but she had become confused and thought she should be awful.

So Ray and Elizabeth would go back to Java, unmourned by anyone except Hat. Elizabeth would be a little disappointed at not seeing any more plays and not going to Palm Beach, and wouldn't like having to pack so late at night. But in a silently communicable way she would understand. In a sense she would be glad. She even guessed that it was the children Ray was running to—to save them and shield them from all the walking dead.

When they went back to their seats for the third act the party from "21" were no longer there—nor did they come in later. It had clearly been another game of Run, Sheep, Run.

THREE HOURS BETWEEN PLANES

[BETWEEN PLANES]

It was a wild chance but Donald was in the mood—healthy and bored, with a sense of tiresome duty done. He was now rewarding himself. Maybe.

When the plane landed he stepped out into a midwestern summer night and headed for the isolated pueblo airport, conventionalized as an old red "railway depot." He did not know whether she was alive, or living in this town, or what was her present name. With mounting excitement he looked through the phone book for her father who might be dead too somewhere in these twenty years.

No. Judge Harmon Holmes—Hillside 3194.

A woman's amused voice answered his inquiry for Miss Nancy Holmes.

"Nancy is Mrs. Walter Gifford now. Who is this?"

But Donald hung up without answering—he had found out what he wanted to know and he had only three hours. He did not remember any Walter Gifford and there was another suspended moment while he scanned the phone book. She might have married out of town.

No. Walter Gifford—Hillside 1191. Blood flowed back into his fingertips.

"Hello?"

"Hello. Is Mrs. Gifford there—this is an old friend of hers."

"This is Mrs. Gifford."

He remembered, or thought he remembered, the funny magic in the voice.

"This is Donald Plant. I haven't seen you since I was twelve years old."

"Oh-h-h!" The note was utterly surprised, very polite, but he could distinguish in it neither joy nor certain recognition.

"—*Don*ald!" added the voice. This time there was something more in it than struggling memory.

". . . when did you come back to town?" Then cordially, "Where *are* you?"

"I'm out at the airport—for just a few hours."

"Well, come up and see me."

"Sure you're not just going to bed."

"Heavens, no!" she exclaimed. "I was just sitting here—having a highball by myself. Just tell your taxi-man. . . ."

On his way Donald analyzed the conversation. His words "at the airport" established that he had retained his position in the upper bourgeoisie. Nancy's aloneness might indicate that she had matured into an unattractive woman without friends. Her husband might be either away or in bed. And—because she was always ten years old in his dreams—the highball shocked him. But he adjusted himself with a smile—she was very close to thirty.

At the end of a curved drive he saw a dark little beauty standing against the lighted door, a glass in her hand. Startled by her final materialization, Donald got out of the cab, saying:

"Mrs. Gifford?"

She turned on the porch light and stared at him, wide-eyed and tentative. A smile broke through the puzzled expression.

"Donald—it *is* you—we all change so. Oh, this is re*mark*able!"

As they walked inside their voices jingled the words "all these years," and Donald felt a sinking in his stomach. This derived in part from a vision of their last meeting—when she rode past him on a bicycle, cutting him dead—and in part from fear lest they have nothing to say. It was like a college reunion—but there the failure to find the past was disguised by the hurried boisterous occasion. Aghast, he realized that this might be a long and empty hour. He plunged in desperately.

"You always were a lovely person. But I'm a little shocked to find you as beautiful as you are."

It worked. The immediate recognition of their changed state, the bold compliment, made them interesting strangers instead of fumbling childhood friends.

"Have a highball?" she asked. "No? Please don't think I've become a secret drinker, but this was a blue night. I expected my husband but he wired he'd be two days longer. He's very nice, Donald, and very attractive. Rather your type and coloring." She hesitated, "—and I think he's interested in someone in New York—and I don't know."

"After seeing you it sounds impossible," he assured her. "I was married for six years, and there was a time I tortured myself that way. Then one day I just put jealousy out of my life forever. After my wife died I was very glad of that. It left a very rich memory—nothing marred or spoiled or hard to think over."

She looked at him attentively, then sympathetically as he spoke.

"I'm very sorry," she said. And after a proper moment, "You've changed a lot. Turn your head. I remember Father saying, 'That boy has a brain.'"

"You probably argued against it."

"I was impressed. Up to then I thought everybody had a brain. That's why it sticks in my mind."

"What else sticks in your mind?" he asked smiling.

Suddenly Nancy got up and walked quickly a little away.

"Ah, now," she reproached him. "That isn't fair! I suppose I was a naughty little girl."

"You were not," he said stoutly. "And I *will* have a drink now."

As she poured it, her face still turned from him, he continued:

"Do you think you were the only little girl who was ever kissed?"

"Do you like the subject?" she demanded. Her momentary irritation melted and she said: "What the hell! We *did* have fun. Like in the song."

"On the sleigh ride."

"Yes—and somebody's picnic—Trudy James'. And at Frontenac that—those summers."

It was the sleigh ride he remembered most and kissing her cool cheeks in the straw in one corner while she laughed up at the cold white stars. The couple next to them had their backs turned and he kissed her little neck and her ears and never her lips.

"And the Macks' party where they played Post Office and I couldn't go because I had the mumps," he said.

"I don't remember that."

"Oh, you were there. And you were kissed and I was crazy with jealousy like I never have been since."

"Funny I don't remember. Maybe I wanted to forget."

"But why?" he asked in amusement. "We were two perfectly innocent kids. Nancy, whenever I talked to my wife about the past, I told her you were the girl I loved *al*most as much as I loved her. But I think I really loved you just as much. When we moved out of town I carried you like a cannonball in my insides."

"Were you *that* much—stirred up?"

"My God, yes! I—" He suddenly realized that they were standing just two feet from each other, that he was talking as if he loved her in the present, that she was looking up at him with her lips half-parted, a clouded look in her eyes.

"Go on," she said, "I'm ashamed to say—I like it. I didn't know you were so upset *then*. I thought it was *me* who was upset."

"You!" he exclaimed. "Don't you remember throwing me over at the drug store?" He laughed. "You stuck out your tongue at me."

"I don't remember at all. It seemed to me *you* did the throwing over." Her hand fell lightly, almost consolingly on his arm. "I've got a photograph book upstairs I haven't looked at for years. I'll dig it out."

Donald sat for five minutes with two thoughts—first the hopeless impossibility of reconciling what different people remembered about the same event—and secondly that, in a frightening way, Nancy moved him as a woman as she had moved him as a child. Half an hour had developed an emotion that he had not known since the death of his wife—that he had never hoped to know again.

Side by side on a couch they opened the book between them. Nancy looked at him, smiling and very happy.

"Oh, this is *such* fun," she said. "Such fun that you're so nice, that you remember me so—beautifully. Let me tell you—I wish I'd known it then! After you'd gone I hated you."

"What a pity," he said gently.

"But not now," she reassured him, and then impulsively: "Kiss and make up—

". . . that isn't being a good wife," she said after a minute. "I really don't think I've kissed two men since I was married."

He was excited—but most of all confused. Had he kissed Nancy? or a memory? or this lovely trembly stranger who looked away from him quickly and turned a page of the book?

"Wait!" he said. "I don't think I could *see* a picture for a few seconds."

"We won't do it again. I don't feel so very calm myself."

Donald said one of those trivial things that cover so much ground. "Wouldn't it be awful if we fell in love again."

"Stop it!" She laughed, but very breathlessly. "It's all over. It was a moment. A moment I'll have to forget."

"Don't tell your husband," Donald said.

"Why not? Usually I tell him everything."

"It'll hurt him. Don't ever tell a man such things."

"All right I won't."

"Kiss me once more," he said inconsistently, but Nancy had turned a page and was pointing eagerly at a picture.

"Here's you," she cried. "Right away!"

He looked. It was a little boy in shorts standing on a pier with a sailboat in the background.

"I remember—" she laughed triumphantly, "—the very day it was taken. Kitty took it and I stole it from her."

For a moment Donald failed to recognize himself in the photo—then, bending closer—he failed *ut*terly to recognize himself.

"That's not me," he said.

"Oh yes. It was at Frontenac—the summer we—we used to go to the cave."

"What cave? I was only three days in Frontenac." Again he strained his eyes at the slightly yellowed picture. "And that isn't me. That's Donald *Bowers*. We did look rather alike."

Now she was staring at him—leaning back, seeming to lift away from him.

“But you’re Donald Bowers!” she exclaimed. Her voice rose a little: “No, you’re not. You’re Donald *Plant*.”

“I told you on the phone.”

She was on her feet—her face faintly horrified.

“Plant! Bowers! I must be crazy. Or was it that drink? I was mixed up a little when I first saw you. Look here! What have I told you?”

He tried for a monkish calm as he turned a page of the book.

“Nothing at all,” he said. Pictures that did not include him formed and re-formed before his eyes—Frontenac—a cave—Donald Bowers— “You threw *me* over!”

Nancy spoke from the other side of the room.

“You’ll never tell this story,” she said. “Stories have a way of getting around.”

“There isn’t any story,” he insisted. But he thought: so she *was* a bad little girl.

And now suddenly he was filled with wild raging jealousy of little Donald Bowers—he who had banished jealousy from his life forever. In the few steps he took across the room he crushed out twenty years and the existence of Walter Gifford with his stride.

“Kiss me again, Nancy,” he said, sinking to one knee beside her chair, putting his hand upon her shoulder. But Nancy strained away.

“You said you had to catch a plane.”

“It’s nothing. I can miss it. It’s of no importance.”

“Please go,” she said in a cool voice. “And please try to imagine how I feel.”

“But you act as if you don’t remember me,” he cried, “—as if you don’t remember Donald *Plant!*”

“I do. I remember you too. . . . But it was all so long ago.” Her voice grew hard again. “The taxi number is Crestwood 8484.”

. . . On his way to the airport Donald shook his head from side to side. He was completely himself now but he could not digest the experience. Only as the plane roared up into the dark sky and its passengers became a different entity from the corporeal world below did he draw a parallel from the fact of its flight. For five blinding minutes he had lived like a madman in two worlds at once.

He had been a boy of twelve and a man of thirty-two, indissolubly and helplessly commingled.

Donald had lost a good deal too in those hours between the planes—but since the second half of life is a long process of getting rid of things, that part of the experience probably didn't matter.

SECTION II

THE PAT HOBBY SERIES, 1940–1941

PAT HOBBY'S CHRISTMAS WISH

It was Christmas Eve in the studio. By eleven o'clock in the morning, Santa Claus had called on most of the huge population according to each one's deserts.

Sumptuous gifts from producers to stars, and from agents to producers, arrived at offices and studio bungalows; on every stage one heard of the roguish gifts of casts to directors or directors to casts; champagne had gone out from publicity offices to the press. And tips of fifties, tens and fives from producers, directors and writers fell like manna upon the white-collar class.

In this sort of transaction there were exceptions. Pat Hobby, for example, who knew the game from twenty years' experience, had had the idea of getting rid of his secretary the day before. They were sending over a new one any minute—but she would scarcely expect a present the first day.

Waiting for her, he walked the corridor, glancing into open offices for signs of life. He stopped to chat with Joe Hopper from the scenario department.

"Not like the old days," he mourned. "Then there was a bottle on every desk."

"There're a few around."

"Not many." Pat sighed. "And afterwards we'd run a picture—made up out of cutting-room scraps."

"I've heard. All the suppressed stuff," said Hopper.

Pat nodded, his eyes glistening.

"Oh, it was juicy. You darned near ripped your guts laughing—"

He broke off as the sight of a woman, pad in hand, entering his office down the hall recalled him to the sorry present.

"Gooddorf has me working over the holiday," he complained bitterly.

"I wouldn't do it."

"I wouldn't either except my four weeks are up next Friday, and if I bucked him he wouldn't extend me."

As he turned away Hopper knew that Pat was not being extended anyhow. He had been hired to script an old-fashioned horse-opera and the boys who were "writing behind him"—that is, working over his stuff—said that all of it was old and some didn't make sense.

"I'm Miss Kagle," said Pat's new secretary.

She was about thirty-six, handsome, faded, tired, efficient. She went to the typewriter, examined it, sat down and burst into sobs.

Pat started. Self-control, from below anyhow, was the rule around here. Wasn't it bad enough to be working on Christmas Eve? Well—less bad than not working at all. He walked over and shut the door—someone might suspect him of insulting the girl.

"Cheer up," he advised her. "This is Christmas."

Her burst of emotion had died away. She sat upright now, choking and wiping her eyes.

"Nothing's as bad as it seems," he assured her unconvincingly. "What's it anyhow? They going to lay you off?"

She shook her head, did a sniffle to end sniffles, and opened her notebook.

"Who you been working for?"

She answered between suddenly gritted teeth.

"Mr. Harry Gooddorf."

Pat widened his permanently bloodshot eyes. Now he remembered he had seen her in Harry's outer office.

"Since 1921. Eighteen years. And yesterday he sent me back to the department. He said I depressed him—I reminded him he was getting on." Her face was grim. "That isn't the way he talked after hours eighteen years ago."

"Yeah, he was a skirt chaser then," said Pat.

"I should have done something then when I had the chance."

Pat felt righteous stirrings.

"Breach of promise? That's no angle!"

"But I had something to clinch it. Something bigger than breach of promise. I still have too. But then, you see, I thought I was in love with him." She brooded for a moment. "Do you want to dictate something now?"

Pat remembered his job and opened a script.

"It's an insert," he began. "Scene 114 A."

Pat paced the office.

"Ext. Long Shot of the Plains," he decreed. "Buck and Mexicans approaching the hyacenda."

"The what?"

"The hyacenda—the ranch house." He looked at her reproachfully. "114 B. Two Shot: Buck and Pedro. Buck: "'The dirty son-of-a-bitch. I'll tear his guts out!'"

Miss Kagle looked up, startled.

"You want me to write that down?"

"Sure."

"It won't get by."

"I'm writing this. Of course it won't get by. But if I put 'you rat' the scene won't have any force."

"But won't somebody have to change it to 'you rat'?"

He glared at her—he didn't want to change secretaries every day.

"Harry Gooddorf can worry about that."

"Are you working for Mr. Gooddorf?" Miss Kagle asked in alarm.

"Until he throws me out."

"I shouldn't have said—"

"Don't worry," he assured her. "He's no pal of mine anymore. Not at three-fifty a week, when I used to get two thousand. . . . Where was I?"

He paced the floor again, repeating his last line aloud with relish. But now it seemed to apply not to a personage of the story but to Harry Gooddorf. Suddenly he stood still, lost in thought. "Say, what is it you got on him? You know where the body is buried?"

"That's too true to be funny."

"He knock somebody off?"

"Mr. Hobby, I'm sorry I ever opened my mouth."

"Just call me Pat. What's your first name?"

"Helen."

"Married?"

"Not now."

"Well, listen Helen: What do you say we have dinner?"

II

On the afternoon of Christmas Day he was still trying to get the secret out of her. They had the studio almost to themselves—only a skeleton staff of technical men dotted the walks and the commissary. They had exchanged Christmas presents. Pat gave her a five-dollar bill, Helen bought him a white linen handkerchief. Very well he could remember the day when many dozen such handkerchiefs had been his Christmas harvest.

The script was progressing at a snail's pace but their friendship had considerably ripened. Her secret, he considered, was a very valuable asset, and he wondered how many careers had turned on just such an asset. Some, he felt sure, had been thus raised to affluence. Why, it was almost as good as being in the family, and he pictured an imaginary conversation with Harry Gooddorf.

"Harry, it's this way. I don't think my experience is being made use of. It's the young squirts who ought to do the writing—I ought to do more supervising."

"Or—?"

"Or else," said Pat firmly.

He was in the midst of his daydream when Harry Gooddorf unexpectedly walked in.

"Merry Christmas, Pat," he said jovially. His smile was less robust when he saw Helen. "Oh, hello, Helen—didn't know you and Pat had got together. I sent you a remembrance over to the script department."

"You shouldn't have done that."

Harry turned swiftly to Pat.

"The boss is on my neck," he said. "I've got to have a finished script Thursday."

"Well, here I am," said Pat. "You'll have it. Did I ever fail you?"

"Usually," said Harry. "Usually."

He seemed about to add more when a call-boy entered with an envelope and handed it to Helen Kagle—whereupon Harry turned and hurried out.

"He'd better get out!" burst forth Miss Kagle, after opening the envelope. "Ten bucks—just *ten bucks*—from an ex*ec*utive—after eighteen years."

It was Pat's chance. Sitting on her desk he told her his plan.

"It's soft jobs for you and me," he said. "You the head of a script department, me an associate producer. We're on the gravy train for life—no more writing—no more pounding the keys. We might even—we might even—if things go good we could get married."

She hesitated a long time. When she put a fresh sheet in the typewriter Pat feared he had lost.

"I can write it from memory," she said. "This was a letter he typed *himself* on February 3rd, 1921. He sealed it and gave it to me to mail—but there was a blonde he was interested in, and I wondered why he should be so secret about a letter."

Helen had been typing as she talked, and now she handed Pat a note.

To Will Bronson
First National Studios
Personal
Dear Bill:

We killed Taylor. We should have cracked down on him sooner. So why not shut up.

Yours
Harry

Pat stared at it, stunned.

"Get it?" Helen said. "On February 1st, 1921, somebody knocked off William Desmond Taylor, the director. And they've never found out who."

III

For eighteen years she had kept the original note, envelope and all. She had sent only a copy to Bronson, tracing Harry Gooddorf's signature.

"Baby, we're set!" said Pat. "I always thought it was a *girl* got Taylor."

He was so elated that he opened a drawer and brought forth a half-pint of whiskey. Then, with an afterthought, he demanded:

"Is it in a safe place?"

"You bet it is. He'd never guess where."

"Baby, we've got him!"

Cash, cars, girls, swimming pools swam in a glittering montage before Pat's eye.

He folded the note, put it in his pocket, took another drink and reached for his hat.

"You going to see him now?" Helen demanded in some alarm. "Hey, wait till I get off the lot. *I* don't want to get murdered."

"Don't worry! Listen, I'll meet you in The Muncherie at Fifth and La Brea—in one hour."

As he walked to Gooddorf's office he decided to mention no facts or names within the walls of the studio. Back in the brief period when he had headed a scenario department Pat had conceived a plan to put a dictaphone in every writer's office. Thus their loyalty to the studio executives could be checked several times a day.

The idea had been laughed at. But later, when he had been "reduced back to a writer," he often wondered if his plan was secretly followed. Perhaps some indiscreet remark of his own was responsible for the doghouse where he had been interred for the past decade. So it was with the idea of concealed dictaphones in mind, dictaphones which could be turned on by the pressure of a toe, that he entered Harry Gooddorf's office.

"Harry—" he chose his words carefully, "do you remember the night of February 1st, 1921?"

Somewhat flabbergasted, Gooddorf leaned back in his swivel chair.

"*What?*"

"Try and think. It's something very important to you."

Pat's expression as he watched his friend was that of an anxious undertaker.

"February 1st, 1921," Gooddorf mused. "No. How could I remember? You think I keep a diary? I don't even know where I was then."

"You were right here in Hollywood."

"Probably. If you know, tell me."

"You'll remember."

"Let's see. I came out to the coast in 'sixteen. I was with Biograph till 1920. Was I making some comedies? That's it. I was making a piece called 'Knuckleduster'—on location."

"You weren't always on location. You were in town February 1st."

"What is this?" Gooddorf demanded. "The third degree?"

"No—but I've got some information about your doings on that date."

Gooddorf's face reddened; for a moment it looked as if he were going to throw Pat out of the room—then suddenly he gasped, licked his lips and stared at his desk.

"Oh," he said, and after a minute: "But I don't see what business it is of yours."

"It's the business of every decent man."

"Since when have you been decent?"

"All my life," said Pat. "And, even if I haven't, I never did anything like that."

"My foot!" said Harry contemptuously. "*You* showing up here with a halo! Anyhow, what's the evidence? You'd think you had a written confession. It's all forgotten long ago."

"Not in the memory of decent men," said Pat. "And as for a written confession—I've got it."

"I doubt you. And I doubt if it would stand in any court. You've been taken in."

"I've seen it," said Pat with growing confidence. "And it's enough to hang you."

"Well, by God if there's any publicity I'll run you out of town."

"You'll run *me* out of town."

"I don't want any publicity."

"Then I think you'd better come along with me. Without talking to anybody."

"Where are we going?"

"I know a bar where we can be alone."

The Muncherie was in fact deserted, save for the bartender and Helen Kagle who sat at a table, jumpy with alarm. Seeing her, Gooddorf's expression changed to one of infinite reproach.

"This is a hell of a Christmas," he said, "with my family expecting me home an hour ago. I want to know the idea. You say you've got something in my writing."

Pat took the paper from his pocket and read the date aloud. Then he looked up hastily:

"This is just a copy, so don't try and snatch it."

He knew the technique of such scenes as this. When the vogue for Westerns had temporarily subsided he had sweated over many an orgy of crime.

"To William Bronson, Dear Bill: We killed Taylor. We should have cracked down on him sooner. So why not shut up. Yours, Harry."

Pat paused. "You wrote this on February 3rd, 1921."

Silence. Gooddorf turned to Helen Kagle.

"Did *you* do this? Did I dictate that to you?"

"No," she admitted in an awed voice. "You wrote it yourself. I opened the letter."

"I see. Well, what do you want?"

"Plenty," said Pat, and found himself pleased with the sound of the word.

"What exactly?"

Pat launched into the description of a career suitable to a man of forty-nine. A glowing career. It expanded rapidly in beauty and power during the time it took him to drink three large whiskeys. But one demand he returned to again and again. He wanted to be made a producer tomorrow.

"Why tomorrow?" demanded Gooddorf. "Can't it wait?"

There were sudden tears in Pat's eyes—real tears.

"This is Christmas," he said. "It's my Christmas wish. I've had a hell of a time. I've waited so long."

Gooddorf got to his feet suddenly.

"Nope," he said. "I won't make you a producer. I couldn't do it in fairness to the company. I'd rather stand trial."

Pat's mouth fell open.

"What? You won't?"

"Not a chance. I'd rather swing."

He turned away, his face set, and started toward the door.

"All right!" Pat called after him. "It's your last chance."

Suddenly he was amazed to see Helen Kagle spring up and run after Gooddorf—try to throw her arms around him.

"Don't worry!" she cried. "I'll tear it up, Harry! It was a joke, Harry—"

Her voice trailed off rather abruptly. She had discovered that Gooddorf was shaking with laughter.

"What's the joke?" she demanded, growing angry again. "Do you think I haven't got it?"

"Oh, you've got it all right," Gooddorf howled. "You've got it—but it isn't what you think it is."

He came back to the table, sat down and addressed Pat.

"Do you know what I thought that date meant? I thought maybe it was the date Helen and I first fell for each other. That's what I thought. And I thought she was going to raise Cain about it. I thought she was nuts. She's been married twice since then, and so have I."

"That doesn't explain the note," said Pat sternly but with a sinky feeling. "You admit you killed Taylor."

Gooddorf nodded.

"I still think a lot of us did," he said. "We were a wild crowd—Taylor and Bronson and me and half the boys in the big money. So a bunch of us got together in an agreement to go slow. The country was waiting for somebody to hang. We tried to get Taylor to watch his step but he wouldn't. So instead of cracking down on him, we let him 'go the pace.' And some rat shot him—who did it I don't know."

He stood up.

"Like somebody should have cracked down on *you*, Pat. But you were an amusing guy in those days, and besides we were all too busy."

Pat sniffled suddenly.

"I've *been* cracked down on," he said. "Plenty."

"But too late," said Gooddorf, and added: "You've probably got a new Christmas wish by now, and I'll grant it to you. I won't say anything about this afternoon."

When he had gone, Pat and Helen sat in silence. Presently Pat took out the note again and looked it over.

"'So why not shut up?'" he read aloud. "He didn't explain that."

"Why *not* shut up?" Helen said.

A MAN IN THE WAY

Pat Hobby could always get on the lot. He had worked there fifteen years on and off—chiefly off during the past five—and most of the studio police knew him. If tough customers on watch asked to see his studio card he could get in by phoning Lou, the bookie. For Lou also, the studio had been home for many years.

Pat was forty-nine. He was a writer but he had never written much, nor even read all the "originals" he worked from, because it made his head bang to read much. But the good old silent days you got somebody's plot and a smart secretary and gulped benzedrine "structure" at her six or eight hours every week. The director took care of the gags. After talkies came he always teamed up with some man who wrote dialogue. Some young man who liked to work.

"I've got a list of credits second to none," he told Jack Berners. "All I need is an idea and to work with somebody who isn't all wet."

He had buttonholed Jack outside the production office as Jack was going to lunch and they walked together in the direction of the commissary.

"You bring *me* an idea," said Jack Berners. "Things are tight. We can't put a man on salary unless he's got an idea."

"How can you get ideas off salary?" Pat demanded—then he added hastily: "Anyhow I got the germ of an idea that I could be telling you all about at lunch."

Something might come to him at lunch. There was Baer's notion about the boy scout. But Jack said cheerfully:

"I've got a date for lunch, Pat. Write it out and send it around, eh?"

He felt cruel because he knew Pat couldn't write anything out but he was having story trouble himself. The war had just broken out and every producer on the lot wanted to end their current stories with the hero going to war. And Jack Berners felt he had thought of that first for his production.

"So write it out, eh?"

When Pat didn't answer Jack looked at him—he saw a sort of whipped misery in Pat's eye that reminded him of his own father. Pat had been in the money before Jack was out of college—with three cars and a chicken over every garage. Now his clothes looked as if he'd been standing at Hollywood and Vine for three years.

"Scout around and talk to some of the writers on the lot," he said. "If you can get one of them interested in your idea, bring him up to see me."

"I hate to give an idea without money on the line," Pat brooded pessimistically. "These young squirts'll lift the shirt off your back."

They had reached the commissary door.

"Good luck, Pat. Anyhow we're not in Poland."

—Good *you*'re not, said Pat under his breath. They'd slit your gizzard.

Now what to do? He went up and wandered along the cell-block of writers. Almost everyone had gone to lunch and those who were in he didn't know. Always there were more and more unfamiliar faces. And he had thirty credits; he had been in the business, publicity and script-writing, for twenty years.

The last door in the line belonged to a man he didn't like. But he wanted a place to sit a minute so with a knock he pushed it open. The man wasn't there—only a very pretty, frail-looking girl sat reading a book.

"I think he's left Hollywood," she said in answer to his question. "They gave me his office but they forgot to put up my name."

"You a writer?" Pat asked in surprise.

"I work at it."

"You ought to get 'em to give you a test."

"No—I like writing."

"What's that you're reading?"

She showed him.

"Let me give you a tip," he said. "That's not the way to get the guts out of a book."

"Oh."

"I've been here for years—I'm Pat Hobby—and I *know*. Give the book to four of your friends to read it. Get them to tell you what stuck in their minds. Write it down and you've got a picture—see?"

The girl smiled.

"Well, that's very—very original advice, Mr. Hobby."

"Pat Hobby," he said. "Can I wait here a minute? Man I came to see is at lunch."

He sat down across from her and picked up a copy of a photo magazine.

"Oh, just let me mark that," she said quickly.

He looked at the page which she checked. It showed paintings being boxed and carted away to safety from an art gallery in Europe.

"How'll you use it?" he said.

"Well, I thought it would be dramatic if there was an old man around while they were packing the pictures. A poor old man, trying to get a job helping them? But they can't use him—he's in the way—not even good cannon fodder. They want strong young people in the world. And it turns out he's the man who painted the pictures many years ago."

Pat considered.

"It's good but I don't get it," he said.

"Oh, it's nothing, a short short maybe."

"Got any good picture ideas? I'm in with all the markets here."

"I'm under contract."

"Use another name."

Her phone rang.

"Yes, this is Pricilla Smith," the girl said.

After a minute she turned to Pat.

"Will you excuse me? This is a private call."

He got up and walked out, and along the corridor. Finding an office with no name on it he went in and fell asleep on the couch.

II

Late that afternoon he returned to Jack Berners' waiting rooms. He had an idea about a man who meets a girl in an office and he thinks she's a stenographer but she turns out to be a writer. He engages her as a stenographer, though, and they start for the South Seas. It was a beginning, it was something to tell Jack, he thought—and, picturing Pricilla Smith, he refurbished some old business he hadn't seen used for years.

He became quite excited about it—felt quite young for a moment and walked up and down the waiting room mentally rehearsing the first sequence. "So here we have a situation like 'It Happened One Night'—only *new*. I see Hedy Lamarr—"

Oh, he knew how to talk to these boys if he could get to them, with something to say.

"Mr. Berners still busy?" he asked for the fifth time.

"Oh, yes, Mr. Hobby. Mr. Bill Costello and Mr. Bach are in there."

He thought quickly. It was half-past five. In the old days he had just busted in sometimes and sold an idea, an idea good for a couple of grand because it was just the moment when they were very tired of what they were doing at present.

He walked innocently out and to another door in the hall. He knew it led through a bathroom right into Jack Berners' office. Drawing a quick breath he plunged . . .

". . . So that's the notion," he concluded after five minutes. "It's just a flash—nothing really worked out, but you could give me an office and a girl and I could have something on paper for you in three days."

Berners, Costello and Bach didn't even have to look at each other. Berners spoke for them all as he said firmly and gently:

"That's no idea, Pat. I can't put you on salary for that."

"Why don't you work it out further by yourself," suggested Bill Costello. "And then let's see it. We're looking for ideas—especially about the war."

"A man can think better on salary," said Pat.

There was silence. Costello and Bach had drunk with him, played poker with him, gone to the races with him. They'd honestly be glad to see him placed.

"The war, eh," he said gloomily. "Everything is war now, no matter how many credits a man has. Do you know what it makes me think of? It makes me think of a well-known painter in the discard. It's war time and he's useless—just a man in the way." He warmed to his conception of himself, "—but all the time they're carting away *his own paintings* as the most valuable thing worth saving. And they won't even let him help. That's what it reminds me of."

There was again silence for a moment.

"That isn't a bad idea," said Bach thoughtfully. He turned to the others. "You know? In itself?"

Bill Costello nodded.

"Not bad at all. And I know where we could spot it. Right at the end of the fourth sequence. We just change old Ames to a painter. . . ."

Presently they talked money.

"I'll give you two weeks on it," said Berners to Pat. "At two-fifty."

"Two-fifty!" objected Pat. "Say, there was one time you paid me ten times that!"

"That was ten years ago," Jack reminded him. "Sorry. Best we can do now."

"You make me feel like that old painter—"

"Don't oversell it," said Jack, rising and smiling. "You're on the payroll."

Pat went out with a quick step and confidence in his eyes. Half a grand—that would take the pressure off for a month and you could often stretch two weeks into three—sometimes four. He left the studio proudly through the front entrance, stopping at the liquor store for a half-pint to take back to his room.

By seven o'clock things were even better. Santa Anita tomorrow, if he could get an advance. And tonight—something festive ought to be done tonight. With a sudden rush of pleasure he went down to the phone in the lower hall, called the studio and asked for Miss Pricilla Smith's number. He hadn't met anyone so pretty for years . . .

In her apartment Pricilla Smith spoke rather firmly into the phone.

"I'm awfully sorry," she said, "but I couldn't possibly. . . . No—and I'm tied up all the rest of the week."

As she hung up, Jack Berners spoke from the couch.

"Who was it?"

"Oh, some man who came in the office," she laughed, "and told me never to read the story I was working on."

"Shall I believe you?"

"You certainly shall. I'll even think of his name in a minute. But first I want to tell you about an idea I had this morning. I was looking at a photo in a magazine where they were packing up some works of art in the Tate Gallery in London. And I thought—"

"BOIL SOME WATER—LOTS OF IT"

Pat Hobby sat in his office in the Writers' Building and looked at his morning's work, just come back from the script department. He was on a "polish job," about the only kind he ever got nowadays. He was to repair a messy sequence in a hurry, but the word "hurry" neither frightened nor inspired him for Pat had been in Hollywood since he was thirty—now he was forty-nine. All the work he had done this morning (except a little changing around of lines so he could claim them as his own)—all he had actually invented was a single imperative sentence, spoken by a doctor.

"Boil some water—lots of it."

It was a good line. It had sprung into his mind full-grown as soon as he had read the script. In the old silent days Pat would have used it as a spoken title and ended his dialogue worries for a space, but he needed some spoken words for other people in the scene. Nothing came.

"Boil some water," he repeated to himself. "Lots of it."

The word "boil" brought a quick glad thought of the commissary. A reverent thought too—for an old-timer like Pat, what people you sat with at lunch was more important in getting along than what you dictated in your office. This was no art, as he often said—this was an industry.

"This is no art," he remarked to Max Leam who was leisurely drinking at a corridor water cooler. "This is an industry."

Max had flung him this timely bone of three weeks at three-fifty.

"Say look, Pat! Have you got anything down on paper yet?"

"Say I've got some stuff already that'll make 'em—" He named a familiar biological function with the somewhat startling assurance that it would take place in the theatre.

Max tried to gauge his sincerity.

"Want to read it to me now?" he asked.

"Not yet. But it's got the old guts if you know what I mean."

Max was full of doubts.

"Well, go to it. And if you run into any medical snags check with the doctor over at the First Aid Station. It's got to be right."

The spirit of Pasteur shone firmly in Pat's eyes.

"It will be."

He felt good walking across the lot with Max—so good that he decided to glue himself to the producer and sit down with him at the Big Table. But Max foiled his intention by cooing "See you later" and slipping into the barber shop.

Once Pat had been a familiar figure at the Big Table; often in his golden prime he had dined in the private canteens of executives. Being of the older Hollywood he understood their jokes, their vanities, their social system with its swift fluctuations. But there were too many new faces at the Big Table now—faces that looked at him with the universal Hollywood suspicion. And at the little tables where the young writers sat they seemed to take work so seriously. As for just sitting down anywhere, even with secretaries or extras—Pat would rather catch a sandwich at the corner.

Detouring to the Red Cross Station he asked for the doctor. A girl, a nurse, answered from a wall mirror where she was hastily drawing her lips: "He's out. What is it?"

"Oh. Then I'll come back."

She had finished, and now she turned—vivid and young and with a bright consoling smile.

"Miss Stacey will help you. I'm about to go to lunch."

He was aware of an old, old feeling—left over from the time when he had had wives—a feeling that to invite this little beauty to lunch might cause trouble. But he remembered quickly that he didn't have any wives now—they had both given up asking for alimony.

"I'm working on a medical," he said. "I need some help."

"A medical?"

"Writing it—idea about a doc. Listen—let me buy you lunch. I want to ask you some medical questions."

The nurse hesitated.

"I don't know. It's my first day out here."

"It's all right," he assured her. "Studios are democratic; everybody is just 'Joe' or 'Mary'—from the big shots right down to the prop boys."

He proved it magnificently on their way to lunch by greeting a male star and getting his own name back in return. And in the commissary, where they were placed hard by the Big Table, his producer, Max Leam, looked up, did a little "takem" and winked.

The nurse—her name was Helen Earle—peered about eagerly.

"I don't see anybody," she said. "Except, oh, there's Ronald Colman. I didn't know Ronald Colman looked like that."

Pat pointed suddenly to the floor.

"And there's Mickey Mouse!"

She jumped and Pat laughed at his joke—but Helen Earle was already staring starry-eyed at the costume extras who filled the hall with the colors of the First Empire. Pat was piqued to see her interest go out to these nonentities.

"The big shots are at this next table," he said solemnly, wistfully, "directors and all except the biggest executives. They could have Ronald Colman pressing pants. I usually sit over there but they don't want ladies. At lunch, that is, they don't want ladies."

"Oh," said Helen Earle, polite but unimpressed. "It must be wonderful to be a writer too. It's so very interesting."

"It has its points," he said . . . he had thought for years it was a dog's life.

"What is it you want to ask me about a doctor?"

Here was toil again. Something in Pat's mind snapped off when he thought of the story.

"Well, Max Leam—that man facing us—Max Leam and I have a script about a doc. You know? Like a hospital picture?"

"I know." And she added after a moment, "That's the reason that I went into training."

"And we've got to have it *right* because a hundred million people would check on it. So this doctor in the script he tells them to boil some water. He says, 'Boil some water—lots of it.' And we were wondering what the people would do then."

"Why—they'd probably boil it," Helen said, and then, somewhat confused by the question, "What people?"

"Well, somebody's daughter and the man that lived there and an attorney and the man that was hurt—"

Helen tried to digest this before answering.

"—and some other guy I'm going to cut out," he finished.

There was a pause. The waitress set down tuna fish sandwiches.

"Well, when a doctor gives orders they're orders," Helen decided.

"Hm." Pat's interest had wandered to an odd little scene at the Big Table while he inquired absently, "You married?"

"No."

"Neither am I."

Beside the Big Table stood an extra, a Russian Cossack with a fierce moustache. He stood resting his hand on the back of an empty chair between Director Paterson and Producer Leam.

"Is this taken?" he asked, with a thick Central European accent.

All along the Big Table faces stared suddenly at him. Until after the first look the supposition was that he must be some well-known actor. But he was not—he was dressed in one of the many-colored uniforms that dotted the room.

Someone at the table said: "That's taken." But the man drew out the chair and sat down.

"Got to eat somewhere," he remarked with a grin.

A shiver went over the nearby tables. Pat Hobby stared with his mouth ajar. It was as if someone had crayoned Donald Duck into "The Last Supper."

"Look at that," he advised Helen. "What they'll do to him! Boy!"

The flabbergasted silence at the Big Table was broken by Ned Harman, the production manager.

"This table is reserved," he said.

The extra looked up from a menu.

"They told me sit anywhere."

He beckoned a waitress—who hesitated, looking for an answer in the faces of her superiors.

"Extras don't eat here," said Max Leam, still politely. "This is a—"

"I got to eat," said the Cossack doggedly. "I been standing around six hours while they shoot this stinking mess and now I got to eat."

The silence had extended—from Pat's angle all within range seemed to be poised in mid-air.

The extra shook his head wearily.

"I dunno who cooked it up—" he said—and Max Leam sat forward in his chair—"but it's the lousiest tripe I ever seen shot in Hollywood."

—At his table Pat was thinking why didn't they do something? Knock him down, drag him away. If they were yellow themselves they could call the studio police.

"Who is that?" Helen Earle was following his eyes innocently. "Somebody I ought to know?"

He was listening attentively to Max Leam's voice, raised in anger. "Get up and get out of here, buddy, and get out quick!"

The extra frowned.

"Who's telling me?" he demanded.

"You'll see." Max appealed to the table at large: "Where's Cushman—where's the Personnel man?"

"You try to move me," said the extra, lifting the hilt of his scabbard above the level of the table, "and I'll hang this on your ear. I know my rights."

The dozen men at the table, representing a thousand dollars an hour in salaries, sat stunned. Far down by the door one of the studio police caught wind of what was happening and started to elbow through the crowded room. And Big Jack Wilson, another director, was on his feet in an instant coming around the table.

But they were too late—Pat Hobby could stand no more. He had jumped up, seizing a big heavy tray from the serving stand nearby. In two springs he reached the scene of action—lifting the tray he brought it down upon the extra's head with all the strength of his forty-nine years. The extra, who had been in the act of rising to meet Wilson's threatened assault, got the blow full on his face and temple and as he collapsed a dozen red streaks sprang into sight through the heavy grease paint. He crashed sideways between the chairs.

Pat stood over him panting—the tray in his hand.

"The dirty rat!" he cried. "Where does he think—"

The studio policeman pushed past; Wilson pushed past—two aghast men from another table rushed up to survey the situation.

"It was a gag!" one of them shouted. "That's Walter Herrick, the writer. It's his picture."

"My God!"

"He was kidding Max Leam. It was a gag I tell you!"

"Pull him out . . . Get a doctor . . . Look out, there!"

Now Helen Earle hurried over; Walter Herrick was dragged out into a cleared space on the floor and there were yells of "Who did it? Who beaned him?"

Pat let the tray lapse to a chair, its sound unnoticed in the confusion. He saw Helen Earle working swiftly at the man's head with a pile of clean napkins.

"Why did they have to do this to him?" someone shouted.

Pat caught Max Leam's eye but Max happened to look away at the moment and a sense of injustice came over Pat. He alone in this crisis, real or imaginary, had *acted*. He alone had played the man, while those stuffed shirts let themselves be insulted and abused. And now he would have to take the rap—because Walter Herrick was powerful and popular, a three-thousand-a-week man who wrote hit shows in New York. How could anyone have guessed that it was a gag?

There was a doctor now. Pat saw him say something to the manageress and her shrill voice sent the waitresses scattering like leaves toward the kitchen.

"Boil some water! Lots of it!"

The words fell wild and unreal on Pat's burdened soul. But even though he now knew at first hand what came next, he did not think that he could go on from there.

TEAMED WITH GENIUS

"I took a chance in sending for you," said Jack Berners. "But there's a job that you just *may* be able to help out with."

Though Pat Hobby was not offended, either as man or writer, a formal protest was called for.

"I been in the industry fifteen years, Jack. I've got more screen credits than a dog has got fleas."

"Maybe I chose the wrong word," said Jack. "What I mean is, that was a long time ago. About money we'll pay you just what Republic paid you last month—three-fifty a week. Now—did you ever hear of a writer named René Wilcox?"

The name was unfamiliar. Pat had scarcely opened a book in a decade.

"She's pretty good," he ventured.

"It's a man, an English playwright. He's only here in L.A. for his health. Well—we've had a Russian Ballet picture kicking around for a year—three bad scripts on it. So last week we signed up René Wilcox—he seemed just the person."

Pat considered.

"You mean he's—"

"I don't know and I don't care," interrupted Berners sharply. "We think we can borrow Zorina, so we want to hurry things up—do a shooting script instead of just a treatment. Wilcox is inexperienced and that's where you come in. You used to be a good man for structure."

"*Used* to be!"

"All right, maybe you still are." Jack beamed with momentary encouragement. "Find yourself an office and get together with René Wilcox." As Pat started out he called him back and put a bill in his hand. "First of all, get a new hat. You used to be quite a boy around the secretaries in the old days. Don't give up at forty-nine!"

Over in the Writers' Building, Pat glanced at the directory in the hall and knocked at the door of 216. No answer, but he went in to discover a blond, willowy youth of twenty-five staring moodily out the window.

"Hello, René!" Pat said. "I'm your partner."

Wilcox's regard questioned even his existence, but Pat continued heartily: "I hear we're going to lick some stuff into shape. Ever collaborate before?"

"I have never written for the cinema before."

While this increased Pat's chance for a screen credit he badly needed, it meant that he might have to do some work. The very thought made him thirsty.

"This is different from playwriting," he suggested, with suitable gravity.

"Yes—I read a book about it."

Pat wanted to laugh. In 1928 he and another man had concocted such a sucker-trap, "Secrets of Film Writing." It would have made money if pictures hadn't started to talk.

"It all seems simple enough," said Wilcox. Suddenly he took his hat from the rack. "I'll be running along now."

"Don't you want to talk about the script?" demanded Pat. "What have you done so far?"

"I've not done anything," said Wilcox deliberately. "That idiot, Berners, gave me some trash and told me to go on from there. But it's too dismal." His blue eyes narrowed. "I say, what's a boom shot?"

"A boom shot? Why, that's when the camera's on a crane."

Pat leaned over the desk and picked up a blue-jacketed "Treatment." On the cover he read:

"BALLET SHOES"
A Treatment
by
Consuela Martin
An Original from an idea by Consuela Martin

Pat glanced at the beginning and then at the end. "I'd like it better if we could get the war in somewhere," he said frowning. "Have the dancer go as a Red Cross nurse and then she could get regenerated. See what I mean?"

There was no answer. Pat turned and saw the door softly closing.

What is this? he exclaimed. What kind of collaborating can a man do if he walks out? Wilcox had not even given the legitimate excuse—the races at Santa Anita!

The door opened again, a pretty girl's face, rather frightened, showed itself momentarily, said "Oh" and disappeared. Then it returned.

"Why it's Mr. Hobby!" she exclaimed. "I was looking for Mr. Wilcox."

He fumbled for her name but she supplied it.

"Katherine Hodge. I was your secretary when I worked here three years ago."

Pat knew she had once worked with him, but for the moment could not remember whether there had been a deeper relation. It did not seem to him that it had been love—but looking at her now, that appeared rather too bad.

"Sit down," said Pat. "You assigned to Wilcox?"

"I thought so—but he hasn't given me any work yet."

"I think he's nuts," Pat said gloomily. "He asked me what a boom shot was. Maybe he's sick—that's why he's out here. He'll probably start throwing up all over the office."

"He's well now," Katherine ventured.

"He doesn't look like it to me. Come on in my office. You can work for *me* this afternoon."

Pat lay on his couch while Miss Katherine Hodge read the script of "Ballet Shoes" aloud to him. About midway in the second sequence he fell asleep, with his new hat on his chest.

II

Except for the hat, that was the identical position in which he found René next day at eleven. And it was that way for three straight days—one was asleep or else the other—and sometimes both. On the fourth day they had several conferences in which Pat again put forward his idea about the war as a regenerating force for ballet dancers.

"Couldn't we *not* talk about the war?" suggested René. "I have two brothers in the Guards."

"You're lucky to be here in Hollywood."

"That's as it may be."

"Well, what's your idea of the start of the picture?"

"I do not like the present beginning. It gives me an almost physical nausea."

"So then, we got to have something in its place. That's why I want to plant the war—"

"I'm late to luncheon," said René Wilcox. "Good-bye, Mike."

Pat grumbled to Katherine Hodge:

"He can call me anything he likes, but somebody's got to write this picture. I'd go to Jack Berners and tell him—but I think we'd both be out on our ears."

For two days more he camped in René's office, trying to rouse him to action, but with no avail. Desperate on the following day—when the playwright did not even come to the studio—Pat took a benzedrine tablet and attacked the story alone. Pacing his office with the treatment in his hand he dictated to Katherine—interspersing the dictation with a short, biased history of his life in Hollywood. At the day's end he had two pages of script.

The ensuing week was the toughest in his life—not even a moment to make a pass at Katherine Hodge. Gradually, with many creaks, his battered hulk got in motion. Benzedrine and great drafts of coffee woke him in the morning, whiskey anesthetized him at night. Into his feet crept an old neuritis and as his nerves began to crackle he developed a hatred against René Wilcox, which served him as a sort of *ersatz* fuel. He was going to finish the script by himself and hand it to Berners with the statement that Wilcox had not contributed a single line.

But it was too much—Pat was too far gone. He blew up when he was half through and went on a twenty-four-hour bat—and next morning arrived back at the studio to find a message that Mr. Berners wanted to see the script at four. Pat was in a sick and confused state when his door opened and René Wilcox came in with a typescript in one hand, and a copy of Berners' note in the other.

"It's all right," said Wilcox. "I've finished it."

"*What?* Have you been *work*ing?"

"I always work at night."

"What've you done? A treatment?"

"No, a shooting script. At first I was held back by personal worries, but once I got started it was very simple. You just get behind the camera and dream."

Pat stood up aghast.

"But we were supposed to collaborate. Jack'll be wild."

"I've always worked alone," said Wilcox gently. "I'll explain to Berners this afternoon."

Pat sat in a daze. If Wilcox's script was good—but how could a first script be good? Wilcox should have fed it to him as he wrote; then they might have *had* something.

Fear started his mind working—he was struck by his first original idea since he had been on the job. He phoned to the script department for Katherine Hodge and when she came over told her what he wanted. Katherine hesitated.

"I just want to *read* it," Pat said hastily. "If Wilcox is there you can't take it, of course. But he just might be out."

He waited nervously. In five minutes she was back with the script.

"It isn't mimeographed or even bound," she said.

He was at the typewriter, trembling as he picked out a letter with two fingers.

"Can I help?" she asked.

"Find me a plain envelope and a used stamp and some paste."

Pat sealed the letter himself and then gave directions:

"Listen outside Wilcox's office. If he's in, push it under his door. If he's out get a call-boy to deliver it to him, wherever he is. Say it's from the mail room. Then you better go off the lot for the afternoon. So he won't catch on, see?"

As she went out Pat wished he had kept a copy of the note. He was proud of it—there was a ring of factual sincerity in it too often missing from his work.

"Dear Mr. Wilcox:

I am sorry to tell you your two brothers were killed in action today by a long range Tommy-gun. You are wanted at home in England right away.

John Smythe
The British Consulate, New York."

But Pat realized that this was no time for self-applause. He opened Wilcox's script.

To his vast surprise it was technically proficient—the dissolves, fades, cuts, pans and trucking shots were correctly detailed. This simplified everything. Turning back to the first page he wrote at the top:

BALLET SHOES
First Revise
From Pat Hobby and René Wilcox

—presently changing this to read:

From René Wilcox and Pat Hobby.

Then, working frantically, he made several dozen small changes. He substituted the word "Scram!" for "Get out of my sight!" He put "Behind the eight-ball" instead of "In trouble," and replaced "You'll be sorry" with the apt coinage "Or else!" Then he phoned the script department.

"This is Pat Hobby. I've been working on a script with René Wilcox, and Mr. Berners would like to have it mimeographed by half-past three."

This would give him an hour's start on his unconscious collaborator.

"Is it an emergency?"

"I'll say."

"We'll have to split it up between several girls."

Pat continued to improve the script till the call-boy arrived. He wanted to put in his war idea but time was short—still, he finally told the call-boy to sit down, while he wrote laboriously in pencil on the last page.

CLOSE SHOT: Boris and Rita

RITA

What does anything matter now! I have enlisted as a trained nurse in the war.

BORIS (moved)

War purifies and regenerates!

(He puts his arms around her in a wild embrace as the music soars way up and we)

FADE OUT:

Limp and exhausted by his effort he needed a drink so he left the lot and slipped cautiously into the bar across from the studio where he ordered gin and water.

With the glow, he thought warm thoughts. He had done al*most* what he had been hired to do—though his hand had accidentally fallen upon the dialogue rather than the structure. But how could Berners tell that the structure wasn't Pat's? Katherine Hodge would say nothing, for fear of implicating herself. They were all guilty but guiltiest of all was René Wilcox for refusing to play the game. Always, according to his lights, Pat had played the game.

He had another drink, bought breath tablets and for awhile amused himself at the nickel machine in the drug store. Louie, the studio bookie, asked if he was interested in wagers on a bigger scale.

"Not today, Louie."

"What are they paying you, Pat?"

"Thousand a week."

"Not so bad."

"Oh, a lot of us old timers are coming back," Pat prophesied. "In silent days was where you got real training—with directors shooting off the cuff and needing a gag in a split second. Now it's a sis job. They got English teachers working in pictures! What do they know?"

"How about a little something on 'Quaker Girl'?"

"No," said Pat. "This afternoon I got an important angle to work on. I don't want to worry about horses."

At three-fifteen he returned to his office to find two copies of his script in bright new covers.

<u>BALLET SHOES</u>
from
<u>René Wilcox and Pat Hobby</u>
<u>FIRST REVISE</u>

It reassured him to see his name in type. As he waited in Jack Berners' anteroom he almost wished he had reversed the names. With the right director this might be another "It Happened One Night," and if he got his name on something like that it meant a three- or four-year gravy ride. But this time he'd save his money—go to Santa Anita only once a week—get himself a girl along the type of Katherine Hodge, who wouldn't expect a mansion in Beverly Hills.

Berners' secretary interrupted his reverie, telling him to go in. As he entered he saw with gratification that a copy of the new script lay on Berners' desk.

"Did you ever—" asked Berners suddenly "—go to a psychoanalyst?"

"No," admitted Pat. "But I suppose I could get up on it. Is it a new assignment?"

"Not exactly. It's just that I think you've lost your grip. Even larceny requires a certain cunning. I've just talked to Wilcox on the phone."

"Wilcox must be nuts," said Pat, aggressively. "I didn't steal anything from him. His name's on it, isn't it? Two weeks ago I laid out all his structure—every scene. I even wrote one whole scene—at the end about the war."

"Oh yes, the war," said Berners as if he was thinking of something else.

"But if you like Wilcox's ending better—"

"Yes, I like his ending better. I never saw a man pick up this work so fast." He paused. "Pat, you've told the truth just once since you came in this room—that you didn't steal anything from Wilcox."

"I certainly did not. I *gave* him stuff."

But a certain dreariness, a grey *malaise*, crept over him as Berners continued:

"I told you we had three scripts. You used an old one we discarded a year ago. Wilcox was in when your secretary arrived, and he sent one of them to you. Clever, eh?"

Pat was speechless.

"You see, he and that girl like each other. Seems she typed a play for him this summer."

"They like each other," said Pat incredulously. "Why, he—"

"Hold it, Pat. You've had trouble enough today."

"He's responsible," Pat cried. "He wouldn't collaborate—and all the time—"

"—he was writing a swell script. And he can write his own ticket if we can persuade him to stay here and do another."

Pat could stand no more. He stood up.

"Anyhow thank you, Jack," he faltered. "Call my agent if anything turns up." Then he bolted suddenly and surprisingly for the door.

Jack Berners signaled on the Dictograph for the president's office.

"Get a chance to read it?" he asked in a tone of eagerness.

"It's swell. Better than you said. Wilcox is with me now."

"Have you signed him up?"

"I'm going to. Seems he wants to work with Hobby. Here, you talk to him."

Wilcox's rather high voice came over the wire.

"Must have Mike Hobby," he said. "Grateful to him. Had a quarrel with a certain young lady just before he came, but today Hobby brought us together. Besides, I want to write a play about him. So give him to me—you fellows don't want him anymore."

Berners picked up his secretary's phone.

"Go after Pat Hobby. He's probably in the bar across the street. We're putting him on salary again but we'll be sorry."

He switched off, switched on again.

"Oh! Take him his hat. He forgot his hat."

PAT HOBBY AND ORSON WELLES

"Who's this Welles?" Pat asked of Louie, the studio bookie. "Every time I pick up a paper they got about this Welles."

"You know, he's that beard," explained Louie.

"Sure, I know he's that beard, you couldn't miss that. But what credits's he got? What's he done to draw one hundred and fifty grand a picture?"

What indeed? Had he, like Pat, been in Hollywood over twenty years? Did he have credits that would knock your eye out, extending up to—well, up to five years ago when Pat's credits had begun to be few and far between?

"Listen—they don't last long," said Louie consolingly. "We've seen 'em come and we've seen 'em go. Hey, Pat?"

Yes—but meanwhile those who had toiled in the vineyard through the heat of the day were lucky to get a few weeks at three-fifty. Men who had once had wives and Filipinos and swimming pools.

"Maybe it's the beard," said Louie. "Maybe you and I should grow a beard. My father had a beard but it never got him off Grand Street."

The gift of hope had remained with Pat through his misfortunes—and the valuable alloy of his hope was proximity. Above all things one must stick around, one must be there when the glazed, tired mind of the producer grappled with the question "Who?" So presently Pat wandered out of the drug store, and crossed the street to the lot that was home.

As he passed through the side entrance an unfamiliar studio policeman stood in his way.

"Everybody in the front entrance now."

"I'm Hobby, the writer," Pat said.

The Cossack was unimpressed.

"Got your card?"

"I'm between pictures. But I've got an engagement with Jack Berners."

"Front gate."

As he turned away Pat thought savagely: "Lousy Keystone Cop!" In his mind he shot it out with him. Plunk! The stomach. Plunk! Plunk! Plunk!

At the main entrance too there was a new face.

"Where's Ike?" Pat demanded.

"Ike's gone."

"Well, it's all right, I'm Pat Hobby. Ike always passes me."

"That's why he's gone," said the guardian blandly. "Who's your business with?"

Pat hesitated. He hated to disturb a producer.

"Call Jack Berners' office," he said. "Just speak to his secretary."

After a minute the man turned from the phone.

"What about?" he said.

"About a picture."

He waited for an answer.

"She wants to know what picture?"

"To hell with it," said Pat disgustedly. "Look—call Louie Griebel. What's all this about?"

"Orders from Mr. Kasper," said the clerk. "Last week a visitor from Chicago fell in the wind machine—Hello. Mr. Louie Griebel?"

"I'll talk to him," said Pat, taking the phone.

"I can't do nothing, Pat," mourned Louie. "I had trouble getting my boy in this morning. Some twirp from Chicago fell in the wind machine."

"What's that got to do with me?" demanded Pat vehemently.

He walked, a little faster than his wont, along the studio wall to the point where it joined the back lot. There was a guard there but there were always people passing to and fro and he joined one of the groups. Once inside he would see Jack and have himself excepted from this absurd ban. Why, he had known this lot when the first shacks were rising on it, when this was considered the edge of the desert.

"Sorry mister, you with this party?"

"I'm in a hurry," said Pat. "I've lost my card."

"Yeah? Well, for all I know you may be a plainclothes man." He held open a copy of a photo magazine under Pat's nose. "I wouldn't let you in even if you told me you was this here Orson Welles."

II

There is an old Chaplin picture about a crowded street car where the entrance of one man at the rear forces another out in front. A similar image came into Pat's mind in the ensuing days whenever he thought of Orson Welles. Welles was in; Hobby was out. Never before had the studio been barred to Pat and though Welles was on another lot it seemed as if his large body, pushing in brashly from nowhere, had edged Pat out the gate.

"Now where do you go?" Pat thought. He had worked in the other studios but they were not his. At this studio he never felt unemployed—in recent times of stress he had eaten property food on its stages—half a cold lobster during a scene from "The Divine Miss Carstairs"; he had often slept on the sets and last winter made use of a Chesterfield overcoat from the costume department. Orson Welles had no business edging him out of this. Orson Welles belonged with the rest of the snobs back in New York.

On the third day he was frantic with gloom. He had sent note after note to Jack Berners and even asked Louie to intercede—now word came that Jack had left town. There were so few friends left. Desolate he stood in front of the automobile gate with a crowd of staring children, feeling that he had reached the end at last.

A great limousine rolled out, in the back of which Pat recognized the great overstuffed Roman face of Harold Marcus. The car rolled toward the children and, as one of them ran in front of it, slowed down. The old man spoke into the tube and the car halted. He leaned out blinking.

"Is there no policeman here?" he asked of Pat.

"No, Mr. Marcus," said Pat quickly. "There should be. I'm Pat Hobby, the writer—could you give me a lift down the street?"

It was unprecedented—it was an act of desperation but Pat's need was great.

Mr. Marcus looked at him closely.

"Oh yes, I remember you," he said. "Get in."

He might possibly have meant get up in front with the chauffeur. Pat compromised by opening one of the little seats. Mr. Marcus was one of the most powerful men in the whole picture world. He did not occupy himself with production any longer. He spent most of his time rocking from coast to coast on fast trains, merging and launching, launching and merging, like a much divorced woman.

"Someday those children'll get hurt."

"Yes, Mr. Marcus," agreed Pat heartily. "Mr. Marcus—"

"They ought to have a policeman there."

"Yes, Mr. Marcus. Mr. Marcus—"

"Hm-m-m!" said Mr. Marcus. "Where do you want to be dropped?"

Pat geared himself to work fast.

"Mr. Marcus, when I was your press agent—"

"I know," said Mr. Marcus. "You wanted a ten-dollar-a-week raise."

"What a memory!" cried Pat in gladness. "What a memory! But Mr. Marcus, now I don't want anything at all."

"This is a miracle."

"I've got modest wants, see, and I've saved enough to retire."

He thrust his shoes slightly forward under a hanging blanket. The Chesterfield coat effectively concealed the rest.

"That's what I'd like," said Mr. Marcus gloomily. "A farm—with chickens. Maybe a little nine-hole course. Not even a stock ticker."

"I want to retire, but different," said Pat earnestly. "Pictures have been my life. I want to watch them grow and grow—"

Mr. Marcus groaned.

"Till they explode," he said. "Look at Fox! I cried for him." He pointed to his eyes: "Tears!"

Pat nodded very sympathetically.

"I want only one thing." From the long familiarity he went into the foreign locution. "I should go on the lot any time. From nothing. Only to be there. Should bother nobody. Only help a little from nothing if any young person wants advice."

"See Berners," said Marcus.

"He said see you."

"Then you did want something," Marcus smiled. "All right, all right by me. Where do you get off now?"

"Could you write me a pass?" Pat pleaded. "Just a word on your card?"

"I'll look into it," said Mr. Marcus. "Just now I've got things on my mind. I'm going to a luncheon." He sighed profoundly. "They want I should meet this new Orson Welles that's in Hollywood."

Pat's heart winced. There it was again—that name, sinister and remorseless, spreading like a dark cloud over all his skies.

"Mr. Marcus," he said, so sincerely that his voice trembled, "I wouldn't be surprised if Orson Welles is the biggest menace that's come to Hollywood for years. He gets a hundred and fifty grand a picture and I wouldn't be surprised if he was so radical that you had to have all new equipment and start all over again like you did with sound in 1928."

"Oh my God!" groaned Mr. Marcus.

"And me," said Pat. "All I want is a pass and no money—to leave things as they are."

Mr. Marcus reached for his card case.

III

To those grouped together under the name "talent," the atmosphere of a studio is not unfailingly bright—one fluctuates too quickly between high hope and grave apprehension. Those few who decide things are happy in their work and sure that they are worthy of their hire—the rest live in a mist of doubt as to when their vast inadequacy will be disclosed.

Pat's psychology was, oddly, that of the masters and for the most part he was unworried even though he was off salary. But there was one large fly in the ointment—for the first time in his life he began to feel a loss of identity. Due to reasons that he did not quite understand, though it might have been traced to his conversation, a number of people began to address him as "Orson."

Now to lose one's identity is a careless thing in any case. But to lose it to an enemy, or at least to one who has become scapegoat for our misfortunes—that is a hardship. Pat was *not* Orson. Any resemblance must be faint and far-fetched and he was aware of the fact. The final effect was to make him, in that regard, something of an eccentric.

"Pat," said Joe the barber, "Orson was in here today and asked me to trim his beard."

"I hope you set fire to it," said Pat.

"I did." Joe winked at waiting customers over a hot towel. "He asked for a singe so I took it all off. Now his face is as bald as yours. In fact you look a bit alike."

This was the morning the kidding was so ubiquitous that, to avoid it, Pat lingered in Mario's bar across the street. He was not drinking—at the bar, that is, for he was down to his last thirty cents, but he refreshed himself frequently from a half-pint in his back pocket. He needed the stimulus, for he had to make a touch presently and he knew that money was easier to borrow when one didn't have an air of urgent need.

His quarry, Jeff Boldini, was in an unsympathetic state of mind. He too was an artist, albeit a successful one, and a certain great lady of the screen had just burned him up by criticizing a wig he had made for her. He told the story to Pat at length and the latter waited until it was all out before broaching his request.

"No soap," said Jeff. "Hell, you never paid me back what you borrowed last month."

"But I got a job now," lied Pat. "This is just to tide me over. I start tomorrow."

"If they don't give the job to Orson Welles," said Jeff humorously.

Pat's eyes narrowed but he managed to utter a polite, borrower's laugh.

"Hold it," said Jeff. "You know I think you look like him?"

"Yeah."

"Honest. Anyhow I could make you look like him. I could make you a beard that would be his double."

"I wouldn't be his double for fifty grand."

With his head on one side Jeff regarded Pat.

"I could," he said. "Come on in to my chair and let me see."

"Like hell."

"Come on. I'd like to try it. You haven't got anything to do. You don't work till tomorrow."

"I don't want a beard."

"It'll come off."

"I don't want it."

"It won't cost you anything. In fact I'll be paying *you*—I'll loan you the ten smackers if you'll let me make you a beard."

Half an hour later Jeff looked at his completed work.

"It's perfect," he said. "Not only the beard but the eyes and everything."

"All right. Now take it off," said Pat moodily.

"What's the hurry? That's a fine muff. That's a work of art. We ought to put a camera on it. Too bad you're working tomorrow—they're using a dozen beards out on Sam Jones' set and one of them went to jail in a homo raid. I bet with that muff you could get the job."

It was weeks since Pat had heard the word "job" and he could not himself say how he managed to exist and eat. Jeff saw the light in his eye.

"What say? Let me drive you out there just for fun," pleaded Jeff. "I'd like to see if Sam could tell it was a phony muff."

"I'm a writer, not a ham."

"Come on! Nobody would never know you back of that. And you'd draw another ten bucks."

As they left the make-up department Jeff lingered behind a minute. On a strip of cardboard he crayoned the name Orson Welles in large block letters. And outside without Pat's notice, he stuck it in the windshield of his car.

He did not go directly to the back lot. Instead he drove not too swiftly up the main studio street. In front of the Administration Building he stopped on the pretext that the engine was missing, and almost in no time a small but definitely interested crowd began to gather. But Jeff's plans did not include stopping anywhere long, so he hopped in and they started on a tour around the commissary.

"Where are we going?" demanded Pat.

He had already made one nervous attempt to tear the beard from him, but to his surprise it did not come away.

He complained of this to Jeff.

"Sure," Jeff explained. "That's made to last. You'll have to soak it off."

The car paused momentarily at the door of the commissary. Pat saw blank eyes staring at him and he stared back at them blankly from the rear seat.

"You'd think I was the only beard on the lot," he said gloomily.

"You can sympathize with Orson Welles."

"To hell with him."

This colloquy would have puzzled those without, to whom he was nothing less than the real McCoy.

Jeff drove on slowly up the street. Ahead of them a little group of men were walking—one of them, turning, saw the car and drew the attention of the others to it. Whereupon the most elderly member of the party threw up his arms in what appeared to be a defensive gesture, and plunged to the sidewalk as the car went past.

"My God, did you see that?" exclaimed Jeff. "That was Mr. Marcus."

He came to a stop. An excited man ran up and put his head in the car window.

"Mr. Welles, our Mr. Marcus has had a heart attack. Can we use your car to get him to the infirmary?"

Pat stared. Then very quickly he opened the door on the other side and dashed from the car. Not even the beard could impede his streamlined flight. The policeman at the gate, not recognizing the incarnation, tried to have words with him but Pat shook him off with the ease of a triple-threat back and never paused till he reached Mario's bar.

Three extras with beards stood at the rail, and with relief Pat merged himself into their corporate whiskers. With a trembling hand he took the hard-earned ten-dollar bill from his pocket.

"Set 'em up," he cried hoarsely. "Every muff has a drink on me."

PAT HOBBY'S SECRET

Distress in Hollywood is endemic and always acute. Scarcely an executive but is being gnawed at by some insoluble problem and in a democratic way he will let you in on it, with no charge. The problem, be it one of health or of production, is faced courageously and with groans at from one to five thousand a week. That's how pictures are made.

"But this one has got me down," said Mr. Banizon, "—because how did the artillery shell get in the trunk of Claudette Colbert or Betty Field or whoever we decide to use? We got to explain it so the audience will believe it."

He was in the office of Louie the studio bookie and his present audience also included Pat Hobby, venerable script-stooge of forty-nine. Mr. Banizon did not expect a suggestion from either of them but he had been talking aloud to himself about the problem for a week now and was unable to stop.

"Who's your writer on it?" asked Louie.

"R. Parke Woll," said Banizon indignantly. "First I buy this opening from another writer, see. A grand notion but only a notion. Then I call in R. Parke Woll, the playwright, and we meet a couple of times and develop it. Then when we got the end in sight, his agent horns in and says he won't let Woll talk anymore unless I give him a contract—eight weeks at $3,000! And all I need him for is one more day!"

The sum brought a glitter into Pat's old eyes. Ten years ago he had camped beatifically in range of such a salary—now he was lucky to get a few weeks at $250. His inflamed and burnt-over talent had failed to produce a second growth.

"The worse part of it is that Woll told me the ending," continued the producer.

"Then what are you waiting for?" demanded Pat. "You don't need to pay him a cent."

"I forgot it!" groaned Mr. Banizon. "Two phones were ringing at once in my office—one from a working director. And while I was talking Woll had to run along. Now I can't remember it and I can't get him back."

Perversely Pat Hobby's sense of justice was with the producer, not the writer. Banizon had almost outsmarted Woll and then been cheated by a tough break. And now the playwright, with the insolence of an Eastern snob, was holding him up for twenty-four grand. What with the European market gone. What with the war.

"Now he's on a big bat," said Banizon. "I know because I got a man tailing him. It's enough to drive you nuts—here I got the whole story except the pay-off. What good is it to me like that?"

"If he's drunk maybe he'd spill it," suggested Louie practically.

"Not to me," said Mr. Banizon. "I thought of it but he would recognize my face."

Having reached the end of his current blind alley, Mr. Banizon picked a horse in the third and one in the seventh and prepared to depart.

"I got an idea," said Pat.

Mr. Banizon looked suspiciously at the red old eyes.

"I got no time to hear it now," he said.

"I'm not selling anything," Pat reassured him. "I got a deal almost ready over at Paramount. But once I worked with this R. Parke Woll and maybe I could find what you want to know."

He and Mr. Banizon went out of the office together and walked slowly across the lot. An hour later, for an advance consideration of fifty dollars, Pat was employed to discover how a live artillery shell got into Claudette Colbert's trunk or Betty Field's trunk or whosoever's trunk it should be.

II

The swath which R. Parke Woll was now cutting through the City of the Angels would have attracted no special notice in the twenties; in the fearful forties it rang out like laughter in church. He was easy to follow: his absence had been requested from two hotels but he had settled down into a routine where he carried his sleeping quarters in his elbow. A small but alert band of rats and weasels were furnishing him moral support in his journey—a journey which Pat caught up with at two a.m. in Conk's Old-Fashioned Bar.

Conk's Bar was haughtier than its name, boasting cigarette girls and a doorman-bouncer named Smith who had once stayed a full hour with Tarzan White. Mr. Smith was an embittered man who expressed himself by goosing the patrons on their way in and out and this was Pat's introduction. When he recovered himself he discovered R. Parke Woll in a mixed company around a table, and sauntered up with an air of surprise.

"Hello, good looking," he said to Woll. "Remember me—Pat Hobby?"

R. Parke Woll brought him with difficulty into focus, turning his head first on one side, then on the other, letting it sink, snap up and then lash forward like a cobra taking a candid snapshot. Evidently it recorded for he said:

"Pat Hobby! Sit down and wha'll you have. Genlemen, this is Pat Hobby—best left-handed writer in Hollywood. Pat h'are you?"

Pat sat down, amid suspicious looks from a dozen predatory eyes. Was Pat an old friend sent to get the playwright home?

Pat saw this and waited until a half-hour later when he found himself alone with Woll in the washroom.

"Listen Parke, Banizon is having you followed," he said. "I don't know why he's doing it. Louie at the studio tipped me off."

"You don't know why?" cried Parke. "Well, I know why. I got something he wants—that's why!"

"You owe him money?"

"Owe him money. Why that — — — —— he owes *me* money! He owes me for three long, hard conferences—I outlined a whole damn picture for him." His vague finger tapped his forehead in several places. "What he wants is in here."

An hour passed at the turbulent orgiastic table. Pat waited—and then inevitably in the slow limited cycle of the lush, Woll's mind returned to the subject.

"The funny thing is I told him who put the shell in the trunk and why. And then the Master Mind forgot."

Pat had an inspiration.

"But his secretary remembered."

"She did?" Woll was flabbergasted. "Secretary—don't remember secretary."

"She came in," ventured Pat uneasily.

"Well then by God he's got to pay me. He's got to pay me or I'll sue him."

"Banizon says he's got a better idea."

"The hell he has. My idea was a pip. Listen—"

He spoke for two minutes.

"You like it?" he demanded. He looked at Pat for applause—then he must have seen something in Pat's eye that he was not intended to see. "Why you little skunk," he cried. "You've talked to Banizon—he sent you here."

He got jerkily to his feet—simultaneously Pat rose and tore like a rabbit for the door. He would have been out into the street before Woll could overtake him had it not been for the intervention of Mr. Smith, the doorman.

"Where you going?" he demanded, catching Pat by his lapels.

"Hold him!" cried Woll, coming up. He aimed a blow at Pat which missed and landed full in Mr. Smith's mouth.

It has been mentioned that Mr. Smith was an embittered as well as a powerful man. He dropped Pat, picked up R. Parke Woll by crotch and shoulder, held him high and then in one gigantic pound brought his body down against the floor. Three minutes later Woll was dead.

III

Except in great scandals like the Arbuckle case the industry protects its own—and the industry included Pat, however intermittently. He was let out of prison next morning without bail, wanted only as a material witness. If anything, the publicity was advantageous—for the first time in a year his name appeared in the trade journals. Also his conscience was clean—within five minutes after the accident he had white-washed himself of all blame. Moreover he was now the only living man who knew how the shell got into Claudette Colbert's—or Betty Field's—trunk.

"When can you come up and see me?" said Mr. Banizon.

"After the inquest tomorrow," said Pat enjoying himself. "I feel kind of shaken—it gave me an earache."

That too indicated power. Only those who were "in" could speak of their health and be listened to.

"Woll really did tell you?" questioned Banizon.

"He told me," said Pat. "And it's worth more than fifty smackers. I'm going to get me a new agent and bring him to your office."

"I tell you a better plan," said Banizon hastily. "I'll get you on the payroll. Four weeks at your regular price."

"What's my price?" demanded Pat gloomily. "I've drawn everything from four thousand to zero." And he added ambiguously, "As Shakespeare says, 'Every man has his price.'"

The attendant rodents of R. Parke Woll had vanished with their small plunder into convenient rat-holes, leaving as the defendant Mr. Smith, and, as witnesses, Pat and two frightened cigarette girls. Mr. Smith's defense was that he had been attacked. At the inquest one cigarette girl agreed with him—one condemned him for unnecessary roughness. Pat Hobby's turn was next, but before his name was called he started as a voice spoke to him from behind.

"You talk against my husband and I'll twist your tongue out by the roots."

A huge dinosaur of a woman, fully six feet tall and broad in proportion, was leaning forward against his chair.

"Pat Hobby, step forward please . . . now Mr. Hobby tell us exactly what happened."

The eyes of Mr. Smith were fixed balefully on his and he felt the eyes of the bouncer's mate reaching in for his tongue through the back of his head. He was full of natural hesitation.

"I don't know exactly," he said, and then with quick inspiration: "All I know is everything went white!"

"*What?*"

"That's the way it was. I saw white. Just like some guys see red or black I saw white."

There was some consultation among the authorities.

"Well, what happened from when you came into the restaurant—up to the time you saw white?"

"Well—" said Pat fighting for time. "It was all kind of that way. I came and sat down and then it began to go black."

"You mean white."

"Black *and* white."

There was a general titter.

"Witness dismissed. Defendant remanded for trial."

What was a little joking to endure when the stakes were so high—all that night a mountainous Amazon pursued him through his dreams and he needed a strong drink before appearing at Mr. Banizon's office next morning. He was accompanied by one of the few Hollywood agents who had not yet taken him on and shaken him off.

"A flat sum of five hundred," offered Banizon. "Or four weeks at two-fifty to work on another picture."

"How bad do you want this?" asked the agent. "My client seems to think it's worth three thousand."

"Of my own money?" cried Banizon. "And it isn't even *his* idea. Now that Woll is dead it's in the Public Remains."

"Not quite," said the agent. "I think like you do that ideas are sort of in the air. They belong to whoever's got them at the time—like balloons."

All three considered this idea.

"Well, how much?" asked Mr. Banizon fearfully. "How do I know he's got the idea?"

The agent turned to Pat.

"Shall we let him find out—for a thousand dollars?"

After a moment Pat nodded. Something was bothering him.

"All right," said Banizon. "This strain is driving me nuts. One thousand."

There was silence.

"Spill it Pat," said the agent.

Still no word from Pat. They waited. When Pat spoke at last his voice seemed to come from afar.

"Everything is white," he gasped.

"*What?*"

"I can't help it—everything has gone white. I can see it—white. I remember going into the joint but after that it all goes white."

For a moment they thought he was holding out. Then the agent realized that Pat actually had drawn a psychological blank. The secret of R. Parke Woll was safe forever.

Too late Pat realized that a thousand dollars was slipping away and tried desperately to recover.

"I remember, I remember! It was put in by some Nazi dictator."

"Maybe the girl put it in the trunk herself," said Banizon ironically. "For her bracelet."

For many years Mr. Banizon would be somewhat gnawed by this insoluble problem. And as he glowered at Pat, placing on him the blame and the attendant hex, he wished that writers could be dispensed with altogether. If only ideas could be plucked from the inexpensive air!

PAT HOBBY, PUTATIVE FATHER

[PAT HOBBY'S YOUNG VISITOR]

Most writers look like writers whether they want to or not. It is hard to say why—for they model their exteriors whimsically on Wall Street brokers, cattle kings or English explorers—but they all turn out looking like writers, as definitely typed as "The Public" or "The Profiteers" in the cartoons.

Pat Hobby was the exception. He did not look like a writer. And only in one corner of the republic could he have been identified as a member of the entertainment world. Even there the first guess would have been that he was an extra down on his luck, or a bit player who specialized in the sort of father who should *never* come home. But a writer he was: he had collaborated in over two dozen moving picture scripts, most of them, it must be admitted, prior to 1929.

A writer? He had a desk in the Writers' Building at the studio; he had pencils, paper, a secretary, paper clips, a pad for office memoranda. And he sat in an overstuffed chair, his eyes not so very bloodshot, taking in the morning's "Reporter."

"I got to get to work," he told Miss Raudenbush at eleven. And again at twelve:

"I got to get to work."

At quarter to one, he began to feel hungry—up to this point every move, or rather every moment, was in the writers' tradition. Even to the faint irritation that no one had annoyed him, no one had bothered him, no one had interfered with the long empty dream which constituted his average day.

He was about to accuse his secretary of staring at him when the welcome interruption came. A studio guide tapped at his door and brought him a note from his boss, Jack Berners:

Dear Pat:

Please take some time off and show these people around the lot.

Jack

"My God!" Pat exclaimed. "How can I be expected to get anything done and show people around the lot at the same time. Who are they?" he demanded of the guide.

"I don't know. One of them seems to be kind of colored. He looks like the extras they had at Paramount for 'Bengal Lancer.' He can't speak English. The other—"

Pat was putting on his coat to see for himself.

"Will you be wanting me this afternoon?" asked Miss Raudenbush.

He looked at her with infinite reproach and went out in front of the Writers' Building.

The visitors were there. The sultry person was tall and of a fine carriage, dressed in excellent English clothes except for a turban. The other was a youth of fifteen, quite light of hue. He also wore a turban with beautifully cut jodhpurs and riding coat.

They bowed formally.

"Hear you want to go on some sets," said Pat. "You friends of Jack Berners?"

"Acquaintances," said the youth. "May I present to you my uncle: Sir Singrim Dak Raj."

Probably, thought Pat, the company was cooking up a "Bengal Lancers," and this man would play the heavy who owned the Khyber Pass. Maybe they'd put Pat on it—at three-fifty a week. Why not? He knew how to write that stuff:

<ins>Beautiful Long Shot. The Gorge</ins>. Show Tribesman firing from behind rocks.
<ins>Medium Shot</ins>. Tribesman hit by bullet making nose dive over high rock. (use stunt man)
<ins>Medium Long Shot. The Valley</ins>. British troops wheeling out cannon.

"You going to be long in Hollywood?" he asked shrewdly.

"My uncle doesn't speak English," said the youth in a measured voice. "We are here only a few days. You see—I am your putative son."

II

"—And I would very much like to see Bonita Granville," continued the youth. "I find she has been borrowed by your studio."

They had been walking toward the production office and it took Pat a minute to grasp what the young man had said.

"You're my what?" he asked.

"Your putative son," said the young man, in a sort of sing-song. "Legally I am the son and heir of the Rajah Dak Raj Indore. But I was born John Brown Hobby."

"Yes?" said Pat. "Go on! What's this?"

"My mother was Delia Brown. You married her in 1926. And she divorced you in 1927 when I was a few months old. Later she took me to India, where she married my present legal father."

"Oh," said Pat. They had reached the production office. "You want to see Bonita Granville."

"Yes," said John Hobby Indore, "if it is convenient."

Pat looked at the shooting schedule on the wall.

"It may be," he said heavily. "We can go and see."

As they started toward Stage 4, he exploded.

"What do you mean 'my potato son'? I'm glad to see you and all that, but say, are you really the kid Delia had in 1926?"

"Putatively," John Indore said. "At that time you and she were legally married."

He turned to his uncle and spoke rapidly in Hindustani, whereupon the latter bent forward, looked with cold examination upon Pat and threw up his shoulders without comment. The whole business was making Pat vaguely uncomfortable.

When he pointed out the commissary, John wanted to stop there "to buy his uncle a hot dog." It seemed that Sir Singrim had conceived a passion for them at the World's Fair in New York, whence they had just come. They were taking ship for Madras tomorrow.

"—whether or not," said John, somberly, "I get to see Bonita Granville. I do not care if I *meet* her. I am too young for her. She is already an old woman by our standards. But I would like to *see* her."

It was one of those bad days for showing people around. Only one of the directors shooting today was an old timer, on whom Pat could count for a welcome—and at the door of that stage he received word that the star kept blowing up in his lines and had demanded that the set be cleared.

In desperation he took his charges out to the back lot and walked them past the false fronts of ships and cities and village streets and medieval gates—a sight in which the boy showed a certain interest but which Sir Singrim found disappointing. Each time that Pat led them around behind to demonstrate that it was all phony Sir Singrim's expression would change to disappointment and faint contempt.

"What's he say?" Pat asked his offspring, after Sir Singrim had walked eagerly into a Fifth Avenue jewelry store, to find nothing but carpenter's rubble inside.

"He is the third richest man in India," said John. "He is disgusted. He says he will never enjoy an American picture again. He says he will buy one of our picture companies in India and make every set as solid as the Taj Mahal. He thinks perhaps the actresses just have a false front too, and that's why you won't let us see them."

The first sentence had rung a sort of carillon in Pat's head. If there was anything he liked it was a good piece of money—not this miserable, uncertain two-fifty a week which purchased his freedom.

"I'll tell you," he said with sudden decision. "We'll try Stage 4, and peek at Bonita Granville."

Stage 4 was double locked and barred, for the day—the director hated visitors, and it was a process stage besides. "Process" was a generic name for trick photography in which every studio competed with other studios, and lived in terror of spies. More specifically it meant that a projecting machine threw a moving background upon a transparent screen. On the other side of the screen, a scene was played and recorded against this moving background. The projector on one side of the screen and the camera on the other were so synchronized that the result could show a star standing on his head before an indifferent crowd on 42nd Street—a *real* crowd and a *real* star—and the poor eye could only conclude that it was being deluded and never quite guess how.

Pat tried to explain this to John, but John was peering for Bonita Granville from behind the great mass of coiled ropes and pails where they hid. They had not got there by the front entrance, but by a little side door for technicians that Pat knew.

Wearied by the long jaunt over the back lot, Pat took a pint flask from his hip and offered it to Sir Singrim who declined. He did not offer it to John.

"Stunt your growth," he said solemnly, taking a long pull.

"I do not want any," said John with dignity.

He was suddenly alert. He had spotted an idol more glamorous than Siva not twenty feet away—her back, her profile, her voice. Then she moved off.

Watching his face, Pat was rather touched.

"We can go nearer," he said. "We might get to that ballroom set. They're not using it—they got covers on the furniture."

On tiptoe they started, Pat in the lead, then Sir Singrim, then John. As they moved softly forward Pat heard the word "Lights" and stopped in his tracks. Then, as a blinding white glow struck at their eyes and the voice shouted "Quiet! We're rolling!" Pat began to run, followed quickly through the white silence by the others.

The silence did not endure.

"*Cut!*" screamed a voice. "What the living, blazing hell!"

From the director's angle something had happened on the screen which, for the moment, was inexplicable. Three gigantic silhouettes, two with huge Indian turbans, had danced across what was intended to be a New England harbor—they had blundered into the line of the process shot. Prince John Indore had not only seen Bonita Granville—he had acted in the same picture. His silhouetted foot seemed to pass miraculously through her blonde young head.

III

They sat for some time in the guard-room before word could be gotten to Jack Berners, who was off the lot. So there was leisure for talk. This consisted of a longish harangue from Sir Singrim to John, which the latter—modifying its tone if not its words—translated to Pat.

"My uncle says his brother wanted to do something for you. He thought perhaps if you were a great writer he might invite you to come to his kingdom and write his life."

"I never claimed to be—"

"My uncle says you are an ignominious writer—in your own land you permitted him to be touched by those dogs of the policemen."

"Aw—bananas," muttered Pat uncomfortably.

"He says my mother always wished you well. But now she is a high and sacred lady and should never see you again. He says we will go to our chambers in the Ambassador Hotel and meditate and pray and let you know what we decide."

When they were released, and the two moguls were escorted apologetically to their car by a studio yes-man, it seemed to Pat that it had been pretty well decided already. He was angry. For the sake of getting his son a peek at Miss Granville, he had quite possibly lost his job—though he didn't really think so. Or rather he was pretty sure that when his week was up he would have lost it anyhow. But though it was a pretty bad break he remembered most clearly from the afternoon that Sir Singrim was "the third richest man in India," and after dinner at a bar on La Cienega he decided to go down to the Ambassador Hotel and find out the result of the prayer and meditation.

It was early dark of a September evening. The Ambassador was full of memories to Pat—the Cocoanut Grove in the great days, when directors found pretty girls in the afternoon and made stars of them by night. There was some activity in front of the door and Pat watched it idly. Such a quantity of baggage he had seldom seen, even in the train of Gloria Swanson or Joan Crawford. Then he started as he saw two or three men in turbans moving around among the baggage. So—they were running out on him.

Sir Singrim Dak Raj and his nephew Prince John, both pulling on gloves as if at a command, appeared at the door, as Pat stepped forward out of the darkness.

"Taking a powder, eh?" he said. "Say when you get back there, tell them that one American could lick—"

"I have left a note for you," said Prince John, turning from his uncle's side. "I say, you *were* nice this afternoon and it really was too bad."

"Yes, it was," agreed Pat.

"But we are providing for you," John said. "After our prayers we decided that you will receive fifty sovereigns a month—two hundred and fifty dollars—for the rest of your natural life."

"What will I have to do for it?" questioned Pat suspiciously.

"It will only be withdrawn in case—"

John leaned and whispered in Pat's ear, and relief crept into Pat's eyes. The condition had nothing to do with drink and blondes, really nothing to do with him at all.

John began to get in the limousine.

"Goodbye, putative father," he said, almost with affection.

Pat stood looking after him.

"Goodbye son," he said. He stood watching the limousine go out of sight. Then he turned away—feeling like—like Stella Dallas. There were tears in his eyes.

Potato Father—whatever that meant. After some consideration he added to himself: It's better than not being a father at all.

IV

He awoke late next afternoon with a happy hangover—the cause of which he could not determine until young John's voice seemed to spring into his ears, repeating: "Fifty sovereigns a month, with just one condition—that it be withdrawn in case of war, when all revenues of our state will revert to the British Empire."

With a cry Pat sprang to the door. No "Los Angeles Times" lay against it, no "Examiner"—only "Toddy's Daily Form Sheet." He searched the orange pages frantically. Below the form sheets, the past performances, the endless oracles for endless racetracks, his eye was caught by a one-inch item:

London, September 3rd. On this morning's declaration by Chamberlain, Dougie cables "England to Win, France to Place, Russia to Show."

THE HOMES OF THE STARS

Beneath a great striped umbrella at the side of a boulevard in a Hollywood heat wave sat a man. His name was Gus Venske (no relation to the runner) and he wore magenta pants, cerise shoes and a sport article from Vine Street which resembled nothing so much as a cerulean blue pajama top.

Gus Venske was not a freak nor were his clothes at all extraordinary for his time and place. He had a profession—on a pole beside the umbrella was a placard:

VISIT THE HOMES OF THE STARS

Business was bad or Gus would not have hailed the unprosperous man who stood in the street beside a panting, steaming car, anxiously watching its efforts to cool.

"Hey fella," said Gus, without much hope. "Wanna visit the homes of the stars?"

The red-rimmed eyes of the watcher turned from the automobile and looked superciliously upon Gus.

"I'm *in* pictures," said the man. "I'm in 'em myself."

"Actor?"

"No. Writer."

Pat Hobby turned back to his car, which was whistling like a peanut wagon. He had told the truth—or what was once the truth. Often in the old days his name had flashed on the screen for the few seconds allotted to authorship, but for the past five years his services had been less and less in demand.

Presently Gus Venske shut up shop for lunch by putting his folders and maps into a briefcase and walking off with it under his arm. As the sun grew hotter moment by moment, Pat Hobby took refuge under the faint protection of the umbrella and inspected a soiled folder which had been dropped by Mr. Venske. If Pat had not been down to his last fourteen cents he would have telephoned a garage for aid—as it was, he could only wait.

After awhile a limousine with a Missouri license drew to rest beside him. Behind the chauffeur sat a little white moustached man and a large woman with a small dog. They conversed for a moment—then, in a rather shamefaced way, the woman leaned out and addressed Pat.

"What stars' homes can you visit?" she asked.

It took a moment for this to sink in.

"I mean can we go to Robert Taylor's home and Clark Gable's and Shirley Temple's—"

"I guess you can if you can get in," said Pat.

"Because—" continued the woman, "—if we could go to the very best homes, the most exclusive—we would be prepared to pay more than your regular price."

Light dawned upon Pat. Here together were suckers and smackers. Here was that dearest of Hollywood dreams—the angle. If one got the right angle it meant meals at the Brown Derby, long nights with bottles and girls, a new tire for his old car. And here was an angle fairly thrusting itself at him.

He rose and went to the side of the limousine.

"Sure. Maybe I could fix it." As he spoke he felt a pang of doubt. "Would you be able to pay in advance?"

The couple exchanged a look.

"Suppose we gave you five dollars now," the woman said, "and five dollars if we can visit Clark Gable's home or somebody like that."

Once upon a time such a thing would have been so easy. In his salad days when Pat had twelve or fifteen writing credits a year, he could have called up many people who would have said, "Sure, Pat, if it means anything to you." But now he could only think of a handful who really recognized him and spoke to him around the lots—Melvyn Douglas and Robert Young and Ronald Colman and Young Doug. Those he had known best had retired or passed away.

And he did not know except vaguely where the new stars lived, but he had noticed that on the folder were typewritten several dozen names and addresses with penciled checks after each.

"Of course you can't be sure anybody's at home," he said. "They might be working in the studios."

"We understand that." The lady glanced at Pat's car, glanced away. "We'd better go in our motor."

"Sure."

Pat got up in front with the chauffeur—trying to think fast. The actor who spoke to him most pleasantly was Ronald Colman—they had never exchanged more than conventional salutations but he might pretend that he was calling to interest Colman in a story.

Better still, Colman was probably not at home and Pat might wangle his clients an inside glimpse of the house. Then the process might be repeated at Robert Young's house and Young Doug's and Melvyn Douglas'. By that time the lady would have forgotten Gable and the afternoon would be over.

He looked at Ronald Colman's address on the folder and gave the direction to the chauffeur.

"We know a woman who had her picture taken with George Brent," said the lady as they started off. "Mrs. Horace J. Ives, Jr."

"She's our neighbor," said her husband. "She lives at 372 Rose Drive in Kansas City. And we live at 327."

"She had her picture taken with George Brent. We always wondered if she had to pay for it. Of course I don't know that I'd want to go so far as *that*. I don't know what they'd say back home."

"I don't think we want to go as far as all that," agreed her husband.

"Where are we going first?" asked the lady, cozily.

"Well, I had a couple calls to pay anyhow," said Pat. "I got to see Ronald Colman about something."

"Oh, he's one of my favorites. Do you know him well?"

"Oh yes," said Pat. "I'm not in this business regularly. I'm just doing it today for a friend. I'm a writer."

Sure in the knowledge that not so much as a trio of picture writers were known to the public he named himself as the author of several recent successes.

"That's very interesting," said the man. "I knew a writer once—this Upton Sinclair or Sinclair Lewis. Not a bad fellow even if he was a socialist."

"Why aren't you writing a picture now?" asked the lady.

"Well, you see we're on strike," Pat invented. "We got a thing called the Screen Playwriters' Guild and we're on strike."

"Oh." His clients stared with suspicion at this emissary of Stalin in the front seat of their car.

"What are you striking for?" asked the man uneasily.

Pat's political development was rudimentary. He hesitated.

"Oh, better living conditions," he said finally, "free pencils and paper. I don't know—it's all in the Wagner Act." After a moment he added vaguely, "Recognize Finland."

"I didn't know writers had unions," said the man. "Well, if you're on strike who writes the movies?"

"The producers," said Pat bitterly. "That's why they're so lousy."

"Well, that's what I would call an odd state of things."

They came in sight of Ronald Colman's house and Pat swallowed uneasily. A shining new roadster sat out in front.

"I better go in first," he said. "I mean we wouldn't want to come in on any—on any family scene or anything."

"Does he have family scenes?" asked the lady eagerly.

"Oh, well, you know how people are," said Pat with charity. "I think I ought to see how things are first."

The car stopped. Drawing a long breath Pat got out. At the same moment the door of the house opened and Ronald Colman hurried down the walk. Pat's heart missed a beat as the actor glanced in his direction.

"Hello, Pat," he said. Evidently he had no notion that Pat was a caller for he jumped into his car and the sound of his motor drowned out Pat's response as he drove away.

"Well, he called you 'Pat,'" said the woman, impressed.

"I guess he was in a hurry," said Pat. "But maybe we could see his house."

He rehearsed a speech going up the walk. He had just spoken to his friend Mr. Colman, and received permission to look around.

But the house was shut and locked and there was no answer to the bell. He would have to try Melvyn Douglas whose salutations, on second thought, were a little warmer than Ronald Colman's. At any rate his clients' faith in him was now firmly founded. The "Hello,

Pat," rang confidently in their ears; by proxy they were already inside the charmed circle.

"Now let's try Clark Gable's," said the lady. "I'd like to tell Carole Lombard about her hair."

The leze majesty made Pat's stomach wince. Once in a crowd he had met Clark Gable but he had no reason to believe that Mr. Gable remembered.

"Well, we could try Melvyn Douglas' first and then Bob Young or else Young Doug. They're all on the way. You see Gable and Lombard live way out in the St. Joaquin valley."

"Oh," said the lady disappointed. "I did want to run up and see their bedroom. Well then, our next choice would be Shirley Temple." She looked at her little dog. "I know that would be Boojie's choice too."

"They're kind of afraid of kidnappers," said Pat.

Ruffled, the man produced his business card and handed it to Pat.

DEERING R. ROBINSON
Vice President and
Chairman of the Board
Robdeer Food Products

"Does *that* sound as if I want to kidnap Shirley Temple?"

"They just have to be sure," said Pat apologetically. "After we go to Melvyn—"

"No—let's see Shirley Temple's *now*," insisted the woman. "Really! I told you in the first place what I wanted."

Pat hesitated.

"First I'll have to stop in some drug store and phone about it."

In a drug store he exchanged some of the five dollars for a half-pint of gin and took two long swallows behind a high counter, after which he considered the situation. He could, of course, duck Mr. and Mrs. Robinson immediately—after all he had produced Ronald Colman, with sound, for their five smackers. On the other hand they just *might* catch Miss Temple on her way in or out—and for a pleasant day at Santa Anita tomorrow Pat needed five smackers more. In the glow of the gin his courage mounted, and returning to the limousine he gave the chauffeur the address.

But approaching the Temple house his spirit quailed as he saw that there was a tall iron fence and an electric gate. And didn't guides have to have a license?

"Not here," he said quickly to the chauffeur. "I made a mistake. I think it's the next one, or two or three doors further on."

He decided on a large mansion set in an open lawn and, stopping the chauffeur, got out and walked up to the door. He was temporarily licked but at least he might bring back some story to soften them—say, that Miss Temple had mumps. He could point out her sick-room from the walk.

There was no answer to his ring but he saw that the door was partly ajar. Cautiously he pushed it open. He was staring into a deserted living room on the baronial scale. He listened. There was no one about, no footsteps on the upper floor, no murmur from the kitchen. Pat took another pull at the gin. Then swiftly he hurried back to the limousine.

"She's at the studio," he said quickly. "But if we're quiet we can look at their living room."

Eagerly the Robinsons and Boojie disembarked and followed him. The living room might have been Shirley Temple's, might have been one of many in Hollywood. Pat saw a doll in a corner and pointed at it, whereupon Mrs. Robinson picked it up, looked at it reverently and showed it to Boojie who sniffed indifferently.

"Could I meet Mrs. Temple?" she asked.

"Oh, she's out—nobody's home," Pat said—unwisely.

"*No*body. Oh—then Boojie would so like a wee little peep at her bedroom."

Before he could answer she had run up the stairs. Mr. Robinson followed and Pat waited uneasily in the hall, ready to depart at the sound either of an arrival outside or a commotion above.

He finished the bottle, disposed of it politely under a sofa cushion and then deciding that the visit upstairs was tempting fate too far, he went after his clients. On the stairs he heard Mrs. Robinson.

"But there's only *one* child's bedroom. I thought Shirley had brothers."

A window on the winding staircase looked upon the street, and glancing out Pat saw a large car drive up to the curb. From it stepped a Hollywood celebrity who, though not one of those pursued by Mrs. Robinson, was second to none in prestige and power. It was old Mr. Marcus, the producer, for whom Pat Hobby had been press agent twenty years ago.

At this point Pat lost his head. In a flash he pictured an elaborate explanation as to what he was doing here. He would not be forgiven. His occasional weeks in the studio at two-fifty would now disappear altogether and another finis would be written to his almost entirely finished career. He left impetuously and swiftly—down the stairs, through the kitchen and out the back gate, leaving the Robinsons to their destiny.

Vaguely he was sorry for them as he walked quickly along the next boulevard. He could see Mr. Robinson producing his card as the head of Robdeer Food Products. He could see Mr. Marcus' skepticism, the arrival of the police, the frisking of Mr. and Mrs. Robinson.

Probably it would stop there—except that the Robinsons would be furious at him for his imposition. They would tell the police where they had picked him up.

Suddenly he went ricketing down the street, beads of gin breaking out profusely on his forehead. He had left his car beside Gus Venske's umbrella. And now he remembered another recognizing clue and hoped that Ronald Colman did not know his last name.

PAT HOBBY DOES HIS BIT

In order to borrow money gracefully one must choose the time and place. It is a difficult business, for example, when the borrower is cockeyed, or has measles, or a conspicuous shiner. One could continue indefinitely but the inauspicious occasions can be catalogued as one—it is exceedingly difficult to borrow money when one needs it.

Pat Hobby found it difficult in the case of an actor on a set during the shooting of a moving picture. It was about the stiffest chore he had ever undertaken but he was doing it to save his car. To a sordidly commercial glance the jalopy would not have seemed worth saving but, because of Hollywood's great distances, it was an indispensable tool of the writer's trade.

"The finance company—" explained Pat, but Gyp McCarthy interrupted.

"I got some business in this next take. You want me to blow up on it?"

"I only need twenty," persisted Pat. "I can't get jobs if I have to hang around my bedroom."

"You'd save money that way—you don't get jobs anymore."

This was cruelly correct. But working or not Pat liked to pass his days in or near a studio. He had reached a dolorous and precarious forty-nine with nothing else to do.

"I got a rewrite job promised for next week," he lied.

"Oh, nuts to you," said Gyp. "You better get off the set before Hilliard sees you."

Pat glanced nervously toward the group by the camera—then he played his trump card.

"Once—" he said, "—once I paid for you to have a baby."

"Sure you did!" said Gyp wrathfully. "That was sixteen years ago. And where is it now—it's in jail for running over an old lady without a license!"

"Well I paid for it," said Pat. "Two hundred smackers."

"That's nothing to what it cost me. Would I be stunting at my age if I had dough to lend? Would I be working at all?"

From somewhere in the darkness an assistant director issued an order:

"Ready to go!"

Pat spoke quickly.

"All right," he said. "Five bucks."

"No."

"All right then," Pat's red-rimmed eyes tightened. "I'm going to stand over there and put the hex on you while you say your line."

"Oh, for God's sake!" said Gyp uneasily. "Listen, I'll give you five. It's in my coat over there. Here, I'll get it."

He dashed from the set and Pat heaved a sigh of relief. Maybe Louie, the studio bookie, would let him have ten more.

Again the assistant director's voice:

"Quiet! . . . We'll take it now! . . . Lights!"

The glare stabbed into Pat's eyes, blinding him. He took a step the wrong way—then back. Six other people were in the take—a gangster's hide-out—and it seemed that each was in his way.

"All right . . . Roll 'em . . . We're turning!"

In his panic Pat had stepped behind a flat which would effectually conceal him. While the actors played their scene he stood there trembling a little, his back hunched—quite unaware that it was a "trolley shot," that the camera, moving forward on its track, was almost upon him.

"You by the window—hey you, *Gyp!* hands up."

Like a man in a dream Pat raised his hands—only then did he realize that he was looking directly into a great black lens—in an instant it also included the English leading woman, who ran past him and jumped out the window. After an interminable second Pat heard the order "Cut!"

Then he rushed blindly through a property door, around a corner, tripping over a cable, recovering himself and tearing for the entrance. He heard footsteps running behind him and increased his gait, but in the doorway itself he was overtaken and turned defensively.

It was the English actress.

"Hurry up!" she cried. "That finishes my work. I'm flying home to England."

As she scrambled into her waiting limousine she threw back a last irrelevant remark. "I'm catching a New York plane in an hour."

Who cares! Pat thought bitterly, as he scurried away.

He was unaware that her repatriation was to change the course of his life.

II

And he did not have the five—he feared that this particular five was forever out of range. Other means must be found to keep the wolf from the two doors of his coupé. Pat left the lot with despair in his heart, stopping only momentarily to get gas for the car and gin for himself, possibly the last of many drinks they had had together.

Next morning he awoke with an aggravated problem. For once he did not want to go to the studio. It was not merely Gyp McCarthy he feared—it was the whole corporate might of a moving picture company, nay of an industry. To have actually interfered with the shooting of a movie was somehow a major delinquency, compared to which expensive fumblings on the part of producers or writers went comparatively unpunished.

On the other hand zero hour for the car was the day after tomorrow and Louie, the studio bookie, seemed positively the last resource and a poor one at that.

Nerving himself with an unpalatable snack from the bottom of the bottle, he went to the studio at ten with his coat collar turned up and his hat pulled low over his ears. He knew a sort of underground railway through the makeup department and the commissary kitchen which might get him to Louie's suite unobserved.

Two studio policemen seized him as he rounded the corner by the barber shop.

"Hey, I got a pass!" he protested. "Good for a week—signed by Jack Berners."

"Mr. Berners specially wants to see you."

Here it was then—he would be barred from the lot.

"We could sue you!" cried Jack Berners. "But we couldn't recover."

"What's one take?" demanded Pat. "You can use another."

"No we can't—the camera jammed. And this morning Lily Keatts took a plane to England. She thought she was through."

"Cut the scene," suggested Pat—and then on inspiration: "I bet I could fix it for you."

"You fixed it, all right!" Berners assured him. "If there was any way to fix it back I wouldn't have sent for you."

He paused, looked speculatively at Pat. His buzzer sounded and a secretary's voice said "Mr. Hilliard."

"Send him in."

George Hilliard was a huge man and the glance he bent upon Pat was not kindly. But there was some other element besides anger in it and Pat squirmed doubtfully as the two men regarded him with almost impersonal curiosity—as if he was a candidate for a cannibal's frying pan.

"Well, good-bye," he suggested uneasily.

"What do you think, George?" demanded Berners.

"Well—" said Hilliard, hesitantly, "we could black out a couple of teeth."

Pat rose hurriedly and took a step toward the door, but Hilliard seized him and faced him around.

"Let's hear you talk," he said.

"You can't beat me up," Pat clamored. "You knock my teeth out and I'll sue you."

There was a pause.

"What do you think?" demanded Berners.

"He can't talk," said Hilliard.

"You damn right I can talk!" said Pat.

"We can dub three or four lines," continued Hilliard, "and nobody'll know the difference. Half the guys you get to play rats can't talk. The point is this one's got the physique and the camera will pull it out of his face too."

Berners nodded.

"All right, Pat—you're an actor. You've got to play the part this McCarthy had. Only a couple of scenes but they're important. You'll have papers to sign with the Guild and Central Casting and you can report for work this afternoon."

"What is this!" Pat demanded. "I'm no ham—" Remembering that Hilliard had once been a leading man, he recoiled from this attitude: "I'm a writer."

"The character you play is called 'The Rat,'" continued Berners. He explained why it was necessary for Pat to continue his impromptu appearance of yesterday. The scenes which included Miss Keatts had been shot first, so that she could fulfill an English engagement. But in the filling out of the skeleton it was necessary to show how the gangsters reached their hide-out, and what they did after Miss Keatts dove from the window. Having irrevocably appeared in the shot with Miss Keatts, Pat must appear in half a dozen other shots, to be taken in the next few days.

"What kind of jack is it?" Pat inquired.

"We were paying McCarthy fifty a day—wait a minute Pat—but I thought I'd pay you your last writing price, two-fifty for the week."

"How about my reputation?" objected Pat.

"I won't answer that one," said Berners. "But if Benchley can act and Don Stewart and Lewis and Wilder and Woollcott, I guess it won't ruin you."

Pat drew a long breath.

"Can you let me have fifty on account," he asked, "because really I earned that yester—"

"If you got what you earned yesterday you'd be in a hospital. And you're not going on any bat. Here's ten dollars and that's all you see for a week."

"How about my car—"

"To hell with your car."

III

"The Rat" was the diehard of the gang, who were engaged in sabotage for an unidentified government of N-zis. His speeches were simplicity itself—Pat had written their like many times. "Don't finish him till the Brain comes"; "Let's get out of here"; "Fella, you're going out feet first." Pat found it pleasant—mostly waiting around as in all picture work—and he hoped it might lead to other openings in this line. He was sorry that the job was so short.

His last scene was on location. He knew "The Rat" was to touch off an explosion in which he himself was killed, but Pat had watched such scenes and was certain he would be in no slightest danger. Out on the back lot he was mildly curious when they measured him around the waist and chest.

"Making a dummy?" he asked.

"Not exactly," the prop man said. "This thing is all made but it was for Gyp McCarthy and I want to see if it'll fit you."

"Does it?"

"Just exactly."

"What is it?"

"Well—it's a sort of protector."

A slight draught of uneasiness blew in Pat's mind.

"Protector for what? Against the explosion?"

"Heck no! The explosion is phony—just a process shot. This's something else."

"What is it?" persisted Pat. "If I got to be protected against something I got a right to know what it is."

Near the false front of a warehouse a battery of cameras were getting into position. George Hilliard came suddenly out of a group and toward Pat and putting his arm on his shoulder steered him toward the actors' dressing tent. Once inside he handed Pat a flask.

"Have a drink, old man."

Pat took a long pull.

"There's a bit of business, Pat," Hilliard said. "Needs some new costuming. I'll explain it while they dress you."

Pat was divested of coat and vest, his trousers were loosened and in an instant a hinged iron doublet was fastened about his middle, extending from his armpits to his crotch very much like a plaster cast.

"This is the very finest strongest iron, Pat," Hilliard assured him. "The very best in tensile strength and resistance. It was built in Pittsburgh."

Pat suddenly resisted the attempts of two dressers to pull his trousers up over the thing and to slip on his coat and vest.

"What's it for?" he demanded, arms flailing. "I want to know. You're not going to shoot at me if that's what—"

"No shooting."

"Then what *is* it? I'm no stunt man—"

"You signed a contract just like McCarthy's to do anything within reason—and our lawyers have certified this."

"What *is* it?" Pat's mouth was dry.

"It's an automobile."

"You're going to hit me with an automobile."

"Give me a chance to tell you," begged Hilliard. "Nobody's going to hit you. The auto's going to pass over you, that's all. This case is so strong—"

"Oh no!" said Pat. "Oh no!" He tore at the iron corselet. "Not on your—"

George Hilliard pinioned his arms firmly.

"Pat, you almost wrecked this picture once—you're not going to do it again. Be a man."

"That's what I'm going to be. You're not going to squash me out flat like that extra last month."

He broke off. Behind Hilliard he saw a face he knew—a hateful and dreaded face—that of the collector for the North Hollywood Finance and Loan Company. Over in the parking lot stood his coupé, faithful pal and servant since 1934, companion of his misfortunes, his only certain home.

"Either you fill your contract," said George Hilliard, "—or you're out of pictures for keeps."

The man from the finance company had taken a step forward. Pat turned to Hilliard.

"Will you loan me—" he faltered, "—will you advance me twenty-five dollars?"

"Sure," said Hilliard.

Pat spoke fiercely to the credit man:

"You hear that? You'll get your money, but if this thing breaks, my death'll be on your head."

The next few minutes passed in a dream. He heard Hilliard's last instructions as they walked from the tent. Pat was to be lying in a shallow ditch to touch off the dynamite—and then the hero would drive the car slowly across his middle. Pat listened dimly. A picture of himself, cracked like an egg by the factory wall, lay athwart his mind.

He picked up the torch and lay down in the ditch. Afar off he heard the call "Quiet," then Hilliard's voice and the noise of the car warming up.

"Action!" called someone. There was the sound of the car growing nearer—louder. And then Pat Hobby knew no more.

IV

When he awoke it was dark and quiet. For some moments he failed to recognize his whereabouts. Then he saw that stars were out in the California sky and that he was somewhere alone—no—he was held tight in someone's arms. But the arms were of iron and he realized that he was still in the metallic casing. And then it all came back to him—up to the moment when he heard the approach of the car.

As far as he could determine he was unhurt—but why out here and alone?

He struggled to get up but found it was impossible and after a horrified moment he let out a cry for help. For five minutes he called out at intervals until finally a voice came from far away, and assistance arrived in the form of a studio policeman.

"What is it fella? A drop too much?"

"Hell no," cried Pat. "I was in the shooting this afternoon. It was a lousy trick to go off and leave me in this ditch."

"They must have forgot you in the excitement."

"Forgot me! *I* was the excitement. If you don't believe me then feel what I got on!"

The cop helped him to his feet.

"They was upset," he explained. "A star don't break his leg every day."

"What's that? Did something happen?"

"Well, as I heard, he was supposed to drive the car at a bump and the car turned over and broke his leg. They had to stop shooting and they're all kind of gloomy."

"And they leave me inside this—this stove. How do I get it off tonight? How'm I going to drive my car?"

But for all his rage Pat felt a certain fierce pride. He was Something in this set-up—someone to be reckoned with after years of neglect. He had managed to hold up the picture once more.

PAT HOBBY'S PREVIEW

"I haven't got a job for you," said Berners. "We've got more writers now than we can use."

"I didn't ask for a job," said Pat with dignity. "But I rate some tickets for the preview tonight—since I got a half credit."

"Oh yes, I want to talk to you about that," Berners frowned. "We may have to take your name off the screen credits."

"*What?*" exclaimed Pat. "Why, it's already on! I saw it in the 'Reporter.' 'By Ward Wainwright and Pat Hobby.'"

"But we may have to take it off when we release the picture. Wainwright's back from the East and raising hell. He says that you claimed lines where all you did was change 'No' to 'No sir' and 'crimson' to 'red,' and stuff like that."

"I been in this business twenty years," said Pat. "I know my rights. That guy laid an egg. I was called in to revise a turkey!"

"You were not!" Berners assured him. "After Wainwright went to New York I called you in to fix one small character. If I hadn't gone fishing you wouldn't have got away with sticking your name on the script." Jack Berners broke off, touched by Pat's dismal, red-streaked eyes. "Still, I was glad to see you get a credit after so long."

"I'll join the Screen Writers Guild and fight it."

"You don't stand a chance. Anyhow, Pat, your name's on it tonight at least, and it'll remind everybody you're alive. And I'll dig you up some tickets—but keep an eye out for Wainwright. It isn't good for you to get socked if you're over fifty."

"I'm in my forties," said Pat, who was forty-nine.

The Dictograph buzzed. Berners switched it on.

"It's Mr. Wainwright."

"Tell him to wait." He turned to Pat: "That's Wainwright. Better go out the side door."

"How about the tickets?"

"Drop by this afternoon."

To a rising young screen poet this might have been a crushing blow but Pat was made of sterner stuff. Sterner not upon himself, but on the harsh fate that had dogged him for nearly a decade. With all his experience, and with the help of every poisonous herb that blossoms between Washington Boulevard and Ventura, between Santa Monica and Vine—he continued to slip. Sometimes he grabbed momentarily at a bush, found a few weeks' surcease upon the island of a "patch job," but in general the slide continued at a pace that would have dizzied a lesser man.

Once safely out of Berners' office, for instance, Pat looked ahead and not behind. He visioned a drink with Louie, the studio bookie, and then a call on some old friends on the lot. Occasionally, but less often every year, some of these calls developed into jobs before you could say "Santa Anita." But after he had had his drink his eyes fell upon a lost girl.

She was obviously lost. She stood staring very prettily at the trucks full of extras that rolled toward the commissary. And then gazed about helpless—so helpless that a truck was almost upon her when Pat reached out and plucked her aside.

"Oh, thanks," she said. "Thanks. I came with a party for a tour of the studio and a policeman made me leave my camera in some office. Then I went to Stage Five where the guide said, but it was closed."

She was a "Cute Little Blonde." To Pat's liverish eye, cute little blondes seemed as much alike as a string of paper dolls. Of course they had different names.

"We'll see about it," said Pat.

"You're very nice. I'm Eleanor Carter from Boise, Idaho."

He told her his name and that he was a writer. She seemed first disappointed—then delighted.

"A writer? . . . Oh, of course. I knew they had to have writers but I guess I never heard about one before."

"Writers get as much as three grand a week," he assured her firmly. "Writers are some of the biggest shots in Hollywood."

"You see, I never thought of it that way."

"Bernud Shaw was out here," he said, "—and Einstein, but they couldn't make the grade."

They walked to the Bulletin Board and Pat found that there was work scheduled on three stages—and one of the directors was a friend out of the past.

"What did you write?" Eleanor asked.

A great male Star loomed on the horizon and Eleanor was all eyes till he had passed. Anyhow the names of Pat's pictures would have been unfamiliar to her.

"Those were all silents," he said.

"Oh. Well, what did you write last?"

"Well, I worked on a thing at Universal—I don't know what they called it finally—" He saw that he was not impressing her at all. He thought quickly. What did they know in Boise, Idaho? "I wrote 'Captains Courageous,'" he said boldly. "And 'Test Pilot' and 'Wuthering Heights' and—and 'The Awful Truth' and 'Mr. Smith Goes to Washington.'"

"Oh!" she exclaimed. "Those are all my favorite pictures. And 'Test Pilot' is my boyfriend's favorite picture and 'Dark Victory' is mine."

"I thought 'Dark Victory' stank," he said modestly. "Highbrow stuff," and he added to balance the scales of truth: "I been here twenty years."

They came to a stage and went in. Pat sent his name to the director and they were passed. They watched while Ronald Colman rehearsed a scene.

"Did you write this?" Eleanor whispered.

"They asked me to," Pat said, "but I was busy."

He felt young again, authoritative and active, with a hand in many schemes. Then he remembered something.

"I've got a picture opening tonight."

"You *have?*"

He nodded.

"I was going to take Claudette Colbert but she's got a cold. Would you like to go?"

II

He was alarmed when she mentioned a family, relieved when she said it was only a resident aunt. It would be like old times walking with a cute little blonde past the staring crowds on the sidewalk. His car was Class of 1933 but he could say it was borrowed—one of his Jap servants had smashed his limousine. Then what? He didn't quite know, but he could put on a good act for one night.

He bought her lunch in the commissary and was so stirred that he thought of borrowing somebody's apartment for the day. There was the old line about "getting her a test." But Eleanor was thinking only of getting to a hairdresser to prepare for tonight, and he escorted her reluctantly to the gate. He had another drink with Louie and went to Jack Berners' office for the tickets.

Berners' secretary had them ready in an envelope.

"We had trouble about these, Mr. Hobby."

"Trouble? Why? Can't a man go to his own preview? Is this something new?"

"It's not that, Mr. Hobby," she said. "The picture's been talked about so much, every seat is gone."

Unreconciled, he complained, "And they just didn't think of me."

"I'm sorry." She hesitated. "These are really Mr. Wainwright's tickets. He was so angry about something that he said he wouldn't go—and threw them on my desk. I shouldn't be telling you this."

"These are *his* seats?"

"Yes, Mr. Hobby."

Pat sucked his tongue. This was in the nature of a triumph. Wainwright had lost his temper, which was the last thing you should ever do in pictures—you could only pretend to lose it—so perhaps his apple-cart wasn't so steady. Perhaps Pat ought to join the Screen Writers Guild and present his case—if the Screen Writers Guild would take him in.

This problem was academic. He was calling for Eleanor at five o'clock and taking her "somewhere for a cocktail." He bought a two-dollar shirt, changing into it in the shop, and a four-dollar Alpine hat—thus halving his bank account which, since the Bank Holiday of 1933, he carried cautiously in his pocket.

The modest bungalow in West Hollywood yielded up Eleanor without a struggle. On his advice she was not in evening dress but she was as trim and shining as any cute little blonde out of his past. Eager too—running over with enthusiasm and gratitude.

He must think of someone whose apartment he could borrow for tomorrow.

"You'd like a test?" he asked as they entered the Brown Derby bar.

"What girl wouldn't?"

"Some wouldn't—for a million dollars." Pat had had setbacks in his love life. "Some of them would rather go on pounding the keys or just hanging around. You'd be surprised."

"I'd do almost anything for a test," Eleanor said.

Looking at her two hours later he wondered honestly to himself if it couldn't be arranged. There was Harry Gooddorf—there was Jack Berners—but his credit was low on all sides. He would do *some*thing for her, he decided. He would try at least to get an agent interested—if all went well tomorrow.

"What are you doing tomorrow?" he asked.

"Nothing," she answered promptly. "Hadn't we better eat and get to the preview?"

"Sure, sure."

He made a further inroad on his bank account to pay for his six whiskeys—you certainly had the right to celebrate before your own preview—and took her into the restaurant for dinner. They ate little. Eleanor was too excited—Pat had taken his calories in another form.

It was a long time since he had seen a picture with his name on it. Pat Hobby. As a man of the people he always appeared in the credit titles as Pat Hobby. It would be nice to see it again and though he did not expect his old friends to stand up and sing "Happy Birthday to You," he was sure there would be back-slapping and even a little turn of attention toward him as the crowd swayed out of the theatre. That would be nice.

"I'm frightened," said Eleanor as they walked through the alley of packed fans.

"They're looking at you," he said confidently. "They look at that pretty pan and try to think if you're an actress."

A fan shoved an autograph album and pencil toward Eleanor but Pat moved her firmly along. It was late—the equivalent of "all aboard" was being shouted around the entrance.

"Show your tickets, please sir."

Pat opened the envelope and handed them to the doorman. Then he said to Eleanor:

"The seats are reserved—it doesn't matter that we're late."

She pressed close to him, clinging—it was, as it turned out, the high point of her debut. Less than three steps inside the theatre a hand fell on Pat's shoulder.

"Hey Buddy, these aren't tickets for here."

Before they knew it they were back outside the door, glared at with suspicious eyes.

"I'm Pat Hobby. I wrote this picture."

For an instant credulity wandered to his side. Then the hard-boiled doorman sniffed at Pat and stepped in close.

"Buddy you're drunk. These are tickets to another show."

Eleanor looked and felt uneasy but Pat was cool.

"Go inside and ask Jack Berners," Pat said. "He'll tell you."

"Now listen," said the husky guard. "These are tickets for a burlesque down in L. A." He was steadily edging Pat to the side. "You go to your show, you and your girlfriend. And be happy."

"You don't understand. I wrote this picture."

"Sure. In a pipe dream."

"Look at the program. My name's on it. I'm Pat Hobby."

"Can you prove it? Let's see your auto license."

As Pat handed it over he whispered to Eleanor, "Don't worry!"

"This doesn't say Pat Hobby," announced the doorman. "This says the car's owned by the North Hollywood Finance and Loan Company. Is that you?"

For once in his life Pat could think of nothing to say—he cast one quick glance at Eleanor. Nothing in her face indicated that he was anything but what he thought he was—all alone.

III

Though the preview crowd had begun to drift away, with that vague American wonder as to why they had come at all, one little cluster found something arresting and poignant in the faces of Pat and Eleanor. They were obviously gate-crashers, outsiders like themselves, but the crowd resented the temerity of their effort to get in—a temerity which the crowd did not share. Little jeering jests were audible. Then, with Eleanor already edging away from the distasteful scene, there was a flurry by the door. A well-dressed six-footer strode out of the theatre and stood gazing about till he saw Pat.

"There you are!" he shouted.

Pat recognized Ward Wainwright.

"Go in and look at it!" Wainwright roared. "Look at it. Here's some ticket stubs! I think the prop boy directed it! Go and look!" To the doorman he said: "It's all right! *He* wrote it. I wouldn't have my name on an inch of it."

Trembling with frustration, Wainwright threw up his hands and strode off into the curious crowd.

Eleanor was terrified. But the same spirit that had inspired "I'd do anything to get in the movies" kept her standing there—though she felt invisible fingers reaching forth to drag her back to Boise. She had been intending to run—hard and fast. The hard-boiled doorman and the tall stranger had crystallized her feelings that Pat was "rather simple." She would never let those red-rimmed eyes come close to her—at least for any more than a doorstep kiss. She was saving herself for somebody—and it wasn't Pat. Yet she felt that the lingering crowd was a tribute to her—such as she had never exacted before. Several times she threw a glance at the crowd—a glance that now changed from wavering fear into a sort of queenliness.

She felt exactly like a star.

Pat, too, was all confidence. This was *his* preview; all had been delivered into his hands: his name would stand alone on the screen when the picture was released. There had to be *some*body's name, didn't there?—and Wainwright had withdrawn.

SCREENPLAY BY PAT HOBBY.

He seized Eleanor's elbow in a firm grasp and steered her triumphantly towards the door:

"Cheer up, baby. That's the way it is. You see?"

NO HARM TRYING

Pat Hobby's apartment lay athwart a delicatessen shop on Wilshire Boulevard. And there lay Pat himself, surrounded by his books—the "Motion Picture Almanac" of 1928 and "Barton's Track Guide, 1939"—by his pictures, authentically signed photographs of Mabel Normand and Barbara LaMarr (who, being deceased, had no value in the pawn shops)—and by his dogs in their cracked leather oxfords, perched on the arm of a slanting settee.

Pat was at "the end of his resources"—though this term is too ominous to describe a fairly usual condition in his life. He was an old timer in pictures; he had once known sumptuous living, but for the past ten years jobs had been hard to hold—harder to hold than glasses.

"Think of it," he often mourned. "Only a writer—at forty-nine."

All this afternoon he had turned the pages of the "Times" and the "Examiner" for an idea. Though he did not intend to compose a motion picture from this idea, he needed it to get him inside a studio. If you had nothing to submit it was increasingly difficult to pass the gate. But though these two newspapers, together with "Life," were the sources most commonly combed for "originals," they yielded him nothing this afternoon. There were wars, a fire in Topanga Canyon, press releases from the studios, municipal corruptions, and always the redeeming deeds of "The Trojums," but Pat found nothing that competed in human interest with the betting page.

—If I could get out to Santa Anita, he thought—I could maybe get an idea about the nags.

This cheering idea was interrupted by his landlord, from the delicatessen store below.

"I told you I wouldn't deliver any more messages," said Nick, "and *still* I won't. But Mr. Carl Le Vigne is telephoning in person from the studio and wants you should go over right away."

The prospect of a job did something to Pat. It anesthetized the crumbled, struggling remnants of his manhood, and inoculated him instead with a bland, easygoing confidence. The set speeches and attitudes of success returned to him. His manner as he winked at a studio policeman, stopped to chat with Louie, the bookie, and presented himself to Mr. Le Vigne's secretary indicated that he had been engaged with momentous tasks in other parts of the globe. By saluting Le Vigne with a facetious "Hel-*lo* Captain!" he behaved almost as an equal, a trusted lieutenant who had never really been away.

"Pat, your wife's in the hospital," Le Vigne said. "It'll probably be in the papers this afternoon."

Pat started.

"My wife?" he said. "What wife?"

"Estelle. She tried to cut her wrists."

"Estelle!" Pat exclaimed. "You mean Es*telle*? Say, I was only married to her three weeks!"

"She was the best girl you ever had," said Le Vigne grimly.

"I haven't even heard of her for ten years."

"You're hearing about her now. They called all the studios trying to locate you."

"I had nothing to do with it."

"I know—she's only been here a week. She had a run of hard luck wherever it was she lived—New Orleans? Husband died, child died, no money. . . ."

Pat breathed easier. They weren't trying to hang anything on him.

"Anyhow she'll live," Le Vigne reassured him superfluously, "—and she was the best script girl on the lot once. We'd like to take care of her. We thought the way was to give you a job. Not exactly a job, because I know you're not up to it." He glanced into Pat's red-rimmed eyes. "More of a sinecure."

Pat became uneasy. He didn't recognize the word, but "sin" disturbed him and "cure" brought a whole flood of unpleasant memories.

"You're on the payroll at two-fifty a week for three weeks," said Le Vigne, "—but one-fifty of that goes to the hospital for your wife's bill."

"But we're divorced!" Pat protested. "No Mexican stuff either. I've been married since, and so has—"

"Take it or leave it. You can have an office here, and if anything you can do comes up we'll let you know."

"I never worked for a hundred a week."

"We're not asking you to work. If you want you can stay home."

Pat reversed his field.

"Oh, I'll work," he said quickly. "You dig me up a good story and I'll show you whether I can work or not."

Le Vigne wrote something on a slip of paper.

"All right. They'll find you an office."

Outside Pat looked at the memorandum.

"Mrs. John Devlin," it read. "Good Samaritan Hospital."

The very words irritated him.

"Good Samaritan!" he exclaimed. "Good gyp joint! One hundred and fifty bucks a week!"

II

Pat had been given many a charity job but this was the first one that made him feel ashamed. He did not mind not *earn*ing his salary, but not getting it was another matter. And he wondered if other people on the lot who were obviously doing nothing were being fairly paid for it. There were, for example, a number of beautiful young ladies who walked aloof as stars, and whom Pat took for stock girls, until Eric, the call-boy, told him they were imports from Vienna and Budapest, not yet cast for pictures. Did half their paychecks go to keep husbands they had only had for three weeks?

The loveliest of these was Lizzette Starheim, a violet-eyed little blonde with an ill-concealed air of disillusion. Pat saw her alone at tea almost every afternoon in the commissary—and made her acquaintance one day by simply sliding into a chair opposite.

"Hello, Lizzette," he said. "I'm Pat Hobby, the writer."

"Oh, hel*lo!*"

She flashed such a dazzling smile that for a moment he thought she must have heard of him.

"When they going to cast you?" he demanded.

"I don't know." Her accent was faint and poignant.

"Don't let them give you the run-around. Not with a face like yours." Her beauty roused a rusty eloquence. "Sometimes they just keep you under contract till your teeth fall out, because you look too much like their big star."

"Oh no," she said distressfully.

"Oh yes!" he assured her. "I'm telling *you*. Why don't you go to another company and get borrowed? Have you thought of that idea?"

"I think it's wonderful."

He intended to go further into the subject but Miss Starheim looked at her watch and got up.

"I must go now, Mr.—"

"Hobby. Pat Hobby."

Pat joined Dutch Waggoner, the director, who was shooting dice with a waitress at another table.

"Between pictures, Dutch?"

"Between pictures hell!" said Dutch. "I haven't done a picture for six months and my contract's got six months to run. I'm trying to break it. Who was the little blonde?"

Afterwards, back in his office, Pat discussed these encounters with Eric the call-boy.

"All signed up and no place to go," said Eric. "Look at this Jeff Manfred, now—an associate producer! Sits in his office and sends notes to the big shots—and I carry back word they're in Palm Springs. It breaks my heart. Yesterday he put his head on his desk and boo-hoo'd."

"What's the answer?" asked Pat.

"Changa management," suggested Eric, darkly. "Shake-up coming."

"Who's going to the top?" Pat asked, with scarcely concealed excitement.

"Nobody knows," said Eric. "But wouldn't I like to land uphill! Boy! I want a writer's job. I got three ideas so new they're wet behind the ears."

"It's no life at all," Pat assured him with conviction. "I'd trade with you right now."

In the hall next day he intercepted Jeff Manfred who walked with the unconvincing hurry of one without a destination.

"What's the rush, Jeff?" Pat demanded, falling into step.

"Reading some scripts," Jeff panted without conviction.

Pat drew him unwillingly into his office.

"Jeff, have you heard about the shake-up?"

"Listen now, Pat—" Jeff looked nervously at the walls. "What shakeup?" he demanded.

"I heard that this Harmon Shaver is going to be the new boss," ventured Pat. "Wall Street control."

"Harmon Shaver!" Jeff scoffed. "He doesn't know anything about pictures—he's just a money man. He wanders around like a lost soul." Jeff sat back and considered. "Still—if you're *right*, he'd be a man you could get to." He turned mournful eyes on Pat. "I haven't been able to see Le Vigne or Barnes or Bill Behrer for a month. Can't get an assignment, can't get an actor, can't get a story." He broke off. "I've thought of drumming up something on my own. Got any ideas?"

"Have I?" said Pat. "I got three ideas so new they're wet behind the ears."

"Who for?"

"Lizzette Starheim," said Pat, "with Dutch Waggoner directing—see?"

III

"I'm with you all a hundred per-cent," said Harmon Shaver. "This is the most encouraging experience I've had in pictures." He had a bright bond-salesman's chuckle. "By God, it reminds me of a circus we got up when I was a boy."

They had come to his office inconspicuously like conspirators—Jeff Manfred, Waggoner, Miss Starheim and Pat Hobby.

"You like the idea, Miss Starheim?" Shaver continued.

"I think it's wonderful."

"And you, Mr. Waggoner?"

"I've heard only the general line," said Waggoner with director's caution, "but it seems to have the old emotional socko." He winked at Pat. "I didn't know this old tramp had it in him."

Pat glowed with pride. Jeff Manfred, though he was elated, was less sanguine.

"It's important nobody talks," he said nervously. "The Big Boys would find some way of killing it. In a week, when we've got the script done, we'll go to them."

"I agree," said Shaver. "They've run the studio so long that—well, I don't trust my own secretaries—I sent them to the races this afternoon."

Back in Pat's office Eric, the call-boy, was waiting. He did not know that he was the hinge upon which swung a great affair.

"You like the stuff, eh?" he asked eagerly.

"Pretty good," said Pat with calculated indifference.

"You said you'd pay more for the next batch."

"Have a heart!" Pat was aggrieved. "How many call-boys get seventy-five a week?"

"How many call-boys can write?"

Pat considered. Out of the two hundred a week Jeff Manfred was advancing from his own pocket, he had naturally awarded himself a commission of sixty per-cent.

"I'll make it a hundred," he said. "Now check yourself off the lot and meet me in front of Benny's bar."

At the hospital, Estelle Hobby Devlin sat up in bed, overwhelmed by the unexpected visit.

"I'm glad you came, Pat," she said. "You've been very kind. Did you get my note?"

"Forget it," Pat said gruffly. He had never liked this wife. She had loved him too much—until she found suddenly that he was a poor lover. In her presence he felt inferior.

"I got a guy outside," he said.

"What for?"

"I thought maybe you had nothing to do and you might want to pay me back for all this jack—"

He waved his hand around the bare hospital room.

"You were a swell script girl once. Do you think if I got a typewriter you could put some good stuff into continuity?"

"Why—yes. I suppose I could."

"It's a secret. We can't trust anybody at the studio."

"All right," she said.

"I'll send this kid in with the stuff. I got a conference."

"All right—and—oh Pat—come and see me again."

"Sure, I'll come."

But he knew he wouldn't. He didn't like sick rooms—he lived in one himself. From now on he was done with poverty and failure. He admired strength—he was taking Lizzette Starheim to a wrestling match that night.

IV

In his private musings Harmon Shaver referred to the showdown as "the surprise party." He was going to confront Le Vigne with a *fait accompli* and he gathered his coterie before phoning Le Vigne to come over to his office.

"What for?" demanded Le Vigne. "Couldn't you tell me now—I'm busy as hell."

This arrogance irritated Shaver—who was here to watch over the interest of Eastern stockholders.

"I don't ask much," he said sharply. "I let you fellows laugh at me behind my back and freeze me out of things. But now I've got something and I'd like you to come over."

"All right—all right."

Le Vigne's eyebrows lifted as he saw the members of the new production unit but he said nothing—sprawled into an armchair with his eyes on the floor and his fingers over his mouth.

Mr. Shaver came around the desk and poured forth words that had been fermenting in him for months. Simmered to its essentials, his protest was: "You would not let me play, but I'm going to play anyhow." Then he nodded to Jeff Manfred—who opened the script and read aloud. This took an hour, and still Le Vigne sat motionless and silent.

"There you are," said Shaver triumphantly. "Unless you've got any objection I think we ought to assign a budget to this proposition and get going. I'll answer to my people."

Le Vigne spoke at last.

"You like it, Miss Starheim?"

"I think it's wonderful."

"What language you going to play it in?"

To everyone's surprise Miss Starheim got to her feet.

"I must go now," she said with her faint poignant accent.

"Sit down and answer me," said Le Vigne. "What language are you playing it in?"

Miss Starheim looked tearful.

"Wenn I gute teachers hätte konnte ich dann thees role gut spielen," she faltered.

"But you like the script."

She hesitated.

"I think it's wonderful."

Le Vigne turned to the others.

"Miss Starheim has been here eight months," he said. "She's had three teachers. Unless things have changed in the past two weeks she can say just three sentences. She can say, 'How do you do'; she can say 'I think it's wonderful'; and she can say 'I must go now.' Miss Starheim has turned out to be a pinhead—I'm not insulting her because she doesn't know what it means. Anyhow—there's your Star."

He turned to Dutch Waggoner, but Dutch was already on his feet.

"Now Carl—" he said defensively.

"You force me to it," said Le Vigne. "I've trusted drunks up to a point, but I'll be goddam if I'll trust a hophead."

He turned to Harmon Shaver.

"Dutch has been good for exactly one week apiece on his last four pictures. He's all right now but as soon as the heat goes on he reaches for the little white powders. Now Dutch! Don't say anything you'll regret. We're carrying you in *hopes*—but you won't get on a stage till we've had a doctor's certificate for a year."

Again he turned to Harmon.

"There's your director. Your supervisor, Jeff Manfred, is here for one reason only—because he's Behrer's wife's cousin. There's nothing against him but he belongs to silent days as much as—as much as—" His eyes fell upon a quavering broken man, "—as much as Pat Hobby."

"What do you mean?" demanded Jeff.

"You trusted Hobby, didn't you? That tells the whole story." He turned back to Shaver. "Jeff's a weeper and a wisher and a dreamer. Mr. Shaver, you have bought a lot of condemned building material."

"Well, I've bought a good story," said Shaver defiantly.

"Yes. That's right. We'll make that story."

"Isn't that something?" demanded Shaver. "With all this secrecy how was I to know about Mr. Waggoner and Miss Starheim? But I do know a good story."

"Yes," said Le Vigne absently. He got up. "Yes—it's a good story . . . come along to my office, Pat."

He was already at the door. Pat cast an agonized look at Mr. Shaver as if for support. Then, weakly, he followed.

They walked in silence down a long corridor.

"Sit down, Pat."

Pat sat down.

"That Eric's got talent, hasn't he?" said Le Vigne. "He'll go places. How'd you come to dig him up?"

Pat felt the straps of the electric chair being adjusted.

"Oh—I just dug him up. He—came in my office."

"We're putting him on salary," said Le Vigne. "We ought to have some system to give these kids a chance."

He took a call on his dictograph, then swung back to Pat.

"But how did you ever get mixed up with this goddam Shaver. *You*, Pat—an old timer like you."

"Well, I thought—"

"Why doesn't he go back East?" continued Le Vigne disgustedly. "Getting all you poops stirred up!"

Blood flowed back into Pat's veins. He recognized his signal, his dog-call.

"Well, I got you a story, didn't I?" he said, with almost a swagger. And he added, "How'd you know about it?"

"I went down to see Estelle in the hospital. She and this kid were working on it. I walked right in on them."

"Oh," said Pat.

"I knew the kid by sight. Now, Pat, tell me this—did Jeff Manfred think you wrote it—or was he in on the racket?"

"Oh God," Pat mourned. "What do I have to answer that for?"

Le Vigne leaned forward intensely.

"Pat, you're sitting over a trap door!" he said with savage eyes. "Do you see how the carpet's cut? I just have to press this button and drop you down to hell! Will you *talk?*"

Pat was on his feet, staring wildly at the floor.

"Sure I will!" he cried. He believed it—he believed such things.

"All right," said Le Vigne relaxing. "There's whiskey in the sideboard there. Talk quick and I'll give you another month at two-fifty. I kinda like having you around."

A PATRIOTIC SHORT

Pat Hobby, the Writer and the Man, had his great success in Hollywood in an era described by Irvin Cobb as "when you had to have a shin-bone of St. Sebastian for a clutch lever." You had to have a pool too and Pat had one—at least he had one for the first few hours after it was filled every week, before it stubbornly seeped away through the cracks in the cement.

"But it was a pool," he assured himself one afternoon more than ten years later. Now he was more than grateful for a small chore at two-fifty a week, but all the years of failure could not take the beautiful memory away.

He was working on a humble "short." It was precariously based on the career of General Fitzhugh Lee who fought for the Confederacy and later for the U.S. against Spain—so it would offend neither North nor South. In conference Pat had tried to cooperate.

"I was thinking—" he suggested to Jack Berners, "—that it might be a good thing nowadays if we could give it a Jewish touch."

"What do you mean?" demanded Jack Berners quickly.

"Well I thought—the way things are and all, it would be a sort of good thing to show that there were Jews in it too."

"In what?"

"In the Civil War." Quickly Pat reviewed his meager history. "They were, weren't they?"

"I suppose so," said Berners, with some impatience. "I suppose everybody was in it—except Quakers."

"Well, my idea was that we could have this Fitzhugh Lee in love with a Jewish girl. He's going to be shot at curfew so she grabs the church bell—"

Jack Berners leaned forward earnestly.

"Say, Pat, you want this job, don't you?"

"Sure, I do."

"Well, I told you the story we want. The Jews can take care of themselves, and if you thought up this tripe to please me you're losing your grip."

Was that a way to treat a man who had once owned a pool? The reason Pat kept thinking about his long-lost pool was because of the President of the United States. Pat was remembering a certain day, a decade ago, in every detail. On that day word had gone around that the President was going to visit the lot. It seemed to mark a new era in pictures because the President of the United States had never visited a studio before. The executives of the company were all dressed up with ties and there were flags over the commissary door . . .

The voice of Ben Brown, the head of the shorts department, broke in on Pat's reverie.

"Jack Berners just phoned me," he said. "We don't want any new angles, Pat. We got a history. Fitzhugh Lee was in the cavalry. He was a nephew of Robert E. Lee and we want to show him surrendering at Appomax, pretty sore and all that. And then show how he got reconciled—we'll have to be careful because Virginia is still lousy with Lees—and how he finally accepts a U.S. commission from McKinley. And clean up the stuff about Spain—the guy that wrote it was a Red and he's got all the Spanish officers having ants in their pants."

In his office Pat looked at the script of "True to Two Flags." The first scene showed General Fitzhugh Lee at the head of his cavalry receiving word that Petersburg had been evacuated. In the script Lee took the blow in lively pantomime, but Pat was getting two-fifty a week—so, casually and without effort, he wrote in one of his favorite lines of dialogue.

LEE (To his officers)
Well, what are you standing here
gawking for? Do something!

6. MEDIUM SHOT. OFFICERS—popping up, slapping each other on back etc.

Dissolve to:

Dissolve to what? Pat's mind dissolved once more into the glamorous past. On that great day ten years before, his phone in the office had rung at noon. It was Mr. Moskin.

"Pat, the President is lunching in the Executives' Dining Room. Doug Fairbanks can't come so there's a place empty and anyhow we think there ought to be one writer there."

His memory of the luncheon was palpitant with glamour. The great man had asked questions about pictures and told a joke, and Pat had laughed uproariously with the others—all of them solid men together—rich, happy, successful.

Afterwards the President was to see some scenes taken on a set, and still later he was going to Mr. Moskin's house to meet several women stars at tea. Pat was not invited to that party, but his Beverly Hills home was next door to Mr. Moskin's mansion and he went home early. From his verandah he saw the cortège drive up, with Mr. Moskin beside the President in the back seat. He was proud of pictures then—of the position he had won in them—of the President of the happy country where pictures were born . . .

Pat sighed. Returning once more to reality he looked down at the script of "True to Two Flags" and wrote slowly and thoughtfully:

> INSERT: A CALENDAR—with the years plainly marked and the sheets blowing off in a cold wind, to indicate that Fitzhugh Lee is growing older and older.

Pat's labors had made him thirsty—not for water, but he knew better than to take anything else his first day on the job. He went out into the hall and along the corridor to the cooler—and as he walked he slipped back into his reverie of things past . . .

It had been a lovely California afternoon so Mr. Moskin had taken his exalted guest and the coterie of stars into his garden, adjoining Pat's garden. Pat went out his back door and followed a low privet hedge, keeping out of sight—and then accidentally came face-to-face with the Presidential party.

The President smiled and nodded. Mr. Moskin smiled and nodded.

"You met Mr. Hobby at lunch," Mr. Moskin said to the President. "He's one of our writers."

"Oh yes," said the President. "You write the pictures?"

"Yes I do," said Pat.

The President glanced over into Pat's property.

"I suppose—" he said, "—that you get lots of inspiration sitting by the side of that fine pool."

"Yes," said Pat. "Yes, I do."

. . . Pat filled his cup at the cooler in the hall. Down the hall there was a group approaching—Jack Berners, Ben Brown and several other executives and with them a girl to whom they were very attentive and deferential. He recognized her face—she was the girl of the year, the It Girl, the Oomph Girl, the Glamour Girl, the girl for whose services every studio was in heavy competition.

Pat lingered over his drink. He had seen many phonies break in and break out again, but this girl was someone to stir every pulse in the nation. His heart beat faster—as the procession drew near, he put down the cup, dabbed at his hair with his hand and took a step into the corridor.

The girl looked at him—he looked at the girl. Then she took one arm of Jack Berners' and one of Ben Brown's and, without the suggestion of an introduction, the party walked right through him—so that he had to take a step back against the wall.

An instant later Jack Berners turned around and called back, "Hello, Pat." And one of the others glanced around but no one else spoke, so interested were they in the girl.

In his office Pat looked gloomily at the scene where President McKinley offers a United States commission to Fitzhugh Lee. Berners had written on the margin: "Have McKinley plug democracy and Cuban-American friendship—but no cracks at Spain as market may improve." Pat gritted his teeth and bore down on his pencil as he wrote:

LEE

Mr. President, you can take your commission and go straight to Hell.

Then Pat bent down over his desk, his shoulders shaking miserably as he thought of that happy day when he had owned a swimming pool.

ON THE TRAIL OF PAT HOBBY

The day was dark from the outset, and a California fog crept everywhere. It had followed Pat in his headlong, hatless flight across the city. His destination, his refuge, was the studio, where he was not employed but which had been home to him for twenty years.

Was it his imagination or did the policeman at the gate give him and his pass an especially long look? It might be the lack of a hat—Hollywood was full of hatless men but Pat felt marked, especially as there had been no opportunity to part his thin grey hair.

In the Writers' Building he went into the lavatory. Then he remembered: by some inspired ukase from above, all mirrors had been removed from the Writers' Building a year ago.

Across the hall he saw Bee McIlvaine's door ajar, and discerned her plump person.

"Bee, can you loan me your compact box?" he asked.

Bee looked at him suspiciously, then frowned and dug it from her purse.

"You on the lot?" she inquired.

"Will be next week," he prophesied. He put the compact on her desk and bent over it with his comb. "Why won't they put mirrors back in the johnnies? Do they think writers would look at themselves all day?"

"Remember when they took out the couches?" said Bee. "In nineteen thirty-two. And they put them back in 'thirty-four."

"I worked at home," said Pat feelingly.

Finished with her mirror he wondered if she were good for a loan—enough to buy a hat and something to eat. Bee must have seen the look in his eyes for she forestalled him.

"The Finns got all my money," she said. "And I'm worried about my job. Either my picture's going to start tomorrow or it's going to be shelved. We haven't even got a title."

She handed him a mimeographed bulletin from the scenario department and Pat glanced at the headline.

TO ALL DEPARTMENTS:
TITLE WANTED—FIFTY DOLLARS REWARD
SUMMARY FOLLOWS

"I could use fifty," Pat said. "What's it about?"

"It's written there. It's about a lot of stuff that goes on in tourist cabins."

Pat started and looked at her wild-eyed. He had thought to be safe here behind the guarded gates but news traveled fast. This was a friendly or perhaps not so friendly warning. He must move on. He was a hunted man now, with nowhere to lay his hatless head.

"I don't know anything about that," he mumbled and walked hastily from the room.

II

Just inside the door of the commissary Pat looked around. There was no guardian except the girl at the cigarette stand but obtaining another person's hat was subject to one complication: it was hard to judge the size by a cursory glance, while the sight of a man trying on several hats in a check room was unavoidably suspicious.

Personal taste also obtruded itself. Pat was beguiled by a green fedora with a sprightly feather but it was too readily identifiable. This was also true of a fine white Stetson for the open spaces. Finally he decided on a sturdy grey Homburg which looked as if it would give him good service. With trembling hands he put it on. It fitted. He walked out—in painful, interminable slow motion.

His confidence was partly restored in the next hour by the fact that no one he encountered made references to tourists' cabins. It had been a lean three months for Pat. He had regarded his job as night clerk for the Selecto Tourist Cabins as a mere fill-in, never to be mentioned to his friends. But when the police squad came this morning they held up the raid long enough to assure Pat, or Don Smith as he called himself, that he would be wanted as a witness.

The story of his escape lies in the realm of melodrama, how he went out a side door, bought a half-pint of what he so desperately needed at the corner drug store, hitch-hiked his way across the great city, going limp at the sight of traffic cops and only breathing free when he saw the studio's high-flown sign.

After a call on Louie, the studio bookie, whose great patron he once had been, he dropped in on Jack Berners. He had no idea to submit, but he caught Jack in a hurried moment flying off to a producers' conference and was unexpectedly invited to step in and wait for his return.

The office was rich and comfortable. There were no letters worth reading on the desk, but there were a decanter and glasses in a cupboard and presently he lay down on a big soft couch and fell asleep.

He was awakened by Berners' return, in high indignation.

"Of all the damn nonsense! We get a hurry call—heads of all departments. One man is late and we wait for him. He comes in and gets a bawling out for wasting thousands of dollars worth of time. Then what do you suppose: Mr. Marcus has lost his favorite hat!"

Pat failed to associate the fact with himself.

"All the department heads stop production!" continued Berners. "Two thousand people look for a grey Homburg hat!" He sank despairingly into a chair. "I can't talk to you today, Pat. By four o'clock, I've got to get a title to a picture about a tourist camp. Got an idea?"

"No," said Pat. "No."

"Well, go up to Bee McIlvaine's office and help her figure something out. There's fifty dollars in it."

In a daze Pat wandered to the door.

"Hey," said Berners, "don't forget your hat."

III

Feeling the effects of his day outside the law and of a tumbler full of Berners' brandy, Pat sat in Bee McIlvaine's office.

"We've got to get a title," said Bee gloomily.

She handed Pat the mimeograph offering fifty dollars reward and put a pencil in his hand. Pat stared at the paper unseeingly.

"How about it?" she asked. "Who's got a title?"

There was a long silence.

"'Test Pilot' has been used, hasn't it?" he said vaguely.

"Wake up! This isn't about aviation."

"Well, I was just thinking it was a good title."

"So's 'The Birth of a Nation.'"

"But not for this picture," Pat muttered. "'Birth of a Nation' wouldn't suit this picture."

"Are you ribbing me?" demanded Bee. "Or are you losing your mind. This is serious."

"Sure—I know." Feebly he scrawled words at the bottom of the page. "I've had a couple of drinks that's all. My head'll clear up in a minute. I'm trying to think what have been the most successful titles. The trouble is they've all been used, like 'It Happened One Night.'"

Bee looked at him uneasily. He was having trouble keeping his eyes open and she did not want him to pass out in her office. After a minute she called Jack Berners.

"Could you possibly come up?" she asked. "I've got some title ideas."

Jack arrived with a sheaf of suggestions sent in from here and there in the studio, but digging through them yielded no ore.

"How about it, Pat? Got anything?"

Pat braced himself to an effort.

"I like 'It Happened One Morning,'" he said—then looked desperately at his scrawl on the mimeograph paper, "or else—'Grand Motel.'"

Berners smiled.

"'Grand Motel,'" he repeated. "By God! I think you've got something. 'Grand Motel.'"

"I said 'Grand Hotel,'" said Pat hastily.

"No, you didn't. You said 'Grand Motel'—and for my money it wins the fifty."

"I've got to go lie down," announced Pat. "I feel sick."

"There's an empty office across the way. That's a funny idea Pat, 'Grand Motel'—or else 'Motel Clerk.' How do you like that?"

As the fugitive quickened his step out the door Bee pressed the hat into his hands.

"Good work, old timer," she said.

Pat seized the hat, retched suddenly into it with a roar and stood holding it there like a bowl of soup.

"Feel—better—now," he mumbled after a moment. "Be right back."

And carrying his dripping burden he shambled toward the lavatory like a hunted man.

FUN IN AN ARTIST'S STUDIO

This was back in 1938 when few people except the Germans knew that they had already won their war in Europe. People still cared about art and tried to make it out of everything from old clothes to orange peel and that was how the Princess Dignanni found Pat. She wanted to make art out of him.

"No, not you, Mr. DeTinc," she said. "I can't paint you. You are a very standardized product, Mr. DeTinc."

Mr. DeTinc, who was a power in pictures and had even been photographed with Mr. Duchmann, the Secret Sin specialist, stepped smoothly out of the way. He was not offended—in his whole life Mr. DeTinc had never been offended—but especially not now, for the Princess did not want to paint Clark Gable or Spencer Rooney or Vivien Leigh either.

She saw Pat in the commissary and found he was a writer, and asked that he be invited to Mr. DeTinc's party. The Princess was a pretty woman born in Boston, Massachusetts, and Pat was forty-nine with red-rimmed eyes and a soft purr of whiskey on his breath.

"You write scenarios, Mr. Hobby?"

"I help," said Pat. "Takes more than one person to prepare a script."

He was flattered by this attention and not a little suspicious. It was only because his supervisor was a nervous wreck that he happened to have a job at all. His supervisor had forgotten a week ago that he had hired Pat, and when Pat was spotted in the commissary and told he was wanted at Mr. DeTinc's house, the writer had passed a *mauvais quart d'heure*. It did not even look like the kind of party that Pat had known in his prosperous days. There was not so much as a drunk passed out in the downstairs toilet.

"I imagine scenario writing is very well-paid," said the Princess.

Pat glanced around to see who was within hearing. Mr. DeTinc had withdrawn his huge bulk somewhat, but one of his apparently independent eyes seemed fixed glittering on Pat.

"Very well-paid," said Pat—and he added in a lower voice, "—if you can get it."

The Princess seemed to understand and lowered her voice too.

"You mean writers have trouble getting work?"

He nodded.

"Too many of 'em get in these unions." He raised his voice a little for Mr. DeTinc's benefit. "They're all Reds, most of these writers."

The Princess nodded.

"Will you turn your face a little to the light?" she said politely. "There, that's fine. You won't mind coming to my studio tomorrow, will you? Just to pose for me an hour?"

He scrutinized her again.

"Naked?" he asked cautiously.

"Oh no," she averred. "Just the head."

Mr. DeTinc moved nearer, nodding vigorously.

"You ought to go. Princess Dignanni is going to paint some of the biggest stars here. Going to paint Jack Benny and Baby Sandy and Hedy Lamarr—isn't that a fact, Princess?"

The artist didn't answer. She was a pretty good portrait painter and she knew just how good she was and just how much of it was her title. She was hesitating between her several manners—Picasso's rose period with a flash of Boldini, or straight Reginald Marsh. But she knew what she was going to call it. She was going to call it Hollywood and Vine.

II

In spite of the reassurance that he would be clothed Pat approached the rendezvous with uneasiness. In his young and impressionable years he had looked through a peep-hole into a machine where two dozen postcards slapped before his eyes in sequence. The story unfolded was "Fun in an Artist's Studio." Even now with the striptease a legalized municipal project, he was a little shocked at the remembrance, and when he presented himself next day at the

Princess' bungalow at the Beverly Hills Hotel it would not have surprised him if she had met him in a turkish towel. He was disappointed. She wore a smock and her black hair was brushed straight back like a boy's.

Pat had stopped off for a couple of drinks on the way, but his first words: "How'ya Duchess?" failed to set a jovial note for the occasion.

"Well, Mr. Hobby," she said coolly, "it's nice of you to spare me an afternoon."

"We don't work too hard in Hollywood," he assured her. "Everything is 'Manana'—in Spanish that means tomorrow."

She led him forthwith into a rear apartment where an easel stood with a square of canvas by the window. There was a couch and they sat down.

"I want to get used to you for a minute," she said. "Did you ever pose before?"

"Do I look that way?" He winked, and when she smiled he felt better and asked: "You haven't got a drink around, have you?"

The Princess hesitated. She had wanted him to look as if he *needed* one. Compromising she went to the ice box and fixed him a small highball. She returned to find that he had taken off his coat and tie and lay informally upon the couch.

"That *is* better," the Princess said. "That shirt you're wearing. I think they make them for Hollywood—like the special prints they make for Ceylon and Guatemala. Now drink this and we'll get to work."

"Why don't you have a drink too and make it friendly?" Pat suggested.

"I had one in the pantry," she lied.

"Married woman?" he asked.

"I have been married. Would you mind sitting on this stool?"

Reluctantly Pat got up, took down the highball, somewhat thwarted by the thin taste, and moved to the stool.

"Now sit very still," she said.

He sat silent as she worked. It was three o'clock. They were running the third race at Santa Anita and he had ten bucks on the nose. That made sixty he owed Louie, the studio bookie, and Louie stood determinedly beside him at the pay window every Thursday. This dame had good legs under the easel—her red lips pleased him and the way her bare arms moved as she worked. Once upon a time he wouldn't have looked at a woman over twenty-five, unless it was a secretary right in the office with him. But the kids you saw around now were snooty—always talking about calling the police.

"Please sit still, Mr. Hobby."

"What say we knock off," he suggested. "This work makes you thirsty."

The Princess had been painting half an hour. Now she stopped and stared at him a moment.

"Mr. Hobby, you were loaned me by Mr. DeTinc. Why don't you act just as if you were working over at the studio? I'll be through in another half-hour."

"What do I get out of it?" he demanded. "I'm no poser—I'm a writer."

"Your studio salary hasn't stopped," she said, resuming her work. "What does it matter if Mr. DeTinc wants you to do this?"

"It's different. You're a dame. I've got my self-respect to think of."

"What do you expect me to do—flirt with you?"

"No—that's old stuff. But I thought we could sit around and have a drink."

"Perhaps later," she said, and then: "Is this harder work than the studio? Am I so difficult to look at?"

"I don't mind looking at you but why couldn't we sit on the sofa?"

"You don't sit on the sofa at the studio."

"Sure you do. Listen, if you tried all the doors in the Writers' Building you'd find a lot of them locked and don't you forget it."

She stepped back and squinted at him.

"Locked? To be undisturbed?" She put down her brush. "I'll get you a drink."

When she returned she stopped for a moment in the doorway—Pat had removed his shirt and stood rather sheepishly in the middle of the floor holding it toward her.

"Here's that shirt," he said. "You can have it. I know where I can get a lot more."

For a moment longer she regarded him; then she took the shirt and put it on the sofa.

"Sit down and let me finish," she said. As he hesitated she added, "Then we'll have a drink together."

"When'll that be?"

"Fifteen minutes."

She worked quickly—several times she was content with the lower face—several times she deliberated and started over. Something that she had seen in the commissary was missing.

"Been an artist a long time?" Pat asked.

"Many years."

"Been around artists' studios a lot?"

"Quite a lot—I've had my own studios."

"I guess a lot goes on around those studios. Did you ever—"

He hesitated.

"Ever what?"

"Did you ever paint a naked man?"

"Don't talk for one minute, please." She paused with brush uplifted, seemed to listen, then made a swift stroke and looked doubtfully at the result.

"Do you know you're difficult to paint?" she said, laying down the brush.

"I don't like this posing around," he admitted. "Let's call it a day." He stood up. "Why don't you—why don't you slip into something so you'll be comfortable?"

The Princess smiled. She would tell her friends this story—it would sort of go with the picture, if the picture was any good, which she now doubted.

"You ought to revise your methods," she said. "Do you have much success with this approach?"

Pat lit a cigarette and sat down.

"If you were eighteen, see, I'd give you that line about being nuts about you."

"But why any line at all?"

"Oh, come off it!" he advised her. "You wanted to paint me didn't you?"

"Yes."

"Well, when a dame wants to paint a guy—" Pat reached down and undid his shoe strings, kicked his shoes onto the floor, put his stockinged feet on the couch, "—when a dame wants to see a guy about something or a guy wants to see a dame, there's a payoff, see."

The Princess sighed.

"Well I seem to be trapped," she said. "But it makes it rather difficult when a dame just wants to paint a guy."

"When a dame wants to paint a guy—" Pat half closed his eyes, nodded and flapped his hands expressively. As his thumbs went suddenly toward his suspenders, she spoke in a louder voice.

"Officer!"

There was a sound behind Pat. He turned to see a young man in khaki with shining black gloves, standing in the door.

"Officer, this man is an employee of Mr. DeTinc's. Mr. DeTinc lent him to me for the afternoon."

The policeman looked at the staring image of guilt upon the couch.

"Get fresh?" he inquired.

"I don't want to prefer charges—I called the desk to be on the safe side. He was to pose for me in the nude and now he refuses." She walked casually to her easel. "Mr. Hobby, why don't you stop this mock-modesty—you'll find a turkish towel in the bathroom."

Pat reached stupidly for his shoes. Somehow it flashed into his mind that they were running the eighth race at Santa Anita—

"Shake it up, you," said the cop. "You heard what the lady said."

Pat stood up vaguely and fixed a long poignant look on the Princess.

"You told me—" he said hoarsely, "you wanted to paint—"

"You told me I meant something else. Hurry please. And officer, there's a drink in the pantry."

. . . A few minutes later as Pat sat shivering in the center of the room his memory went back to those peep-shows of his youth—though at the moment he could see little resemblance. He was grateful at least for the turkish towel, even now failing to realize that the Princess was not interested in his shattered frame but in his face. It wore the exact expression that had wooed her in the commissary, the expression of "Hollywood and Vine," the other self of Mr. DeTinc—and she worked fast while there was still light enough to paint by.

TWO OLD-TIMERS

Phil Macedon, once the Star of Stars, and Pat Hobby, *scriptwriter*, had collided out on Sunset near the Beverly Hills Hotel. It was five in the morning and there was liquor in the air as they argued and Sergeant Gaspar took them around to the station house. Pat Hobby, a man of forty-nine, showed fight, apparently because Phil Macedon failed to acknowledge that they were old acquaintances. He accidentally bumped Sergeant Gaspar, who was so provoked that he put him in a little barred room while they waited for the captain to arrive.

Chronologically Phil Macedon belonged between Eugene O'Brien and Robert Taylor. He was still a handsome man in his early fifties and he had saved enough from his great days for a hacienda in the San Fernando Valley; there he rested as full of honors, as rollicksome and with the same purposes in life as Man o' War.

With Pat Hobby life had dealt otherwise. After twenty-one years in the industry, script and publicity, the accident found him driving a 1933 car which had lately become the property of the North Hollywood Finance and Loan Company. And once, back in 1928, he had reached a point of getting bids for a private swimming pool.

He glowered from his confinement, still resenting Macedon's failure to acknowledge that they had ever met before.

"I suppose you don't remember Colman," he said sarcastically. "Or Connie Talmadge or Bill Crocker or Allan Dwan."

Macedon lit a cigarette with the sort of timing in which the silent screen has never been surpassed, and offered one to Sergeant Gaspar.

"Couldn't I come in tomorrow?" he asked. "I have a horse to exercise—"

"I'm sorry, Mr. Macedon," said the cop—sincerely for the actor was an old favorite of his. "The Captain is due here any minute. After that we won't be holding *you*."

"It's just a formality," said Pat, from his cell.

"Yeah, it's just a—" Sergeant Gaspar glared at Pat. "It may not be any formality for *you*. Did you ever hear of the sobriety test?"

Macedon flicked his cigarette out the door and lit another.

"Suppose I come back in a couple of hours," he suggested.

"No," regretted Sergeant Gaspar. "And since I have to detain you, Mr. Macedon, I want to take the opportunity to tell you what you meant to me once. It was that picture you made, 'The Final Push'—it meant a lot to every man who was in the war."

"Oh, yes," said Macedon, smiling.

"I used to try to tell my wife about the war—how it was, with the shells and the machine guns—I was in there seven months with the 26th New England—but she never understood. She'd point her finger at me and say 'Boom! You're dead,' and so I'd laugh and stop trying to make her understand."

"Hey, can I get out of here?" demanded Pat.

"You shut up!" said Gaspar fiercely. "You probably wasn't in the war."

"I was in the Motion Picture Home Guard," said Pat. "I had bad eyes."

"Listen to him," said Gaspar disgustedly. "That's what all them slackers say. Well, the war was *some*thing. And after my wife saw that picture of yours I never had to explain to her. She knew. She always spoke different about it after that—never just pointed her finger at me and said 'Boom!' I'll never forget the part where you was in that shell-hole. That was so real it made my hands sweat."

"Thanks," said Macedon graciously. He lit another cigarette. "You see, I was in the war myself and I knew how it was. I knew how it felt."

"Yes sir," said Gaspar appreciatively. "Well, I'm glad of the opportunity to tell you what you did for me. You—you explained the war to my wife."

"What are you talking about?" demanded Pat Hobby suddenly. "That war picture Bill Corker did in 1925?"

"There he goes again," said Gaspar. "Sure—'The Birth of a Nation.' Now you pipe down till the captain comes."

"Phil Macedon knew me then all right," said Pat resentfully. "I even watched him work on it one day."

"I just don't happen to remember you, old man," said Macedon politely. "I can't help that."

"You remember the day Bill Corker shot that shell-hole sequence don't you? Your first day on the picture?"

There was a moment's silence.

"When will the Captain be here?" Macedon asked.

"Any minute now, Mr. Macedon."

"Well, I remember," said Pat, "—because I was there when he had that shell-hole dug. He was out there on the back lot at nine o'clock in the morning with a gang of hunkies to dig the hole and four cameras. He called you up from a field telephone and told you to go to the costumer and get into a soldier suit. Now you remember?"

"I don't load my mind with details, old man."

"You called up that they didn't have one to fit you and Corker told you to shut up and get into one anyhow. When you got out to the back lot you were sore as hell because your suit didn't fit."

Macedon smiled charmingly.

"You have a most remarkable memory. Are you sure you have the right picture—and the right actor?" he asked.

"Am I!" said Pat grimly. "I can see you right now. Only you didn't have much time to complain about the uniform because that wasn't Corker's plan. He always thought you were the toughest ham in Hollywood to get anything natural out of—and he had a scheme. He was going to get the heart of the picture shot by noon—before you even knew you were acting. He turned you around and shoved you down into that shell-hole on your fanny, and yelled 'Camera.'"

"That's a lie," said Phil Macedon. "I *got* down."

"Then why did you start yelling?" demanded Pat. "I can still hear you: 'Hey, what's the idea! Is this some ____ ____ gag? You get me out of here or I'll walk out on you!'

"—and all the time you were trying to claw your way up the side of that pit, so damn mad you couldn't see. You'd almost get up and then you'd slide back and lie there with your face working—till finally you began to bawl and all this time Bill had four cameras on you. After about twenty minutes you gave up and just lay there, heaving. Bill took a hundred feet of that and then he had a couple of prop men pull you out."

The police captain had arrived in the squad car. He stood in the doorway against the first grey of dawn.

"What you got here, sergeant? A drunk?"

Sergeant Gaspar walked over to the cell, unlocked it and beckoned Pat to come out. Pat blinked a moment—then his eyes fell on Phil Macedon and he shook his finger at him.

"So you see I *do* know you," he said. "Bill Corker cut that piece of film and titled it so you were supposed to be a doughboy whose pal had just been killed. You wanted to climb out and get at the Germans in revenge, but the shells bursting all around and the concussions kept knocking you back in."

"What's it about?" demanded the captain.

"I want to prove I know this guy," said Pat. "Bill said the best moment in the picture was when Phil was yelling 'I've al*ready* broken my first fingernail!' Bill titled it 'Ten Huns will go to hell to shine your shoes!'"

"You've got here 'collision with alcohol,'" said the captain looking at the blotter. "Let's take these guys down to the hospital and give them the test."

"Look here now," said the actor, with his flashing smile, "my name's Phil Macedon."

The captain was a political appointee and very young. He remembered the name and the face but he was not especially impressed because Hollywood was full of has-beens.

They all got into the squad car at the door.

. . . After the test Macedon was held at the station-house until friends could arrange bail. Pat Hobby was discharged but his car would not run, so Sergeant Gaspar offered to drive him home.

"Where do you live?" he asked as they started off.

"I don't live anywhere tonight," said Pat. "That's why I was driving around. When a friend of mine wakes up I'll touch him for a couple of bucks and go to a hotel."

"Well now," said Sergeant Gaspar, "I got a couple of bucks that ain't working."

The great mansions of Beverly Hills slid by and Pat waved his hand at them in salute.

"In the good old days," he said, "I used to be able to drop into some of those houses day or night. And Sunday mornings—"

"Is that all true you said in the station," Gaspar asked, "—about how they put him in the hole?"

"Sure, it is," said Pat. "That guy needn't have been so upstage. He's just another old-timer like me."

MIGHTIER THAN THE SWORD

The swarthy man, with eyes that snapped back and forward on a rubber band from the rear of his head, answered to the alias of Dick Dale. The tall, spectacled man who was put together like a camel without a hump—and you missed the hump—answered to the name of E. Brunswick Hudson. The scene was a shoeshine stand, insignificant unit of the great studio. We perceive it through the red-rimmed eyes of Pat Hobby, who sat in the chair beside Director Dale.

The stand was out-of-doors, opposite the commissary. The voice of E. Brunswick Hudson quivered with passion but it was pitched low so as not to reach passers-by.

"I don't know what a writer like me is doing out here anyhow," he said, with vibrations.

Pat Hobby, who was an old-timer, could have supplied the answer, but he had not the acquaintance of the other two.

"It's a funny business," said Dick Dale, and to the shoeshine boy: "Use that saddle soap."

"Funny!" thundered E., "It's *sus*pect! Here against my better judgment I write just what you tell me—and the office tells me to get out because we can't seem to agree."

"That's polite," explained Dick Dale. "What do you want me to do—knock you down?"

E. Brunswick Hudson removed his spectacles.

"Try it!" he suggested. "I weigh a hundred and sixty-two and I haven't got an ounce of flesh on me." He hesitated and redeemed himself from this extremity. "I mean *fat* on me."

"Oh, to hell with that!" said Dick Dale contemptuously. "I can't mix it up with you. I got to figure this picture. You go back East and write one of your books and forget it." Momentarily he looked at Pat Hobby, smiling as if *he* would understand, as if anyone would understand except E. Brunswick Hudson. "I can't tell you all about pictures in three weeks."

Hudson replaced his spectacles.

"When I *do* write a book," he said, "I'll make you the laughing-stock of the nation."

He withdrew, ineffectual, baffled, defeated. After a minute Pat spoke.

"Those guys can never get the idea," he commented. "I've never seen one get the idea and I been in this business, publicity and script, for twenty years."

"You on the lot?" Dale asked.

Pat hesitated.

"Just finished a job," he said.

That was five months before.

"What screen credits you got?" Dale asked.

"I got credits going all the way back to 1920."

"Come up to my office," Dick Dale said. "I got something I'd like to talk over—now that bastard is gone back to his New England farm. Why do they have to get a New England farm—with the whole West not settled?"

Pat gave his second-to-last dime to the bootblack and climbed down from the stand.

II

We are in the midst of technicalities.

"The trouble is this composer Reginald De Koven didn't have any color," said Dick Dale. "He wasn't deaf like Beethoven or a singing waiter or get put in jail or anything. All he did was write music and all we got for an angle is that song 'Oh, Promise Me.' We got to weave something around that—a dame promises him something and in the end he collects."

"I want time to think it over in my mind," said Pat. "If Jack Berners will put me on the picture—"

"He'll put you on," said Dick Dale. "From now on I'm picking my own writers. What do you get—fifteen hundred?" He looked at Pat's shoes: "Seven-fifty?"

Pat stared at him blankly for a moment; then out of thin air, produced his best piece of imaginative fiction in a decade.

"I was mixed up with a producer's wife," he said, "and they ganged up on me. I only get three-fifty now."

In some ways it was the easiest job he had ever had. Director Dick Dale was a type that, fifty years ago, could be found in any American town. Generally he was the local photographer, usually he was the originator of small mechanical contrivances and a leader in bizarre local movements, almost always he contributed verse to the local press. All the most energetic embodiments of this "Sensation Type" had migrated to Hollywood between 1910 and 1930, and there they had achieved a psychological fulfillment inconceivable in any other time or place. At last, and on a large scale, they were able to have their way. In the weeks that Pat Hobby and Mabel Hatman, Mr. Dale's script girl, sat beside him and worked on the script, not a movement, not a word went into it that was not Dick Dale's coinage. Pat would venture a suggestion, something that was "Always good."

"Wait a minute! Wait a minute!" Dick Dale was on his feet, his hands outspread. "I seem to see a dog."

They would wait, tense and breathless, while he saw a dog.

"Two dogs."

A second dog took its place beside the first in their obedient visions.

"We open on a dog on a leash—pull the camera back to show another dog—now they're snapping at each other. We pull back further—the leashes are attached to tables—the tables tip over. See it?"

Or else, out of a clear sky:

"I seem to see De Koven as a plasterer's apprentice."

"Yes." This hopefully.

"He goes to Santa Anita and plasters the walls, singing at his work. Make a note of that, Mabel."

In a month they had the requisite hundred and twenty pages. Reginald De Koven, it seemed, though not an alcoholic, was too fond of "The Little Brown Jug." The father of the girl he loved had died of drink, and after the wedding when she found him drinking from the Little Brown Jug, nothing would do but that she should go away for twenty years. He became famous and she sang his songs as Maid Marian but he never knew it was the same girl.

The script, bound in yellow paper, and marked "Temporary Complete. From Pat Hobby," went up to the head office. The schedule called for Dale to begin shooting in a week.

Twenty-four hours later he sat with his staff in his office, in an atmosphere of blue gloom. Pat Hobby was the least depressed. Four weeks at three-fifty, even allowing for the two hundred that had slipped away at Santa Anita, was a far cry from the twenty cents he had owned on the shoe-shine stand.

"That's pictures, Dick," he said consolingly. "You're up—you're down—you're in, you're out. Any old-timer knows."

"Yes," said Dick Dale absently. "Mabel, get on the phone and call that E. Brunswick Hudson. He's on his New England farm—maybe milking bees."

In a few minutes Miss Hatman reported.

"He flew into Hollywood this morning, Mr. Dale. I've located him at the Beverly Wilshire Hotel."

Dick Dale pressed his ear to the phone. His voice was bland and friendly as he said:

"Mr. Hudson, there was one day here you had an idea I liked. You said you were going to write it up. It was about this De Koven stealing his music from a sheepherder up in Vermont. Remember?"

"Yes."

"Well, Berners wants to go into production right away, or else we can't have the cast, so we're sort of on the spot, if you know what I mean. Do you happen to have that stuff?"

"You remember when I brought it to you?" Hudson asked. "You kept me waiting two hours—then you looked at it for two minutes. Your neck hurt you—I think it needed wringing. God, how it hurt you. That was the only nice thing about that morning."

"In picture business—"

"I'm so glad you're stuck. I wouldn't tell you the story of 'The Three Bears' for fifty grand."

As the phones clicked Dick Dale turned to Pat.

"Goddamn writers!" he said savagely. "What do we pay you for? Millions—and you write a lot of tripe I can't photograph and get sore if we don't read your lousy stuff! How can a man make pictures when they give me two bastards like you and Hudson. How? How do you think—you old whiskey bum!"

Pat rose—took a step backward toward the door. He didn't know, he said.

"Get out of here!" cried Dick Dale. "You're off the payroll. Get off the lot."

Fate had not dealt Pat a farm in New England, but there was a café just across from the studio where bucolic dreams blossomed in bottles if you had the money. He did not like to leave the lot, which for many years had been home for him, so he came back at six and went up to his office. It was locked. He saw that they had already allotted it to another writer—the name on the door was E. Brunswick Hudson.

He spent an hour in the commissary, made another visit to the bar, and then some instinct led him to a stage where there was a bedroom set. He passed the night upon a couch occupied by Claudette Colbert in the fluffiest ruffles only that afternoon.

Morning was bleaker, but he had a little in his bottle and almost a hundred dollars in his pocket. The horses were running at Santa Anita and he might double it by night.

On his way out of the lot he hesitated beside the barber shop but he felt too nervous for a shave. Then he paused and turned, for from the direction of the shoeshine stand, he heard Dick Dale's voice.

"Miss Hatman found your other script, and it happens to be the property of the company."

E. Brunswick Hudson stood at the foot of the stand.

"I won't have my name used," he said.

"That's good. I'll put her name on it. Berners thinks it's great, if the De Koven family will stand for it. Hell—the sheepherder never would have been able to market those tunes anyhow. Ever hear of any sheepherder drawing down jack from ASCAP?"

Hudson took off his spectacles.

"I weigh a hundred and sixty-three—"

Pat moved in closer.

"Join the army," said Dale contemptuously. "I got no time for mixing it up. I got to make a picture." His eyes fell on Pat. "Hello old-timer."

"Hello Dick," said Pat smiling. Then knowing the advantage of the psychological moment he took his chance.

"When do we work?" he said.

"How much?" Dick Dale asked the shoeshine boy—and to Pat: "It's all done. I promised Mabel a screen credit for a long time. Look me up someday when you got an idea."

He hailed someone by the barber shop and hurried off. Hudson and Hobby, men of letters who had never met, regarded each other. There were tears of anger in Hudson's eyes.

"Authors get a tough break out here," Pat said sympathetically. "They never ought to come."

"Who'd make up the stories—these feebs?"

"Well anyhow, not authors," said Pat. "They don't want authors. They want writers—like me."

PAT HOBBY'S COLLEGE DAYS

The afternoon was dark. The walls of Topanga Canyon rose sheer on either side. Get rid of it she must. The clank clank in the back seat frightened her. Evylyn did not like the business at all. It was not what she came out here to do. Then she thought of Mr. Hobby. He believed in her, trusted her—and she was doing this for him.

But the mission was arduous. Evylyn Lascalles left the canyon and cruised along the inhospitable shores of Beverly Hills. Several times she turned up alleys, several times she parked beside vacant lots—but always some pedestrian or loiterer threw her into a mood of nervous anxiety. Once her heart almost stopped as she was eyed with appreciation—or was it suspicion—by a man who looked like a detective.

—He had no right to ask me this, she said to herself. Never again. I'll tell him so. Never again.

Night was fast descending. Evylyn Lascalles had never seen it come down so fast. Back to the canyon then, to the wild, free life. She drove up a paint-box corridor which gave its last pastel shades to the day. And reached a certain security at a bend overlooking plateau land far below.

Here there could be no complication. As she threw each article over the cliff it would be as far removed from her as if she was in a different state of the Union.

Miss Lascalles was from Brooklyn. She had wanted very much to come to Hollywood and be a secretary in pictures—now she wished that she had never left her home.

On with the job though—she must part with her cargo—as soon as this next car passed the bend . . .

II

. . . Meanwhile her employer, Pat Hobby, stood in front of the barber shop talking to Louie, the studio bookie. Pat's four weeks at two-fifty would be up tomorrow and he had begun to have that harassed and aghast feeling of those who live always on the edge of solvency.

"Four lousy weeks on a bad script," he said. "That's all I've had in six months."

"How do you live?" asked Louie—without *too* much show of interest.

"I don't live. The days go by, the weeks go by. But who cares? Who cares—after twenty years."

"You had a good time in your day," Louie reminded him.

Pat looked after a dress extra in a shimmering lamé gown.

"Sure," he admitted, "I had three wives. All anybody could want."

"You mean *that* was one of your wives?" asked Louie.

Pat peered cautiously after the disappearing figure.

"No-o. I didn't say *that* was one. But I've had plenty of them feeding out of my pocket. Not now though—a man forty-nine is not considered human."

"You've got a cute little secretary," said Louie. "Look Pat, I'll give you a tip—"

"Can't use it," said Pat definitely. "I got fifty cents."

"I don't mean that kind of tip. Listen—Jack Berners wants to make a picture about U.W.C. because he's got a kid there that plays basketball. He can't get a story. Why don't you go over and see the Athaletic Superintendent named Doolan at U.W.C.? That superintendent owes me three grand on the nags, and he could maybe give you an idea for a college picture. And then you bring it back and sell it to Berners. You're on salary, ain't you?"

"Till tomorrow," said Pat gloomily.

"Go and see Jim Kresge that hangs out in the Campus Sport Shop. He'll introduce you to the Athaletic Superintendent. Look, Pat, I got to make a collection now. Just remember, Pat, that Doolan owes me three grand."

III

It didn't seem hopeful to Pat but it was better than nothing. Returning for his coat to his room in the Writers' Building he was in time to pick up a plainting telephone.

"This is Evylyn," said a fluttering voice. "I can't get rid of it this afternoon. There's cars on every road—"

"I can't talk about it here," said Pat quickly. "I got to go right over to U.W.C. on a notion."

"I've tried," she wailed, "—and *tried!* And every time, some car comes along—"

"Aw, please!" He hung up—he had enough on his mind.

For years Pat had followed the deeds of "the Trojums" of U.S.C. and the almost as fabulous doings of "the Roller Coasters," who represented the Univ. of the Western Coast. His interest was not so much physiological, tactical or intellectual as it was mathematical—but the Rollers had cost him plenty in their day—and it was with a sense of vague proprietorship that he stepped upon the half De Mille, half Aztec campus.

He located Kresge who conducted him to Superintendent Kit Doolan. Mr. Doolan, a famous ex-tackle, was in excellent humor. With five colored giants in this year's line, none of them quite old enough for pensions, but all men of experience, his team was in a fair way to conquer his section.

"Glad to be of help to your studio," he said. "Glad to help Mr. Berners—or Louie. What can I do for you? You want to make a picture? . . . Well, we can always use publicity. Mr. Hobby, I got a meeting of the Faculty Committee in five minutes and perhaps you'd like to tell them your notion."

"I don't know," said Pat doubtfully. "What I thought was maybe I could have a spiel with you. We could go somewhere and hoist one."

"Afraid not," said Doolan jovially. "If those smarties smelt liquor on me—Boy! Come on over to the meeting—somebody's been getting away with watches and jewelry on the campus and we're sure it's a student."

Mr. Kresge, having played his role, got up to leave.

"Like something good for the fifth tomorrow?"

"Not me," said Mr. Doolan. "You, Mr. Hobby?"

"Not me," said Pat.

IV

Ending their alliance with the underworld, Pat Hobby and Superintendent Doolan walked down the corridor of the Administration Building. Outside the dean's office Doolan said:

"As soon as I can, I'll bring you in and introduce you."

As an accredited representative neither of Jack Berners nor of the studio, Pat waited with a certain *malaise*. He did not look forward to confronting a group of highbrows but he remembered that he bore an humble but warming piece of merchandise in his threadbare overcoat. The dean's assistant had left her desk to take notes at the conference so he repleted his calories with a long, gagging draught.

In a moment, there was a responsive glow and he settled down in his chair, his eye fixed on the door marked:

SAMUEL K. WISKITH
DEAN OF THE STUDENT BODY

It might be a somewhat formidable encounter.

. . . but why? They were stuffed shirts—everybody knew that. They had college degrees but they could be bought. If they'd play ball with the studio they'd get a lot of good publicity for U.W.C. And that meant bigger salaries for them, didn't it, and more jack?

The door to the conference room opened and closed tentatively. No one came out but Pat sat up and readied himself. Representing the fourth biggest industry in America, or *al*most representing it, he must not let a bunch of highbrows stare him down. He was not without an inside view of higher education—in his early youth he had once been the "Buttons" in the D.K.E. House at the University of Pennsylvania. And with encouraging chauvinism he assured himself that Pennsylvania had it over this pioneer enterprise like a tent.

The door opened—a flustered young man with beads of sweat on his forehead came tearing out, tore through—and disappeared. Mr. Doolan stood calmly in the doorway.

"All right, Mr. Hobby," he said.

Nothing to be scared of. Memories of old college days continued to flood over Pat as he walked in. And instantaneously, as the juice of confidence flowed through his system, he had his idea . . .

". . . it's more of a realistic idea," he was saying five minutes later. "Understand?"

Dean Wiskith, a tall, pale man with an earphone, seemed to understand—if not exactly to approve. Pat hammered in his point again.

"It's up-to-the-minute," he said patiently, "what we call 'a topical.' You admit that young squirt who went out of here was stealing watches, don't you?"

The faculty committee, all except Doolan, exchanged glances, but no one interrupted.

"There you are," went on Pat triumphantly. "You turn him in to the newspapers. But here's the twist. In the picture we make, it turns out he steals the watches to support his young *bro*ther—and his young brother is the mainstay of the football team! He's the climax runner. We probably try to borrow Tyrone Power but we use one of *your* players as a double."

Pat paused, trying to think of everything.

"—of course, we've got to release it in the southern states, so it's got to be one of your players that's white."

There was an unquiet pause. Mr. Doolan came to his rescue.

"Not a bad idea," he suggested.

"It's an appalling idea," broke out Dean Wiskith. "It's—"

Doolan's face tightened slowly.

"Wait a minute," he said. "Who's telling *who* around here? You listen to *him!*"

The Dean's assistant, who had recently vanished from the room at the call of a buzzer, had reappeared and was whispering in the dean's ear. The latter started.

"Just a minute, Mr. Doolan," he said. He turned to the other members of the committee.

"The proctor has a disciplinary case outside and he can't legally hold the offender. Can we settle it first? And then get back to this—" he glared at Mr. Doolan, "—to this pre*pos*terous idea?"

At his nod the assistant opened the door.

This proctor, thought Pat, ranging back to his days on the vine-clad, leafy campus, looked like all proctors, an intimidated cop, a scarcely civilized beast of prey.

"Gentlemen," the proctor said, with delicately modulated respect, "I've got something that can't be explained away." He shook his head, puzzled, and then continued: "I know it's all wrong—but *I* can't seem to get to the point of it. I'd like to turn it over to *you*—I'll just show you the evidence and the offender. . . . Come in, you."

As Evylyn Lascalles entered, followed shortly by a big clinking pillow cover which the proctor deposited beside her, Pat thought once more of the elm-covered campus of the University of Pennsylvania. He wished passionately that he were there. He wished it more than anything in the world. Next to that he wished that Doolan's back, behind which he tried to hide by a shifting of his chair, were broader still.

But Evylyn Lascalles had seen him. And:

"There you are!" she cried gratefully. "Oh, Mr. Hobby—Thank God! I couldn't get rid of them—and I couldn't take them home—my mother would kill me. So I came here to find you—and this man peeked into the back seat of my car!"

"What's in that sack?" demanded Dean Wiskith. "Bombs? What?"

Seconds before the proctor had picked up the sack and bounced it on the floor, so that it gave out a clear unmistakable sound, Pat could have told them. There were dead soldiers—pints, half-pints, quarts—the evidence of four strained weeks at two-fifty—empty bottles collected from his office drawers. Since his contract was up tomorrow he had thought it best not to leave such witnesses behind.

Seeking for escape his mind reached back for the last time to those careless days of fetch and carry at the University of Pennsylvania.

"I'll take it," he said rising.

Slinging the sack over his shoulder, he faced the faculty committee and said surprisingly:

"Think it over."

V

"We did," Mr. Doolan told his wife that night. "But we never made head nor tail of it."

"It's kind of spooky," said Mrs. Doolan. "I hope I don't dream tonight. The poor man with that sack! I keep thinking he'll be down in purgatory—and they'll make him carve a ship in *every one* of those bottles—before he can go to heaven."

"Don't!" said Doolan quickly. "You'll have *me* dreaming. There were plenty bottles."

RECORD OF VARIANTS

The tables below record emendations adopted from the surviving textual witnesses. Editorial emendations are also given in these tables. For each story, a headnote describes the extant evidence. Sigla indicate the sources of the emendations; entries are keyed by page and line to the Cambridge text. The reading to the left of the bracket is the emended reading; the reading to the right is the rejected reading.

The following symbols are used:

~	the same word
¶	new paragraph
∧	space or the absence of punctuation
FSF	Fitzgerald
TS/TSS	typescript/s
Esq	*Esquire* magazine text
ed	an independent editorial emendation
FSF/MSS	*F. Scott Fitzgerald Manuscripts* (New York: Garland, 1991)

"Three Acts of Music"

A carbon TS of an early version of this story is filed in the Tearsheets box of the FSF Papers at Princeton, together with an unmarked set of tearsheets. This TS is a separate version of the story, too early to collate but useful in establishing the accidental texture.

5.11	dive,] ed; ~∧ Esq
5.30	Yonkers] ed; Yonkers' Esq
7.21	women's] ed; woman's Esq

"The Ants at Princeton"

Fitzgerald sold a ribbon TS of this story to *Esquire* in February 1936. Later he sent in a carbon copy of this TS, revised in his hand; this revised carbon has been used in establishing the text here. These two TSS survive in the FSF Additional Papers and the FSF Papers at Princeton.

10.10	all∧] ed; ~, TS, Esq
10.11	industry∧] ed; ~, TS, Esq

10.13 possible,] ed; ~∧ TS, Esq
10.15 Trustees,] ed; ~∧ TS, Esq
10.25 large,] ed; ~∧ TS, Esq
10.30 varsity∧] ed; ~, TS, Esq
11.31 Addicts,] ed; ~∧ TS, Esq
11.37 Harvard;] ed; ~∧ TS, Esq
13.24 eyes,] ed; ~∧ TS, Esq
13.30 foot] Esq; feet TS
14.11 Saltonville?] TS; ~, Esq

"'I Didn't Get Over'"

Two TSS are present at Princeton in the FSF Additional Papers—an early version entitled "'I Never Got Over'" and a revised version, which functioned as setting copy and which has been used to establish the Cambridge text. Also extant at Princeton is a set of page proofs marked by the *Esquire* copy-editor.

15.21 arrival:] ed; ~, TS, Esq
16.27 cap,] ed; ~∧ TS, Esq
18.37 and,] ed; ~∧ TS, Esq
20.3 snapped] Esq; snapped out TS
20.7 jammed] TS; jammed that Esq
20.16 calm∧] ed; ~, TS, Esq
20.32 and his] Esq; and every trace of TS
21.3 they] TS; they're Esq
21.32 lingered] Esq; lingered for a minute TS
22.14–15 never even] TS; never Esq
22.16 place once] TS; place Esq

"An Alcoholic Case"

The only surviving TS, in the FSF Additional Papers at Princeton, is the *Esquire* setting copy. This TS has been used to establish the text here; the copy-editor transferred FSF's late revisions, mailed to the magazine, onto this copy. Also extant at Princeton is a set of proofs, corrected by the *Esquire* copy-editor.

Changes made in the story by the editor Malcolm Cowley for its first reprinting are disallowed. For discussion, see the introduction, pp. xxiii–xxvi.

23.4 are you] TS; are Esq
23.10 to . . . have] Esq; to have TS
23.19 get] Esq; have TS
24.7–8 the . . . game] Esq; the story of the Yale-Dartmouth game TS
24.9 come in] Esq; come TS
24.13 chiffonier] Esq; writing table TS
24.33 framed] Esq; framed at the five-and-ten TS

24.35 remembered the] Esq; the TS
25.28 utterly senseless] Esq; senseless TS
25.29 it while] Esq; it TS
25.35 this . . . night] Esq; this hour TS
26.5 me about it] Esq; me TS
26.6 cartoonist who lives] Esq; cartoonist TS
29.34–35 doing? Do . . . man?] TS; doing? Esq
30.1 then:] ed; ~, TS, Esq
30.9 copper plate] Esq; spot TS
30.12 hardboiled] Esq; strong TS
30.29 she had dropped] ed; he had thrown TS, Esq
31.5 sprained] ed; strained TS, Esq

"The Long Way Out"

The setting-copy TS is extant in the FSF Additional Papers and is the source for the TS emendations below. A set of proofs also survives bearing the title "Oubliette," and with markings by the *Esquire* copy-editor but no change in the title.

32.2 Louis XI] ed; Louis VI Esq
32.3 Balue] ed; Ballou Esq
33.3 illness,] ed; ~∧ Esq
33.31 Then they] Esq; They they TS
34.9 operator,] ed; ~∧ Esq
34.16 There's] TS; There is Esq
34.32 King,] TS; ~∧ Esq
35.11 child's] ed; child Esq
35.17 on,] ed; ~∧ Esq
35.31 room—] TS; room. Esq
36.20 and next] TS; and the next Esq
36.26 accepted] Esq; accept TS

"The Guest in Room Nineteen"

A holograph, entitled "Room Nineteen," survives in the Marie Shank Additions at Princeton, together with the TS setting copy, also in the Additional Papers. This setting copy bears revisions in FSF's hand—also minor corrections in the hand of the *Esquire* copy-editor.

39.12–13 get back into] Esq; into TS
39.36 awaited] TS; waited Esq
40.8 Cass. And] ed; Cass, and Esq
40.16 watchman] ed; man Esq
40.34 disease,] ed; ~∧ Esq
41.20 said quietly] Esq; said TS

42.1 stoop] Esq; stoup TS
42.5 to . . . small] Esq; to fill the TS
42.33 said.] ed; ~, Esq

"In the Holidays"

Only an unmarked set of tearsheets survives at Princeton. The four emendations below are editorial.

43.28 left,] ed; ~∧ Esq
45.34 Say,] ed; ~∧ Esq
47.18 There] ed; Then Esq
47.28 Collins,] ed; ~∧ Esq

"Financing Finnegan"

Only an unmarked set of tearsheets survives at Princeton. The emendations below are editorial.

50.2 us,] ed; ~∧ Esq
50.4 publisher,] ed; ~∧ Esq
51.8 brilliantly,] ed; ~∧ Esq
51.28 fact,] ed; ~∧ Esq
56.6 shiver,] ed; ~∧ Esq
56.15 it,] ed; ~∧ Esq
56.18 into] ed; in Esq
57.19 as if] ed; as Esq
57.19 errand,] ed; ~∧ Esq
58.33 first—] ed; ~∧ Esq

"Design in Plaster"

The setting-copy TS survives in the FSF Additional Papers at Princeton; two carbons of this same TS are present in the FSF Papers. The setting copy has been used in establishing the Cambridge text. Also surviving at Princeton are a set of page proofs, marked by the *Esquire* copy-editor, and a set of unmarked tearsheets.

59.18 "it] ed; "—it TS, Esq
59.19 bed,] ed; ~∧ TS, Esq
60.26–27 were in need of being] Esq; needed to be TS
61.19 that,] Esq; ~∧ TS
62.4 quarter] TS; a quarter Esq
62.8 come] Esq; come along TS
62.17 go. *space break*] TS; go. *no space break* Esq
62.19 truth,] ed; ~∧ TS, Esq

62.33 bell rings] Esq; peals of the bell TS
62.36 cautiously:] ed; ~. TS, Esq
63.25 quickly,] ed; ~. TS, Esq
63.28 orthopedist] Esq; orthopedician TS

"The Lost Decade"

The setting-copy TS survives in the FSF Additional Papers; two carbons of this TS are present in the FSF Papers. The setting copy has been used to establish the Cambridge text.

65.5 "Jack-o-Lantern"] ed; *Jack-a-Lantern* TS, Esq
66.7 street,] ed; ~∧ TS, Esq
66.14 Do . . . rather] Esq; Rather TS
66.26 curiosity,] ed; ~∧ TS, Esq
66.28 been,] ed; ~∧ TS, Esq
67.2 they] ed; They TS, Esq
67.2 Fifties∧] ~. TS, Esq
67.26–27 off . . . manner] Esq; off TS
67.33 Building.] ed; ~, TS, Esq
67.33 rubber-necked] Esq; stopped and rubber-necked TS
68.5 now] Esq; this afternoon TS
68.15 awhile,] ed; ~∧ TS, Esq

"On an Ocean Wave"

Five TSS are present in the FSF Papers at Princeton. The earliest is entitled "The Ocean Wave." The pseudonym "Paul Elgin" is present on the next three TSS in sequence but is not on the final TS of the five, which has no by-line. Collations indicate that FSF sold an early TS of the story to *Esquire*, then sent in one or two revised TSS. The Cambridge text is based on the final TS in the sequence, which is a carbon of the setting copy.

69.14 wife∧] TS; ~, Esq
70.33 chair∧] ed; ~, TS, Esq
71.25 bed . . . what's] Esq; bed. What's TS
71.30 blushed] ed; stood up, blushing
72.23 Dollard,] ed; ~∧ TS, Esq

"The Woman from '21'"

Four early TSS survive at Princeton in the FSF Papers. One bearing heavy holograph revisions has been facsimiled in FSF/MSS, 6, 3: 429–35. The setting copy is present in the *Esquire* Additional Papers and is the basis of the Cambridge text.

73.4 59th Street∧] ed; ~ ~, Esq
73.13 Old] ed; old Esq
73.24 outside,] ed; ~∧ Esq
74.14 God!"— . . . play—] ed; ~!" . . . ~, Esq
74.25 Run, Sheep, Run] ed; ~ ~ ~ Esq

"Three Hours between Planes" ["Between Planes"]

Five TSS, representing various stages of composition, are extant at Princeton in the FSF Papers. Two more TSS survive in the Additional Papers; the second of these is the setting copy used at *Esquire*. The Cambridge text is based on this TS. All surviving TSS bear the title "Between Planes." The change to "Three Hours between Planes" was made in a copy-editor's hand on the setting copy. The story was submitted to *Esquire* under the by-line "John Darcy" but was published, after FSF's death, under his own name.

77.1 mood—] TS; ~, Esq
77.14 answering—he] TS ~. He Esq
77.14 he had] TS; had Esq
78.8 was just] TS; was Esq
78.17 dark] TS; dark-haired Esq
79.2 drinker,] TS; ~∧ Esq
79.5 York—] Esq; ~∧ TS
79.23 little girl] TS; girl Esq
80.1 Post Office] ed; post office Esq, post-office TS
80.3 that.] ed; ~∧ TS, Esq
81.16 husband," Donald said.] TS; husband." Esq
82.5 was it] ed; it was TS, Esq
82.19 few] TS; five Esq
82.34 corporeal] ed; corporate TS, Esq

"Pat Hobby's Christmas Wish"

The only surviving pre-publication document is the setting-copy TS in the FSF Additional Papers. The Cambridge text is based on this TS.

87.4 producers,] ed; ~∧ TS, Esq
87.5 offices] ed; office TS, Esq
87.25 it∧] TS; ~, Esq
88.36 That's] Esq; that's TS

89.9–11 hyacenda] *stet* (deliberate error)
89.18 course∧] ed; ~, TS, Esq
90.28 hello,] ed; ~∧ TS, Esq
91.1 it.] TS; ~∧ Esq
91.9 Pat's] Esq; Mike's TS
92.18 Listen,] ed; ~∧ TS, Esq
93.7 were] Esq; was TS
95.13 joke,] ed; ~∧ TS, Esq
95.19 You've] Esq; you've TS

"A Man in the Way"

FSF sold an eight-page ribbon TS to *Esquire*, then sent in pp. 1, 4, 5, and 6 of a carbon copy bearing his handwritten revisions. The copy-editors at the magazine substituted these mailed-in carbons for the corresponding leaves in the ribbon copy, and this became the setting copy, which survives in the FSF Additional Papers, and which is the basis for the Cambridge text. A clean carbon is extant in the FSF Papers as well.

97.21–22 be . . . lunch] Esq; tell you at lunch TS
98.24 pretty,] Esq; ~∧ TS
100.25 didn't] TS; did not Esq
101.15 Say,] ed; ~∧ TS, Esq
101.35 up∧] Esq; ~, TS

"'Boil Some Water—Lots of It'"

A heavily revised early TS survives in the FSF Papers. A clean TS, made from this early TS, was submitted to *Esquire*. Later FSF sent in a revised carbon TS, which was used as setting copy. The Cambridge text is based on this setting copy.

103.12 had read] Esq; read TS
103.22 was leisurely] Esq; was TS
104.28 had had] Esq; had TS
105.9 Except,] ed; ~∧ TS, Esq
105.22 too. It's . . . interesting.] Esq; too. TS
105.31 into] TS; in Esq
106.2 hurt—] ed; hurt. TS, Esq
106.11 extra, a] TS; extra. A Esq
107.12 attentively . . . anger.] Esq; to Max Leam's voice. TS
107.25 feet in an instant] Esq; feet TS
108.2 up . . . situation.] Esq; up. TS

"Teamed with Genius"

An early two-page fragment, together with two eleven-page carbon TSS of the setting copy, survive in the FSF Papers. The setting copy is preserved in the FSF Additional Papers and is the basis for the Cambridge text. A set of proofs, marked by the *Esquire* copy-editor, is also extant at Princeton.

109.7 is,] Esq; is∧ TS
110.1 Building,] ed; ~∧ TS, Esq
111.4 —What] TS; ∧~ Esq
111.29 asleep,] TS; ~∧ Esq
112.22 short,] Esq; ~∧ TS
114.30 between] Esq; among TS
117.5 see,] Esq; ~∧ TS
117.18 asked . . . eagerness] Esq; asked TS
117.26 Besides,] ed; ~∧ TS, Esq
117.30 we'll] Esq; it's a cinch we'll TS

"Pat Hobby and Orson Welles"

The setting copy (bearing late revisions in FSF's hand) survives in the FSF Additional Papers, together with a set of proofs marked by the magazine's copy-editor. Also extant is a carbon of the setting copy, in the FSF Papers. The Cambridge text is based on the setting copy.

118.30 unimpressed] Esq; undismayed TS
119.18 waited . . . answer] Esq; waited TS
119.19 wants to know] Esq; says TS
121.5 any longer] Esq; anymore TS
121.31 nodded very] Esq; nodded TS
122.10 said,] ed; ~∧ TS, Esq
122.23 Those] Esq; The TS
123.10 a bit] Esq; something TS
123.15 stimulus,] ed; ~∧ TS, Esq
124.23 writer, not a] Esq; writer," said Pat feebly. "I'm no TS
124.35 tour] Esq; leisurely tour TS
125.6 The car] Esq; He TS
125.15 turning,] Esq; ~∧ TS
125.17 party∧] ed; ~, TS, Esq
125.18 as] Esq; just as TS

"Pat Hobby's Secret"

The setting copy is extant in the Additional Papers. Also at Princeton is a list of changes, mailed in by FSF on 15 March 1940. The Cambridge text is based on the setting copy; all changes in the list are present in the Cambridge text. Also surviving at Princeton, in the FSF Papers, is an early TS of the story and a carbon of the setting copy.

126.4 problem,] Esq; ~∧ TS
126.7 got] TS; get Esq
127.5 producer,] Esq; ~∧ TS
128.14 side,] ed; ~∧ TS, Esq
128.20 playwright] Esq; playmate TS
129.5 me. He's . . . me or] TS; me or Esq
129.14 He . . . Pat] TS; Pat Esq
129.31–33 journals. Also . . . blame.] TS; journals Esq
131.22 All . . . idea.] TS; *cut in Esq text*
131.34 Everything is] TS; Everything's Esq
132.5 tried desperately] Esq; desperately he tried TS
132.10–11 Pat, placing . . . hex,] TS; Pat, Esq

"Pat Hobby, Putative Father"

An early version survives in the FSF Papers; the setting copy is extant in the Additional Papers, together with galleys marked by the *Esquire* copy-editor. The Cambridge text is based on the setting copy.

133.25 constituted] Esq; was TS
135.5 I would] TS; I'd Esq
136.30 peek] Esq; get a peek TS
137.23 word] ed; words TS, Esq
138.16 will] Esq; do TS
139.13 questioned] Esq; said TS
139.18 began] Esq; started TS
139.22 Dallas] Esq; Dallas, that was it TS

"The Homes of the Stars"

The only surviving pre-publication version is the setting copy, preserved among the Additional Papers, together with a set of proofs corrected by the *Esquire* copy-editor. Fitzgerald sent in a list of corrections to Gingrich. The Cambridge text is based on the setting copy and the list of corrections.

142.5 woman] Esq; woman smugly TS
143.24 all that] Esq; that TS
144.14 what . . . an] Esq; an TS
144.29 woman,] ed; ~∧ TS, Esq
146.4 electric] Esq; obvious electric TS
146.6 mistake] Esq; mistake about the number TS

146.12 walk] Esq; sidewalk TS
146.19 can] Esq; can get a TS
147.20 up.] Esq; up. They would— TS

"Pat Hobby Does His Bit"

Two TSS, one early and one late, survive in the FSF Papers. The second TS is a carbon of the setting copy, which is not extant. A set of unmarked proofs is among the Additional Papers. The Cambridge text is based on the second TS.

148.16 it?] Esq; ~. TS
149.34 rushed] Esq; ran TS
150.5 New York plane] Esq; plane to New York TS
150.18 To have actually] TS; Actually to have Esq
150.35 was] TS; were Esq
151.8 him] Esq; him lightly TS
152.31 gang,] ed; ~∧ TS, Esq
153.4 killed,] ed; ~∧ TS, Esq
153.17 This's] TS; This is Esq
153.31 very much like] Esq; like TS
155.5 noise] Esq; sound TS
155.9 IV] Esq; *space break* TS
155.21 away,] ed; ~; TS, Esq
156.2 tonight?] Esq; ~. TS

"Pat Hobby's Preview"

The setting copy and a set of proofs marked by the copy-editor are among the Additional Papers. Two carbons of this setting copy survive in the FSF Papers. The Cambridge text has been established from the setting copy.

160.16 much, every] Esq; much that every TS
160.23 This] TS; The Esq
161.3 entered] Esq; sat down in TS
163.5 gazing about] TS; gazing Esq
163.16 movies∧] ed; ~, TS, Esq

"No Harm Trying"

The setting copy, among the Additional Papers, is the only TS version to survive and serves as the basis of the Cambridge text. A set of proofs marked by the copy-editor is also present in the Additional Papers.

165.29 was to] ed; was TS, Esq
166.21 nothing∧] ed; ~, TS, Esq

171.10 are you] Esq; you TS
171.26 Dutch was] Esq; the latter was TS
171.30 goddam] Esq; Goddamned TS
172.19 They . . . corridor.] TS; *cut in Esq text*
172.21 Pat sat down.] TS; *cut in Esq text*

"A Patriotic Short"

The setting copy for the unrevised version, published in *Esquire* in December 1940, is extant in the Bertie Barr Additions. The revised version, sent in too late by Fitzgerald, is represented by a ribbon TS in the *Esquire* Additions and a carbon in the FSF Papers. The ribbon TS serves as the basis for the revised version published in this Cambridge volume.

174.5 week,] ed; ~∧ TS
175.13 department,] ed; ~∧ TS
176.2 before,] ed; ~∧ TS
176.31 hedge,] ed; ~∧ TS

"On the Trail of Pat Hobby"

The setting copy (on which the Cambridge text is based) survives in the Additional Papers; also extant is a set of galleys, corrected by the copy-editor. A carbon of the setting copy is among the FSF Papers.

178.29 picture's going to start] TS; picture starts Esq
181.5 "'Test Pilot' has been] ed; "'Test Pilot's' been TS; "*Test Pilot's* been Esq
181.5 vaguely] TS; with a vague tone Esq
181.21 up?" she asked. "I've] TS; up? I've Esq
181.33 Pat hastily] TS; Pat Esq
182.6–11 Pat . . . man.] TS; ¶ Pat seized Mr. Marcus' hat, and stood holding it there like a bowl of soup. ¶ "Feel—better—now," he mumbled after a moment. "Be back for the money." ¶ And carrying his burden he shambled toward the lavatory. Esq

"Fun in an Artist's Studio"

The setting copy is extant in the Additional Papers, together with a set of galleys corrected by the copy-editor. An early version bearing FSF's revisions is found among the FSF Papers, together with a carbon of the setting copy. The Cambridge text is based on the setting copy.

184.18 nodding vigorously] TS; and nodded Esq
185.13 with] ed; on TS, Esq
185.31 Would] TS; Now would Esq
186.17 hasn't] TS; has not Esq
187.18 what?"] TS; ~?" she queried. Esq

"Two Old-Timers"

The setting copy is extant in the *Esquire* Additions and serves as the basis of the Cambridge text. Also surviving is a set of galleys marked by the copy-editor. Two carbons of the setting copy are among the FSF Papers.

190.7 Gaspar,] ed; ~∧ TS, Esq
194.6 another] TS; an Esq

"Mightier than the Sword"

The setting copy is present in the Additional Papers, together with a set of galleys corrected by the copy-editor. The Cambridge text is based on the setting copy. Two carbons of the setting copy survive in the FSF Papers.

195.7 Hobby,] ed; ~∧ TS, Esq
195.23 spectacles] TS; glasses Esq
199.1 Goddamn] TS; Goddam Esq

"Pat Hobby's College Days"

The setting copy, which survives in the Additional Papers, is the basis of the Cambridge text. No proofs appear to survive. Three carbons of the setting copy are among the FSF Papers. One of these carbons appears to bear corrections dictated by FSF and inscribed on the TS in his secretary's hand.

205.19 make,] ed; ~∧ TS, Esq

"Dearly Beloved"

Four TSS survive in the FSF Papers, one bearing the pseudonymous by-line "John Darcy." The Cambridge text has been established from the last TS in the sequence.

257.13 radiance, . . . kind,] ed; ~; . . . ~∧ TS
257.25 parents,] ed; ~; TS
258.22 remember,] ed; ~∧ TS

EXPLANATORY NOTES

Annotated here are references in the stories to persons, places, movie stars, directors, film titles, dramatic and prose works, hotels, restaurants, businesses, newspapers, and popular songs.

"Three Acts of Music"

3.7 'No, No, Nanette' by Vincent Youmans

This 1925 musical was a success for the American composer Vincent Youmans (1898–1946). It was a lighthearted comedy about a millionaire Bible publisher and his wild-hearted young ward, Nanette. The hit song of the production was "Tea for Two," with lyrics by Irving Caesar. Youmans also collaborated with the lyricists Otto Harbach, Ira Gershwin, and Oscar Hammerstein II. He is remembered today for his score for *Flying Down to Rio* (1933), the first of the Fred Astaire – Ginger Rogers movies.

4.19–21 "All Alone" and "Remember" and "Always" and "Blue Skies" and "How About Me"

Songs by the composer and lyricist Irving Berlin (1888–1989), all written during the 1920s. "All Alone" and "Blue Skies" were recorded by Al Jolson; "Always" was written as a wedding present for Ellin Mackay, who is glossed in the next note. Fitzgerald includes lyrics from "Remember," "Always," and "Blue Skies" in the story. He misremembers the lyric from "Blue Skies": it should be blue skies "all day long" or "from now on," instead of "overhead."

5.21 this Mackay girl

The poor boy – rich girl story of Irving Berlin and Ellin Mackay (1903–88) would have appealed to Fitzgerald. Berlin, a Russian Jewish immigrant, grew up as Israel Baline on the Lower East Side. Mackay was the daughter of the millionaire Clarence Mackay, a prominent Catholic and New York socialite. Ellin's father disapproved of Berlin and sent her to Europe, hoping that she would meet other beaux, but she returned and eloped with Berlin in 1926. Her father severed relations with her for five years; later they were reconciled. Ellin remained married to Berlin until her death, less than a year before his own.

5.30 Yonkers girl

The woman in the story is of low social class; her origins show in her accent. Yonkers is a large manufacturing city on the east bank of the Hudson, north of the Bronx.

7.4 Duke's hospital

The woman in the story is employed at Duke University Hospital, which opened in July 1930 in Durham, North Carolina—to the east of Asheville, where Fitzgerald was then living. The hospital was operated in conjunction with a medical school and a school of nursing.

7.32 Jerome Kern

This American composer (1885–1945) began as a pianist for a New York music publisher; soon he was contributing songs to Broadway musicals. He teamed with Oscar Hammerstein II in the 1927 musical *Show Boat* (adapted from the novel by Edna Ferber) to create "Old Man River," "Can't Help Lovin' Dat Man," and "Why Do I Love You?" In 1935 Kern moved to Hollywood and spent most of the rest of his career there. The two Kern songs that Fitzgerald uses in this story are "Smoke Gets in Your Eyes" and "Lovely to Look At," both of which he probably knew from the 1935 movie version of the musical *Roberta*, starring Irene Dunne, Fred Astaire, and Ginger Rogers. Kern had teamed with the lyricist Otto Harbach on the first tune, which was part of the 1933 Broadway version of *Roberta*. For the 1935 film, Kern added two new songs, one of which was "Lovely to Look At," with lyrics by Dorothy Fields and Jimmy McHugh. Fitzgerald remembers one of the lyrics incorrectly: it should be "Lovely to look at / Delightful to know . . ." not "Romantic to know."

8.5 Dr. Kelly

Howard Atwood Kelly (1858–1943) was a well-known gynecologist, radiologist, and surgeon at the Johns Hopkins medical school. He was a pioneer in the use of radium in cancer treatment and invented the Kelly cytoscope, which lit the inside of the body during surgery. Fitzgerald probably learned of Kelly during the years in which he and Zelda lived in Baltimore, where she was receiving treatment at Johns Hopkins.

"The Ants at Princeton"

11.3 Fritz Crisler

Herbert Orin "Fritz" Crisler (1899–1982) coached the football team at the University of Minnesota during the 1930–31 season, then came east to coach at Princeton from 1932 to 1937. Crisler's teams used the two-platoon system, with separate units of players on offense and defense. He was successful at Princeton: during his years there his teams won thirty-five games, lost nine, and tied five. Fitzgerald wrote a spoof letter to Crisler in 1934 and had it published in the *Princeton Athletic News* (16 June 1934). In the letter Fitzgerald suggests among other things that Crisler use "a member of the Board of Trustees at left tackle" and that he not revive "that variation of the 'Mexican' shift that I suggested last year." The letter has been reprinted in *F. Scott Fitzgerald in His Own Time: A Miscellany*, ed. Matthew J. Bruccoli and Jackson R. Bryer (Kent, Ohio: Kent State University Press, 1971): 174–75. Princeton football historian Jay Dunn writes that for a time during the 1930s Fitzgerald regularly telephoned Crisler with advice before big games. "Once before a Harvard game [Fitzgerald] told Crisler to use red ants and black ants. Let the red ants (red on red) wear down the Crimson, then send the black ants (true Princeton sons) out to finish the job." See Jay Dunn, *The Tigers of Princeton: Old Nassau Football* (Huntsville, Alabama: Strode Publishers, 1977): 166–67. The satire in "The Ants at Princeton" probably has its origins in the ill feeling between Princeton and Harvard over an incident after the 1926 game between the two schools. Princeton won the contest 12–0. After the game, copies of the Harvard *Lampoon* circulated outside the stadium; the issue contained a cartoon depicting the Princeton players as "convicts, sots, delts and muckers." An editorial in the same issue charged that the Princeton honor system was a device for cheating and maintained that the Harvard student body wanted to drop Princeton as a football opponent. As a result of this incident, the two schools did not play each other in football for the next seven years. The series was resumed in 1934, at Fritz Crisler's insistence, with elaborate demonstrations of sportsmanship on both sides—but some ill feeling remained (Dunn, 148–51).

11.12 Hillebrand, Biffy Lea, Big Bill Edwards and the Poes

Famous football players at Princeton in the 1880s and 1890s. Arthur R. T. "Doc" Hillebrand was an All-American tackle, as was Langdon "Biff" Lea. Hillebrand, Lea, and guard William H. "Big Bill" Edwards all returned to coach at Princeton after they had graduated. The Poes were six brothers who played football at Princeton. John Prentiss Poe, Jr., a member of Fitzgerald's class at Princeton, left school to enlist in the Royal Highland infantry; he was killed in action in France in September 1915. Fitzgerald mentions him in "Princeton" (1927), an essay included in the Cambridge edition of *My Lost City* (2005): 8.

11.30–31 Lawrenceville Seconds and the New Jersey School for Drug Addicts

The "breather" games were played against inferior opponents, but Fitzgerald is not being serious here. The Lawrenceville Seconds would be the B-team from Lawrenceville School, a prep school five miles southwest of Princeton. The New Jersey School for Drug Addicts is fictitious.

12.5 old Groton man

Groton, an Episcopal prep school in Groton, Massachusetts, was then a feeder school for Harvard, Princeton, Yale, and other prestigious institutions. The character in chapter 3 of *Trimalchio* whose "Oxford mush-mouth" accent Fitzgerald satirizes has entered his son in advance for admission to Groton. See the Cambridge edition of *Trimalchio* (2000): 38. This passage was deleted in galleys and does not appear in *The Great Gatsby*.

12.9–10 a Maeterlinck . . . an Adams

The Belgian writer Maurice Maeterlinck (1862–1949), winner of the Nobel Prize for Literature in 1911, was the author of several philosophical books about nature, including *The Life of the White Ant* (*La Vie des termites*), first published in 1926. When Fitzgerald attended the Newman School as a teenager, he met the Boston author Henry Adams (1838–1918). Fitzgerald is probably alluding here to *The Education of Henry Adams*, privately printed in 1906 and published in 1918. The character Thornton Hancock in *This Side of Paradise* is based on Adams.

14.12 the son of John Harvard

Students at Harvard were known as "the sons of John Harvard" after the seventeenth-century clergyman from Charlestown, Massachusetts, after whom the university is named. At his death John Harvard (1607–38), who was childless, bequeathed half of his estate (a sum of £779) and his 400-volume library to the institution, then known as New College. The school renamed itself Harvard College the following year.

14.21 Harkness Chair of Insectology at Yale

The Chair of Insectology is an invention, but Fitzgerald must have known that members of the Harkness family were among the great benefactors of Yale. Harkness Tower (a bell tower in the divinity school), Mary S. Harkness Auditorium (in the school of medicine), Edward S. Harkness Memorial Hall (a dormitory), and William L. Harkness Hall (an academic building) are named for members of the family.

"'I Didn't Get Over'"

15.1 'sixteen in college

The narrator means that he was a member of the class of 1916. He would have joined the armed forces in the spring of 1917 when the US declared war on Germany and her allies.

16.2 a blue M. P. band

A member of the Military Police—known as an "M. P."—would sometimes wear a blue band on his arm or helmet to differentiate himself from the other soldiers.

16.6 Leavenworth

Fitzgerald went through army training camp at Fort Leavenworth, on the Missouri River in Kansas, where he wrote much of "The Romantic Egotist," the unpublished novel from which he took Book I of *This Side of Paradise*. Fort Leavenworth is the site of a large military prison, established there in 1874.

16.10 D.S.C.

The Distinguished Service Cross is a US Army decoration, awarded for extraordinary heroism in battle and ranking just below the Congressional Medal of Honor in prestige. The DSC was established by President Woodrow Wilson during the First World War.

17.23 that story about 'what killed the dog.'

A vaudeville and Ziegfeld Follies sketch called "No News, or, What Killed the Dog," performed by the comedian Nat Wills (1873–1917). Wills played a servant reporting to his absent employer on the telephone: "There's no news . . . except that you don't have to bring home any dog food . . . well, because the dog died . . . he was trying to save the baby . . . from the fire . . . the one your wife started when she ran off with the chauffeur . . ." and so forth.

17.29–18.1 Stokes mortar . . . one-pounder

A light mortar used by the Allied forces in the First World War, named for its inventor, F. W. S. Stokes. The weapon, effective in trench warfare, fired a 4.5 kg shell and had a maximum range of 1,200 yards. A one-pounder was a light artillery piece, easily transported.

18.7 Stonewall Jackson

General Thomas J. "Stonewall" Jackson (1824–63), one of the most able commanders in the Confederate army during the American Civil War, earned the name "Stonewall" for his steadfastness at First Manassas. He is remembered today for his tactics in the Shenandoah Valley Campaign of 1862.

18.35 to wigwag

To signal with flags, using a system similar to the Morse code of dots and dashes for letters of the alphabet. Wigwag signaling, developed in the 1850s, was first employed in the American Civil War. Each letter consisted of a combination of three motions; Fitzgerald, as an officer candidate, would have studied the system in training camp during the First World War.

21.12 Brest

Prisoners of war taken by the Allied forces were held at Brest, a port city in the west of France, before being transported to prisons in Great Britain. Brest was the major port of disembarkation for American troops headed for the front. After the war it became a major calling port for transatlantic liners.

"An Alcoholic Case"

23.27 "Gone with the Wind"

This extraordinarily popular novel by Margaret Mitchell (1900–49) was first published in 1936 and won the Pulitzer Prize for that year. During his last three weeks on the MGM payroll in Hollywood, late in 1938, Fitzgerald worked on the dialogue for the film version of the novel. His marked copy of the screenplay survives at Princeton. In a January 1939 letter to his daughter, Scottie, he wrote that *Gone with the Wind* was "not very original" but that it was "interesting, surprisingly honest, consistent and workmanlike throughout" (*The Letters of F. Scott Fitzgerald*, ed. Andrew Turnbull [New York: Scribners, 1963]: 49–50).

26.6 Forest Park Inn

When he wrote this story Fitzgerald was living at the Grove Park Inn in Asheville, North Carolina. Zelda was undergoing psychiatric treatment at a nearby sanitarium. The original Inn, built in 1912–13, consisted of five sections joined end-to-end and extending along a mountain ridge. The wall surfaces and chimneys of the structure are of uncut granite boulders from nearby Sunset Mountain. The Inn is also the likely setting of "The Guest in Room Nineteen," later in this volume.

27.26–27 the movie she had just seen about Pasteur and the book they had all read about Florence Nightingale

Probably *The Story of Louis Pasteur* (1935), starring Paul Muni and Josephine Hutchinson, a Warner Brothers "biopic" that won the Oscar for best screenplay in the year of its release. The film tells the story of Pasteur's "germ theory" and his struggles with the French Academy, which was dismissive of his findings. The nurse trainees would have read one of the many popular biographies of Florence Nightingale, among whose accomplishments was the founding of the Nightingale School for Nurses at St. Thomas' Hospital, London, in 1860.

"The Long Way Out"

32.1–3 Touraine . . . Louis XI . . . Cardinal Balue

The French cardinal Jean Balue (ca. 1421–91), an adviser to Louis XI, entered into an unsuccessful conspiracy against the king with Charles the Bold of Burgundy. Louis, known as the "Spider King," took revenge on Cardinal Balue by holding him prisoner from 1469 to 1480, reportedly in an iron cage in his castle in Touraine, a province in central France.

32.28 hair waves

During the first few decades of the twentieth century, many American women styled their hair with the "permanent wave" or "perm," a chemical treatment that produced artificial curls. Permanent waves were popular with women who wore the fashionable short hair styles of the 1920s and 1930s.

"The Guest in Room Nineteen"

37.3–4 a half-finished picture puzzle

In a typical resort hotel of the period, jigsaw puzzles were left in progress on tables in the lobby or lounge. Guests would work on the puzzles for diversion; the activity was a social solvent, allowing people to meet each other.

"Financing Finnegan"

50.20 Dillinger

John Dillinger (1902–1934) was the most famous American bank robber of the 1930s. He and his gang terrorized the Midwest in 1933: he was captured twice but escaped both times and was eventually held responsible for sixteen killings. Dillinger was declared "Public Enemy Number One" by the Federal Bureau of Investigation and was shot to death by FBI agents in Chicago in July 1934.

54.8 four-flusher

A bluffer, one who makes empty claims—from the practice of bluffing a flush, in stud poker, with four cards of the same suit showing but no fifth card of that suit in the hole.

55.2 three Bryn Mawr anthropologists

Satire by Fitzgerald. Bryn Mawr, then as now, was an academically rigorous women's college of Quaker origins located ten miles northwest of Philadelphia. Bryn Mawr is one of the Seven Sisters—the most prestigious women's colleges in the country.

"Design in Plaster"

64.9 ethylene gas

An unsaturated hydrocarbon used as a general anesthetic.

"The Lost Decade"

65.4–5 Dartmouth "Jack-o-Lantern"

The campus humor magazine at Dartmouth University. Budd Schulberg (b. 1914), the young Hollywood scriptwriter who befriended Fitzgerald in 1939, is the original for the character Orrison Brown in the story. Schulberg had been one of the editors of the *Jack-o-Lantern* during the 1930s. Fitzgerald wrote humorous items for the *Princeton Tiger*, a comparable publication, during his college years; he served on the editorial board of the *Tiger* in 1915.

65.21 '21'

The "21" Club, known simply as "21"—rendered always with numerals—is a fashionable New York restaurant at 21 West 52nd Street, between Fifth and Sixth Avenues. It opened as a speakeasy in 1922 and was the most exclusive of the nightclubs that served alcohol during Prohibition. On a rainy night Robert Benchley uttered one of his best-remembered wisecracks at the restaurant: "Get me out of this wet coat and into a dry Martini." This is the restaurant referred to in "The Woman from '21,'" a story included later in this volume.

66.1 Empire State Building

Fitzgerald uses New York skyscrapers as symbols in this story. The Empire State Building, on Fifth Avenue between 33rd and 34th Streets, was erected as a speculative venture; construction began in late 1929, and the building opened on 1 May 1931. Fitzgerald also uses the Empire State Building in a symbolic way in his 1935 essay "My Lost City," recently published in the final revised version in the Cambridge edition of *My Lost City* (2005): 106–15.

66.18 Moriarty's

A famous Irish pub in central Philadelphia, popular with politicians and members of the press. The establishment was known for its 65-foot mahogany bar, installed in 1937, and for its heavily decorated dining room on the second floor.

66.27 Admiral Byrd's hideout

In 1929, Rear Admiral Richard E. Byrd (1888–1957) established a scientific base on the Ross Ice Shelf in Antarctica and called it "Little America." He made four expeditions to the Antarctic in all: on his second trip, in 1933, he established a base far inland, which he occupied alone for five months. He was almost killed by toxic carbon monoxide gas from his heater but eventually identified the problem and saved himself. Fitzgerald probably knew of Byrd's adventures from magazine coverage during the mid-1930s, or he might have read Byrd's book *Alone: The Classic Polar Adventure* (1938).

66.34 Crêpe ties

Men's ties made of crinkled silk or cotton, popular for summer wear during the 1910s and early 1920s but falling out of favor when silk ties with regimental stripes became fashionable around 1925.

67.13–14 Cole Porter

This famous American composer (1891–1964) moved to Paris in 1917 and stayed there until 1928, when his songs began to find success in London and New York. *Gay Divorcée* (1932) and *Anything Goes* (1934) were his first big Broadway hits.

67.18 Carnegie Hall

The most famous concert hall in New York, on the southeast corner of 57th and Seventh Avenue, built between 1889 and 1891. The Main Hall, for symphony orchestras and other large groups of performers, has been much praised for its acoustical properties and its ambience.

67.30–32 Rockefeller Center . . . Chrysler Building . . . Armistead Building

Rockefeller Center, a complex of commercial buildings at Fifth Avenue and 52nd Street, and the Chrysler Building, an Art Deco skyscraper at 405 Lexington Avenue, were (with the Empire State Building) among the most famous architectural structures in New York during the 1930s. All three were identified with the 1920s and with the American will to achieve, to rise, to compete. The Armistead Building, which Trimble has designed in the story, is fictitious.

"On an Ocean Wave"

70.27 Cherbourg

The major French seaport on the English Channel and a primary docking point for transatlantic passenger liners in the 1920s and 1930s.

"The Woman from '21'"

73.3–4 the frozen music of Fifth Avenue and 59th Street

The address tells the reader that Raymond Torrence and his wife are staying at the Plaza Hotel, then the most famous caravanserai in the city and the setting for Jay Gatsby's face-off with Tom Buchanan in *The Great Gatsby* (1925).

73.6 Javanese

Elizabeth is from the island of Java, adjacent to Sumatra and Borneo, all three part of the Dutch East Indies in the 1930s. The chief exports of Java were sugar, rubber, tea, coffee, and tobacco.

73.10 Stork Club

An upscale restaurant and night spot at 3 East 53rd Street and a favorite hangout for journalists such as Walter Winchell and Damon Runyon. Winchell described the club as "the New Yorkiest place in New York."

73.13–14 Old Westbury

A community for the wealthy near Hempstead, Long Island, about twenty-two miles from Manhattan, known for its fox-hunting and polo events. Members of the Vanderbilt, Whitney, and Du Pont families were among the residents in the 1930s.

73.16 the children in Suva

The Torrences live in Suva, the Europeanized capital city of the Fiji Islands.

73.18–19 a girl sick with yaws

An infection of the skin, bones, and joints, found in tropical climates and most commonly contracted by children between the ages of six and ten. Yaws is caused by the bacterium *Treponema pertenue* and is transmitted by eye gnats or by skin contact with an infected person.

73.20 a play by William Saroyan

Fitzgerald probably had in mind Saroyan's *The Time of Your Life* (1939), which won both the New York Drama Critics Circle Award and the Pulitzer Prize for Drama (which he refused). Saroyan (1908–81) had another drama staged on Broadway in 1939—*My Heart's in the Highlands*, also a hit.

73.21 "21"

The "21" Club is glossed in the notes for "The Lost Decade."

74.21 Mrs. Jiggs

This is Maggie, the wife of Jiggs in the cartoon strip "Bringing Up Father," popularly known as "Jiggs and Maggie." Maggie is a social climber, anxious to rise; Jiggs is an Irish immigrant who prefers simple pleasures such as the pool hall, a poker game, and a dish of corned beef and cabbage. The comic strip was drawn by George McManus for the King Features newspaper syndicate.

74.25 Run, Sheep, Run

A children's game in which one child is the Fox, one is the Shepherd, and the rest are Sheep. The Sheep hide as a group; the Fox attempts to find them; the Shepherd warns the Sheep, with prearranged word signals, when the Fox approaches the hiding place. The object is for the Sheep to flee to safety in the Pen. The Shepherd attempts to lure the Fox away from the hiding place, and when the Shepherd thinks that the Sheep can make it to safety, he shouts: "Run, Sheep, Run!"

"Pat Hobby's Christmas Wish"

93.10–11 "I was with Biograph till 1920."

The American Mutoscope and Biograph Company, one of the earliest cinema studios, was headquartered on East 14th Street in New York City in 1906. Lillian Gish appeared as a child actress in some of its films, and D. W. Griffith directed his first movie there—*The Adventures of Dollie*, in 1908. Among the stars at Biograph were Mary Pickford, Mack Sennett, Billy Quirk, and Lionel Barrymore. The company migrated to California in 1910 and flourished for a time (also maintaining studios back east in the Bronx), but its refusal to produce feature-length films brought about its downfall in 1916. Gooddorf's recollection that he was with Biograph "till 1920" would mean that he worked for the company after it was acquired by Empire Trust, its chief creditor.

"A Man in the Way"

97.9 benzedrine

This amphetamine, long used as a stimulant by writers and musicians, was a favorite drug of the Beats a decade or so later. Benzedrine pills, known as "bennies," were produced in laboratories across the Mexican border, just south of Los Angeles, and were easily procurable in Hollywood.

98.6 Hollywood and Vine

The intersection of Hollywood Boulevard and Vine Street was famous in the 1930s for its proximity to many sites associated with the film industry—including the Pantages Theatre, the Hollywood Plaza Hotel, the Lasky-Paramount Studios, and the Taft Building, where the offices of the Academy of Motion Pictures Arts and Sciences were located.

99.22 a short short

A "short," also called a "short subject," was a two- or three-reel film lasting approximately thirty minutes. Shorts were shown before feature-length films, together with cartoons and newsreels. Hollywood studios used shorts to train beginning directors, actors, and other personnel, and to experiment with sound and color. A "short short" would have been a one-reeler, lasting about ten minutes.

100.8–9 'It Happened One Night'

This 1934 feature-length movie, one of director Frank Capra's most memorable films, was a screwball romantic comedy starring Claudette Colbert and Clark Gable, both of whom won Oscars for their performances. The screenplay was written by Fitzgerald's friend Samuel Hopkins Adams, who based the script on his own short story "Night Bus."

100.9 Hedy Lamarr

This Austrian beauty, born Hedwig Eva Maria Kiesler in 1913, specialized in femme-fatale roles. Before coming to Hollywood, she caused an international sensation by appearing in the nude in a Czech film called *Ekstase* (1933). She starred in the film *Algiers* with Charles Boyer in 1938; later she appeared in *White Cargo* (1942) and *Samson and Delilah* (1949). Fitzgerald probably saw her on the Metro-Goldwyn-Mayer film lot; she was under contract to the studio in 1938, while he was working there.

101.27 Santa Anita

Betting on horse races was legalized in California in 1933. Santa Anita Park, an elaborate racetrack about twenty miles from Hollywood, opened for business on Christmas Day 1934. Pat, who likes to take a flutter on the ponies, goes to Santa Anita frequently in these stories. Sometimes he places his wagers off-track with Lou, the studio bookie.

102.7 Tate Gallery

This famous London art museum, named for the benefactor Henry Tate, was opened in 1897 on the former site of Millbank Prison in Pimlico.

"'Boil Some Water—Lots of It'"

105.9–10 Ronald Colman

Ronald Colman (1891–1958) is mentioned frequently in the Pat Hobby stories and has one line in "The Homes of the Stars." Colman enjoyed a long career in Hollywood, beginning in silent films and making the transition to talking pictures in the late 1920s. In one of his best silent films, *Stella Dallas* (1925), he appeared as the wealthy father of Laurel Dallas—a role played by Lois Moran, the actress on whom Fitzgerald based Jenny Prince in his 1927 story "Jacob's Ladder," and Rosemary Hoyt in *Tender Is the Night* (1934).

106.24 "The Last Supper"

This mural by Leonardo da Vinci, one of the most famous works in Western art, was completed in 1498 and is located in the convent of Santa Maria delle Grazie in Milan. Donald Duck is one of Walt Disney's wackiest animated characters.

"Teamed with Genius"

110.18 if pictures hadn't started to talk

The first movies with full sound tracks were released in 1928. Some silent-film actors remained popular in the talkies, but others (the senior Douglas Fairbanks, for example) did not make the transition well. Screenwriters like Pat who were competent with structure but inept at dialogue saw their careers fade. Fiction-writers and dramatists who had sold silent-movie rights to the film studios realized a windfall when a court ruling allowed them to sell the sound rights, of those same stories and plays, to Hollywood a second time.

110.29 BALLET SHOES

In March 1936 Fitzgerald attempted without success to sell a movie treatment called "Ballet Shoes" to the film magnate Samuel Goldwyn. Fitzgerald wanted "Ballet Shoes" to be a starring vehicle for the Russian ballerina Olga Spessivtzeva, whom Goldwyn was trying to sign to a movie contract. "Ballet Shoes," which survives in typescript, was published in the *Fitzgerald/Hemingway Annual 1976*, pp. 5–7.

115.21 the nickel machine

Pat is amusing himself with a nickel slot machine, a legal form of gambling in California during the late 1930s. Nickel slots were everywhere in Los Angeles during the 1930s, even in drug stores, where liquor was also sold.

115.30–31 a sis job

In the context of this story, Pat means that the invention of dialogue for movie scripts is a job for "sissies," or gay men.

115.33 'Quaker Girl'

Here the name of a racehorse, but Fitzgerald is recalling *The Quaker Girl* (1911), a musical comedy that enchanted him at the age of fifteen during a trip to New York City from his prep school in Hackensack, New Jersey. Ina Claire starred in that production as an English girl who wins the heart of an American visitor to her home town. Fitzgerald mentions *The Quaker Girl* in his 1935 essay "My Lost City," first published in *The Crack-Up* (1945) and collected in the Cambridge edition of *My Lost City* (2005): 106.

"Pat Hobby and Orson Welles"

118.0 Orson Welles

The bearded actor, director, and producer Orson Welles (1915–85) was called the "boy wonder" of the movies in 1940, though his greatest triumphs in film lay ahead of him. After a successful early career in the theatre, he came to Hollywood in 1940 with a contract from RKO that granted him total artistic freedom. He directed *Citizen Kane* (1941), *The Magnificent Ambersons* (1942), and *Touch of Evil* (1958). His best film performances came in *Jane Eyre* (1943) and *The Third Man* (1949).

118.5 credits

The key to success for a Hollywood scriptwriter was to earn as many screen credits as possible. The scriptwriter's name would appear in the opening credits as author or co-author of the screenplay; this would help to keep the scriptwriter's name visible and his or her services in demand. A "script doctor" or "structure man" like Pat might be called in to work briefly on a movie but would rarely earn a credit. During his last stint in Hollywood, Fitzgerald earned only one screen credit—as co-author with E. E. Paramore of the script for *Three Comrades* (1938).

118.15–16 Filipinos and swimming pools

Many of the domestic servants employed by Hollywood movie people were from the Philippine Islands; a swimming pool on one's property was a sign of money and elevated status.

118.18–19 ". . . it never got him off Grand Street."

Louie's father was likely a Jewish immigrant living on the Lower East Side of Manhattan. Grand Street, which ran east-to-west through the Jewish ghetto, was a busy thoroughfare crowded with sweatshops, small businesses, and pushcart peddlers.

119.4 "Lousy Keystone Cop!"

The Keystone Cops, a slapstick troupe in police uniforms, were featured in many of the zany Mack Sennett comedies of the silent-movie era. They specialized in fantastic chase scenes and custard-pie battles.

120.15–16 "The Divine Miss Carstairs"

Fitzgerald is probably thinking of *Captivating Mary Carstairs* (1915), a romantic comedy that starred Norma Talmadge, Allan Forrest, and Bruce M. Mitchell.

121.25 stock ticker

A ticker-tape machine, or "stock ticker," conveyed stock prices over long distances via the telegraph. These machines printed information in "ticker symbols" on thin rolls of tape. Mr. Marcus wants a place where he can escape from worry about his stock portfolio.

121.29 "Look at Fox! I cried for him."

Wilhelm Fried (1879–1952) was a Hungarian Jew from the Lower East Side who changed his name to William Fox and entered the moving-picture business in 1904. He built a chain of movie theatres and made a fortune in distributing motion pictures during the 1920s. Fox lost his wealth in a series of anti-trust lawsuits; his studios were merged with Twentieth Century to form Twentieth Century Fox, which prospered with the films of Will Rogers and Shirley Temple during the 1930s. Mr. Marcus, in the story, is thinking of the charges pending against Fox in 1940 for allegedly bribing a judge in a bankruptcy hearing. Fox was convicted in 1941 and served six months in a Pennsylvania penitentiary.

"Pat Hobby's Secret"

126.8–9 Claudette Colbert or Betty Field

Both women were popular cinema actresses during the late 1930s and 1940s. Claudette Colbert (1905–96) starred in sophisticated comedies, including *It Happened One Night* (1934), mentioned above, *I Met Him in Paris* (1937), *Zaza* (1939), and *Midnight* (1940). Betty Field (1913–73) was a stage performer who was praised for her acting in *Of Mice and Men* (1940). In 1949 she appeared in the second movie version of *The Great Gatsby*, playing in a cast that included Alan Ladd, Ruth Hussey, and Shelley Winters.

127.23 Paramount

Paramount traced its roots to the Famous Players Film Company and its founder, Adolph Zukor. By the 1930s Paramount was one of the major studios in Hollywood; its stars included Marlene Dietrich, Mae West, Gary Cooper, Bing Crosby, and the Marx Brothers.

128.6 Tarzan White

Arthur P. "Tarzan" White was an All-American football player (and a Phi Beta Kappa) at the University of Alabama. Later he played professional football for the New York Giants and the Chicago Cardinals and, in the off-seasons, was a professional wrestler. "Mr. Smith" in Fitzgerald's story must have encountered White in the wrestling ring.

129.27 great scandals like the Arbuckle case

Roscoe C. "Fatty" Arbuckle (1887–1933) was a popular comedian in silent films whose career was ruined in 1921 when he was charged with murdering a young actress at a drinking party in San Francisco. Two trials ended with hung juries; in a third trial he was acquitted, but his films had been banned, and he never again appeared on the cinema screen.

130.12–13 "As Shakespeare says, 'Every man has his price.'"

Not Shakespeare but the eighteenth-century British statesman Sir Robert Walpole, generally thought of as the first Prime Minister. Edward

Bulwer-Lytton wrote a comedy in three acts entitled *Walpole; or, Every Man Has His Price* (1869).

"Pat Hobby, Putative Father" ["Pat Hobby's Secret"]

133.17 the morning's "Reporter"

The *Hollywood Reporter*, edited by W. R. "Billy" Wilkerson, was a daily trade newspaper for the film industry. Launched in 1930, it was a colorful rag filled with reviews, feature stories, and gossip. Many film moguls detested the *Reporter* and banned it from their studio lots. The *Reporter* is mentioned also in "Pat Hobby's Preview."

134.8 the extras . . . for 'Bengal Lancer'

Jack Berners means *The Lives of a Bengal Lancer*, a hit movie released by Paramount in 1935, starring Gary Cooper, Franchot Tone, and Richard Cromwell as British soldiers defending the borders of India from nomadic raiders. Paramount hired hundreds of Piute Indians from reservations in California, along with Hindu olive-pickers from the Napa Valley, to play the warlike tribesmen.

135.18 Bonita Granville

A pretty film actress (1923–88), best-known in the late 1930s for playing the teenaged girl detective/reporter Nancy Drew in a string of movies for Warner Brothers.

135.33 World's Fair in New York

This best-known of the New York World's Fairs was erected on Flushing Meadows and featured two landmark structures known as the Trylon and the Perisphere. The fair included a futuristic car-based city, a speech synthesizer, and an early television. It opened in April 1939 and closed in October 1940, having drawn some 45 million visitors.

137.16–17 an idol more glamorous than Siva

Siva, or Shiva, is one of the three supreme gods of Hinduism. Siva worship is associated with the phallus; the god is sometimes depicted wearing a garland of skulls, though Fitzgerald might have had in mind another incarnation, as Lord of the Cosmic Dance, in which the Siva figure, four-armed, is poised on one foot over the body of a prostrate demon.

138.27–30 Ambassador Hotel . . . Cocoanut Grove

The Ambassador, on Wilshire Boulevard, had an interior that mimicked the Alhambra, with colorful tile floors, Moorish arches, and elaborate stone fireplaces. In 1927 Fitzgerald stayed at the Ambassador with Zelda while he was writing "Lipstick," a screen treatment intended for Constance Talmadge. The Cocoanut Grove (in the next paragraph) was a dining and dancing club in the Ambassador, famous for its papier-mâché palm trees and cocoanuts, which had been rescued from the set of Rudolph Valentino's film *The Sheik*. The club featured an indoor waterfall and a large mural depicting a moonwashed Hawaiian landscape.

139.22 like Stella Dallas

A reference to the title character in the 1925 silent movie *Stella Dallas*, mentioned above in the note on Ronald Colman. The film, directed by Henry King and released by United Artists, was based on the 1923 novel of the same title by Olive Higgins Prouty. Stephen Dallas, a man of education and refinement, marries a woman of low class named Stella Martin. Together they have a daughter whom they name Laurel. Stella becomes a social embarrassment to her husband; he divorces her and moves to New York City. When Laurel reaches her teens, Stella realizes that Stephen can provide her with advantages and opportunities that she cannot, so she bids goodbye to Laurel, who joins her father in the city and eventually marries into polite society. Colman played the role of Stephen Dallas; Stella was played by Belle Bennett. Lois Moran, the young actress of whom Fitzgerald was enamored in the mid-1920s, took the role of Laurel; Douglas Fairbanks, Jr., in a breakthrough role, appeared as her suitor and eventual husband. The movie was remade as a talkie in 1937, with Barbara Stanwyck as Stella and Anne Shirley in the role of Laurel. The scene in the 1925 version in which Stella bids farewell to Laurel is lachrymose and touching—hence the reference here.

139.32–33 "Los Angeles Times" . . . "Examiner" . . . "Toddy's Daily Form Sheet"

The *Times* was the major Republican newspaper in Los Angeles; the *Examiner*, a Hearst paper, was Democratic and pro-labor. Pat's political awareness is rudimentary: *Toddy's*, a tip sheet for racetrack betters, would be the most important of the three publications to him.

140.3 September 3rd

The Second World War began on 1 September 1939, when Germany invaded Poland. On 3 September, England and France declared war on Germany.

"The Homes of the Stars"

141.2–3 no relation to the runner

Gene Venske was a successful US middle-distance runner during the 1930s. He was the college national champion in the mile run as a student at the University of Pennsylvania in 1934 and, in 1936, ran on a four-man team that set a world record in the four-mile relay. Venske ran in the 1936 Berlin Summer Olympics and retired from competition after the Second World War.

142.18 Brown Derby

The original Brown Derby restaurant, on Wilshire Boulevard across from the Ambassador Hotel, was a favorite dining establishment for movie people. In 1937 the Brown Derby moved one block, to 3347 Wilshire, into a new building that was built in the shape of a brown derby hat. A neon sign on top invited customers to "Eat in the Hat."

142.26–34 Clark Gable . . . Melvyn Douglas . . . Robert Young . . . Ronald Colman . . . Young Doug

All popular leading men of the period. Clark Gable (1901–60), known for his big ears and thin mustache, made thirty-nine films in the 1930s. His most famous movie, *Gone with the Wind*, was released in 1939, the year before "Homes of the Stars" was published in *Esquire*. Melvyn Douglas (1901–81) played sophisticated, witty characters; he starred with Claudette Colbert in *She Married Her Boss* (1935) and with Greta Garbo in *Ninotchka* (1939). The earnest, likeable Robert Young (1907–98) appeared opposite Joan Crawford in *Today We Live* (1933) and was matched with Barbara Stanwyck in *Red Salute* (1935). He was one of the stars of *Three Comrades* (1938), for which Fitzgerald co-wrote the script. Douglas Fairbanks, Jr. (1909–2000), mentioned above in the gloss for Stella Dallas, was best known for playing the leads in *The Prisoner of Zenda* (1937) and *Gunga Din* (1939). Ronald Colman is glossed in the notes for "'Boil Some Water—Lots of It.'"

143.21 George Brent

The Irish-born leading man George Brent (1904–79) was an actor of limited range but dependable virility; he starred in eleven films with Bette Davis—all shot at Warner Brothers during the 1930s. He also played opposite Ginger Rogers, Myrna Loy, and Olivia de Havilland at various times during his career.

143.36 Upton Sinclair or Sinclair Lewis

These writers were often confused with one another. Both were still publishing during the late 1930s—Lewis (1885–1951) had won the Nobel Prize for Literature in 1930 and was best-known for his novels *Main Street* (1920) and *Babbitt* (1922). The prolific Sinclair (1878–1968) was still famous in the 1930s for *The Jungle* (1906), his exposé of the Chicago meat-packing industry.

144.3 Screen Playwriters' Guild

Pat, confused, is blending the names of two labor organizations. The Screen Writers Guild, founded in 1921, was a writers' union (affiliated with the Authors League of America) that agitated in Hollywood during the 1930s for improved working conditions, better pay, and a fair system for awarding screen credits. The Screen Playwrights was a company union, organized by the Academy of Motion Pictures Arts and Sciences in order to undercut the efforts of the Screen Writers Guild. Hollywood was beset by labor problems during the 1930s, some of which are mentioned in *The Last Tycoon* (1941).

144.9–10 —it's all in the Wagner Act. . . . Recognize Finland.

More confusion by Pat. The National Labor Relations Act of 1935, known as the "Wagner Act," affirmed the right of labor to organize, to bargain with management, and to go on strike. As for Finland, Pat is aware in some fashion of the Soviet–Finnish "Winter War" of 1939–40. The Soviet Union attacked Finland in November 1939; the Finnish forces held off the Soviets for a time and appealed to France, England, and the US for assistance. France and England were preparing to send troops to Finland when a treaty was signed in March 1940, ending the war. The US was under pressure from France and England in the early months of 1940 to recognize the plight of the Finns and to send military aid. Sympathizers with Finland collected money to send to Finnish civilians. In "On the Trail of Pat Hobby," which appears later in this volume, Pat tries to touch his writer-friend Bee McIlvaine for a loan. She refuses, telling him, "The Finns got all my money."

145.3–4 Carole Lombard

This popular and glamorous actress, born in 1908, married Clark Gable in 1939. A talented comedienne, she appeared in *True Confession* in 1937 and *Fools for Scandal* in 1938; Mrs. Robinson might want to give her some advice about her platinum-blonde hair. Lombard died in a plane crash in January 1942.

146.22 Shirley Temple

Shirley Temple (b. 1928), the most popular child star in Hollywood, had a string of hit movies during the 1930s that included *The Little Colonel* (1935), *Captain January* (1936), *Heidi* (1937), *Rebecca of Sunnybrook Farm* (1938), and *The Little Princess* (1939). Fitzgerald visited Shirley and her mother on 11 July 1940; he tried without success to persuade Mrs. Temple to allow Shirley to play Honoria in a film version of his story "Babylon Revisited" (1931).

"Pat Hobby Does His Bit"

152.1 papers to sign with the Guild

If Pat is to appear in a movie he will need to join the Screen Actors Guild, a labor union officially incorporated in 1933 to combat poor working conditions and low pay for actors.

152.19–20 Benchley . . . Don Stewart . . . Lewis and Wilder and Woollcott

Prominent authors of Fitzgerald's approximate generation who wrote for the screen and appeared on stage and in movies as well. Fitzgerald knew them all socially: Robert Benchley (1889–1945), Donald Ogden Stewart (1894–1980), Sinclair Lewis (1885–1951), Thornton Wilder (1897–1975), and Alexander Woollcott (1887–1943).

"Pat Hobby's Preview"

159.10 Universal

Still one of the major studios in Hollywood during the 1930s, though in precarious financial condition during those years. Universal specialized in thrillers such as *Dracula* (1931), *Frankenstein* (1931), and *The Mummy*

(1932). The studio also turned out the comedies of W. C. Fields and the Sherlock Holmes films starring Basil Rathbone.

159.13–17 'Captains Courageous' . . . 'Test Pilot' . . . 'Wuthering Heights' . . . 'The Awful Truth' . . . 'Mr. Smith Goes to Washington' . . . 'Dark Victory'

Hit movies of the late 1930s. *Captains Courageous* (1937) starred Spencer Tracy, Freddie Bartholomew, and Mickey Rooney; *Test Pilot* (1938) featured Clark Gable and Myrna Loy; *Wuthering Heights* (1939) starred Merle Oberon and Laurence Olivier; *The Awful Truth* (1937) had Irene Dunne and Cary Grant in the leading roles; *Mr. Smith Goes to Washington* (1939) featured James Stewart, Jean Arthur, and Claude Rains; *Dark Victory* (1939) starred Bette Davis, George Brent, and Humphrey Bogart.

160.32–33 Bank Holiday of 1933

Pat's confidence in banks seems to have evaporated during the so-called "bank holiday" of 1933, a mandatory four-day closing of all banks ordered by the US Congress on 6 March 1933, the day after Franklin D. Roosevelt was inaugurated as President. The holiday was later extended until 13 March. During this period federal inspectors examined some 5,000 banks and closed the ones that were insolvent. The measure was meant to restore faith in banking institutions, but it was not altogether successful.

"No Harm Trying"

164.19 "Life"

This large-format glossy magazine, launched in November 1936 by Henry Luce, concentrated on photojournalism. *Life* devoted more space to pictures than to words; it specialized in feature stories, human-interest tales, and celebrities. Its pictorial coverage of the Second World War built support for the American war effort.

164.20–21 a fire in Topanga Canyon

Fitzgerald is thinking of an enormous forest fire in Topanga Canyon that began on 23 November 1938 and destroyed some 200 houses, many of them belonging to people in the movie business. See "Forest Fires Invade Coast Movie Colonies," *New York Times*, 24 November 1938, p. 1.

"A Patriotic Short"

174.2 Irvin Cobb

Irvin S. Cobb (1876–1944) was a humorist, satirist, journalist, screenwriter, radio personality, and Hollywood actor. He wrote hundreds of short stories and published nearly sixty books during his career; his best-known character was a Kentuckian named Judge Priest. Most of his screenplays, written during the 1930s, were filmed by MGM; Fitzgerald probably knew Cobb while he was under contract to that studio in 1937 and 1938.

175.25 General Fitzhugh Lee

Fitzhugh Lee (1835–1905), a grandson of "Light Horse Harry Lee" and a nephew of Robert E. Lee, was a Confederate cavalry general during the American Civil War. He resigned his commission in the US army in 1861 and returned to his home state of Virginia to join the Southern cause. He participated in J. E. B. Stuart's ride around McClellan's army early in the war and successfully covered the Confederate retreat from Antietam in 1862. After the war, Fitzhugh Lee devoted himself to reconciliation between the North and South. From 1886 to 1890 he served as Governor of Virginia and in April 1896 was appointed Consul-general of Havana by President Grover Cleveland. He was retained in that post by President William McKinley and re-entered the US army during the Spanish–American War as a commander of volunteers.

177.10 the It Girl

The original "It" Girl was Clara Bow (1905–65), who starred in many of the classic silent films of the Jazz Age, including *Grit* (1924), for which Fitzgerald wrote the story line, and in which she played a character called Orchid McGonigle. Her breakthrough film was *Mantrap* (1926); she continued to act in the talkies, but her Brooklyn accent did not translate well into the sound era. The "It" she possessed was sex appeal.

"On the Trail of Pat Hobby"

181.5–33 'Test Pilot' . . . 'The Birth of a Nation' . . . 'It Happened One Night' . . . 'Grand Hotel'

Four classic movies, among the best produced by the US movie industry to that point. *Test Pilot* and *It Happened One Night* are glossed above. *The Birth of a Nation* (1915) is the film for which the director D. W. Griffith is most frequently remembered—more for the innovative camera techniques than for the plot line. *Grand Hotel* (1932) featured an all-star cast that included Greta Garbo, John Barrymore, Joan Crawford, Wallace Beery, and Jean Hersholt. The film was conceived by the MGM producer Irving Thalberg, on whom Fitzgerald based Monroe Stahr in *The Last Tycoon* (1941).

"Fun in an Artist's Studio"

183.9 Mr. Duchmann, the Secret Sin specialist

Probably Marius Duchmann, a German cinematographer whose movies included *Durch Leid zum Licht* (1918), *Das Mysteriöse Bett* (1920), and *Des Toten Rach* (1920). German films of this period were more sexually explicit than their American counterparts.

183.12–13 Spencer Rooney or Vivien Leigh

Pat is mixing the names of Spencer Tracy (1900–67) and Mickey Rooney (b. 1920), both major Hollywood stars of the period. (To prevent the *Esquire* copy-editor from correcting the error, Fitzgerald put a note at the foot of this page of the setting copy: "Note to Printer: The mistake 'Spencer Rooney' is deliberate.") Vivien Leigh (1913–67) was an English actress, best remembered for her Oscar-winning performances as Scarlett O'Hara in *Gone with the Wind* (1939) and Blanche du Bois in *A Streetcar Named Desire* (1951).

184.20–21 Jack Benny and Baby Sandy and Hedy Lamarr

The comedian and film star Jack Benny (1894–1974) performed in vaudeville after the First World War and graduated to movies in 1929. In the late 1930s he appeared in *Artists and Models Abroad* (1938) and *Man about Town* (1939). "Baby Sandy," whose real name was Sandra Lee Henville (b. 1938), was Universal's answer to Shirley Temple in the late 1930s and early 1940s. She made a series of popular movies and was named "Baby of the Year" by *Parents* magazine. She retired from acting at the age of five. Her films included *Unexpected Father* (1939), *Little Accident* (1939), and *Sandy Gets Her Man* (1940). Hedy Lamarr is glossed in the notes for "A Man in the Way."

184.25 Boldini . . . Reginald Marsh

Giovanni Boldini (1842–1931), an Italian painter of portraits and genre scenes, had reached his greatest success in Paris in the 1880s and 1890s. Boldini was known as the "Master of Swish"; he posed his subjects in graceful attitudes and used a bravura style of brushwork. His 1886 portrait of Giuseppe Verdi hangs in the National Gallery of Modern Art in Rome. The American painter and illustrator Reginald Marsh (1898–1954) was known for his illustrations in *Vanity Fair*, *Harper's Bazaar*, and the *New Yorker*. He is remembered for a series of New York street scenes executed in the 1930s, including the etching "Tattoo-Haircut-Shave" (1932), at the Art Institute of Chicago, and the painting "In 14th Street" (1934), at the Museum of Modern Art, New York.

185.1 Beverly Hills Hotel

This luxury hotel, built in 1912 on a hill overlooking Sunset Boulevard, was patronized by film people. It was the scene, from time to time, of scandalous behavior and was a favorite place for dealmakers to meet and negotiate. Its pink façade, set behind a rampart of shrubbery and masonry, caused it to be known as "The Pink Palace."

"Two Old-Timers"

190.10–11 between Eugene O'Brien and Robert Taylor

Eugene O'Brien (1882–1966) was a popular leading man on the stage and in silent movies, often cast opposite Norma Talmadge. He appeared regularly in feature films from 1915 to 1928 and played roles in *Rebecca of Sunnybrook Farm* (1917) and *Graustark* (1925). Robert Taylor (1911–69), a matinée idol of the 1930s, was known as "The Man with the Perfect Profile." He was cast opposite Jean Harlow, Greta Garbo, and Ava Gardner; in 1938 he appeared in *A Yank at Oxford* and *Three Comrades*—both of which Fitzgerald labored on as a screenwriter.

190.14 Man o' War

By the 1930s this famous racehorse was out to stud—the implication Fitzgerald wants here. Man o' War competed only in 1919–20, as a two- and three-year-old, but during this short period he won twenty of twenty-one races and collected almost $250,000 in purses. He was equally impressive as a sire, producing 64 stakes winners and some 200 other champions. He sired War Admiral, the winner of the 1937 Triple Crown, and was the grandfather of Seabiscuit.

190.23 Connie Talmadge . . . Allan Dwan

All from the silent-movie era: Constance Talmadge (1900–73) broke into movies in 1916 and by the mid-1920s was a major star, earning almost

$100,000 for each film in which she appeared. "Bill Crocker," a character in the 1909 D. W. Griffith one-reeler *Eradicating Aunty*, was played by the actor Herbert Prior, who eventually appeared in over 300 films. Allan Dwan (1885–1981) directed more than 400 movies, most of them one- and two-reelers made during the early years of the film industry. He specialized in action films and mounted a camera on a moving car, thus creating, in *David Harum* (1915), the first dolly shot in the history of cinema.

191.7–8 'The Final Push'

A fictitious title, but meant to suggest *The Big Parade* (1924), the movie that established King Vidor (1894–1982) as a leading Hollywood director. The film is remembered for its choreographed combat sequences and for the performance of John Gilbert (1899–1936) as James Apperson, a spoiled rich boy thrust into combat. In a 25 December 1939 letter, preserved at Princeton, Fitzgerald wrote to Gingrich: "Did you know that last story was the way 'The Big Parade' was really made? King Vidor pushed John Gilbert in a hole—believe it or not."

"Mightier than the Sword"

196.25 Reginald De Koven

Henry Louis Reginald De Koven (1861–1920) was an American music critic and composer of light operas. His most famous song was "Oh, Promise Me" (1889); his operettas include *Robin Hood* and *The Mandarin*. In 1902 he founded the Washington Symphony Orchestra.

197.36 "The Little Brown Jug"

Overly fond of the bottle. "Little Brown Jug" was a popular tune by the American songwriter Joseph Winner (1837–1918). Fitzgerald probably knew the big-band arrangement recorded by the Glenn Miller orchestra in April 1939.

198.19 Beverly Wilshire Hotel

This famous hotel, built in the Spanish Mission style, is located at 9500 Wilshire Boulevard in Beverly Hills. It was popular with movie people and was the scene of frequent parties and receptions.

199.34 ASCAP

The American Society of Composers, Authors, and Publishers, established in 1914, is an organization that monitors performances of music, live and recorded, and collects royalties and licensing fees for its members.

"Pat Hobby's College Days"

201.2 clank clank

Fitzgerald based this story on his hiring of Frances Kroll (b. 1918) as his secretary in April 1939. From time to time he asked her to dispose of his empty gin bottles. See Frances Kroll Ring, *Against the Current: As I Remember F. Scott Fitzgerald* (Berkeley, Calif.: Creative Arts Book Co., 1985).

203.17–18 half De Mille, half Aztec campus

Fitzgerald means that the campus is built on a grand scale. Cecil B. De Mille (1881–1959) was known for directing "epic" films based on stories from the Bible, Roman history, or the American West. His most famous silent movie is *The Ten Commandments* (1923); in the sound era he made *Dynamite* (1929), *The Sign of the Cross* (1932), and *Cleopatra* (1934). De Mille was a showman with a knack for spectacle and storytelling. The Aztecs were known for their monumental architecture.

204.30 D.K.E. House

Delta Kappa Epsilon, a men's social fraternity at many American colleges, whose members are known as Dekes.

205.22 Tyrone Power

Tyrone Power (1913–58) appeared in almost fifty films during a career that began in 1932 and lasted into the late 1950s. He usually played the romantic lead; his films during the late 1930s include *Suez* (1938), *Rose of Washington Square* (1939), and *The Mark of Zorro* (1940).

"Dearly Beloved"

256.5–6 Rosicrucian Brotherhood

The Ancient Mystic Order of Rosae Crucis, probably founded in Germany in 1115, is a nonsectarian and essentially nonreligious fraternal body, devoted to the transmutation of the gross elements of human behavior into high spiritual qualities. Its name derives from its symbol: a cross with a red rose at its center.

ILLUSTRATIONS

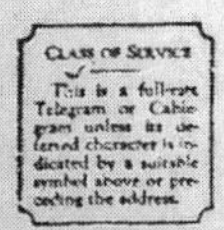

CLASS OF SERVICE
This is a full-rate Telegram or Cablegram unless its deferred character is indicated by a suitable symbol above or preceding the address.

WESTERN UNION

R. B. WHITE, PRESIDENT — NEWCOMB CARLTON, CHAIRMAN OF THE BOARD — J. C. WILLEVER, FIRST VICE-PRESIDENT

SYMBOLS
DL = Day Letter
NL = Night Letter
LC = Deferred Cable
NLT = Cable Night Letter
Ship Radiogram

The filing time shown in the date line on telegrams and day letters is STANDARD TIME at point of origin. Time of receipt is STANDARD TIME at point of destination

Received at

SA4 80 NL 2 EXTRA=TDS ENCINO CALIF 16 — 1939 JUL 17 AM 2 17

ARNOLD GINGRICH.CARE ESQUIRE MAGAZINE=
919 NORTH MICHIGAN AVE CHGO=

BEEN SICK IN BED FOUR MONTHS AND WRITTEN AMONG OTHER THINGS TWO GOOD SHORT STORIES ONE 2300 WORDS AND 1800 BOTH TYPED AND READY FOR AIR MAIL STOP WOULD LIKE TO GIVE YOU FIRST LOOK AND AT SAME TIME TOUCH YOU FOR 100 WIRED TO BANK OF AMERICA CULVERCITY CALIFORNIA STOP EVEN IF ONLY ONE SUITED YOU I WOULD STILL BE FINANCIALLY ADVANCED IN YOUR BOOKS PLEASE WIRE IMMEDIATELY 5521 AMESTOY AVENUE ENCINO CALIFORNIA AS AM RETURNING STUDIO MONDAY MORNING=
THAT GHOST SCOTT FITZGERALD.

2300 1800 100 5521.

THE COMPANY WILL APPRECIATE SUGGESTIONS FROM ITS PATRONS CONCERNING ITS SERVICE

Figure 1 Cable from Fitzgerald to Arnold Gingrich, 17 July 1939, reestablishing Fitzgerald's relationship with *Esquire*. The two stories mentioned in the cable are "Design in Plaster" and "The Lost Decade," published by Gingrich in the issues for November and December 1939. *Esquire* Additions, Fitzgerald Papers, Princeton University Libraries.

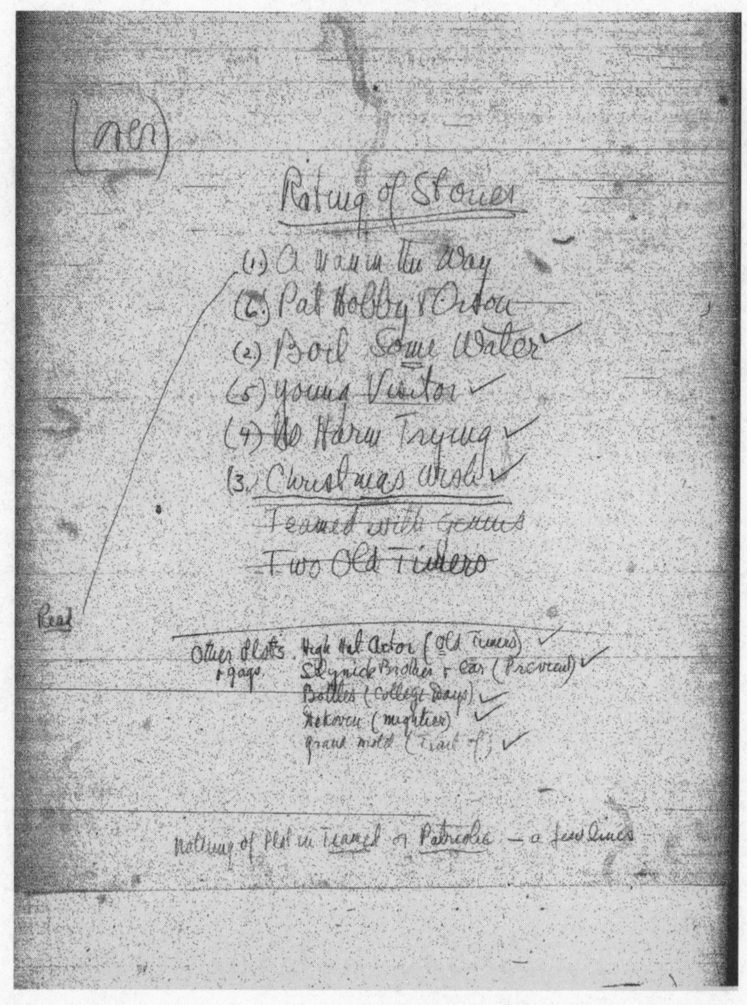

(over)

Rating of Stories

(1.) A Man in the Way
(6.) Pat Hobby & Orson
(2.) Boil Some Water
(5.) Young Visitor
(4.) No Harm Trying
(3.) Christmas Wish
~~Teamed with Genius~~
~~Two Old Timers~~

Read

Other plots & gags. High Hat Actor (Old Timers)
Selznick Brother & Car (Preview)
Bottles (College Days)
[illegible] (mighties)
[illegible] (Trait of)

Nothing of Plot in Travel or Patriotic — a few lines

Figure 2 Fitzgerald's "Rating of Stories" for the Pat Hobby Series, together with his notes on other stories about the character. Fitzgerald Papers, Princeton University Libraries.

Figure 3 Arnold Gingrich, founding editor of *Esquire*, ca. 1938. Arnold Gingrich Papers, Bentley Historical Library, University of Michigan.

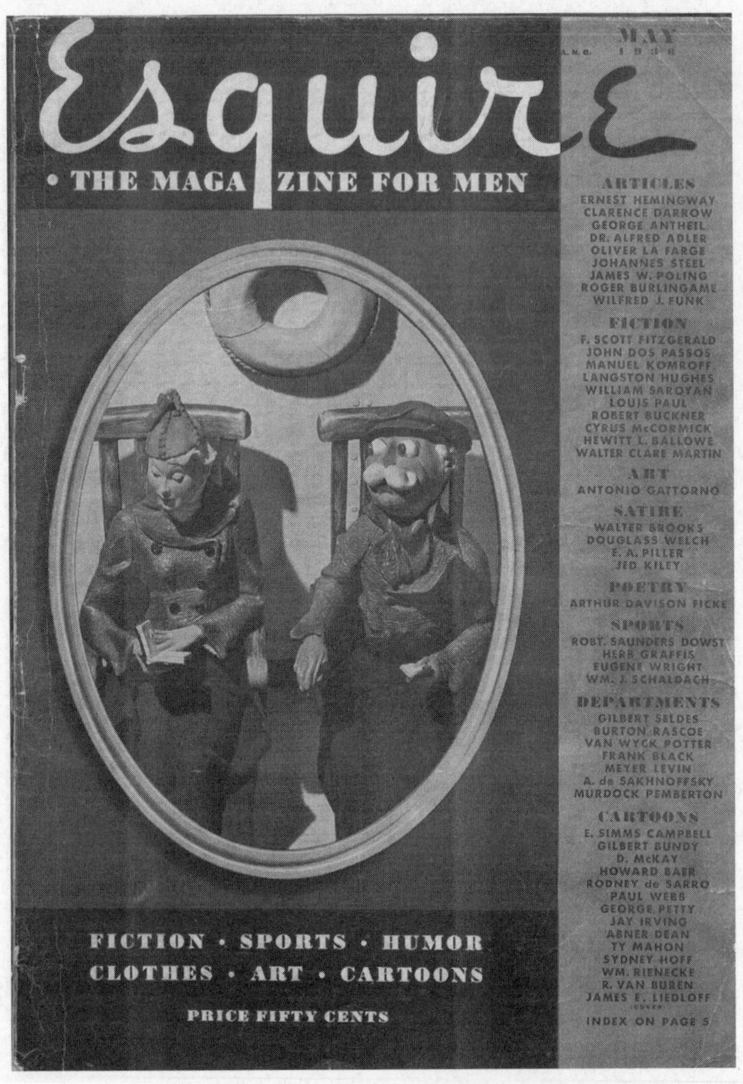

Figure 4 Cover for the May 1936 issue of *Esquire*, containing Fitzgerald's story "Three Acts of Music." Other contributors include Ernest Hemingway, Clarence Darrow, George Antheil, John Dos Passos, Langston Hughes, and William Saroyan. Thomas Cooper Library, University of South Carolina.

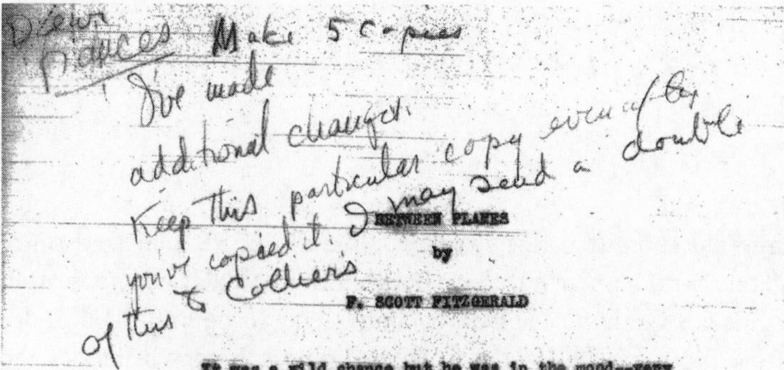

BETWEEN PLANES

by

F. SCOTT FITZGERALD

It was a wild chance but he was in the mood--very healthy and somewhat bored, with a sense of much tiresome duty done. He was now rewarding himself. Maybe.

When the plane landed he stepped out into ten o'clock of a mid-western summer night, and headed for the isolated pueblo airport, conventionalized as an old red "railway depot." He did not know whether she was alive, or living in this town, or what was her present name. With mounting excitement he looked through the phone book for her father who might be dead too, somewhere in these twenty years. No. Judge Harmon Holmes --Hillside 3194.

An amused woman's voice answered his inquiry for Miss Nancy Holmes.

"Nancy is Mrs. Walter Gifford now. Who is this?"

But he hung up without answering--having found out what he wanted to know and having only three hours. He did not remember any Walter Gifford and there was another suspended moment while he scanned the phone book, for she might have married out of town.

No. Walter Gifford--Hillside 1191. Blood flowed back into

Figure 5 First page of a typescript of "Three Hours between Planes," here entitled "Between Planes," with a note in Fitzgerald's hand suggesting that he might submit the story also to *Collier's* magazine. "Three Hours between Planes" appeared after Fitzgerald's death in the July 1941 *Esquire*. Fitzgerald Papers, Princeton University Libraries.

APPENDIX 1

"DEARLY BELOVED"

Fitzgerald submitted this story to Gingrich on 23 February 1940, together with a poem entitled "Beloved Infidel" that he had written for Sheilah Graham. He wanted both items to be published under his pseudonym, "John Darcy," but Gingrich accepted neither the story nor the poem. "Dearly Beloved" was first published in the *Fitzgerald/Hemingway Annual 1969*, pp. 1–3, and was reprinted in *The Short Stories of F. Scott Fitzgerald: A New Collection* (New York: Scribners, 1989): 773–75. Four typescripts of the story are extant at Princeton; the text below has been established from the last in the sequence of typescripts. For emendations in the text, see the Record of Variants; for annotations, see the Explanatory Notes.

DEARLY BELOVED

O my Beauty Boy—reading Plato so divine! O, dark, oh fair, colored golf champion of Chicago. Over the rails he goes at night, steward of the club car, and afterwards in the dim smoke by the one light and the smell of stale spittoons, writing west to the Rosicrucian Brotherhood. Seeking ever.

O Beauty Boy here is your girl, not one to soar like you, but a clean swift serpent who will travel as fast on land and look toward you in the sky.

Lilymary loved him, oft invited him and they were married in St. Jarvis' Church in North Englewood. For years they bettered themselves, running along the tread-mill of their race, becoming only a little older and no better than before. He was loaned the "Communist Manifesto" by the wife of the advertising manager of a Chicago daily but for preference give him Plato—the "Phaedo" and the "Apologia," or else the literature of the Rosicrucian Brotherhood of Sacramento, California, which burned in his ears as the rails clicked past Alton, Springfield and Burlington in the dark.

Bronze lovers, never never canst thou have thy bronze child—or so it seemed for years. Then the clock struck, the gong rang and Dr. Edwin Burch of South Michigan Avenue agreed to handle the whole thing for two hundred dollars. They looked so nice—so delicately nice, neither of them ever hurting the other and gracefully expert in the avoidance. Beauty Boy took fine care of her in her pregnancy—paid his sister to watch with her while he did double work on the road and served for caterers in the city; and one day the bronze baby was born.

O Beauty Boy, Lilymary said, here is your beauty boy. She lay in a four-bed ward in the hospital with the wives of a prize fighter, an undertaker and a doctor. Beauty Boy's face was so twisted with radiance, his teeth shining so in his smile and his eyes so kind, that it seemed that nothing and nothing could ever.

Beauty Boy sat beside her bed when she slept and read Thoreau's "Walden" for the third time. Then the nurse told him he must leave. He went on the road that night and in Alton going to mail a letter for a passenger he slipped under the moving train and his leg was off above the knee.

Beauty Boy lay in the hospital and a year passed. Lilymary went back to work again cooking. Things were tough, there was even trouble about his workman's compensation, but he found lines in his books that helped them along for awhile when all the human beings seemed away.

The little baby flourished but he was not beautiful like his parents, not as they had expected in those golden dreams. They had only spare-time love to give the child so the sister more and more and more took care of him. For they wanted to get back where they were, they wanted Beauty Boy's leg to grow again so it would all be like it was before. So that he could find delight in his books again and Lilymary could find delight in hoping for a little baby.

Some years passed. They were so far back on the tread-mill that they would never catch up. Beauty Boy was a night-watchman now but he had six operations on his stump and each new artificial limb gave him constant pain. Lilymary worked fairly steadily as a cook. Now they had become just ordinary people. Even the sister had long since forgotten that Beauty Boy was formerly colored golf champion of Chicago. Once in cleaning the closet she threw out all his books—the "Apologia" and the "Phaedo" of Plato, and the Thoreau and the Emerson and all the leaflets and correspondence with the Rosicrucian Brotherhood. He didn't find out for a long time that they were gone. And then he just stared at the place where they had been and said "Say, man . . . say man."

For things change and get so different that we can hardly recognize them and it seems that only our names remain the same. It seemed wrong for them still to call each other Beauty Boy and Lilymary long after the delight was over.

Some years later they both died in an influenza epidemic and went to heaven. They thought it was going to be all right then—indeed things began to happen in exactly the way that they had been told as children. Beauty Boy's leg grew again and he became golf champion of all heaven, both white and black, and drove the ball powerfully from cloud to cloud through the blue fairway. Lilymary's breasts became young and firm, she was respected among the other angels, and her pride in Beauty Boy became as it had been before.

In the evening they sat and tried to remember what it was they missed. It was not his books, for here everyone knew all those things by heart, and it was not the little boy for he had never really been one of them. They couldn't remember, so after a puzzled time they would give up trying, and talk about how nice the other one was, or how fine a score Beauty Boy would make tomorrow.

So things go.

APPENDIX 2

PUBLICATION AND EARNINGS

Fitzgerald received $200 per contribution for the first nonfiction pieces that he published in *Esquire*. By the time he began to sell short stories to the magazine, his price had been raised to $250. Fitzgerald handled all dealings with *Esquire* himself and paid no commission to Harold Ober, his literary agent. Much of the information in this appendix appeared first in Bryant Mangum's *A Fortune Yet: Money in the Art of F. Scott Fitzgerald's Short Stories* (New York: Garland, 1991).

Title	Publication Date	Price in *Esquire*
"Three Acts of Music"	May 1936	$250
"The Ants at Princeton"	June 1936	$250
"'I Didn't Get Over'"	October 1936	$250
"An Alcoholic Case"	February 1937	$250
"The Long Way Out"	September 1937	$250
"The Guest in Room Nineteen"	October 1937	$250
"In the Holidays"	December 1937	$250
"Financing Finnegan"	January 1938	$250
"Design in Plaster"	November 1939	$250
"The Lost Decade"	December 1939	$250
"Pat Hobby's Christmas Wish"	January 1940	$250
"A Man in the Way"	February 1940	$250
"'Boil Some Water—Lots of It'"	March 1940	$250
"Teamed with Genius"	April 1940	$250
"Pat Hobby and Orson Welles"	May 1940	$250
"Pat Hobby's Secret"	June 1940	$250
"Pat Hobby, Putative Father"	July 1940	$250
"The Homes of the Stars"	August 1940	$250
"Pat Hobby Does His Bit"	September 1940	$250
"Pat Hobby's Preview"	October 1940	$250
"No Harm Trying"	November 1940	$250
"A Patriotic Short"	December 1940	$250

"On the Trail of Pat Hobby"	January 1941	$250
"Fun in an Artist's Studio"	February 1941	$250
"On an Ocean Wave"	February 1941	$250
"Two Old-Timers"	March 1941	$250
"Mightier than the Sword"	April 1941	$250
"Pat Hobby's College Days"	May 1941	$250
"The Woman from '21'"	June 1941	$250
"Three Hours between Planes"	July 1941	$250